Solace
of
Dusk

DUSK AND EMBERS
BOOK 1

SOLACE OF DUSK

K. V. MEADOWS

For the ones the world deems *Undesirable*,
and those struggling to believe in their *own* magic.

Kingdom of Erleya

The Verge

Moicriach

Glinrew

Dubh
Carrig

Uldarvik

MAINLAN

Fiada
Purlieu

Content Warnings

This book is an adult fantasy novel. Some content may not be suitable for all readers.

- Violence (real world weapons, prolonged torture, magic wielding), blood without gore, and violent killing
- Child abandonment, infant death (not detailed), and a brief mention of miscarriage
- Unmanaged severe mental illness, anxiety and anxiety attacks, suicidal ideation
- Sensual and sexual content (on page, non-explicit)
- Grief and loss, mentions of parental death, terminal illness
- Disability prejudice, ableism, classism
- Profanity

If you need to put down this book at any moment, whether it is temporarily or permanently, please do so. Take care of yourself first!

Disclaimer

The signed language depicted in this book matches the grammatical rules of spoken English to make the dialogue more seamless to read. The language itself is specific to this fantasy world, and is not intended to match a signed language in our world. I have worked with a Deaf sensitivity reader, and intend no offense or thoughtlessness through my portrayal. This story is uniquely Durvla's story and is not intended to represent the entire population of d/Deaf/HOH individuals.

Prologue

CROUCHING WITHIN THE HEART of eternity, she waits. Claws retracted, fangs withdrawn.

She pumps ire through the veins of her successor, knitting flesh together with despair, filling her successor's marrow with tendrils of yearning and void.

She is the embodiment of chaos.

A cold persistence. The icy exterior wherein flames dance in the shadows.

With every breath, she waits, a dagger poised for the attack.

Her pulse beats within the chest of her successor, providing kindling for the inevitable.

One day shadowfire will purify the realm, she purrs. *Balance will be restored. It will be the dawn of a new day. A new world. Patience. One day, it will all be well. But rest now. For when you wake, the world will burn.*

Chapter 1
DURVLA

COLD DREAD DANCES ALONG *my spine as I shove a tome of fairytales beneath my mattress and sprint across my cottage. My little brother teeters around the house, oblivious to the doom outside our door. I snatch his knitted earflap hat off the armchair and shove it onto his head before hoisting him into my arms. "Sorry, sweet boy. Time to go play in your secret space."*

I rush over to our drying rack where small articles of clothing hang, and I overturn the whole thing. There's a trapdoor beneath the sheepskin rug, but before I can even get it open, a Forayer barges into my home, sneering, torch ablaze. "Durvla Garrick, you've been caught harboring an Undesirable!" he shouts. "You'll be hanged, along with that monstrosity."

He points at my brother and marches toward us.

"Please. He's not a monstrosity. He's a child."

The Forayer yanks his sword from his belt and raises it, set to bring it down upon us. He swings and—

I jolt awake.

Cold sweat trickles down my back, sending a tremor through me. My heart competes with my lungs, and I wheeze as I try to get my breathing under control.

There are no Forayers here.

No torchlights.

The room is dark and I'm in bed. Beside me, my five-year-old brother stirs, his little body tangled in the sheets, his curls spilling over his face.

Thank the goddess Sunlagh, it was just a dream.

I fight to steady my breathing, and my heart rate gradually calms as Taig rolls onto his stomach. I place my hand on his back. If he wakes fully, that will be the end of our night.

For a while longer, I stare at him, at the steady rise and fall of his back as he drifts into deep slumber.

Tomorrow, I need to be awake before the crack of dawn, as always. I need to sleep. I slip under the covers again and curl up close to Taig.

Eventually, sleep takes me again.

This time without any nightmares.

In the morning, Taig hobbles in circles, repeatedly squeezing his little hands together. Our fluffy sheepdog, Finn, licks remnants of breakfast off the floor. I try to finish getting dressed for the fourth time, wrestling my hair into thick braids and pinning the stray curls in place at the back of my head. Loose coils still fall across my forehead and temples, but this process has been interrupted so many times by Taig getting into mischief that I don't bother to wrangle them. My head is pounding, no doubt from my restless night, but there's no rest for the weary on this side of the bridge.

I regard Taig for a moment before approaching my desk. Last night, he was eager for my constant attention, and I left my desk completely disorganized. I meant to clean up after I finally managed to get him to sleep, but I'd just been so tired that I left it all in disarray. I've already fallen behind on work this week because I've been wrapped in the vise grip of my malady. I'm usually able to manage the daily headaches and other nuisances, but every now and then an unyielding episode attacks my body and flays me into submission. I'm still recovering from the mild episode I had a few days ago, and it's a bleak reminder of who I am. Of *what* I am to the crown.

Undesirable.

Unable to perceive any sounds by now, I'm not sure how much longer I can hide in plain sight.

Regret nudges me as I stare at the bundles of various plant samples and incomplete drawings scattered among my finished catalogue notes. My scissors are hiding beneath this mess somewhere …

Finn appears at my side as soon as I sit, shoving his shaggy black and white head against my leg. I jump to my feet, expecting the worst as Finn runs toward the door. His tail wags eagerly and he paws at the wood.

I tug the sleeve of my tunic down over my leather bracelet and smooth my hands over my hips as I try to steady my erratic pulse. When I open the door, I'm met with bright blue eyes and an even brighter smile. Finn leaps onto Osheen, his tail slapping so hard against my thigh that it stings. Osheen manages to give Finn enough attention to satisfy him, and the dog runs off to continue his quest for stale breadcrumbs on the kitchen floor.

"Good morning!" Osheen hand signs as he speaks—a habit he's developed for my sake over the years.

"Good morning," I respond, also speaking aloud as I sign. "Aren't you late for your post?"

"Yes." He runs his fingers through his deep auburn hair. Behind him, ribbons of pink streak the brightening morning sky. "Bhugearan must truly be struggling because there isn't much to harvest yet. I'm almost sure I'll be home early despite arriving late."

We've already had a tough winter, but the crops aren't bouncing back as they should. Even nature is as reluctant as Mainland to ensure our survival.

He scratches his close-trimmed, auburn beard and continues. "I have bad news. You're needed in the greenhouse."

My stomach sinks and I quickly glance over my shoulder at Taig who is now making a beeline for my desk. I hold up a finger to Osheen before rushing away and sweeping Taig off his feet. His skinny little body shakes with laughter, his brown eyes lighting up with glee. I spin him once just for fun and my head screams at me. Bad idea. I set him down and close my eyes for a moment.

When I open them, Osheen's concerned gaze is on me. "Are you alright?" he asks.

"Never better." I rub my forehead and sign one-handed. "Why am I needed in the greenhouse?"

"I'm not sure. My mother just asked me to get the message to you. I can stop by and feed Taig lunch later and get him in a fresh nappy if you'd like." He studies me cautiously.

I hesitate. "Well … are you sure? Wouldn't Granny wonder where you are?"

"It's not a big deal, Durvla."

I loose a breath. "Well, if it really isn't too much trouble—" I stop abruptly to intercept Taig as he turns to head back to my desk. Taking his hand, I walk him over to his safe space on the opposite side of our humble abode—an enclosure made with wooden slats and a sliding gate. It's a glorified cage, really, but a rather comfortable one filled with his favorite toys, fluffy pillows, and blankets. A little haven to keep him busy while I'm out.

Whenever a raid is expected, that enclosure is very easily disguised as an indoor nesting area for newborn animals in need of additional care. It's the perfect excuse in an agricultural town.

I pick up my boots from their spot beside the door and shove my feet into them. As I bend to lace them up quickly, my head protests the position. Osheen stands there, still scrutinizing me as I stand upright again.

"Are you sure you're alright? I can tell the girls that—"

"I'm fine." I give him a tight smile. Taig is walking around, tilting his head side to side as though he's dancing to imaginary music. A grin is plastered on his face, but already his unruly curls have tumbled into his eyes. He scrunches up his little nose and swats the curls away. I freeze, considering going back to fix his hair—annoyed about this deviation from my planned schedule. Unease settles into my bones, and when Osheen lays his hand on my shoulder, I nearly leap out of my skin.

"I'll fix his hair. You go ahead," he motions.

This time, my smile is genuine. "Are you sure you aren't a Mind Whisperer?"

He laughs. "I just know you."

It's hard to deny. "Make sure you burn any soiled nappies. I'd hate to be bested by poo."

Osheen smiles. "Durvla, I know the drill."

I sigh and speak aloud without signing. "I'm leaving, sweet boy." I glance over my shoulder at Taig as I grab my triangular shawl from the rack near the door. I drape it over my shoulders, wrapping it around my torso twice and fastening it with my leather belt to keep it in place. I thank Osheen again, rising onto the balls of my feet to kiss him on the cheek, and step out into the crisp air. It's spring, but early mornings still feel wintry.

I wrap my arms around myself and inhale the fresh, damp air. Already, the village has come alive. Women and children of different ages are outside hanging laundry on clotheslines. Their lips move as they chat amicably with each other. Toddlers run around barefooted, unbothered by the cold, wet soil. I can imagine their giggles and it makes me smile.

My boots sink into the earth and moisture seeps into the weathered leather. I need new ones, but I also need to put food on the table. I hurry past an elderly man who's polishing a pair of worn-down shoes even worse than mine. A mother straightening her young daughter's apron lifts her head to smile at me, and a few other people busy themselves repairing the holes in their roofs.

The mud turns to green grass. Cows and sheep graze leisurely in a massive expanse of meadow to my right. Osheen's mother stands in the pathway ahead of me. She waves both arms above her head, a bright smile on her face.

"Good morning, Orla," I say when I'm within her hearing range.

"Good morning, dear." She doesn't know how to sign, and it's not safe in public, but she always makes sure to face me so I can easily read her lips. "Sorry to pull you away from your cataloguing, but we seem to have a problem. Quite a few of our plants are withering, so we could use your expertise."

I simply nod and Orla's thin lips curl into a tender smile before sadness glosses over her eyes. Her fading auburn hair blows in the breeze that sweeps across the path, and she ties it back with a ribbon as we begin the short trek to the greenhouse.

Orla wasn't always in the gardening and botany trade; until recently, she was a shepherd and shearer. An old knee injury that progressively worsened made it impossible for her to keep up with the physical demands of her old post.

"It's raid week," she says. "Are you prepared?"

Raid week—at some point in the next seven days, people hired by the crown will search our homes for what they consider the greatest threat: magic. If they find none, they seek something else or *someone* incriminating, especially those unable to contribute to society. Unfortunately, both Taig and I would be lumped into that category.

I shrug at Orla. "I'll survive." I hope.

"You always do. Have you gotten a chance to start a sweater for yourself?"

I've lost track of how many times Orla has tried convincing me to make myself a sweater. There was one year when my mother and I made our entire family sweaters for the winter solstice. These days, however, I'm usually working on expanding Taig's wardrobe. He's a growing child, after all.

"No, but I may get started on it soon." I won't.

"I can't wait to see. You're talented, you know. You really ought to relocate to Ballybaeg."

Not this again.

"For all you know, you'll get commissioned to make sweaters for Mainland. Imagine how different your life could be!"

I wrinkle my nose. "I'm fine here."

"But are you happy?"

I hesitate and cringe inwardly at her knowing smile. "I'm alive. And safe." More importantly, Taig is safe. "Are *you* ready for the raid this week?"

"Am I ever?" she asks, her lips tugging downward. "During the last Quarterly, Shon was taken away for the possession of a scroll. An incantation or something. Foolish boy. So young too. Such a shame."

Shon was Orla's neighbor. A boy of just sixteen. He'd been living on his own after both parents were arrested for harboring an Undesirable—his younger sister. Nothing out of the ordinary there, but I can't imagine losing two parents and a sibling at once. Losing one loved one at a time is painful enough.

The cool air summons goose bumps along the back of my neck as we walk down the broken stone pathway toward the large, domed greenhouse. It's seen better days. A combination of small and large windows—some spider-webbed with cracks, some completely broken—make up the walls. It's a wonder the structure remains standing. Orla opens the door, letting me in first. The humidity hits me, despite all the cracks, as soon as I step inside.

The scents of moist soil, flowers, and savory herbs fill the interior. It's almost overwhelming but oddly comforting at the same time. I push my loose curls off my forehead, trying to tuck them into my braids as we make our way across the cracked brick floor. Beams of sunlight filter in through the large, overarching floor to ceiling windows, illuminating the racks of bundled plants mounted to panels between the glass. Wooden shelves stand akilter, packed to capacity with gardening supplies.

Two dark-haired young women raise their heads from where they're bent over some plant boxes. The taller of the two, Grawnye, waves to me and the other, Eemer, beckons me to them. Eemer says something that I can't decipher from her distance. I glance sidelong at Orla who relays the message. "She says it's about time you showed up."

I nod my thanks and respond to the women, "Better late than never."

We cross the greenhouse to meet up with them. Grawnye holds scissors in one hand, her other pressed against a visibly pregnant belly. Eemer gestures toward a small clump of leaves and white buds; half of the leaves are a sickly yellowing color, the other half, darker green as they should be.

"It didn't look so bad yesterday," Grawnye says.

The row of the other primrose clusters mirror the same unhealthy appearance. With a frown, I fiddle with my stray curls. "We can prune the diseased parts and lay down fresh soil. It'll take a while, but that may solve it. It'll just be a matter of trying a few different solutions."

Eemer's brown eyes are wide, but I swear I can see my words going into one ear and out the other. Grawnye, however, nods in understanding and holds up the scissors. "I better get started then."

We all grab pruning scissors from the shelves and take responsibility for one planter box each. Carefully, we sever the diseased parts of the plant from the parts that still appear healthy. Hopefully, they'll continue to grow normally. Replacing the soil is a longer and messier task, but together, we get it done.

I glance up often to ensure that I catch any ongoing conversations, sometimes adjusting my position to read someone's lips. I still miss bits and pieces, but years of gradual hearing loss have gifted me with the ability to piece together clues to draw the right conclusions.

I happen to lift my head just as Grawnye speaks again. "The raid should happen any day now. Did you hear about the Renwicks? Turns out they've been harboring an Undesirable."

Here we go. I steel my face and swipe the back of my dirty hand across my sweaty forehead.

"No way." Eemer's eyes go wide again.

"Yes, the wee lad has a strange little face. Doesn't look quite human, if you know what I mean."

Eemer nods.

"But they want to keep him. They say he's their son and that they love him. Heart-wrenching really. You should see how the babe's ma clung to him when a neighbor noticed his face. I'm surprised no one's reported them."

I turn away, focusing on the soil beneath my hands and ignoring the heat that seeps into my veins. Their chatter goes on in the background, fully masked by my lack of focus. Here in the Grounds—across the bridge from Mainland where the royal family and other nobles live— we are all lowborn laborers. Many Grounders live rewarding lives, raising families and building connections with others, even though we work from the moment we can handle a spade or milk a cow.

But Undesirables—individuals with debilitating illnesses, children who don't develop on schedule, and those deemed unable to adequately contribute to society—are sent to the Wastelands. Outcast. Left for dead. People say that life in the Wastelands is so harsh that it's impossible. It's a death sentence. Those who don't bring their Undesirable loved ones forward are sentenced to death for withholding truths from the crown.

And then there are those accused of being Mages—possessing abilities of sorcery or wielding elemental magic. Whether there have been any true Mages in recent years is a different story.

Cold water sloshes over my hands, soaking through my tunic sleeves. I yelp and scramble to hold onto the bucket that Eemer had unexpectedly shoved into my arms. Her thin brows rise, her eyes even larger than usual.

"Sorry," I say to her confused face. "Lost in thought."

"As always." She smiles warmly.

I can't find it in me to smile back, so I water my section and get to my feet. My head feels as though it weighs a ton. "Is that all? I need to get back to cataloguing."

My tone must have come out sharper than I intended, because Grawnye and Eemer exchange glances and Orla's eyebrows rise toward her hairline. She stands and takes me aside, away from the girls. "The dye plants are scheduled to be delivered to Ballybaeg today."

My heart clenches as I read between the lines. Grawnye is well into her pregnancy, Eemer simply cannot be trusted to find her way out of town and back without getting lost, and Orla's knees are awful—so that leaves me responsible for making the delivery. Of course, on a day that I already had to be away from Taig.

The day just gets better and better ...

Chapter 2
DURVLA

TIME DRAGS AS WE cut and bundle various plants, change out the soil, and plant new seasonal flowers and herbs. The sun is high in the sky by the time we finish. We've all had to remove our overcoats and shawls. Sweat gathers on the small of my back and my undershirt sticks to my chest. It will be a relief to get out of the greenhouse, even though I still have to make the trek to Ballybaeg.

We used to have an additional gardener that could've done the delivery, but she was apprehended for treason. I don't even remember what *treasonous* deed she committed, but it leaves us with one less helper.

My stomach rumbles as we step from the hot greenhouse into the cool air. Amusement sparks in Orla's blue eyes. "Whoa, hungry there, lass?"

I smile sheepishly. "Starving."

Her ruddy face is splotchy from our hard labor. She pulls a handkerchief from her skirt pocket and mops her forehead. "Why don't you stop by? Granny insisted I bring you over for some fresh bread."

I hesitate. I want to check on Taig before I head to Ballybaeg and I'm running out of time. I don't even know if Osheen made it back to look after him.

Orla regards me with wide, expectant eyes, much like her son's.

I glance at the wagon that I'm toting around, filled with bundled plants that I still need to categorize and label before delivering them. "I have to get—"

"I'll hurry her along. And with luck, Osheen may be able to accompany you on your journey."

My teeth sink into my lower lip as I consider my options. It'll be suspicious and impolite if I still refuse. I've known the Oakley family for most of my twenty-three years of life, and they've been kinder than ever since my mother died. The least I can do is appease the elderly matriarch. "Alright, but I can't stay long."

Orla beams. "Great!"

I follow Orla to her house, walking right past my own. *Sorry, Taig.* My heart physically tries to tug me toward him, but I clench my hand on the handle of the wagon and keep in step with Orla. Osheen said he'd be there.

But what if he's not?

Sweat slicks my palms. I really need to hurry. Before we even head up the pathway of worn-down grass, the mouthwatering aroma of fresh-baked bread reaches me. Sourdough. My stomach growls again, the traitor. Ahead of me, Orla's shoulders shake with laughter.

She opens the door and I salivate, my knees wobbling.

A stout, elderly woman approaches, practically running toward us. Before I can prepare myself, I'm crushed against her ample chest.

"Hi, Granny," I say—she refuses to be called anything but. My mouth waters from the scent of dough and meat clinging to her shirt.

"Why has it been so long?" She holds me at arm's length, her thick brows raised. Lustrous waves of silver hair caress her shoulders, and fine lines wander from the corners of her eyes and mouth. It's obvious she's laughed a lot in her lifetime. How is she able to look beyond the gloom of this existence and find such joy? I wish I knew.

I smile awkwardly under Granny's scrutiny.

"You are too skinny," she declares, and I resist the urge to peer down at my soft middle and broad hips. "You need more meat on your bones. Let me get you some soup. Sit, sit."

My stomach lurches as she shuffles off, her movements surprisingly quick for her size and age. "No, no. Granny …"

But she's stopped listening to me.

"Ma, she needs to go to Ballybaeg to deliver dye plants before dark. We can't have the workshops blaming her for slow fabric production, now can we?"

Thank you, Orla!

Granny's shoulders slump. She turns away from the fireplace and the large pot warming over it, and shuffles over to the dining table instead. A golden sourdough loaf sits there, steam still wafting off the crust. The knife slices through the bread, eliciting the phantom sound of a satisfying crunch in my memory. My mother baked bread frequently when she was alive.

Granny returns to me with a generous chunk of sourdough wrapped in cheesecloth.

It takes all my self-restraint not to unwrap it and devour the whole thing. "Thank you."

"Come back for supper." Granny smiles and, before I can reject the offer, ushers me toward the door. I wince. Granny's hands are deceptively strong from years of laboring in the fields.

I bid her and Orla farewell and shove the bread through the slit in my overskirt into the pocket underneath. Taking up the handle of the wagon again, I make my way back toward my house.

As I open the door, Finn nearly knocks me over. I pat his shaggy head and he returns to where Osheen sits on the floor in front of Taig. My shoulders relax and I step inside. "You're here," I sign. It's a relief to not have to focus on reading lips as I have been doing all day. The exhaustion rushes in all at once, but I try not to focus on it.

My job isn't complete yet.

Osheen smiles. "Did you doubt me?" He rips off a piece of the bread that he'd been feeding Taig before my arrival.

I know I shouldn't, but doubt is rooted in my very being. After pulling the wagon carefully over the threshold, I crouch to remove my shoes then drop a kiss atop Taig's chestnut curls. He glances briefly at me before turning back to Osheen for more bread.

My hands are stained green and blue, even though I've washed them more times than I can remember before leaving the greenhouse. One by one, I take the bundles over to my table. When they're laid out neatly, I cut strips of parchment and ready my quill and twine, my scissors on standby.

As quickly as I can, I take note of the expected dye colors and their corresponding plants. I hate that I have to leave my home again, and especially that I have to rely on someone else to look after Taig in my absence. It's foolish and risky.

Osheen taps on my shoulder, and I turn to him, blowing hair out of my face with a big sigh.

"Do you want me to make the delivery?" His face says he knows my answer already.

It's kind, but I need the deeds to count toward my record, especially since I'm even more behind on my work now. Taig spins slowly on his bottom and I almost smile. "It's *my* task," I say, speaking only. I tear my gaze away from my little brother and back to Osheen's worried face, signing again. "I have to go."

He helps me load the bundles back into the wagon, and just as I'm putting my shoes on, he brings me a waterskin. "For the road," he motions.

I smile at him. He's the absolute sweetest. "Thank you."

"Anything for you, Durvla. Hurry back, yes?"

No, I was planning to take my time, I want to say with bitter sarcasm.

I smile tightly before stepping out of the house again to set off on my unexpected journey.

Travelers, soldiers seeking shelter, and even Forayers have casually called my village, Ballybaeg, and Ballygort *the Big Three*. Together, we provide food and clothing to Mainland, while our people struggle to survive on the bare minimum. If I were to leave Cluain Baile, Ballybaeg is where I would go, but each time the itch to escape my village surfaces, I push it away. It isn't a possibility and it's foolish to think otherwise.

The sun is sinking as I head back home with undyed hanks of imperfect wool that a worker from the mill so graciously gave me. I can already picture the sweater I want to make for Taig.

My breath puffs out in tiny clouds as I hurry across the sodden land. I take a slightly different pathway, cutting across someone's property, when I spot a basket sitting on the side of the road. A bundle of fabric peeks out from inside the woven wicker. Releasing my grip on the wagon handle, I approach the basket with caution.

A tiny foot and the pale profile of a little face pokes out from the fabric.

My stomach drops.

My knees squelch into the moist soil, and I don't even hesitate before lifting the baby out of the basket. Her eyes are closed, a small cleft bisecting one side of otherwise full lips to her button nose. The foot peeking out is clubbed, turned fully inward. Every little detail is so precious that I find myself memorizing it because, clearly, no one else cares. There's hardly any color left in her face and she's cool to the touch, her breathing labored.

Anger and pain for this little life squeezes my heart. Gods, how could a parent abandon their child like this? I hold the baby against my chest, desperately trying to warm her little body. Her respirations grow slower, less frequent, and I hum a tune from my memories, a prayer asking the Great Rhianu to escort the little one's soul into Lugda's hands and begging the Underworld god to grant her a place in paradise. It's perhaps more superstition than anything in this age, but ... I hope with all my being.

Eventually, the baby takes a shallow breath and then no more. I cradle her little body in my arms, silent tears streaming down my face, until my joints ache from sitting still for so long in the chilly elements.

Her forehead is cold when I press my lips to it. It's nonsensical to wrap her up again, but I can't stand the idea of leaving her little body open to the cold air. It's only then that I release the sob I'd been holding, the built-up tension in my chest releasing.

Yet another innocent life commended to Lugda because of fear driven by the foolish laws of the land.

My skirt is a muddy mess when I stand, cold wind whipping my braids free from their pins. I wipe my tears and then hug myself as I walk away from the infant's body, reclaiming the wagon before resuming my journey home. My legs are heavy, my heart even heavier. The poor babe. She didn't deserve such an end. More tears leak down my face every now and then, but I press on. I just need to get home and wrap my arms around Taig again. He could've easily been that babe.

By the time I reach my village, Cluain Baile, there is one streak of orange left in the sky. Barely enough light for me to see my own feet, but I trudge on. Behind me, the wheels of the wagon keep sinking into the wet ground and I have to yank violently on the handle to get it moving. Seeing Taig's little face again is the only thing keeping me from spiraling after that little one died in my arms.

As I get home, Osheen and Finn greet me at the door. Taig is happily playing with a little wooden toy, gnawing on it without a care in the world. It does my heart well to find him safe and sound.

"Welcome back," Osheen motions. "Taig was perfect."

He answers before I can even ask. "Thank you. You better get back home. I'll get Taig fed and bathed."

My voice must've sounded as flat as I imagined because Osheen regards me carefully. He doesn't speak for a moment, but at last, he says, "I'll bring over some food and look after Taig a while longer so you can relax for a moment. You've just gotten home. You need a break."

I laugh humorlessly as I step toward Taig and lightly ruffle his hair. Finn trots by and licks Taig's cheek, pulling wide-mouthed giggles from him. I turn back to Osheen. "I don't have time for breaks."

"Read that fancy book you like so much," he signs, as if I hadn't already responded.

My lips quirk up. It's not a *fancy* book; it's a book of fairytales.

"Get some knitting done. Or wash up and go to bed."

I lower my brows. "I've already been gone all day. I want to spend some time with Taig."

"Durvla." He rests his hands for a moment as he carefully considers his next words. "You have to take a break sometime. You're either working or looking after Taig. You can trust my family, you know. You don't have to take on this burden all by yourself."

Heat pours into my chest and I sign sharply. "He's *not* a burden."

Osheen throws up his hands in surrender, forgetting to sign for a moment. "Wrong choice of words." He remembers himself and resumes signing. "I wasn't implying that *Taig* is a burden. I just mean that I know he is …" His mouth snaps shut, and his hands pause. "I know Taig requires a lot of energy, and there's a lot more you have to deal with. You have your own ailment, and you're only just on the mend from that episode you had a few days ago."

"Thank you for the reminder."

"The point is I want to help. My family would want to help. You know they love you."

"I know they do, but I refuse to put them in danger. The less they know, the better. Your mother already knows about my ailment and my deafness. That's more than enough, thank you."

Osheen's chest heaves with a deep sigh. "How about I bring you some pork and potatoes, and I can feed Taig while you change your clothes and freshen up. Then I'll leave you alone."

Pork and potatoes? Pork is a rare meal in Cluain Baile, so it's a tempting offer. All I have in the house is stale bread and questionable cheese. I glance over at Taig. He's playing with a wooden toy. "Fine," I sign. He wins this time. "Thank you."

He smiles, a little too pleased with himself.

Osheen sees his way out and I sit on the floor, soaking up Taig's presence. He crawls away, grabbing a pillow, which he squishes into his face with a gleeful expression. His joy is undeniable, but also inexplicable. For a child who's had it so hard, who's not seen the outdoors in the past three years, never interacted with other children, and only recently learned to walk at the age of five, he's so very happy. I could learn a thing or two from him.

Taig glances up at me from his beloved pillow, his big brown eyes peering through runaway coils of hair. I move closer to him and push his hair back. Our complexions are the same, light brown with a bronze undertone, but his hair color is like Ma's. Mine is dark brown like Da's. Sometimes I see Ma's face in his. Does he remember her?

"Are you ready for dinner?" I ask aloud. Taig smiles at me and chucks the pillow aside, crawling away to do who knows what.

He's clearly more than alright. Calm even. Maybe I can get a bit of work done on the gown my mother had guided me through. I get to my feet again and fetch fresh clothing to change into before heading into the washroom. Leaving the door open, I quickly relieve my bladder before peeling off my sordid work clothing and sponging off with the chilly basin water. My heart races as I expect Osheen to walk in at any moment, but I manage to get into a fresh skirt, tunic, and socks. From my wardrobe, I remove a garment cover containing a knitted dress. Ma and I had been working on it for so long.

The door flies open, blasting cool wind from outside, and I drop the garment cover in surprise. Osheen rushes into the house, his usually ruddy complexion stark white.

"Raid!" he signs.

Chapter 3
DURVLA

PANIC SPEARS INTO THE depths of my belly and for a moment I'm rooted where I stand. A second passes, then two, and finally I jump into action. "Let Finn out," I shout to Osheen as I run across my house. Finn is protective of us and I'm certain they won't hesitate to kill him if he attacks. I snatch up a knitted hat with reinforced earflaps, and as I shove the hat on over Taig's head, he swats at me. Rightfully so. "I'm sorry, Taig. Time to go play in your secret place."

Osheen has already let Finn out and races past me, yanking open the crawl space hidden in the floorboards. He helps me get Taig in there, making sure the padding is secure and that there is some entertainment available. I don't have time to think of much else as I close the trapdoor and cover it with a linen sheet and a sheepskin rug. "Go," I tell Osheen as he starts to help me replace the drying rack on top of it all.

He nods and runs out of the house. He can't be here when the Forayers—glorified mercenaries—arrive. He has to care for his own family.

He's barely gone a couple of minutes before my door flies open again.

Forayers dressed in black uniforms storm into my home, and I flinch and back myself against a wall. Vibration radiates through the floor as they empty cabinets, overturn smaller pieces of furniture, and destroy almost everything their hands touch. I gawk at the eerie dance of the torches as indistinct words pass between the Forayers, and I pray to all the gods that Taig isn't panicking below the floorboards.

My heart threatens to break through my ribcage and my ears start ringing as I force myself to watch the destruction unfolding before me. I shakily tug down my sleeve over the leather bracelet on my wrist, needing to keep my hands busy as I try to focus on steadying the wild cadence of my heart. What would I even do if they found the concealed door? Shout at them? Jump on their backs? I'm powerless.

One of the men appears in front of me, a scroll in hand. He unrolls it and asks, "Durvla Garrick?"

I focus on his lips and nod.

"You live here alone, correct?"

Another nod.

"Mother deceased? Father deceased? Younger brother deceased?"

My heart in my throat, I nod once more.

"Is there anything you'd like to confess? Any contraband? Magical practices?"

"No, sir."

"You are aware that a confession will earn you a lifetime of service to the Veilguards rather than a death sentence." It's not a question.

"Yes."

We all know being sentenced to the Veilguards—ordinary citizens forced to guard the Veil to a realm filled with dangerous magical beings and monsters—might as well be a death sentence.

"What do you contribute to your village?"

I point a shaky finger toward my desk. "I'm the botanist. I work with the gardeners, make deliveries to Ballybaeg, and occasionally help shepherd the sheep when necessary. Orla Oakley, Grawnye Aron, and Eemer Riley can vouch for me." It should be enough to deem me a worthy contribution to Cluain Baile.

The man rolls up the scroll and scans me from head to toe, assessing for impediments. Assessing my worth. I push my shoulders back slightly even as I'm quaking on the inside. Satisfied, the mercenary marches off, though he pauses before he gets very far. He picks up a beautifully knitted throw and stares at it for a moment. He pulls a dagger from his belt and tears right through the center of the throw. My heart is ripped to shreds right along with it.

I stare, stupefied, as the ruined blanket that my mother made falls to the floor.

Another Forayer approaches, a different knitted item in her hand that makes my heart skip a beat. The blaze of her torch casts a sinister shadow on her face, making it nearly impossible to discern her words. She repeats the question, shaking the garment in her hand for emphasis. I think she's asking what it is, but all I can focus on is the roar of my pulse and that shrill ringing that slowly devours logic.

"It's a dress." My knitting needles still protrude from the fabric. It's already taken me so long. I can't even calculate how long it's been by now. I bite my lip and will the nausea away.

The fullness in my ears is so painful, the whistling sound growing louder.

"Where did you get the dress from?"

"I made it. It's not finished." I can feel my voice waver. *Breathe.*

"*You* made this." She's doubtful.

I bob my head and my vision jumps back and forth as if I'm intentionally moving my eyes. I firmly focus on the woman, even as my vision goes haywire. I shouldn't have taken the dress out. It's not the type of dress typically owned by residents of Cluain Baile or by anyone in the Grounds for that matter.

Gods, they're going to arrest me for theft. I breathe in deeply as colors creep into the edges of my vision and the back of my head throbs, starting to grow heavier. This is not the time, I tell my body. If I have an episode now …

I squeeze my eyes shut and wait to be apprehended. Or worse.

Nothing happens.

When I open my eyes, everyone's gone, destruction in their wake. I blink and release a shaky breath. My legs are leaden, numb. Deep breath. I slowly count to ten.

Regaining the sensation in my legs, I walk to the window and peer out. Menacing flames are still flickering, just outside of my house. The Forayers are gathered as if having a meeting. There's still an annoying keening note in my ear accompanying that painful water-logged sensation that drives me absolutely mad. I close my eyes again and press my aching forehead against the cool surface of the glass.

A sudden jolt radiates through the window, and I reel back, my heart hammering as Forayers storm into my house again.

Goose bumps break out all over my skin and cold sweat drips down my back. A wave of dizziness hits me so hard that I lose track of where I am in space.

I have no idea what's being said to me, but out of nowhere, I'm flanked on either side, hands wrapping around my upper arms.

The ringing in my ear intensifies. My vision wanes, darkening at the edges again. *Breathe.*

"Please, I'm just a botanist. There must be some mistake."

The Forayers couldn't care any less—they haul me out of my house, away from Taig, even as I dig my heels into the ground.

Outside, villagers gather like spectators. Osheen is front and center, his broad shoulders square as though he intends to intercept.

"Please." Sobs tear from my throat as my feet leave the ground. The Forayer tosses me over his shoulder like a sack of flour. I kick and thrash wildly, having nothing else to lose. "*Please!* Let me go!" I lift my head and desperately search the crowd.

Osheen is running toward me, yelling something. A Forayer catches him in the stomach with a staff mid-run, and he falls to the ground.

I scream his name, and his head snaps up to me. Wishing with all I have that we could read each other's minds, I stare at him and focus my thoughts. *Look after Taig. Look after my brother. Please. Look after Taig, Look after Taig. Look after Taig. Please, please, please understand this.*

Osheen goes still, trying to read the expression on my face. Trying to get anything at all from me. Then he holds his hand to his chest and nods.

A fresh wave of dizziness crests over me as the ringing in my ears becomes unbearable. Darkness consumes my vision until I'm left with no choice but to surrender to oblivion.

Chapter 4
CARYS

"OH, ALL YOUR SUITORS will just swoon when they see you in this dress. Teal compliments you," Lowri gushes.

"The rust-colored dress was better," Ellynne says. "It brings out the amber of your eyes."

My servants are all giggles and grins, but I am not amused by these ridiculous excuses for dresses. They're a bloody bore.

I sigh and smooth out the exaggerated flared skirt of the teal dress I'm currently wearing. Shades of green flatter me but this ... this is rubbish. Before I turn away, I glimpse at my reflection. "Unlace me."

The women exchange expressions and Ellynne unlaces the bodice. My lungs can finally expand again, and I take a deep breath. As soon as the stays are fully unfastened, I pull them away from my body and fling them aside. The bodice lands on the purple velvet cushion of the ornately carved armchair.

"Ellynne, tell me the dressmaker sent something more inspired."
I glance over my shoulder at the redhead behind me.

"No ... " She finishes unbuttoning the rest of the dress.

I can't step out of it fast enough. "Magdin's freezing tits," I mumble. "Of all the dressmakers in this godsforsaken kingdom, I have to get stuck with the incompetent ones." This is the third dressmaker I've had in just three months. There will be a fourth.

I huff and march off in my chemise, dropping onto the bed with a grunt.

"Lowri, pour the princess a glass of wine."

Thank the gods for Ellynne.

I groan with annoyance into my silk sheets.

The bed depresses and I feel Ellynne's familiar touch as she strokes my hair. Her fingers catch on a few knots, and I wince.

"You have the hair of a princess, but the heart of a warrior." The amusement in Ellynne's voice provokes laughter from me. I press my cheek against the sheet, turning to face her.

"A warrior sounds so much more intriguing. At least then I wouldn't have to go to this bloody Feast." Hells, the bloody Feast wouldn't even exist if not for the necessity of my marriage.

"It's nearly time for you to visit Her Majesty," Ellynne reminds me. As though I can possibly forget. "Let's get you looking more presentable."

"Fine." I sigh, sitting up.

"Tomorrow we'll try on more dresses for the Feast. How does that sound?" She's speaking in that ridiculous, soothing tone.

"You're patronizing me."

Ellynne responds with a knowing smile. She's lucky I'm fond of her in all her cheeky glory.

I push myself off the bed and follow her to the wooden vanity, my dark hair swinging well below my backside. Try as I may, I can't help but pout like a petulant toddler as I plop into the vanity chair. "My hair looks awful, doesn't it?" I turn to Lowri as the slight woman hands me a goblet of wine.

"N-no, Your Highness."

I roll my eyes, and I swear Ellynne does as well. Lowri is relatively new to my service after my last lady eloped with another servant, and she's nothing like her sister. Not even in appearance. For what Lowri lacks in curves, Ellynne has it all and more. Long lashes frame Lowri's big blue eyes, giving her the illusion of wearing kohl. Ellynne's eyes are olive green with a perpetual sparkle as fiery as the hair on her head.

I seize the goblet from Lowri and chug the wine before handing it back. The brunette skitters off while I glower at my reflection. Golden strands of hair shine through my black tresses—a physical trait from the grandmother who died before my birth. I've seen paintings of her, with stunning raven hair, golden-streaked like mine, and warm brown eyes like my mother's.

Thanks to many sleepless nights, dark semicircles draw attention to my amber eyes, the freckles scattered across my nose and cheekbones stark against my ivory complexion.

"Why are you scowling at yourself like that?" Ellynne asks as she lifts my brush from the vanity and begins carefully running it through my hair.

I allow silence to fill the space. Now and then, Ellynne tugs harder on the brush, pulling a hiss from me each time. "Should I cut it?" I ask.

"It's up to you." She smiles at me in the mirror's reflection as she continues detangling the knots. "I would miss styling it, though."

I shrug. Perhaps severing myself from my defining feature could also cut away my faults.

Ellynne plaits a small portion on each side, pulling the braids into a halo around my head and securing them with little hairpins. The lower portion of my hair is left loose to cascade down my back. She finishes the look with my favorite diadem—a delicate headpiece of gold, twisted into an intricate design that dips into a V against my forehead. A ruby gem at the center of the V matches the amulet that rests against my chest.

"There." She beams with pride. "Do you like it?"

I turn my head from side to side, admiring my hair from different angles. It's perfect, as is to be expected from Ellynne's gifted hands. "It's lovely," I say, the corner of my lips twitching up into a small smile. I stand and my tresses drop down to the backs of my thighs.

Lowri comes running toward me, a bodice and a sage green gown in hand. Both women help me into the garments, lacing, cinching, and buttoning it all before slipping my favorite heeled shoes onto my feet. The buckle of this pair is adorned with tiny iridescent gems that match any dress I wear. I appear more than presentable, but I am tardy. As usual. I set off with purpose toward my door and Ellynne calls out to me.

"Carys, don't forget your book."

Right. How could I forget that? I halt in my tracks and turn as Ellynne approaches with a leather-bound tome in hand. The cover is nondescript save for a few abstract swirls bordering it. The original cover had the book's title, *Erleyan Folklore and Fairytales*, branded into the leather. Unfortunately, when my book began falling apart last year, my mother had it rebound with this bizarrely dull cover.

I gratefully take the heavy book from her. "What would I do without you?"

She smirks. "You'd be a mess, of course."

"I'm *still* a mess. Utter chaos, in fact." My cheek twitches, a smile threatening to break my resolve. Right now, however, I need to be the ice princess again.

I turn on my heels and open the door before sweeping out of the chamber and nearly colliding with a solid mass. My personal guard, Sir Callum Ferrer, is broad-shouldered, the top of his head not far beneath the top of the doorway. I'm taller than average, but he makes *everyone* look short. Excitement prickles at my skin as I gaze up at those piercing blue eyes beneath his cropped ashy blond hair. He's a dream to look at, but I've seen what he can do with that sword on his hip.

Gods be damned, I've seen what he can do with those hips too.

"Good morning." A slow smile spreads across his lips.

I take a deep breath and vanquish any lustful thoughts as I tear my gaze away from his mouth.

Giggles sound behind me as the sisters exit the bedchamber. Lowri holds her hand over her mouth to contain more giggles, and Ellynne winks at me. I roll my eyes though I'm unable to stop the small smirk that slips past my stony exterior. Both women curtsy before dashing away, and my attention snaps back to Callum.

"Are you ready to go?" he asks.

"No, but let's do this."

Understanding crosses his face.

Visits to my mother's chamber have been increasingly gloomy lately. I look forward to reading with her—or more likely *to* her. As much as it pains me having to face her, it's always refreshing to escape into this book of fairytales where sprites and merrow exist.

Callum extends his hand away from me, as if introducing me to the large corridor. We follow the winding passageway, my heels clacking against the tiles as we walk beneath high stone arches. The hallway opens into the busy concourse where numerous nobles and servants mill about. Ornate stone columns support a massive archway and a foreboding double door leading to the royal chambers. I lift my chin and throw back my shoulders, plowing on across the concourse, acknowledging each greeting with a curt nod.

Just once, I would like to walk these halls without having to interact with others. Without anything being expected of me.

The guards let us through the double door, allowing us into a private hallway. It's another trek through several winding corridors before we arrive at an immense carved door at the very end. Two pairs of guards stand watch, all dressed in maroon. Each wears a black sash with gold embroidery of the sun eclipsing a crown turned on its side. Queen's Guards. All four bow to me before two stand aside while one of the other two opens the door.

As Callum and I enter my mother's bedchamber, I'm hit with the stench of tonic herbs and an odor I can't describe. It seems like hundreds of candles fill the great space, their flames swaying eerily against the floral designs painted on the walls. The fireplace crackles, exuding a suffocating heat in addition to all the candles.

"Good morning, Princess," says Iywan.

I turn my attention to my royal advisor—the queen's friend and right hand. Iywan is tall and slender, with grey hair slicked back and braided at the nape of his neck. His umber skin is a map of wrinkles, and his dark brown eyes are steady and wiser than his sixty years. Once upon a time, he'd been like a second father to me, but we grew apart over this past year. The sight of him makes my stomach sink. He bows, and I frown at him.

"Why are there so many bloody candles in here? It's hotter than Lugda's balls."

I swear his eye twitches.

Language, I remind myself.

"We're hoping to sweat the sickness out," Iywan says. "Briony has informed me that it's a simple yet effective cure."

"Who's Byney?"

A thin young woman with icy blue eyes and a small, upturned nose stands from my mother's bed. Sandy brown hair frames her long face. I've never seen her before. A porcelain bowl against her chest catches my attention.

"Apologies, Your Highness," she says. Her voice is quiet, but not at all timid. "I'm the new healer's apprentice."

Alys didn't tell me anything about a new apprentice. I wave my hand. "You can go now."

"Thank you, Your Highness." The healer's apprentice curtsies and strides past Callum with sure steps.

My mother is asleep in an enormous four-poster bed with heavy canopies of deep maroon draped all around her. She's covered up to her neck in quilted fabric and even her pallor is flushed, her skin beaded with sweat. My heart tugs painfully. Even her once golden hair is rapidly turning silver, as if her sickness is leeching the pigment.

I sit beside her and place the book on my lap. "Good day, Mother."

The healers have already informed us that whatever is ailing her is not contagious, so I lean over to kiss her sweaty brow. She doesn't even stir. A dull ache settles in my chest, but I force myself to take a breath. I need to be brave. For her.

"I've brought our favorite book. What shall we read today?"

Still no response. It's bizarre. Normally she wakes, if even for just one tale. Why in Rhianu's name is she not waking up?

I glance toward Iywan who's standing aside respectfully. "What was in that bowl?" There's no hiding the blame in my voice.

"I requested that Briony give her valbane. Your mother was in a great deal of pain."

Valbane—with the right dosage, it's strong enough to keep a man unconscious through an amputation. Heat floods my veins and I frown. *Now* he tells me.

"You couldn't have waited a damn moment longer until I got a chance to see her?"

"My sincerest apologies, Your Highness. Please know that I had your mother's best interest at heart."

"That *best interest* should've included letting her be awake long enough to see her only surviving child. She looks forward to these moments." We both do.

He inhales to respond but I hold up my hand, intercepting him. He knows he's wrong. I turn my attention back to my mother and brush back damp strands of silver hair from her forehead. "And could you put out some of those bloody candles? She's sweating like a glassblower's arse!" I stand and heavily place the book onto the small decorative table beside the bed before tugging a layer of sheets off my mother. "How long will the valbane last?"

"A few hours, Princess. Shall I summon you when Her Majesty is awake?"

"Of course."

"And what of Audience, Your Highness?"

I freeze, annoyance nipping at me. The last thing I want to do right now is sit in the throne room and listen to people complain about things I cannot control. "You may hold Audience in my stead."

"Very well, Princess."

I turn away from Iywan, rolling my eyes before pressing one last kiss to my mother's brow. "Have her ladies give her a sponge bath with rose oil." My voice trembles and I feel as though I've swallowed fire.

This is not how I expected this visit to go—I'd looked forward to reading with her, to musing over the world that I wish we lived in. A world where magic can do wonders, illnesses can be cured, and happily ever after is possible. I want to scream, cry, smash a few things. Something inside of me entertains the notion of cathartic destruction, but Alys's voice of reason is in my head, reminding me to step back from the situation and evaluate it.

Is this worth my rage?

My mother would hate for me to lose my temper just because Iywan was trying to alleviate her pain. Even though it did leave her unconscious before my visit.

I collect my book, and Callum opens the door for me to storm out of the chamber, my dress and hair swishing around me.

Chapter 5
CARYS

AS SOON AS WE clear the door, the guard closes it behind us. I take a deep breath and it's a big mistake, because tears immediately sting my eyes. Callum discreetly nudges my arm. "Let's go," he urges gently.

I try to swallow around the lump in my throat as I fall into step beside him. We backtrack through the maze of corridors until we finally enter the concourse. I focus on my breathing, blocking out everything and everyone. No weakness. I'm a formidable, unperturbed image of frigidity. Beside me, Callum's posture is rigid and intimidating.

No one dares to approach us.

Good.

We stop at my bedchamber door and Callum dips his head toward me, his face calculating.

"I'm fine," I say.

"Are you sure?"

"No ..." I can't take my eyes off him, the heat of disappointment and anger in my blood morphing into a very different warmth. I need to get my mind off the situation with my mother. My fingers tangle in the black trim of Callum's maroon livery jacket, and my lips lift in a small smile. "I have some time to burn ..."

Callum's gaze drops to my lips, and he clenches his sword hilt as though he isn't sure what else to do with his hand. "I ... should send for Ellynne and Lowri ..." The intensity in his eyes says something else. He doesn't dare to touch me though, even with my grasp on the front of his uniform.

"I don't need Ellynne or Lowri." I take his hands and place them on my waist before running my fingers through his blond hair. "Right now, I need *you*."

He glances around for a moment—we both know that someone else should guard my door in the meanwhile. Yet he opens my door with a grin on his irresistible lips, and I reciprocate as we step into my bedchamber.

· · ○ ☽ ☀ ☾ ○ · ·

A while later, I'm choosing a dress that's easy for me to put on with minimal assistance. I glance over my bare shoulder as Callum buckles his sword belt. His powerful back straightens, his features hardening again. All evidence of lust disappears. "I'll call for your ladies," he says.

Welcome back, sentinel Callum. I shake my head. "No."

He blinks and scratches his chin.

I step into a cobalt blue dress and pull it up over my narrow hips, then slip my arms into the long, tapered sleeves and turn my back to Callum. "Just button me up and I'm set."

As adept as he was at taking the other dress off, he fastens this one just as easily. Once he's finished, I slide my hands over my hair, hoping to tame any frizz. "How do I look?"

That sparkle momentarily returns to his face. "Beautiful."

I can't help but smile. "Flatterer."

He grabs my shoes and I sit on the bed to slip them on. Callum drops to his knees in front of me and takes over the task, tightening the buckle perhaps a bit more taut than necessary. He glances up at me. "It's nearly shift change."

I frown. Not that I have anything against Tiernan; in fact, I hold him in the highest regard. But for obvious reasons, Callum is my favorite.

"I have time to get you to the infirmary and back. Shall we?" He stands, straightening his livery before extending his hand to me.

Glass shatters as I enter the fragrant infirmary, and Alys swears loudly.

"That's rather foul language for a lady," I call out with a grin.

Kneeling on the floor beside shards of glass in a clear puddle, the head healer lifts her face to me. A cheeky grin graces her full lips. "When have I ever claimed to be a lady, dear Carys?"

The new apprentice halts in her rush to Alys's side and drops into a deep curtsy. "Your Highness," she says with a polite smile.

Another healer whose name I can never remember, pauses in the middle of putting fresh linens on a cot. He bows and I nod to him. The infirmary isn't huge: eight cots in two rows of four, large windows with drawn curtains, and rows of shelves with various medicinal supplies fill the moderate space.

The apprentice grabs a cloth from a basket on one of the counters that line the wall and returns to Alys's side. "I've got it, Lady Alys."

Alys hesitates briefly but stands and removes her apron from her full-bodied figure, hanging it on a nearby hook. "Right," she says in that sunshiny tone of hers. She thanks the apprentice and approaches me, regarding me with grey eyes that stand out beautifully against her mahogany skin. A huge smile spreads across her round face and it's so contagious that I cannot resist smiling back. "Alright, dear one. Shall we proceed to your room?"

"Yes." I stare over her shoulder at the new healer's apprentice. "I wasn't aware that you were getting an apprentice."

"Neither was I," she says, keeping her voice down. "But with the recent disease outbreaks across Mainland, Lord Iywan thought I could use the additional help."

"Do we have any more information on that yet?"

The apprentice woman is working unhurriedly, her sidelong stare making me clench my jaw to avoid telling her to stop eavesdropping.

"I'm afraid not," says Alys. "It's very odd."

The apprentice is still listening. I want to throw something at her. "You, apprentice girl. Don't you have other tasks to do?"

"I do, Your Highness."

Alys tilts her head into my view, brows lifted. "Be nice." Her voice is quiet, melodious.

"I am." I flash her a strained smile. "There's something I need to discuss with you. In private." This time I keep my voice lowered.

Alys nods. "Briony, I'll be right back. Please help Vaughn dose out the serums."

"Yes, Lady Alys."

Alys presses her hand gently against the small of my back. "Let's walk."

As we step out into the hall again, Callum flashes a charming smile at Alys. "You look well, Lady Alys."

Big flirt.

Alys laughs lightly. "You are too kind, Callum."

Heat crawls into my chest. Alys is in her fifties and Callum is twenty-five. There's absolutely nothing romantic there. Still, it takes me a moment to ward off the envy. Technically he can flirt with whomever he wants but still ...

We set off for my bedchamber, Callum on one side of me, Alys on the other.

"So, what do you need to discuss?" Alys asks.

Right. "I know my mother is in pain, but I'd prefer if she is not sedated when I'm scheduled to visit."

I slow my pace as fine lines appear between Alys's brows.

"You didn't know."

She shakes her head. For a moment, there's silence, then Alys asks, "Have you been working on grounding?"

"Yes." I smile as convincingly as I can, but Alys always sees right through my lies.

"*Carys.*" She tucks a few loose waves of her salt-and-pepper hair into the huge bun at the back of her head.

"I don't have time."

"You need to find the time, dear one. And remember—"

"—deep breathing and positive thoughts throughout the day," I interject. "I know, Alys."

Alys wrinkles her nose and pats my arm. "Are you ready for the Feast?"

This subject is even more annoying than the apprentice. I frown. "Of course not. I can't even find the right dress."

"Is that really what is bothering you?"

"It's the damn dress *and* this idiotic tradition. My mother is practically knocking on Lugda's door and they're pushing me into marriage. As if my mother hasn't ruled without a king by her side for years now!"

"You are the last heir," she reminds me.

I stop dead in my tracks. "Are you actually defending this tradition?"

"Not defending, dear, just stating the facts. The same facts the Council is going to throw at you if you resist."

I know that I'm the last heir. My brother died when I was only five—sixteen years ago, but it feels like an eternity. Following my brother's death, I remember my mother having two other pregnancies, but no live children to account for. Like the goddess Rhianu had decided my mother couldn't be trusted to keep more children alive. If the gods even have such power in this twisted world anymore.

Perhaps it was just rotten luck.

I cannot remember how my brother died. Sometimes he dominates my dreams. His body falling away, unmoving. My father succumbed to an illness when I was thirteen, shortly after a distressing incident I wish to forget. We've theorized that the same illness is now holding my mother hostage.

By the time we arrive at my bedchamber door, my dark-haired guard, Tiernan, is already guarding it. "Your Highness," he says, his strict, angular eyes not even showing a hint of a smile.

"Hello, Major Kilkenny," I respond just as formally, if only to annoy him.

Tiernan is two years older than Callum and about my height. He's not as broad-shouldered or brawny as Callum, but Ostanha have mercy, his lean, powerful body is damn lethal. I've watched him spar in the training grounds—his skills with almost any weapon are scarily impressive.

He salutes Callum, who returns the gesture before bowing to me and then marching off.

As Tiernan opens the door, Alys and I walk through. I stride across the chamber to my bed as the door closes, and I collapse onto my mattress with a huff.

Gossamer canopy drapes stare back at me as I turn my face up toward the ceiling. "How are we supposed to talk anymore with Byney—"

"—*Briony.*"

"—watching all the time? It'll be suspicious if you're constantly coming to my bedchamber."

Alys shrugs. "Then let her be suspicious." She makes her way toward the desk where a kettle and a tankard has already been set—likely by Ellynne—a small clay cup beside it. Steam wafts from the cup as Alys pours hot water into it. She pulls a small vial from her pocket as I approach and empties tea leaves into the cup.

"Where's the honey?" I ask.

"We're awaiting a delivery from Wynn Odhran."

Eagerness floods my belly and I clear my throat. "So, what's the status of things?" I ask, lowering my voice though there's no one else around.

She lowers hers as well. "The final Quarterly Raid has been completed. There are more captives than there has been in a while, including an entire caravan of young ones."

A chill cuts through me, all anticipation of Wynn's arrival forgotten. This should not be happening. The fear of Otherworldly activity has gotten out of hand—suspicions are higher than ever. But how do I override beliefs that are so deeply rooted in Erleyan ancient history? How do I get the Council to see the error of our ways?

"We've gotten word there's going to be an unscheduled raid on the Big Three villages in a few weeks. An alert has already been sent through rebel networks—they're planning to intercept and rescue as many innocents as possible."

"Lierwen be with them."

Alys nods though I know she doesn't believe in the Protector, the Father of the gods, or any old gods of Erleya for that matter. Just as I don't believe that she's telling me everything. I'm not even certain how she knows all that she does.

"Anything else?" I ask.

"No." Her tone is definitive, though she avoids my gaze. There's no point in pushing her though; she tells me what I need to know. It would likely be dangerous for me to know more than what she's already told me.

"There's a council meeting soon," I say. "I'm not going to be taken by surprise, am I?"

"I've told you all I can, Carys. Now ..." She lifts the small cup, holding it out to me.

My face crumples—I have to drink this disgusting tea without honey. I peer into the cup at the amber liquid inside, the tealeaves sunken to the bottom.

"It won't be that bad," Alys assures me. "One gulp. You'll hardly taste it."

Setting my resolve, I swallow it down with one gulp just before the tealeaves could escape into my mouth. The liquid hits the back of my tongue, the bitterness making me gag slightly. I set the empty cup down so hard it's a wonder it doesn't crack.

Alys chuckles. "It's a fertility suppressant, dear one, not a casual afternoon tea. It's not that bad." She pours me a fresh cup of water. "You can't always have heaps of honey at your disposal."

I don't see why not, but I guzzle down the water, desperate to get the bitterness out of my mouth.

Alys exhales loudly, a smile on her face as she shakes out her arms as though preparing for a fight. "Alright, grounding time. I'm afraid that temper of yours is showing itself very often lately."

"Because I'm surrounded by arseheads." I shrug and Alys laughs.

"Be that as it may, there will come a day when you'll have to remain calm despite the *arseheads* around you. You're to be queen one day. You can't fight fire with fire. You need to learn to quell the flames."

"Hopefully it'll be a while still before I'm queen." My mother is a fighter. She can defeat this mystery illness.

Alys's lips curve upward, but it's that poor-Carys smile that leaves her grey eyes dull. I know it too well. "In the meantime ... You know the routine. Relax your mind, plant your awareness firmly on what your body is doing and not on the world around you. Ready?"

I roll my eyes. "Ready."

Chapter 6
DURVLA

THE STENCH OF URINE and feces forces me back into consciousness. My eyes fly open to darkness, and a band of panic wraps around my chest as the memories pour into my head. Gut roiling, I push myself upright and reach out, grasping for anything. Something dry and gritty grazes my fingertips. Where am I? I push myself backward on my bottom until my back meets something solid that feels like bars.

Slowly, I adjust to the dark, to the hay scattered beneath me along the wooden floor of the horse-drawn prison wagon. There seems to be others within the metal bars, but I can't make out more than their silhouettes. Riders in black uniforms that blend into the night surround our wagon on horseback, their faces distorted from the undulating shadows cast by their torches.

My stomach churns, sending spasms up my throat. I swallow, and immediately, my stomach twists again.

I need to calm myself.

A shallow breath later, I try to gauge my surroundings. Outside the wagon are small, unkempt altars, and textile mills amongst scattered houses. Not much else is decipherable, but I'm certain we're in Ballybaeg.

My back pressed against the bars, I close my eyes and try to force coherent thoughts into my mind. Between my unpredictable body and my pitiful lack of athleticism, I would never get far, even if there was an escape. If my very scant geographical knowledge serves me right, Mainland is about two days away.

Growing up, we all heard stories about Mainland. About the overindulgent banquets upon the tables of the nobles, the colorful garments of silk and lace, and the jewels that bedazzle their entitled necks. They have easily accessible healers and more efficient medicines—even a cure for the outbreak that wiped out so many people years ago. Their luxuries are unattainable in the Grounds.

My heart lurches as the cage rocks hard enough to throw me onto my side. I squint against the glare of the sun as I push myself upright against the bars again.

I must have fallen asleep.

My tongue sticks to the roof of my mouth; I swallow repeatedly in hopes of chasing the dryness away. A massive hole in my sock allows my big toe to peek out, my feet growing stiffer and tingling painfully. The icy breeze that permeates the thin fabric of my clothing does nothing to help, even as I tuck my feet beneath my skirt and wrap my arms around my torso.

As much as I try to ignore the others, I'm still aware of the elderly man across from me, a mother with her arms protectively around a sleeping toddler, and an adolescent girl sitting on one end with a perpetual scowl on her face. I count four others present. What have any of these people done? Or rather, what have they been accused of?

Beyond the bars, the dirt road bisects open pastures, and the houses are farther apart. Shaggy cows graze in the fields, and behind a fence to our left, fat pigs bask in the sunlight.

This must be the livestock region, Ballygort. I've come here once before with Da. That was a long time ago. Sadness whispers through my memories, paving the way for Taig's adorable face to infiltrate in my mind. Osheen is with him. He'll be fine. Right?

It isn't the norm that Osheen looks after Taig for an entire day; does he know the cues when Taig is hungry? Or overwhelmed?

Having a brother who cannot verbally communicate, I've figured out creative ways to tap into his fascinating mind. I can decipher his grunts, headshaking, and hand-wringing. Can Osheen?

My heart races and it's suddenly hard to breathe.

I'm not hungry at all, but my stomach is determined to gnaw on itself.

The cage grows more putrid by the minute. If the stench doesn't kill me, the embarrassment that grips me each time I contribute to the reek certainly will. Restlessness swells among the captives as the day drags on and the sun dips out of sight. No one is familiar, and most just keep to themselves. Every now and then a Forayer offers ladles of sullied water through the bars, pouring directly into our desperate hands.

Another night passes, and by midmorning, almost everyone clambers to their feet like eager children. I'm the last to stand, taking a moment for my vision to clear and my body to stabilize.

I squint at the view up ahead: a grand bridge with lattice sidings of wood and metal. On the other side of the rushing river, the grass is so green that it resembles a painting. Larger, more colorful houses and taller buildings line the streets.

Mainland.

It's about another half hour before we leave behind the jarring gravel roads of the Grounds and cross the bridge into Mainland, where the wheels of the cage wobble only slightly over brick paving. Mainlanders stroll about, some in woolen dress coats tapered at the waist, and others sporting luxurious tweed jackets that look so warm I want to crawl into them. Many stop to stare and jeer at us, their faces twisted with animosity.

A young boy around Taig's age strides forward. His cherubic face seems to have hardly seen the sun, and wisps of platinum blond curls tumble out from beneath his tweed cap. He stops to pick up a small rock and, sneering, flings it—

Oh gods.

I duck, my vision wavering. The stone flies right through the bars and over my head. It strikes an older man on the other side of the cage. Blood spurts through his fingers as he presses them against the wound above his eye. Sickening guilt grips me. The Mainlander boy is now doubled over at the waist, guffawing at the man's expense. A throng of other children gather around him, pointing their little fingers and taunting us while their guardians observe, unperturbed, from a distance.

I'm grateful when we leave that part of the city behind. Time drags on, but eventually we're moving alongside a loch, its dark waters sparkling in the sunlight. Ahead, an ominous iron gate looms, an impressive metal work of intricate whorls depicting a partial sun intersecting a crown turned on its side. The royal insignia. The gate opens to a vast expanse of patchy grass surrounded by stone barracks. Cannons, a host of other jail wagons, and varying structures unfamiliar to me fill the space. Soldiers rush about, all appearing busy with different tasks.

A green plateau—Paramount—looms above the barracks, and at the apex, a stunning fortress of grey stone eclipses the sky.

The Fortress.

Even from this distance, it's foreboding. I gape at the castle's silhouette before my attention drops to the ground.

At the farthest side of the encampment, nestled in the shadow of the Paramount plateau, is Fiada Purlieu. Great Rhianu, have mercy. Even us Grounders know that lush forest is where the Veil resides—the separation between our world and the Otherworld. It's also where the Veilguards, ordinary citizens from the Grounds who are conscripted by the crown, serve as the first line of defense from Otherworldly onslaught.

I didn't expect it to appear so ... ordinary. It's hard to believe that monsters and other beings not of this world can allegedly break through said Veil.

Very hard to believe.

I'm so caught up in my own thoughts that I don't notice we've stopped moving for a while. My head jerks toward the Forayer speaking from the open gate of the cage, but I've already missed half of what he's said. "—May the Great Father Lierwen bestow his favor upon you and Lugda have mercy on your souls."

We stumble out of the cage. My muscles are stiff from sitting for so long, and dirt filters in through the holes in my socks, but I keep moving. The captives are sorted into lines within the encampment, all heading toward barracks where a mixture of Forayers in black and other soldiers in charcoal gather.

Nausea seizes my gut. I could die here ... On what basis was I apprehended? Does it demand my death? With luck, I'll serve as a Veilguard. At least it's not an immediate death sentence. Still, fear latches onto me.

As soon as I step away from the cage, falling into a line of other captives, someone seizes my arm. I flinch and face a woman in a charcoal uniform with a royal insignia pin and a couple of badges over her heart. Her impressive height and breadth obscure my view, and the coppery streaks in her short brown hair catch the sunlight. One of her eyes is deep brown, but the other is cloudy and devoid of pigment. A jagged scar runs from above the eyebrow on that side, down to her russet cheek. Her unnerving gaze nearly has me wilting. My focus darts back and forth between her eyes and her lips, terrified I'll miss something or be too suspicious.

"State your name, girl," she says.

"Durvla Garrick." My throat aches from the utterance.

The woman nods sharply. "I'm Sergeant Angharad. Come with me."

I struggle to keep up with her long strides as she marches across the compact dirt toward a building that overlooks what appear to be training grounds. Most of the other captives are being led in the opposite direction.

My brows furrow. "Where am I going?"

She keeps her pace, and my chest tightens as I'm unable to read her lips. "Pardon?"

Her head snaps to me. "Do not speak."

My heart hiccups and I press my lips together, rapidly nodding.

When she comes to an abrupt halt, I dig my heels into the dirt to stop. My body protests, muscles aching, dizziness setting in. More soldiers in charcoal stand on either side of the entrance to the building. They salute Sergeant Angharad as I hurry in behind her, my threadbare socks catching on the stony floor. Unfinished red brick surrounds us, and the only furniture in sight is a long wooden table bearing a pitcher and tankard, and a rickety wooden chair in the center of the room.

I'm suddenly, staggeringly aware of how much my mouth feels coated with sand.

Sergeant Angharad regards me with apathy when I face her again. We stop in the center of the room, and she says, "Remove your clothing."

I blink at her. "What?"

Her eyes narrow to slits. "Remove. Your. Clothing."

At that moment, a young soldier steps into the room. He's slight and fair-skinned with a bald head. Though he doesn't appear older than sixteen, his brown-black eyes are severe. I turn to Sergeant Angharad again.

"Make haste!" she says.

I flinch. *In front of … him?* My focus shifts back and forth between them.

"Or do you want me to remove them for you?"

"No, I can do it," I mumble.

With shaky hands, I unlace my tunic and pull it off over my head. My skirt joins it on the floor, followed by my undershirt and my socks. With each layer, I lose another splinter of dignity, until at last, I'm naked as the day I was born. Humiliated, I cross my arms over my breasts, grateful for once that there's not much to hide. Sergeant Angharad towers over me, her asymmetrical leer boring right through me.

"Remove your hands."

My cheeks burn as I let my hands fall away from my breasts. I want so much to turn away from the woman, but I need to pay attention to her face in case she gives more orders.

Her callous glare darts over my body, appraising me like I'm livestock. An unpleasant shiver dances across my skin. "Take off the bracelet."

My stomach dips. I never take it off. "My mother gave this to me," I explain. "Please. It's the last thing I have to remember her by."

"Take it off or I will."

I fumble with the ties of the leather bracelet. With reluctance, I remove and relinquish it, struggling to draw a breath without tears spilling down my cheeks. I'm left both bereft and overcome all at once. Like every emotion is trying to cram its way into an already crowded vessel. Ice and heat simultaneously flood my veins, thrumming through my temples. It takes everything within me to remain standing as Sergeant Angharad tucks my bracelet into her pocket.

She steps closer as the boy approaches.

I stop breathing for a heartbeat as he marches toward me, an iron stick in his hand. It glows an angry orange on one end.

Sergeant Angharad grabs my left arm, immobilizing it in her beefy hands at my elbow and wrist where a band of lighter brown skin is the only evidence of the bracelet I once wore. Before I can register what's happening, searing pain shoots from my forearm straight up to my shoulder. I can't stop the scream that escapes me as the soldier continues to hold the metal rod against my flesh. My knees wobble, cold sweat breaks out on my skin, and my breaths come in shallow pants as I turn my head away. Sergeant Angharad releases me. I stumble but somehow keep to my feet. Aghast, I stare down at the raw flesh of my forearm. Bright red against my tawny skin, the royal insignia stares back at me.

I've been *branded*.

I stare at the soldier's back as he walks out of the room. The air chills me, reminding me of my nudity, and I clutch my branded arm to my chest.

I'm shivering uncontrollably now, but not just from the cold. Everything aches, my throat is like the Wastelands. My legs wobble; I'm not sure how much longer I can remain standing.

Sergeant Angharad appears at my side again, shoving clean clothes against my chest. "Get dressed," she says.

I nod, biting back a cry of pain from the fresh burn on my forearm as I slip the tunic over my head and gingerly guide my injured arm through the first sleeve. The excess fabric hangs off me, rubbing against my raw skin with each movement. The trousers prove to be more difficult than I imagined to don; my balance is way off kilter, my toes are still numb, and every movement of my left arms is agonizing.

The incessant whistling in my ear only worsens things. I get one leg in and my foot catches on the inside of the other pant leg. Sergeant Angharad throws her arm out to keep me from toppling over.

"Thank you," I say, but she just folds her burly arms across her chest.

"Cadet Bronn," she calls. I follow her line of sight to where the young soldier has returned with two others in charcoal uniforms.

Immediately, my pulse skitters. They march toward me, manacles in hand. I'm shackled at the wrists in front of my body and flanked by the other two guards. Dizziness swoops in with a vengeance. I'm kept upright only by the grip of the soldiers.

"Please," I beg. I don't even know why I've been brought here. I haven't done anything! The words remain locked in my mind, and Sergeant Angharad turns to walk away. "*Please!* I can't ..." I can't what? Logical words abandon me as bright light flares in my vision. I blink forcibly, clinging to consciousness. I can't faint. Not now. Not when I have no clue what's about to happen to me.

My ears are agonizing, and nausea has my stomach in a chokehold. Which would be worse: vomiting all over these soldiers or collapsing? The absurdity of it forces a sharp, bitter laugh out of me.

Cadet Bronn stands in front of me again, his face distorted with annoyance. I open my mouth to plead again, all the while fighting the darkness that threatens to pull me down. But it's clear my fight is in vain as soon as he lifts his fist.

I hardly feel the strike before the darkness welcomes me back in its embrace.

Chapter 7
CARYS

THE ARCHERY RANGE IS nestled within tall, perfectly manicured hedges in a massive field just beyond the royal gardens. Beneath my feet, the grass has been so trampled that there's more dirt than green. Wiping my hand across my brow, I force myself to focus on my archery master, Gethin, and not on the boredom of target after target that I can hit with my eyes closed. If only he'd give me a greater challenge!

"I believe you're ready to work on hitting targets from horseback," Master Gethin says, shoving wispy white hairs out of his gaunt face.

My eyes widen, and I press my lips together to keep from squealing, but a smile spreads across my face anyway. I set my bow against a boulder and shift on my feet, unable to stand still.

"I'll go set up the targets. In the meantime, try not to shoot your sentinel, hmm?" He turns and hurries off, leaving me surprised at his attempt at humor.

I set my bow and quiver down against a boulder as Tiernan steps closer to me. "Have you considered learning to wield a dagger?" he asks.

"This again?" I prop my fists on my hips.

The corner of his lip twitches, his stern expression softening. "You're impressive with a bow and arrow, but in the event of close combat—"

My heart skitters and I push away the memory of an arrow zipping toward me. With a steadying breath, I summon enough gall to say, "I'm not a warrior or a knight, Tiernan. What close combat must I be prepared for?"

His thoughtful expression and unspoken words uncover the rubble of my past. I wet my lips, which have suddenly gone dry.

"Princess, you *know* there have been—"

I cut him off with a glare. "Security at Paramount has been rectified since that last incident." I try not to remember rough hands around my throat, but it's getting harder to breathe. The archery range fades from my view. I blink away the memories. Hot, reeking breath against my face. Harsh promises of destroying the royal bloodline. The sword running straight through the assassin's middle, forcing him to release his death grip on me. Once I'd caught my breath, it had taken so godsdamned long for me to stop screaming. Even as the assassin lay dead at my feet, even as Tiernan told me over and over that I was safe.

It wasn't the first time he'd saved my arse.

With another blink, the gardens of the past fall away, the archery range clear again as the cool breeze rustles through my hair and pulls me back to the present. Tiernan's sword is still firmly secured at his hip. There's no blood in sight, no dead assassin at my feet. I absently rub my neck, as if the incident happened moments ago rather than three years prior.

The next attempt had been just days later as I stepped beyond the gates to visit Barr na Cahar with Ellynne. The arrow meant for me had whizzed right past Ellynne's ear. I can still remember her shriek that had twisted my gut and left me unwilling to ever leave the castle again.

Tiernan's concerned face comes back into view and I narrow my eyes at him as though my mind hadn't taken a nasty tumble into the past. His lips part, but another voice comes from elsewhere and it takes me a brief moment to return to my senses. I spin, perhaps a little too dramatically, toward Iywan as he approaches. The sun suddenly feels too warm, and I have to remind myself to unclench my jaw and smile politely.

Tiernan's face has gone stony again as he lowers his head in a respectful greeting, but he remains rooted at my side.

"My apologies for interrupting your archery lessons, Princess. But we need to discuss the matter of the Feast and your suitors."

I breathe in and feign a perfectly composed smile. "Can this wait until after my lesson? Lord Gethin has just left to set up targets along the riding path."

He purses his lips briefly, then reluctantly bows before turning to retreat. A few heartbeats pass while Tiernan and I stare at Iywan's back as he moves farther away.

Tiernan finally speaks up. "If you keep putting off this discussion, I'm afraid Lord Iywan will choose a suitor for you. And if he does, I have an inkling it won't be in your favor. He only cares about image."

"He can't do that," I say.

Gethin arrives before Tiernan can rebut. "Ready?" Gethin asks. I turn away from Tiernan and nod to my archery master.

There aren't as many candles burning in my mother's bedchamber today. That apprentice girl—Brenna?—is at my sleeping mother's bedside. Iywan observes from a short distance, but as he sees me, he bows. Brenna, or Bertie, or whatever her name is, has the audacity to smile at me, and I clutch the tome of fairytales against my chest.

She knows something you don't, a voice inside me whispers. *Don't trust her.*

I stiffen, my breath frozen in my chest.

"No valbane today, Your Highness," the apprentice girl says proudly.

My mother's breathing is languid. She's even paler, if possible. I glare at the apprentice healer. "You're dismissed, Blawnid."

She draws a breath to speak but simply curtsies before rushing off.

I approach my mother. "I'd like some alone time with her," I say to Iywan.

Iywan bows again. "Yes, Princess Carys."

As the door shuts behind him, I gently set the tome down on the side table and brush my hand across my mother's clammy forehead. "Mother, it's me. Carys."

My mother's eyes flutter, but they don't fully open. Her lips part as though she intends to say something. No sound emerges until she clears her throat gently. "Water," she rasps after a long pause.

"Water?" Her lips are chapped and peeling, though Brigid just walked off with a bowl. I move toward the table and grab the small pitcher of water, pouring some into a teacup before returning to my mother. "Tiernan, help me."

He nods and leaves his post at the door to help sit my mother up, propping her against the cushioned headboard. She's barely able to keep her head upright, but Tiernan stabilizes her as I hold the cup to her lips so she can sip the water.

A lump rises in my throat and tears threaten to escape as water drips from the queen's mouth. But I steel my resolve, gently wiping my sleeve across her chin to catch the water droplets. My mother's strength lies within her broken body like a trapped flame. When she finally turns to me, the recognition in her brown eyes both shreds and patches my heart. Would it be easier if that stubborn glint in her eyes ceased to exist? Then, at least, there wouldn't be much hope to hold on to. I could let her go. But that's not the case—her illness is as unpredictable as my shifting moods.

I swallow thickly. "It's so good to see you awake." My voice sounds strained.

A ghost of a smile appears on her haggard face. "Good to see you too."

Tiernan's expression is sympathetic as he takes the cup from me. I nod my appreciation and turn back to my mother just as she reaches out for my face. The little strength she's mustered wavers, and I take her cool hand in mine, pressing it against my cheek.

"You're still wearing your amulet," she says, a calculating look on her face.

I blindly clasp the sun-shaped amulet resting against my chest. Its warmth radiates, as though the sun truly lives within, comforting me as always. "Of course." My brows furrow. "Why wouldn't I?"

Her smile turns woeful. "Because you've outgrown it."

The necklace fits perfectly fine, but it's not worth an argument, so I nod. "Alright, Mother. Shall I read you a passage from our favorite book?"

The skin around her eyes crinkles before the smile takes over her lips. "Of course, cariad."

The term of endearment envelops me like a hug. I sink onto the bed beside her, our shoulders touching. I open the book somewhere in the middle, its weight shared across our laps. Stories about selkies, serpentine beasts that hide within our lochs, and the cunning Fair Folk fill the book's pages. Every child grows up hearing about the will-o'-wisps that lead lost souls to their deaths—a warning to keep wee ones from wandering away from safety.

I've always been intrigued by banshees and, as a child, would so often imagine the keening that foretold the death of a loved one. Around the time of my brother's death, I'd imagined seeing a dark, wraithlike creature wandering the halls of the castle.

It was perhaps how my young mind coped.

My favorite tales are the ones about Mages. Particularly the heirs of the sun goddess, Agryna—Lightweavers who saved the realm from destruction by the evil enchantress. It would be so bloody incredible to be a Mage.

I begin reading the well-known tale of "The Enchantress Queen."

Enidwen was a lesser Mage who envied the magical prowess of her siblings. She spent her days mixing potions and tending to fevers in her village, while her siblings flaunted their magical healing abilities, curing diseases and fatal wounds.

One day, Enidwen was bathing in the River Daehan, her golden hair like the very sun that shone upon the waters, when a man rose from its depths to gaze upon her beauty. He was clearly not of this world, but he was immediately smitten with the mortal woman. The Otherworlder, Caedmon, dazzled Enidwen with his display of powers and his captivating physique. He doted on her and treated her like royalty. Enidwen very quickly became enthralled with Caedmon, and he fell deeper in love.

Caedmon told Enidwen tales of the Otherworld, where there was no sickness and no death. Enidwen beseeched him to take her back to his paradise, and he agreed with one condition.

She could never return to the mortal realm again.

Good riddance, Enidwen thought, and she departed the mortal realm with Caedmon to begin life anew in the Otherworld.

The Otherworld was just as Caedmon had described. The land was breathtaking. Gentle beasts of the air and land roamed the realm in peace. Vivid foliage and flowers adorned the terrain without effort. Otherworlders of all tribes lived in harmony with one another, drawing their raw power from the very essence of their land—from the lush forests and shining rivers, the lightning that split the skies, and the gems that bloomed within the caverns.

Gifts from the ancient gods who begat them.

One day, Enidwen asked Caedmon, "Are there no evil beings here?"

Caedmon replied, "In ancient times, there were corrupt beings among us. They were banished hundreds of mortal years ago to the Underworld where they forged their kingdom within Lugda's domain. The leader of the fallen ones, the Underling Prince, is imprisoned within Lugda's hells, never to see the light of day again."

The knowledge tantalized Enidwen. "Aside from the Underling Prince, are the Underlings able to infiltrate the mortal realm as Otherworlders occasionally do?" she asked Caedmon.

"Only when the Veil between our worlds is thin enough."

Enidwen thought back to her life in the mortal realm. She craved imperfection. Craved *more*. She could manipulate fire and light, but had no one to flaunt her newfound powers to. Her siblings would be so jealous. They would finally respect her.

Another day came and Enidwen asked Caedmon, "What about the monsters that dwelled in the Otherworld? I grew up with tales of such creatures."

"They have been dormant since the banishment of the Underlings," Caedmon replied. "They have slept for hundreds of years. Their powers are too great; they would restore corruption to our paradise."

"Are you afraid they may awaken someday?"

"They can only be awoken by an irreversible sacrifice," Caedmon replied.

More time passed and curiosity gnawed at Enidwen's immortal soul. She once again approached Caedmon and asked, "What would happen if something is taken from the Otherworld to the mortal realm?"

Caedmon grew angry and refused to respond.

It was all the answer that Enidwen needed.

I stop reading as my mother's eyelids grow heavier. Sooner than I'd like, her breathing deepens and she gives up the fight to remain awake. I softly close the book and consider her ailing face. A pang settles in my chest, but I have to focus on the reality that she's still here. She's still holding on to life despite the grip Lugda has on her.

But how much longer can she fight?

"I'll come back tomorrow," I whisper as I lean in to press a kiss to her cheek. With a sigh, I stand and head for the door. Once again, I nod to her guards and set off with Tiernan.

As we return to my bedchamber, he diligently takes his place beside my door, and I walk into the silence of solitude.

Left alone, I'm consumed with desolation and excess—contradiction at its finest. My mind buzzes with hundreds of thoughts, overlapping, refusing to be silenced. My Feast dress, suitors, archery and grounding lessons, council meetings, Audience, and other responsibilities that I constantly shirk. Yet, it all feels meaningless. I move to my side table and set the tome down with gentle precision to keep myself from flinging it off the balcony.

What's the point of fairytales when reality is so much louder?

My hand moves to the amulet around my neck, and I press it against my chest, allowing the warmth to envelope me, trying to focus on the grounding techniques that Alys has taught me. I plop down onto my bed and remove my shoes and stockings, pressing my feet against the floor and embracing the cool sensation.

With forced focus, I track the rays of sunlight that filter in through my window and across the floor. I close my eyes and listen to the howl of the wind outside. Slowly, the rampage of thoughts fades away, until my hand finds my amulet again, and memories come eddying back to the tempest that is my mind.

I still remember the day my mother gave me this necklace.

It had been shortly after the death of my brother.

One thing I can never forget about Aneirin is his laugh. It was lighthearted. Musical, almost. He was kind, witty, and a damn good swordsman. He would've made a great king someday. He was ten years my senior, and I was but five years old. A little flame of a child, carefree and too eager to give in to the voice in my head that told me to misbehave. Until Aneirin's death.

Lugda had taken him so suddenly.

An accident, people said. My mother has always refused to share the details of his death, even with me. But I remember the overwhelmingly fragmented feeling that had crawled inside me after he died. I remember my mother hanging the necklace around my neck, the weight of it settling against my chest, quelling the unease.

"To quiet that voice in your head," my mother had said. "And to comfort you in times when you've forgotten your own strength." She'd traced the sun design that surrounded the ruby gem. "Agryna's blessing."

And I'd believed it.

But where's Agryna now?

Chapter 8
CARYS

THE SECOND QUARTERLY RAID started a few days ago, so by now the Forayers should've returned with their plunder. I yank my bedchamber door open and there's Callum standing guard. Something within me unfurls now that I don't have to deal with Tiernan's suffocating logic and sternness. "Good to have you back," I tell him.

He nods, a small smile on his lips. "Happy to serve, Your Highness."

My forehead creases. Why the formality?

But a flash of beige and grey robes moves across my plane of vision as a portly young man comes to an abrupt halt. Surprise lifts his dark brows, and there is stubble across his normally clean-shaven dark brown skin. He bows a tad awkwardly, struggling to balance a stack of leather-bound books in his arms. "Your Highness," he says with a cocky smile.

I resist the urge to scowl at him. The councilors in general are infuriating, but Jac, being the youngest Master Historian ever to sit on the Council, is particularly annoying. "Councilor Jac," I respond with cool, rehearsed politeness. I stare at him a while longer before he bows again and departs.

There aren't normally council members on this side of the fortress. It's odd, but there is always something strange going on around here. I sigh and set off toward my intended destination.

"Where are you off to in such a hurry?" Callum asks, catching up to me with a single stride.

I glance up at him. "The depository."

He smirks. "Bored again, are you?"

"Always. I had to endure Tiernan for the entire morning, you know."

Callum chuckles as we set off for the other side of the castle. "He's not the most jovial, but don't tell him I said that. I'd hate to be on the receiving end of his fury. You have the best of the best guarding you."

I look up at him, my lips curving. "Patting yourself on the back, are you?"

"A tad." He schools his expression into neutrality as we arrive in front of the heavily guarded depository door. The guards bow to me and open the door to an enormous room with bare stone floors and unpainted brick walls. It's filled with all kinds of odds and ends, from ornate chests to unmarked scrolls. Often, it's a tossup whether there's anything valuable or if it's all just rubbish.

"Where are the new things?" I ask a burly guard.

He points and I follow his finger.

It's a dress.

My eyes widen. The hangs over a crooked, rusty nail. I've seen a lot of dresses in my twenty-one years, but they're usually painfully comparable. This one is a breath of fresh air. Why is it in the depository, of all places?

I make a beeline for the knitted garment and stare at it in awe. The embroidery on the bodice beckons me and I cannot resist lightly running my fingers over the design. The embroidery is the same color as the dress itself, but it still somehow stands out perfectly. The point of a knitting needle protrudes from the bottom and the rest of the hem is tragically unraveling.

My focus is fixed on the work of art as I ask no one in particular, "What is a dress doing here?" No one responds. "Callum." I don't have to say anything else for him to appear at my side. The dress hangs well beyond my reach; even Callum has to rise onto the balls of his feet to retrieve it. When he hands it to me, I'm surprised by the weightiness of it as I cradle it in my arms. Still, no one has answered me, and a stab of impatience propels my temper.

"Somebody speak, godsdammit." I fix the guards with a simmering glower and the burly one spits out his words like I'm holding a sword to his throat.

"It was confiscated from a home in one of the Big Three villages, Your Highness."

"Ballybaeg?"

"No. Cluain Baile," the shorter guard says.

My brows furrow. "That can't be right. No one in the agriculture village could possibly have this sense of fashion or talent. Are you certain?"

"Yes, Your Highness. I collected the report. The woman claims she made it."

"What is her trade?"

His face crumples in concentration. "Botanist, I believe, Your Highness."

I stare at the dress in my arms. How could a *botanist* make something this exquisite? "Has Lord Iywan seen this?"

"Not yet, Your Highness."

I take a few strides toward the door, and in the silence of the depository, the clacking of my heels echoes. "This botanist ... Was she arrested or ... ?"

"Yes, she waws arrested, Your Highness."

Theft isn't treason. Moreso, this would be *petty* theft. Not any business of Mainland. I hold it up the dress as high as I can and focus on the knitting needle poking out the bottom. I've been to Barr na Cahar numerous times and I've had countless dresses made for me. This dress is unlike anything worn by Grounders, but it's not a Mainland style either. It could be common to the Outer Isles, perhaps. But I doubt the woman stole it. Whoever this woman is, she has extraordinary talent and she's wasting it in the brig. Or worse ...

I want her in my service.

Immediately.

Chapter 9
DURVLA

PAIN YANKS ME INTO consciousness. My entire body throbs, especially my face. With my first attempt to open my eyes, my skull threatens to split wide open. Beneath me, the surface is rough and a stench that I cannot decipher assaults my senses. Curiosity melds with fear, but I keep my eyes closed. Until something touches my arm.

I'm upright in no time, images of soldiers rising in my mind. My heart pounds as I scoot backward on my bottom, the coarse surface scraping my palms, the injury on my forearm pulling a cry of pain from me.

I squint against the pulsating headache that mars my vision. A woman with deep brown skin and grey-speckled black hair stares back, holding her hands up as if to placate me. Whatever she says is lost on me.

I run my hands over the surface beneath me. There are rough stone walls at my back and sides, and metal bars in the front. Shackles no longer bind my wrists, but I'm in a prison cell, no doubt. Terror wraps around my heart, squeezing until I forget how to breathe. My eyes dart back to the woman, and she rears back slightly as though I've startled her just as much.

Again, she holds her hands up to show she has no ill intent. Then she blinks, thrown off guard. For a moment, her grey gaze lingers, then she snaps herself out of the shock. "I'm not ... hurt you," she says.

Focus Durvla. Breathe, I tell myself. I force my attention to her full lips, willing my mind to pick up what it can in the dim lighting.

"... name is ... tend your wounds."

Wounds? The throbbing in my arm and face becomes more apparent, as if she's summoned them. I lift my hand to my face and my fingertips meet swollen flesh. The skin is rough, as though a scab is forming.

The healer swats my hand away lightly and tilts her head into my line of vision. "Try not to touch it." She hands me a metal tankard. "Drink. *Slowly*." She makes a gesture with her hand to indicate speed.

Frowning, I take the tankard from her and peer into it. My hand is clammy as I hold it tightly. The first sip of the cool, crisp water immediately soothes my parched throat. Keeping the healer's words in mind, I drink slowly, savoring every drop. The healer rummages through a large canvas bag at her side and pulls out a couple of clay jars and a washcloth.

She pauses in her rummaging to focus on me again and says slowly, pantomiming with the flannel, "I'm going to clean your wounds and apply some salve. You should feel much better."

I set the empty tankard aside before pulling back my sleeve and daring to look at the arm that was branded. The skin is violently red and welted, slightly oozy. Nausea grips my gut again and I turn away, swallowing forcibly.

The healer taps my shoulder cautiously and holds up the flannel for me to see. "… prevents festering. It will sting … breathe through it."

I nod, but as soon as the cloth touches my burn, I bite back a yelp and the taste of copper blooms on my tongue. That was quite a *sting*.

"I know." Her expression is empathetic. "… may sting a little less. You have a nasty … your cheek … isn't as severe as the burn."

The memory of Cadet Bronn's fist flying toward my face brings a fresh wave of phantom pain to my cheek, but I breathe in deeply as the healer applies more solution to the cloth. I want to cry. I hate this dim lighting with all my heart. My head pounds from the sheer concentration just to figure out what this kind healer is saying to me.

I reel in my focus again just as she asks, "Where are you from? If you don't mind answering."

"Cluain Baile."

Like she warned, the cut on my cheek stings when the damp cloth touches it, but nothing like the branding. Her brows knit together as she picks up a jar and opens it. "What was your trade in Cluain Baile?"

"Botany."

Is that astonishment that crosses her face? She dips a thick finger into the jar, and then lifts my branded arm with her other hand. I tense up, preparing for more pain, but the clear salve only leaves behind a cool, soothing sensation that travels through my arm. I sigh with relief and the healer smiles.

"There," she says. "You'll be as good as new in no time." She smiles, but I can't smile back.

Good as new in no time, for what purpose? "What's going to happen to me?"

Her smile falters. Well, that's promising …

"Someone will speak to you soon," she says. "… don't know much."

Helpful. "Thank you for ..." *Patching me up, being kind* ... The words remain trapped in my mind as I focus only on breathing through the fear.

"No thanks needed." She gets to her feet and turns toward the bars, her full-bodied figure blurring from the tears gathering in my eyes. A guard steps up to open the gate to my cell and the healer gracefully exits. She's the first kind face I've seen here and I'm sure she'll be the last.

Chapter 10
CARYS

"ARE GROUNDERS REALLY BEING apprehended for petty theft?"
I ask as I barge into Iywan's study. He jumps so hard that he knocks
over his inkwell. He yanks the parchment he was writing on away from
the traveling ink and sets the jar upright again. I grimace—that was
unfortunate.

"I'm not sure what you're referring to, Princess," he says as he
takes a handkerchief from his robes to mop up the ink spillage.

I hold up the dress I've toted to his study. "A guard informed
me that they took this dress from Cluain Baile and apprehended its
maker. This isn't treason, so there shouldn't have been any grounds
for an arrest."

Iywan appears genuinely befuddled. "I was not aware." He stands
and walks over to a basin of water to wash the ink off his hand.

"Do you have the newest arrest and conscription records?"

"Yes." He wipes his long fingers dry before consulting a hefty pile of documents on his massive desk. In silence, he thumbs through the pages. "May I ask why you're interested in this particular case?" He doesn't turn away from the paperwork.

"If she, indeed, made this dress, I'd like her in my service."

Iywan pauses for half a heartbeat. "Wouldn't you prefer a seasoned dressmaker from Barr na Cahar?"

"No. I'm tired of the shi—*rubbish* dresses from those dressmakers."

He pulls out a sheet of paper and his eyes dart across the lines of text. "Her name is Durvla Garrick. A botanist from Cluain Baile. Her sentence is currently under review."

My eyes widen, and Iywan sets the page down slowly. "What is there to review? This dress could not have come from Barr na Cahar. Stylistically, it doesn't fit the standards of recent fashion trends. Therefore, if this botanist girl stole it, it had to be from her own people. That is within *their* jurisdiction, not Mainland's."

"The Grounders are incapable of executing justice—therefore crimes committed by a Grounder fall within the jurisdiction of Mainland if deemed punishable by the Forayers."

He sounds like he's just quoted that from a law book, and it's utter shit. "So now we're giving glorified mercenaries permission to act as judges? That's madness. The raids are supposed to be for the purpose of keeping Erleya safe from the threat of Otherworldly activity. As if there has been any proof of such a thing in centuries. If there's something in need of a *review*, it's these archaic laws."

Iywan's eyes close for a moment, his narrow chest expanding with a deep breath. "Duly noted, Princess. However, the Forayers are not acting as judges. They're arresting individuals based on a crime and bringing the prisoners to Paramount to receive their sentence. It is likely that Durvla Garrick's sentence will be a lifelong service to the Veilguards rather than a death sentence."

I gesture to the heavy knitted dress in my arms. "The Veilguards? For allegedly stealing a *dress?*" My voice echoes in the chamber. I can almost hear Alys in my head, telling me not to fight fire with fire. I take a deep breath and exhale slowly. "Lord Iywan, I'd like you to look at this dress." I hold it up. "There are knitting needles still in it. Even if this woman stole it, what could she do with it? *Stare* at it?"

Iywan's eyes move from the dress to my face. He's unimpressed, making me glance at the garment in my hand. Just a moment ago, it appeared to be the greatest dress I'd ever seen. Now it's obvious that it is flawed, the material isn't the highest quality—the wool is scratchy—the embroidery is nonuniform ... but what more can be expected from something created in the Grounds?

It's not just beautiful and unique despite the flaws. It's beautiful and unique *because* it's flawed. It's more interesting than the hundreds of dresses I've had made by renowned dressmakers. If the creator behind this dress gets her hands on quality material, the result would be stunning. I just know it!

"What if we let her prove that it isn't stolen?" I ask Iywan.

"This is not your responsibility, Princess."

"For Rhianu's sake," I mumble, scrubbing my forehead with the heel of my hand. I huff out a breath and wrangle my temper. "I act on behalf of the reigning queen while she's incapacitated, with your counsel, of course. *Everything* is my responsibility."

Iywan falls silent under the weight of my words, his lips a thin line.

"Let me vouch for ... this woman." I can't even remember her name and I'm willing to vouch for her. My gut tells me it's a good idea. "Let her prove it's not theft. Give her a pair of knitting needles and wool. It's that simple. I even have some in my bedchamber. And if the bloody laws say she needs a sentence, then sentence her to royal servitude. It wouldn't be the first time that's been done."

Iywan exhales heavily and runs his fingers over his neatly braided grey hair. His reluctance is almost palpable as he lowers himself into the seat and takes a fresh sheet of paper. "I will write up an order." He dips his quill into the inkwell and begins rapidly writing. "If she can prove that the dress is indeed her work, you may have her in your service."

"Alright." I try to keep the excitement out of my voice.

"Bear in mind that this woman is from the Grounds and will require lessons in etiquette, as well as how to dress the part. At the moment, I cannot dispatch additional servants to assist in her assimilation. We're a tad short-staffed with the growing rebellion. The necessity of your marriage is becoming glaringly obvious."

"That's fine," I say with a shrug, not entertaining his not-so-inconspicuous nod toward my impending marriage. I'm sure Ellynne and Lowri won't mind helping the botanist with some etiquette.

A satisfying scratch of his signature at the end of the document nearly tugs a smile from me. I press my lips together to mask it, afraid that my enthusiasm might make him change his mind.

He folds the paper and tips a candle, dripping wax onto it to form a seal. He presses the signet of his ring into the wax as he turns his dark gaze to me. "Try not to make this a habit, Princess. You cannot always get what you desire."

"I never said I could." But I can get this one.

"We also must discuss the conditions of your marriage."

My stomach sinks a little. Queens are expected to immediately produce an heir, to ensure the bloodline will thrive. Without an heir, my reign would be at risk. And since no marriage means no heir, remaining unwed also threatens my reign. Somehow the expectation of begetting royal children frightens me even more than ascending the throne.

"I recall that the condition is: I get to choose my groom from your carefully handpicked list of suitors."

His jaw tightens, a vein pulsing visibly in his temple. "Yes, provided you properly weigh the pros and cons and decide which union would be best for the kingdom."

The dress gets heavier in my arms. I drape it over my shoulder and nod to Iywan. "I am aware of the importance of my choice."

"I would hope so. You've been preparing for this since childhood. I trust you'll make the right decision."

My chest tightens and I clear my throat to loosen the tension. "Once I have my new dressmaker, I'll be able to better focus on the *conditions* of my marriage." So romantic. "Much gratitude to you, Lord Iywan."

He stands and bows slightly before I offer him a pinched smile and get the hells out of his study as quickly as I can.

Chapter 11
DURVLA

MY THROAT AND CHEST ache from constantly fighting back tears. I'm not sure how long it's been, but as I'm dozing off yet again, the floor beneath me vibrates slightly. I glance up as the prison guard unlocks the gate and slides it open to let in a foreboding figure.

Sergeant Angharad comes to a halt in front of me and I stare at her mouth. "Good morning. Come along," she says.

I push myself to my feet, ignoring the relentless ache in my head and my blurry vision. At least my arm already hurts less—Mainland's salves are certainly far superior to anything we have in the Grounds. As I follow Sergeant Angharad out of the cell, another guard steps toward me. I instinctively flinch so hard that my muscles throb. The guard holds up manacles, but Sergeant Angharad says something to him that makes him back off.

I'm led down the passageway, my bare feet padding on the cold ground, my head forward to avoid the multitude of prisoner cells I pass. I hasten to keep up with Sergeant Angharad as she rounds the corner and takes a set of steep, rocky stairs down to an even lower level. It's dark, with limited light coming from an oil lamp bracketed to the wall. A lone door stands ajar ahead of us, and Sergeant Angharad grasps my arm to pull me through, marching straight toward a table in the center of the room. A horrid stain stares back at me from the wooden surface, flickering in the flames of the oil lanterns on either side of the room. I force my imagination away from forming theories behind the origin of the stain.

Sergeant Angharad pulls out the chair from behind the table and points. "Sit."

Somehow, I can't convince my legs to move.

Her brawny body goes rigid, her hand moving to her sword hilt. "Now!"

My heart and legs jump into motion, and I drop into the hard chair.

I find myself fixated on the stain on the table. A single thought circles in my mind: it's blood. I swallow down the nausea, but it takes effort. A multitude of scars mar the table. What could've caused them? As my mind starts reeling, Sergeant Angharad shoves something into my hands. A pair of metal knitting needles and the softest skein of wool I've ever touched. I turn my focus to the woman, perplexed.

She says something and I have to reel in my panicking mind to decipher her words.

"Make something?" I ask, hoping I've gotten it right.

"Do not make me repeat myself."

I nod and look down at the items, then up at the woman towering over me, forcing me to *knit*, practically at sword point. Luckily, her sword is safely in a scabbard at her hip. For now. I take a deep breath and set the needles down in my lap for a moment so I can find the end of the wool. My fingers are stiff and slightly numb from the cold, and my dominant arm throbs, my sleeve rubbing against the injured skin with each movement. Still, I get several stitches onto the needle and throw myself into the repetitive task as though my life depends on it.

In fact, I'm certain it does.

Tears blur my vision, and my hands tremble incessantly, but I work through it. Taig relies on me. I can't let him down. Even if I'm not physically there with him, I'm his person.

I knit faster than I ever have before, accidentally jabbing my fingers and palms with the dull tips now and then, but I bite through the mild discomfort of it all. After a while, a beefy hand comes into my vision and shoves the work down so aggressively that it's forced out of my hands. I lift my head, wide-eyed.

"That's enough," says Sergeant Angharad. She snatches my work from me and holds it up. I've made a small swatch with some kind of lacy motif. Whether it's an actual sensible design, I have no clue. Unimpressed, Sergeant Angharad walks over to the door again and has an exchange with another soldier.

Time drags by. I stare at the table again until the stains and damages morph into different shapes. After forever, Sergeant Angharad approaches me. "Let's go."

I stand without argument.

"You are released from your prison sentence," she says.

Hope floods my chest, and I fight the urge to smile. I'm going home.

"The princess has pardoned you, provided you agree to serve as her new dressmaker."

My heart sinks, my shoulders slump—icy dread replaces relief. I'm not going home … Tears prickle behind my eyes and it takes the utmost effort to keep from bawling, from begging them to let me go.

"Do you agree?"

What other choice do I have? It's either accept, or what? Conscription to the Veilguards? Life in prison? Death on the gallows? There are so many questions bombarding me, but I can't convince the words to come out. I nod and the soldier's shoulders sag.

"Follow me," she says.

I force myself to trail behind her out of the room and through a tunnel lit only with a few oil lanterns. We round corner after corner. I swear we're walking in circles.

Will I ever see my home again? Taig must be so confused about where I am. I hope Osheen is taking good care of him. but with the days growing longer, Osheen will be working more hours. What if Taig is subjected to long periods all by himself? My heart lurches and tears stream uncontrolled down my cheeks, even as I try to will them away.

My legs protest, my feet gripping the rough stone floor harder as we ascend through the tunnels. By the time we come upon dark stone stairs, pressure is building in my ears, and my calves and thighs scream louder with each step.

Just when I think I cannot climb any farther, the floor levels out and we head out of the darkness and through a small, empty vestibule toward a door. We step out of the building, and I draw in a sharp breath as my feet sink into the cold, grassy earth. The sun has departed, leaving behind a subtle trace of orange on the horizon and the faint beginnings of the crescent moon. After being in the dark for so long, the brightness of the sun is an assault on my senses. I squint, my vision bleary, my forehead beginning to throb.

Wordlessly, Sergeant Angharad follows the winding path of the plateau, trekking up a series of cliffside steps flanked by bushes. My heart hammers, but as much as I try not to look down, my curiosity pulls my gaze down to the loch below. Dark water wavers beneath the subtle rays of the sun, sending a rush of dizziness straight to my head.

I swallow the bitter acid that creeps into my throat and press my hand against the cobblestone wall. Keeping my body as close as possible to the wall, I follow Sergeant Angharad up one last set of stone steps to where the castle looms ahead. Rosebushes and green hedges border the pathway. We move toward an unguarded door, and Sergeant Angharad uses an iron key to open it. She moves aside to let me in, and my wet feet slip on the tiled floors. Again, the soldier has to steady me.

She fixes me with a glare and huffs with frustration before continuing onward. I follow her more carefully this time, each step calculated.

We walk down the corridor, passing several smaller doors before arriving at a large entrance at the very end. Sergeant Angharad raps on the wood and pushes it open, unleashing a rush of aromatic steam from within. The room is dim with candles all around. A slender woman with dark hair kneels on one of two shallow steps that lead up to a large vat of steaming water. Another woman with a curvaceous figure sets a heap of towels down on the bottom step and turns to face me as the door shuts.

I swallow and blink back tears as the redhead approaches me. She wipes her hands on her apron, her brown dress and underskirt pinned on one side up to her thick thigh, as though she's expecting to wade into the water herself. "Oh, poor dear," she says to me. "You look stunned."

Stunned ... that's one way to put it.

"With the ... and fresh clothing, ... much better. If you will disrobe?"

Not again ... I bite my lip, shaking my head as I step back. The tremor starts in my hands, and my legs follow. I can't breathe, my chest overcrowded with panic. I shut my eyes, and not even a breath later, a light touch against my shoulder causes me to flinch. My eyes fly wide as the redhaired woman pulls her hand away, concern on her face.

"You're safe in here," she says. "Have no fear."

I take one slow breath at a time.

"What do you say? Shall we get you cleaned up?"

Chapter 12
DURVLA

MY HANDS TREMBLE AS I begin removing my prison clothing. At least this time, I'm only wearing trousers and a top, so undressing is less prolonged, less painful.

The redhead's olive green eyes survey my appearance, and she reaches for my left hand, her face dropping. She holds my arm up, scrutinizing my branding, then gently lowers my arm to my side. "Those brig guards are monsters. We are not. Alright?"

I nod.

"I'm Ellynne." She makes an aloof gesture over her shoulder. "And that's my sister, Lowri."

Lowri smiles coyly at me and waves before turning back to her task of dumping something from a vial into the tub.

"Come, let's get you in the water," says Ellynne.

I nod and follow her toward the tub, one arm across my breasts, the other hand in front of my crotch.

"Relax, I've seen my fair share of tits and cunts," says Ellynne.

Well, that's blunt. Warmth floods my cheeks.

"Don't be … ; you have a lovely figure. You're going to look stunning in the dress … for you."

My lips part, but no words come to mind. I climb the marble steps to the tub and dip my toe into the water. It's bordering on too hot, forcing me to grit my teeth as my injured arm submerges for a moment. But as my body sinks beneath the surface—my left arm exempt—the tension in my muscles melts away. I sigh blissfully and close my eyes, reveling in the warmth that I've been denied for the past couple of days. Then someone touches my arm.

I open my eyes, and Ellynne holds up a damp washcloth. "We're going to lather you now."

Water sloshes from the abrupt shift as my body tenses again. "I can do it myself."

Both women laugh. "Don't be …" says Ellynne as she passes the cloth to Lowri.

I sigh. It takes me a moment to decipher her words. Apparently, modesty and privacy are preposterous in Mainland. Understood. I pretend that I'm anywhere but here as Lowri scrubs me clean. Ellynne disappears behind me and tugs on the ribbon and pins lost in my hair. Frizzy curls tumble down onto my shoulders before hot, fragrant water flows into my face, forcing my eyes closed. I hold my breath as a fresh stream pours over my head. Ellynne works her fingers through my hair, massaging my scalp in a way that almost makes me purr like a house cat. My body sinks further into the water and I almost—*almost*—forget that I'm naked in front of strangers.

When Ellynne and Lowri help me out of the tub. I'm not sure what to do with myself as they walk around me, drying my skin with a large towel and bandaging my left forearm before applying fragrant oils and creams to my skin. They dress me with practiced efficiency, donning me in a chemise and petticoat to begin.

Lowri lifts my arms to press a corset against my torso. She holds it in place while Ellynne laces up the front with impressive speed. This thing is squeezing the air out of my lungs. "It's kind of hard to breathe," I say.

Ellynne smiles warmly. "You get used to it."

At last, a mauve gown with loose, long sleeves tapered and ruffled at the wrist covers the layers beneath. The gown is simple in design, but the quality of the fabric is beyond anything I've ever dreamt of wearing. I run my hands over the lower portion of the dress, in awe of its softness.

"Come. Let's see what we can do with these glorious curls." Ellynne takes me by my unbranded right arm and leads me to a chair. I sit gingerly.

"My mum had curls like yours," Ellynne says. "She hated them, but I always found them so beautiful."

She probably hated them because they're a pain in the rear to manage. I smile at Ellynne regardless. "Thank you."

Ellynne stands behind me and pours oil into her hand before running her fingers through my ringlets from roots to tips. She adeptly works through the knots while I grit my teeth against the tugging. She steps back and Lowri slips a pair of knee-high stockings, and the finest ankle boots I've ever worn, onto my feet. "Alright," says Ellynne, appearing in front of me again.

She takes my hands and pulls me to my feet. "Have a look." She gestures toward a full-length mirror against the wall. I approach the mirror and gawk at the stranger in the reflection. There's no sign of the botanist from Cluain Baile. A crown of curls rests atop my head and the stay beneath my dress cinches my waist, the silken fabric embracing the full curve of my hips, my breasts appearing deceptively larger. My cheek is still slightly swollen and discolored from Cadet Bronn's assault, but surprisingly it barely hurts now.

Ellynne and Lowri stand on either side of me, grinning. "You look like you belong here now," Ellynne says.

Looks can be deceiving.

My chest constricts and the corset does nothing to help me draw a full breath again. If anyone finds out that I'm an Undesirable, I'm certain I'll be skipping the Veilguards and going straight to the gallows this time.

"Ready?" Ellynne asks, arching a brow at me.

I can do this; I can play the role of the perfect … dressmaker. I force a smile onto my face and nod before following the ladies out of the bath chamber and into the corridor again.

The plain hallways grow brighter, more sconces with candles lining the walls. We step out of the building and walk across a covered bridge overlooking a garden toward—Holy Rhianu, that's the Fortress on the Mount.

The Castle of Erleya.

My heart picks up speed, surpassing my quick footsteps as I follow Lowri and Ellynne. A mammoth of a door looms ahead of us, a guard standing on each side with a spear in hand.

Ellynne doesn't even say anything, but the guards step forward and turn in unison to push the doors open. My knees turn to water as an enormous room stretches out in front of us. The ceiling *must* be touching the sky. Elaborate chandeliers hang down from the sky-ceiling, crystals iridescent in the candlelight.

Someone nudges me and I flinch. A young woman glides toward me, resplendent in a silken emerald gown that drags slightly on the floor behind her. A golden circlet adorns her head and ink black hair cascades down well below her tiny waist, strands of gold shining through. For a moment, I'm mesmerized by the stark contrast of the golden strands against her dark tresses. Then she levels her piercing amber eyes on me, and I reflexively step back.

My knees lock as my gaze snags on a dark-haired guard beside her. His obsidian eyes glare daggers at me, icy ruthlessness radiating off his body. As if my very existence is offensive.

Then again, isn't that what Mainlanders think of Grounders?

The blood rushes from my face, but I can't convince myself to stop staring back at him—at his high cheekbones, the upward sweep of his eyes, the stubborn set of his jaw. He doesn't appear much older than me and his fair skin is free of wrinkles. But there are silver streaks on the right side of his head that disappear into a bun at the back.

At my side, Ellynne nudges me and I'm almost certain that she whispers something. I tear my focus away from the guard and end up gawking openly at the princess's freckled face. It's like I've lost all sense of decorum and logic. I cannot stop myself from staring at these stunning people.

The princess lifts her chin haughtily, but there's a hint of a smile on her lips. She steps closer to me, and I straighten, my skin prickling with unease.

Breathe.

I subtly suck in a breath.

"You're Durvla Garrick?" the princess asks at last.

I nod, before realizing it must be rude. "Yes, Your Highness." I should curtsy, but my knees are still locked and I'm afraid to fall if I try to move.

"Welcome to the Fortress on the Mount, Durvla. I've asked Ellynne to be your guide. She's been in my service for years now, so you're in excellent hands." She turns abruptly before I can respond and waltzes off, her intimidating guard beside her and Lowri in their shadow.

I release my breath, the tension flowing out of my shoulders. The return of my aching head and ringing ears wrap me in familiarity, reminding me that even though I'm on the other side of the bridge and dressed as a Mainlander, I'm still me.

"Come." Ellynne smiles reassuringly. "You must be hungry."

I nod. I'm not, in fact, hungry, but I don't argue.

"Alright," she says. "Let's head to the dining room first, then I'll give you a proper tour."

My appetite eventually resurfaces as I munch on fresh bread, cheese, and apples.

"You must have a thousand questions," Ellynne says as we set off on a tour of the castle. "I promise that after I give you the grand tour, I'll answer them all."   z`

I nod and keep up with her rapid pace. Ellynne shows me the concourse, the infirmary, and we pause at a door with *library* etched in gold against the dark wood. Ellynne pushes it open, revealing a grand room with a high ceiling. Hundreds, maybe thousands of leather-bound books line the solid wall-to-wall shelves. A round table with a lavish wooden pedestal and tripod base fills the empty space at the center of the library, two ivory-colored velvet armchairs on either side. There are even ladders to reach the upper shelves that tower above the room.

The shelves are almost ominously dark, contrasted by the textured painting of green and gold foliage on an ivory background that fills the spaces between the shelves and extends across the ceiling. Straight toward the back of the main room is an archway leading to another room filled with books. I stare in wonder. I want to get my hands on them all. Every. Single. Book.

Ellynne smiles as I turn to her again. "In awe?"

"I've never seen so many books in my life." I resist the urge to continue gawking at my surroundings and focus on Ellynne's words.

"Are there no libraries in Cluain Baile?"

I shake my head. *Nor large dining halls, nor miscellaneous rooms for no purpose other than for show.* "Most people in my village cannot read. The most books I've seen were in a wool mill in Ballybaeg. And they were all on needlework."

"Intriguing," says Ellynne.

We step out of the library, and I immediately miss the inviting scent of the leather.

"Well …" Ellynne pats the library door. "As someone in Princess Carys's service, you are free to use the library. Take as many books as you want, as long as you return them. Personally, I enjoy the great romances." She winks playfully at me and a smile tugs at my lips.

By the time we arrive at a nondescript door in a secluded hallway, I've forgotten where everything is. Ellynne pushes the door open with little effort and waves me in.

The room is as large as my entire house. If not larger. There's a bed with carved wooden posts, massive double windows, and a desk piled with crafty supplies against the far wall. Beside the table is a small shelf neatly stocked with spools of colorful threads, stacks of fabric, and other materials that I've only dreamed of getting my hands on.

"Welcome to your bedchamber," says Ellynne when I drag my attention back to her.

I blink at her. "Did you say *my* bedchamber?"

Ellynne nods, the skin on the corners of her eyes crinkling slightly. "I did."

I'm at a loss for words. When I do finally move, it's the bed I make a beeline for. The mattress is like a cloud, the sheets are *silk*. Mother above … "This is the most comfortable thing I have ever sat on in my entire life," I say aloud.

Ellynne chuckles. "Well, I'm glad you like it. I'm certain you'll find clothes that fit you in the wardrobe. And …" She points to a door on the opposite side of the desk, and I miss everything she says until she angles her head to me again. "Do you have any questions for me?"

I nod and swallow, trying to tack down one of the dozens of questions flying through my mind. "What exactly is expected of me as Princess Carys's dressmaker? Aside from … well, making her garments?" Saying that aloud is ridiculous. I am no dressmaker.

Is it common practice for dressmakers to be procured from the Grounds? I bite my lip to keep the question from leaping out.

"Princess Carys has instructed me to help you with basic etiquette. So, first things first. When you address someone of a higher station, be sure to state their title. Princess Carys or Your Highness, for example. Lord Iywan because he is the Hand of the Queen and Carys's advisor. Most of the noblemen and women at this court should be addressed as 'Lord' or 'Lady,' including the head healer, Lady Alys."

So that was the healer's name.

"The guards are addressed as Sir, followed by their first names, except for Major Kilkenny, and on the unlikely occasion that you get to interact with the queen herself, you should address her as Your Majesty."

The information is crammed into my head for me to pick apart later. I nod. "Understood."

"Now," Ellynne says with a grin, tossing her wavy red hair over her shoulder. "Show me your curtsy."

I hesitate for a moment. The royals are the only ones who would be worthy of a curtsy, and no royal has visited the Grounds since I was a wee one. I stand, allow my head to adjust to the change in posture, then I place one foot awkwardly behind the other and bend my knees. Ellynne winces and I straighten up right away.

"Let's work on that," she says. But despite her corrections and my repeated attempts, my curtsy remains abysmal.

Ellynne smiles reassuringly. "You'll get it."

I sigh.

"The most important thing is that you do your job and do it well. The princess is counting on you."

"Wonderful."

Ellynne picks up on my sarcasm and chortles. "Just be your genuine self, work well, and stay out of things that aren't your business."

"That won't be a problem."

For a moment, we stand there wordlessly, then I walk around the room, admiring my surroundings, frequently glancing back at Ellynne to make sure she isn't speaking to me. Beneath the plush fur rug that extends through most of the room, the floor is tiled with a dark blue and copper motif. The walls are covered with textured paint in burnt sienna, and on one side is a fireplace.

I imagine Taig tottering around the large room, taking it all in. He would thrive here.

My heart clenches painfully, and I have to force myself to breathe in. Then out.

I turn to Ellynne just as she says, "... be off." She smiles. "Make yourself at home ... someone will collect you ... Her Highness."

I smile uneasily, my heart hiccuping in my chest. "Thank you."

Ellynne heads for the door but as she opens it, she jumps aside, startled.

Standing in my doorway is none other than the princess of the kingdom of Erleya.

Chapter 13
CARYS

TIRED OF PACING MY room for the morning, and overwhelmed with curiosity and impatience, I make my way to the dressmaker's bedchamber. "Are you certain you don't want to summon her to your chamber?" Tiernan asks as he walks beside me.

"We're already heading there," I counter.

He tucks the silver strands within his dark hair behind his ear and turns forward again without any further inquiry. I can almost *feel* his disapproval. Tiernan Kilkenny is a stickler for rules and regulations, protocol and order, but he's certainly relaxed over the years.

We step up to Durvla's door and as I lift my hand to knock, it flies open. Ellynne nearly barrels right into me. "Carys! My apologies!" she says.

I respond with a nonchalant wave of my hand. "It's fine, Ellynne. I just came to see how our new resident is settling in."

"We've only just gotten back from the tour. She's all yours." She smiles and curtsies before walking away.

As I face the new Grounder woman, she hastily dips into a god-sawful curtsy, and I can't help but laugh. She straightens, an awkward smile replacing the brief embarrassment that flooded her features a second ago.

"How do you like your chamber?" I ask.

"It's incredible." Her brown eyes light up, a more genuine smile on her face.

"Is it a suitable environment for creating?"

"Yes." Then she quickly adds, "Your Highness."

"Good, because the Feast is in a month and I'm entrusting you with the task of making my dress."

The woman sways a little on the spot. Her tawny skin blanches, and she presses her hand against one of the front posts of her bed. "One month?"

"That's not a problem, is it?"

"No, Your Highness." She releases the post and flexes her hands at her side.

"I need to look so remarkable that my suitors take one glance at me and drop dead. Even better if that happens in a literal sense."

A line forms between her brows.

"Don't get me wrong, I'd love to find a handsome suitor to bed and wed, preferably in that order, because I'd like to know what I'm getting myself into. These noblemen and royals ... they're often older and have a great bloodline, but their personalities?" I point my thumb down to the ground. "You know what I mean?"

Durvla nods, but she starts to fiddle with her sleeve. She focuses on my mouth often. It isn't uncommon for people to avoid looking me in the eye, but it's irritating all the same.

"The dress that they confiscated from your home is stunning. Can you make a similar one for me?"

She stares at me, dumfounded.

"Have I stunned you?" I snap my fingers, and she finally blinks, smoothing her hands over the sides of her dress.

"Sorry, Your Highness," she says. "I'm just trying to figure out … why me? I'm not a noble or even a Mainlander. It's just surprising that you would choose me of all people."

"Oh." I wave my hand indifferently and huff out a breath. "The dressmakers of Mainland are painfully uninspired. Your dress is the most unique I've ever seen. The stitch, the embroidery. It's incredible that you're just a botanist."

Her lips lift in a pitiful attempt at a smile.

"But if you're a fraud, I'm sending you back to Cluain Baile."

I expect dread, but her face shines with expectancy, her body going still. Does she actually *want* to go back to the cesspool that is the Grounds? That would be utterly absurd. I practically bite my tongue to keep from outright insulting my new dressmaker. "You're lucky, you know. You get to live in luxury. Not many Grounders get to do that. And you just have one simple task: Make me a dress."

She purses her lips, her back rigid. Her expression goes flat.

"Do you understand a thing I'm saying?"

"Yes, Your Highness."

She starts to curtsy, but I hold out my hands to stop her. "Please, don't. Your curtsy is atrocious, and I don't care for it anyway. But before I go, what do you need in order to make my dress?"

"I …" It takes her a moment to find her words. "I need spun fiber, fabric, and your measurements. Your Highness."

"Alright." I turn to head out the door again, and Tiernan steps aside from the open doorway. "You can take my measurements tonight after supper," I throw over my shoulder. "And in the morning, Major Kilkenny will accompany you to Barr na Cahar."

Tiernan gives me a slow nod, but there's no response from Durvla.

I turn to find her gawking cluelessly at me, with no acknowledgment of anything I've just said. Magdin's tits, tell me I didn't land myself yet another incompetent dressmaker. "Did you hear me?"

She blinks as if coming out of a trance. "I didn't. My apologies." She laces her fingers tightly together in front of her and I catch the slightest wince.

I back off. Perhaps there is more damage than just the bruises on her face. Perhaps she's been through enough in one day. "I'll arrange your transport to Barr na Cahar in the morning. That's the fashion district. I'm sure Ellynne has shown you the library—the last dressmaker sometimes took out books on … well, whatever you needlewomen read." I pause. "If you *can* read, that is."

A muscle twitches in her cheek. "I can read," she says, after a brief moment.

"Alright, well … I'd like to see your progress on my dress daily. You have today to settle in, and you can begin your work tomorrow after you return from Barr na Cahar. I'd like to meet for breakfast every day so you can show me your magic."

Her lips press into a straight line, and she swallows visibly. Grounders are raised to believe that even the *mention* of magic is treasonous. Poor woman. "It's just figurative, Durvla." I sigh and shake my head before turning on my heel to exit her chamber.

As the door closes behind me, I turn to Tiernan. He stares back at me with respectful curiosity.

"Is it me," I ask, "or is she a bit doltish? She can't even look me in the eye."

"I think she's just nervous, Princess."

I click my tongue. "I sure hope that's the case."

Chapter 14
DURVLA

LOCKING MY EYES ON the mirror, I still can't believe what I see. The swollen gash on my face is scabbing over and fading from red to dark blue against my light brown skin. It's unsightly but could be far worse, I suppose. My curls are still tame beneath the pins Ellynne strategically placed.

I focus on the nearly unrecognizable reflection as I hold the skirt of this lavish dress and dip into one last curtsy. My legs ache from the repetition, and it's as if I haven't slept in ten years—which does nothing to help my nagging headache—but I don't want to risk another Mainlander laughing in my face the next time I curtsy.

I've been in this room for over an hour now, and I still can't believe that I'm not dreaming. Or having a nightmare. Despite my exhaustion, my nerves crawl every time I try to sit still.

The shadows from the fire in the hearth all resemble Taig's wild hair. I can see his goofy smile and his little grabby hands. It's unnatural that I don't have to get up to prevent him from putting an object into his mouth. There's no supper to cook, no bath to give.

I am utterly useless, unsure of how to function without having to take care of someone.

Giving up on any attempt to relax, I approach the shelf beside the former dressmaker's desk and thumb through the stack of fabrics. There are no spun fibers for knitting, but there is a lot of embroidery thread, measuring tape, and a pincushion. I find a couple of quills, an inkwell, and paper.

Sitting at the table, I dip the quill into the inkwell, but the blank sheet of paper stares back at me. Taunting me. I haven't measured Princess Carys yet, but I have a good idea of what may suit her body type. I'm average height with wide hips and a soft middle, while Princess Carys is statuesque and slender with a nonexistent waist. She's small-chested, which makes designing the bodice easier than if she were heavier up top. She would look great in a gown with a wide skirt or even something formfitting. Honestly, she could pull off anything with her confidence, but what *suits* her?

The quill moves on its own as an image materializes before me. I still need to get a better idea of the princess's likes and dislikes, but for now, I have an inkling. She wants something bold, something unique, something that would cause her suitors to drop dead—literally, apparently. I smile and shake my head to myself. The princess isn't what I expected.

In the paintings I've seen of the royal family, they're often in light colored, full-coverage gowns. Maybe the opposite is exactly what Carys wants. I jot down a few notes, my penmanship somewhat careless in my haste.

I wish I could send a letter to Osheen, but he has always refused to let me teach him how to read or write.

It isn't necessary for my survival, he's always said.

It turns out it just might be necessary for mine.

The evening creeps in as I sit at the window, gazing into the gathering darkness. I can't get my thoughts off Taig. The guilt is predatory, eating away at my conscience. At some point, I change into a flowy night-gown, but I have to keep my mind busy to keep the tears at bay. I light all the candles I can find until the desk is lit up like the starry sky. Then I get back to revising my dress design for the princess.

I'm not sure how much time passes before something touches my shoulder. I recoil so hard that the tip of the pen tears a hole in the paper, the ink bleeding right through part of the design. My heart tries to figure out how to beat normally again as Princess Carys stares down at me with raised brows.

I shove my chair back and push myself out of it, dropping into a curtsy. "Apologies, Your Highness." My words come out in a single, rushed exhalation. "I was a little too focused on …" I stare down at the paper. It's ruined.

I sigh as Carys lifts the paper and peers at it. "Is this my dress?" Her focus briefly flicks to me before returning to the torn, ink-stained paper, her fingers tapping along the back of the parchment.

I nod. "It's just a rough idea for now. I have to take your measurements and get more specifics on what you want."

"Looks like you actually do know what you're doing."

I shrug. Part of me wants to play the fool card in hopes I get sent back home sooner, but doing this job well is the smarter option. "Since you're here, may I take your measurements now?"

"Of course." She analyzes the sketch again.

I open one of the desk drawers and rummage through it for the tape measure. "I'll need your height, waist, bust—"

"I'm aware of how measurements go," she says, impatience hardening her features as she sets my design down and reaches over her shoulder, struggling with the buttons on the back of her dress.

"Right. Apologies."

"Stop apologizing."

I nod as she continues to struggle. "Would you like … help with that?"

She casts me an exasperated glower and I somehow manage to hold my ground. "Would you rather gawk at me while I struggle?"

Before I can think of a response, she turns her narrow back to me. I make quick work of her buttons, praying she doesn't say anything of importance while her back is to me. Mercifully, she's down to her silky shift in no time, her corset tossed aside. When she faces me again, she's restless, idly spinning the sun-shaped amulet of her necklace between her fingers. I take a fresh sheet of paper from the drawer and grab my measuring tape before stepping behind her again.

She remains stationary as I take her height, but as I move on to her waist, her hand taps against the side of her thigh. She's fidgeting with her underdress as I take her bust measurement. By the time I'm done, she's heaved about a dozen sighs, and I'm honestly surprised she didn't walk off whenever I paused to jot down the numbers.

"There," I say with a grimace of a smile as I roll up the tape measure and set it aside.

Her perfectly arched brows rise with surprise, even as she fiddles with her necklace again. "You're finished?"

I nod.

"That was quick."

I've only ever measured Taig, and that is quite a feat. Her impatient fidgeting can hardly compare, but it's also … curious. "What color would you like your dress to be?" I ask, trying to keep my mind on the present.

She purses her lips for a moment. "Not ivory or any other shade of white," she says after a while. "I also have substantial amounts of green and blue in my wardrobe, so something other than those would be great."

I nod.

The princess glances at my sketch again. "I want the neckline to be a little less …"

The last word I don't quite make out and my pulse jumps at the fear that she'll discover my communication challenges.

"Less what?" I ask.

"*Stuffy*. There isn't much to show, but I'm not afraid to show what I *do* have."

"Oh, understood." I chuckle, more relieved than amused.

Carys begins to pace in front of me, but she glances at me often enough for me to read the words on her lips. "I want … that is mysterious and … gerous. People need … that I'm not to be toyed with."

"Mysterious and … dangerous?" I ask. "And that you're not to be toyed with."

Her pacing halts, her eyes narrowing. "Yes," she says, though she clearly wants to pummel me into the ground. I stand firm and breathe through the urge to recoil. I try especially hard to keep myself from asking what constitutes a *dangerous* dress.

"But if you can't do that …" She lets the sentence hang.

I'm not sure I can. I swallow around the lump in my throat.

"Durvla, if you make the dress of my dreams, I'll reward you with anything you want."

That piques my interest. "*Anything?*"

"Name it and it's yours. Within reason, of course." Her smile is slow, almost practiced.

I falter as I consider asking for wealth and comfort—clemency for harboring an Undesirable and being one myself.

"Well?" she demands.

I settle for the safest request that still works in my favor. "I'd like permission to go back home to Cluain Baile. And an exemption from all future Quarterly Raids."

She blinks and stares at me. Have I baffled her? Here I am in the Fortress on the Mount, in the presence of the princess; it should be unlikely that I'd want to leave all of this behind. But my life's purpose is not here in the castle—it's back home with my brother. Not being a dressmaker, but being a caregiver. It's what I do best.

"Very well," says Carys. "But only if you can truly impress me."

I nod. "That sounds fair."

Incredulity crosses her face. "Well then, Durvla. Impress me." She walks backward for a couple of steps, then turns and strides out of my room.

I collapse into the chair, limp with relief. It's possible that I can go back home. It's possible that I'd be able to see Taig, my dog Finn, Osheen, Orla, and Granny again. Even Eemer and Grawnye. I crumple my original sketch and begin afresh, my new motivation propelling me through.

I saunter around my temporary room. It's extravagant yet rigid, lacking the coziness I'm accustomed to, but Taig could flourish here. He lights up any room. His crooked little smile, his too-hard hugs, and his amusing nuzzles with his head against my cheek are guaranteed to lift my mood, even on the most miserable of days. He is the epitome of making the best of a situation—of living life with inexplicable and unapologetic joy despite his limitations.

We began hiding him when he was three years old, aware that the Forayers who raided our homes would notice his atypical behavior and have our heads. Worse, they would've sent him straight to the Wastelands or wherever they send Undesirable children. I shudder to even fathom it.

To the village, we announced Taig's death. It was safer having everyone believe that he no longer lived, safer that the Forayers chronicled his death in their records. The lie saved his life and ours. Osheen kept the secret from his parents. He's the most loyal person I know. When my mother died, he stepped up without even being asked. There wasn't much time for grief—I had another little human being to look after. Keeping Taig alive meant being his person all day, every day.

The older he got, the more attention he needed, and the more I dove deeper and deeper, latching on to my caregiver role. I wouldn't trade it. I wouldn't trade my brother. Not for all the luxury in the world.

Chapter 15
DURVLA

IN THE MORNING, I wake to an orange glow behind my eyelids. I dare to open my eyes and I'm practically blinded by the rays of the sun. I squint, straining to make out a face, but there's only a silhouette against the brightness—a mane of wavy hair that throws hope in to mix with my confusion for a moment.

But it's not Taig. It's Ellynne. I catch the end of her sentence.

"... a heavy sleeper."

I rub my bleary eyes. "I am. Apologies." As I scrub my hand over my face, I draw in a sharp breath, wincing. I'd forgotten all about my injuries and my face throbs, but last night I'd had the best sleep of my life. Guilt settles into the pit of my stomach.

"Well, you better get going. One of Carys's guards, Major Kilkenny, is going to accompany you to Barr na Cahar this morning. He's already waiting outside your door."

If my confusion is visible, Ellynne doesn't react. Instead, she heads over to my closet and rummages through it. She looks questioningly over her shoulder at me.

"Apologies ... still half asleep," I say. I stand and pad over to her, illogically self-conscious about my bare feet and thin nightgown when she's already seen me stark naked.

Ellynne glances at me. "Do you have a favorite color?"

I frown. *Do I?* "Not really." I've never had much of a choice. It's been shades of brown, greys and whites my whole life. "I suppose green?" Like foliage. Like the plants I'd so diligently tended to in the greenhouse.

She turns to me, handing over a forest green linen dress. "Perfect."

I hold it up, admiring it. "It's very pretty."

"There's a ..." With her face angled to the wardrobe, I miss the rest of what she says. A moment of later, she pulls out a beige woolen coat with brass buttons down the front. It's tapered at the waist, a gown in coat form. Stunning really. "I'll leave it on the bed for you," says Ellynne. "I have to get to Princess Carys, but I just wanted to make sure you were settled in and ready for your first full day here."

"That's very kind of you. Thank you."

Ellynne smiles and rushes out. Meanwhile, I get dressed as quickly as possible, and I sit on the bed to slip my boots on. There are some hair accessories on my side table now—a couple of clips and a few ribbons. Ellynne must've brought them in for me. I smile and unbraid my hair, finger-combing through my dark curls and tying half up with a ribbon before checking my appearance in the mirror.

I touch my fingertips to my cheek. It's darker blue than yesterday and a little stiff, but hopefully it won't draw too much attention.

I toss my coat on before grabbing my sketch from the desk and folding it. Cautiously opening the door, I find the princess's dark-haired guard standing rigid. I shrink back as his onyx gaze homes in on my face.

"Good morning," he says.

"Good morning." I slip the sketch into my pocket, my focus still on the guard's chiseled face.

He extends his right hand to me, and I automatically reach out with my dominant hand, making for an awkward, impossible arm clasp. My face heats.

Great first impression, Durvla.

I clear my throat. "A pleasure to meet you, Major Kilkenny."

His gaze sweeps from my hair down to my boots, scrutinizing my appearance. When he finds my face again, he says, "Are you able to ride a horse in that?"

I frown. I'm not able to ride a horse at all. Unsure of what to say, I just stand there.

Major Kilkenny raises a brow. "Well, if you're comfortable in that …" he begins. An uneasy tension fills the wordless space until he says, "Alright, let's get going then." He starts walking and I follow, barely keeping up with his stride.

He's only as tall as the princess, but far more intimidating. The silver streaks in his dark brown hair suit him somehow. A sword is secured at his waist, and he keeps his hand on the hilt as though he expects us to get attacked at any moment.

Does he expect us to get attacked? I gulp.

We walk through the castle, through an area that Ellynne didn't show me during our tour yesterday. Major Kilkenny doesn't speak, which is a relief as it would be especially difficult to focus on the movement of his lips with my pulse scurrying. I don't know what to expect from this excursion. All I know is that there's an armed guard beside me who isn't particularly fond of me, and I'm not sure if he's assigned to protect me or keep me captive.

When we reach the stables, a petite young man with unruly blond hair stands between two horses. The stench of manure wafts to my nostrils and I'm overcome with nostalgia, remembering the hundreds of times I've fertilized the greenhouse plants. I try not to spiral, bidding my mind to focus on the present instead of where I'd rather be. Out of my peripheral vision, Major Kilkenny glances in my direction, his brows raised as if awaiting a response from me.

Gods, I really need to pay better attention if I'm going to make it out of here alive.

"Have you ridden a horse before?" he asks, not for the first time, I'm sure.

I shake my head. "No."

He turns forward again and continues toward the horses—one with black hair gleaming in the sunlight, and the other chestnut brown with a cream-colored mane and tail. They're beautiful, but I stop a short distance from them. Up close, they are *huge*. I've seen horses before, of course, but not consistently, and I've certainly never ridden one. The thought makes my stomach sink.

Major Kilkenny greets the stableboy and thanks him before turning his attention back to me, beckoning me closer. I take a breath before moving toward him.

Major Kilkenny rubs the sable and cream-colored horse and arches a brow at me as though I'm a mystery. It does nothing to stop my stomach from sinking further.

"This is Mirren," he says. "She has a gentle temperament and is perfect for beginners. Ghendor here is the opposite." He moves on to stroke the black horse's muscular back. "He can be a nasty fellow, but we have a civil agreement." Ghendor huffs as though he understands.

Major Kilkenny encourages me to let Mirren sniff my open palm, but she bypasses my offering and sticks her snout right into my neck. I hold my breath and root my feet. This horse is going to *eat* me. At the least, she'll bite me. Can a person die from a horse bite?

My fears are quelled when the mare nudges my arm. She seems harmless.

"Alright," says Major Kilkenny when I turn to him again. "Let's get you in the saddle."

My chest tightens. "I'm afraid of heights."

He pauses, brows lowered, dark eyes brooding. "Going to Barr na Cahar on foot will take the entire morning. We're already running behind schedule."

Sorry, I was busy recuperating from being arrested, forced to sit in filthy conditions for days, manhandled, and thrown in jail before being unexpectedly assigned to Princess Carys's service. I press my tongue against the roof of my mouth to keep the words from flying out. "How do I ... ?" I gesture to Mirren.

Major Kilkenny instructs me to slip one boot into the stirrup and push myself up. My muscles are still sore and stiff, my arms trembling slightly as I maintain the position. My other leg still dangles, and for a moment, I fear I'll be stuck awkwardly half standing in the stirrup, my arms grasping the saddle like a lifeline. Major Kilkenny appears on the other side of the horse and places a steady hand atop mine.

After my experience with Mainlanders in the past few days, my heart quickens with apprehension, but there is no ill intent on Major Kilkenny's face. Only mild annoyance.

"Get your other leg over before Mirren loses her patience," he says.

Alright, maybe more than *mild* annoyance. Is it truly the horse he's concerned will lose patience?

I fully hoist myself up, swinging my leg over the horse. Major Kilkenny dodges my foot, barely evading a boot to the face. I'm fully seated now, but my other leg dangles, my vision swimming before me. Major Kilkenny firmly grasps my ankle and slides my foot into the stirrup for me. There's a tug on my dress and my eyes fly open as he smooths the material down over the side of Mirren, ensuring I retain my modesty.

The gesture is so … unexpected.

"Let's get going," he says. "Try to look ahead instead of down." He hands me the reins and quickly instructs me on some basics.

I am going to fall off this horse. Great Mother, help me.

Major Kilkenny mounts Ghendor, and the horse sets off at a walk. As Mirren follows, I grab on to the reins a little too hard and she reels back. My heart leaps.

I'm going to fall, I'm going to fall, I'm going—

Major Kilkenny shouts something beside me. He says something else and I just gawk at him, beyond flustered. He gestures with the reins in his hand, telling me to let up on them.

I immediately drop the reins and he presses his lips together and turns his face to the sky for a second as if praying for patience.

My heart is racing, and my palms are sweating. I take a deep breath and slowly exhale as Major Kilkenny takes Mirren's reins along with Ghendor's. Mirren resumes walking as Ghendor does, and I hold on to the pommel with all my might. Major Kilkenny observes me for a while, then says, "Eyes ahead of you."

I can say the same to you, I want to tell him.

Eventually, we graduate to a trot, then a canter. I adjust. Slowly, as always, but I do adjust. A while later, I no longer have to grip the pommel like my life depends on it, and I even manage to hold the reins on my own. Mirren veers off course a couple of times thanks to my shoddy leading skills, but I successfully steer her back each time.

We trot through cobblestone streets, passing houses far larger than any homes in the Grounds. There isn't a lot of open land, but there are statues of the old deities and fountains scattered among the grand two-story homes of refined stone. We pass a circle of carved boulders in an overgrown field, moss and vines creeping up the stony altar at the center. Even in Mainland the temples have been forsaken. Interesting.

At some point, the residential area falls behind, paving the way for small shops with breathtaking dresses, jewelry, and pottery displayed in their windows. I stare at every storefront we pass, amazed that the citizens of Mainland can just walk into any shop and purchase things rather than laboring for them. No, that's the job of my people across the bridge.

Out of the shop runs a little girl with rich brown skin and curly black hair piled atop her head. Her gown of ivory and gold shimmers in the sunlight as she pouts and folds her arms across her chest.

I can't make out what she's saying, but her mother exits the shop right after her, trying to reason with her. The little girl points to a necklace in the shop window and stomps. The sight is so unbelievable that I almost laugh. I try to imagine being upset because I couldn't get *jewelry*. Half the time I can't even get food on our table.

Gods, I hope Taig is eating well.

I swallow and turn my attention to the road ahead, but Major Kilkenny is staring at me. I face him fully.

"Let's pick up the pace," he says. "We can't be away all day."

As if any of this is my choice.

"We're nearly there."

"Great," I say, forcing a smile onto my face.

He doesn't even feign a smile back. Of course he doesn't.

We pass a few more shops before Major Kilkenny pulls gently on Ghendor's reins to halt him.

I do the same, maybe a little too harshly, because Mirren reels back again. "Sorry!" I call out, and she settles again.

We're in front of a shop with hanks of colorful wool and patterned fabrics visible through the frosted window. I'm so busy staring that I'm startled when Kilkenny reaches up to help me off Mirren's back. He guides me down, but even with his steady grasp on my upper arms, I stumble. It's like my legs have forgotten how to support me.

Kilkenny peers down at me, his face a mask that gives away nothing. "Those legs of yours are like a newborn foal's ..." he says plainly.

I gawk at him, unsure of how to interpret that. "Thank you?"

There's the tiniest spark in his gloomy eyes. His cheek twitches and he presses his lips together firmly. With a curt nod, he releases me and steps back, putting space between us.

It's good to be on solid ground again. Except the earth might as well still be moving. I hold on to Mirren's saddle, waiting for my body to adjust again and trying not to focus on the throbbing in my temples. Major Kilkenny doesn't move either. Is it out of the fear that I'll run or out of concern? Once I gather my composure, rubbing at my left temple, we walk toward the store, and with each step I'm a little less likely to trip over my own feet.

I glance up at him. "Do I have a spending limit?"

He shakes his head and holds the door open. "No limit."

My eyes flare wide. It's unfathomable, but I nod and step into the aroma of fresh linens within the shop. I inhale deeply and glance at my surroundings. It's a needlewoman's paradise, with embroidery thread of every color imaginable on display, different fabrics lined up in rows, and shelves upon shelves of spun fiber. Naturally, I gravitate toward the skeins, drawn like a sailor to a siren's song. I keep my hands at my side as it's almost sacrilegious to touch the wool.

No, not just wool. *Silk*.

The skeins of silk have varying thickness, and so many different color choices. The things I could make for Taig. Colorful sweaters, trousers, socks. He needs a new hat. A lump forms in my throat. I take a deep breath and push thoughts of Taig away. I need to focus on the task at hand.

Skeins of black draw me away from the lighter shades of silk fibers. The color of Carys's hair minus the golden streaks. My teeth dig into my lower lip as I stroll down the shelves of fibers and come upon a section of knitting needles. I grab a few different sizes and turn to find the princess's earnest guard.

He stands a short distance from me, his intense stare following my every move. Goose bumps arise on my skin, and I rub the sleeve of the coat I'm wearing, taming the strange, prickling sensation from being watched so closely. It takes effort to ignore his stare, so I focus on piling bundles of black silk fibers into my arms.

I can hardly hold them all, and as I turn to head back toward Major Kilkenny, I nearly collide with a table containing spools of embroidery thread. Gold thread reminiscent of the streaks in Princess Carys's hair draws my attention, and countless possibilities arise in my mind, until one idea thwarts the others.

With under a month to work, there is no way I can fully knit a floor-length gown, but I can still give the princess something bold and unique. I just need to exercise my creative muscles more than I ever have before. Part of me is intrigued by this challenge and I navigate away from the guilt that rises again—away from the thoughts that remind me to remain miserable in the face of this injustice.

I reach for the gold embroidery thread, but that throws off the balance of the stack of yarns in my arms. The skeins start to tumble from me, but Major Kilkenny appears at my side, his hands brushing against mine as he catches everything. I glance up at him and smile sheepishly. "Thank you."

He only nods and my eyes shift from his sharp jawline to those silver streaks in his hair. When his brows raise, and I realize that I'm openly staring at him. Heat crawls up my neck and I'm suddenly unsure what to do with my empty hands.

His attention shifts, and I follow his line of vision to a tall, mahogany grandfather clock at the far end of the shop.

Noon. It's been about half an hour since we arrived.

Major Kilkenny looks back to me, worry etched into his features. "We need to get going."

"Alright. I just need the shopkeeper to cut a few yards of fabric for me."

His lips form a straight line for a moment. "Anything else?"

"No."

"Alright," he says.

We make our way toward the counter, but as we're about to pass a table of adornments, I stop abruptly. Buttons, broaches, and beads stare back at me. A set of gold beads calls to me. I *need* them. I take some of the gold buttons as well, just for good measure. I'm not entirely sure how I'll use any of them, but they'll be used one way or another because they're perfect.

"For Rhianu's sake," says Major Kilkenny. "I've never seen someone take so long to select such tedious items."

My excitement dissipates. What a killjoy he is … "Apologies, I'm done," I say.

Major *Killjoy* regards me. "Are you certain this time?" The corners of his eyes crinkle slightly, though he doesn't smile. Does he ever smile?

"I'm certain, yes."

"At long last." The fine crinkles are gone, and he nods upward to the counter, wordlessly urging me to hurry.

Moments later, the materials are loaded into the pack attached to Major Kilkenny's black stallion, Ghendor, and we're back on the road to Paramount. For a split second, I consider riding off straight to Cluain Baile. But I can hardly handle Mirren at a canter, and there's no way Major Killjoy would let me escape. I sigh and accept my fate as we head back to the castle.

At least I have a task to keep me busy. Even if it is daunting.

Chapter 16
CARYS

I SLAM MY PLAYING cards down on the table and glare at Ellynne. "You cheated!"

Ellynne laughs. "I most certainly did *not*! You are just a sore loser."

She's not wrong, but I glower at her as she gathers all the cards together to reshuffle them. It's our third game and she's won all of them.

"I'm with you," Lowri chimes in. "She must be cheating."

"Or I just *know* things." Ellynne wiggles her fingers before her face and Lowri giggles. "How about something different?"

"How about … you tell me my fortune instead, oh divine oracle?" I lean back in my chair and smirk at her.

A spark of delight appears in Ellynne's olive green eyes. She's rubbish at reading others, so her false divination is top-notch entertainment. I'd love to hear how my breasts are going to mysteriously grow two sizes bigger. Or how enchanted rain is going to pour from Rhianu and Lierwen's perfect Overworld and end the spreading disease.

Ellynne draws in a breath to respond, but there's a robust knock on the door. "Your Highness, Major Kilkenny and Durvla Garrick have returned," Callum announces from outside of my door.

"Finally." I jump from my seat. "Rain check," I say to Ellynne, who lunges forward to catch my chair before it topples.

She rights it again with a playful smirk. "I look forward to it."

We arrive at Durvla's door and Callum knocks, announcing my presence as he does so. But there's no response. He knocks again. Still no response. He turns his perplexed face to me. "Tiernan says he escorted her back to her bedchamber."

I nudge him aside and bang on the door with the heel of my hand.

"Maybe she went to the bathing chamber or something," says Callum.

I shove the door open and there she is, standing beside her bed, her back to the door. She turns, and as she spots me, she yelps, nearly falling over.

"Your Highness," she says, slightly breathless. She dips into a hurried, yet surprisingly passable curtsy. "Apologies, I was caught up in—" She gestures to the bed, and I approach to take a better look. There are hanks of black wool, deep purple fabric, beads, and black … whatever that underskirt material for adding volume is called.

I pluck some of the black wool and … it's not wool, but the sleekest silk. "I like your color choice," I say, sliding my thumb over the soft fibers.

She smiles, validated. "I'm happy to hear that."

I set the silken fibers down and bend to slide my hand over purple fabric, also silk. "This shade is gorgeous."

"I thought so too."

As I straighten again, Durvla's stomach growls, and her hand flies to her abdomen as though she intends to muffle the sound. "Pardon me," she says, a flush shining through her tawny complexion.

I wave my hand dismissively. "You can't help your own bodily functions. Hells, not even royalty can hold back the occasional fart, belch, or stomach gurgle. Have you had breakfast?"

She shakes her head. "I munched on an apple, but it's alright. I don't eat much."

"Don't be ridiculous. You have full access to the dining hall." As I turn, my own stomach growls. "Actually, you can come along. I'd like to hear more about your plans for my dress, anyway. Do you have a favorite meal?"

No response. I halt midway to her door and turn back to her.

Durvla blinks as though she hasn't registered my question.

"So, do you?"

Confusion washes over her face. "Do I …" Her throat bobs.

I frown. Something is so off with her, and I can't quite put my finger on it. At least the bruising on her cheek is surprisingly minimal, and the way her perfect curls beautifully frame her face makes me somewhat envious.

"I'm heading to the dining hall if you want to come along."

She smiles. "I'd like that."

I sigh and walk out of her bedchamber. Mercifully, Durvla follows, and Callum falls into step at my side as we make our way toward the kitchen. We walk briskly and Durvla easily keeps up, taking in our surroundings. We arrive in the dining hall where a grand table that seats twenty is the focal point. Several chandeliers hang down from the beams in the ceiling, all twinkling with candlelight.

Durvla is still wide-eyed as Eefa strides in, shapely hips swaying, her honey blond braid draped over her shoulder. The woman's lips curve up into a smile, her large green eyes sparkling with intrigue as they land on Durvla. "Ooh, a new face," she drawls.

Confusion furrows Durvla's brows and she glances from Eefa to me. "This is Eefa. Apprentice to the head cook. She's ... exceptionally sociable and far too confident for her own good."

She winks and I can't help but laugh even as I roll my eyes.

"Eefa, this is Durvla Garrick, my new dressmaker."

Eefa slides her hands over the apron atop her simple beige dress before extending her arm to Durvla. They clasp forearms briefly before Eefa steps back. "Nice to meet you, Durvla." Her round face and flawless olive complexion give her a youthful appearance, reminding me that she's just nineteen. Her uncanny haughtiness gives her the air of a woman who has experienced quite a lot. I clear my throat as my mind tries to wander off to less appropriate things that *I* have experienced with her.

Durvla's stomach growls again, and she presses her hands against her abdomen once more. Eefa laughs lightly. "Sit, I'll get you something to eat," she says before disappearing behind the double doors into the kitchen.

Soon, there's a plate with roasted guinea fowl, stewed carrots and potatoes, and some hearty bread in front of Durvla. I receive a plate with much of the same. Durvla eats, but she often glances up at me as though she's afraid I'd smite her while her head is down. I focus on my meal, letting her enjoy probably the best one she's ever had.

Wait until she tastes Eefa's lemon cake. It's to die for.

Soon, Durvla finishes her meal and washes it down with a goblet of water. "Thank you," she says after daintily wiping her lips on a cloth napkin.

I shrug. "*I* didn't cook it. Come on." I stand and she does so as well. "I heard you were excited about the library. Would you like to visit? I go there nearly every day; especially if I need a quick getaway or time to myself."

A smile brightens that sullen face of hers. "Absolutely," she says.

I'm practically following *her* across the castle to the library. It's strangely amusing. As we enter the library, Durvla stares in awe. There's something childlike and refreshing in the way she takes in this new environment. Her hands clench and unclench eagerly, as if she's ready to grab every book from the shelves. Absolutely relatable.

"This is probably my favorite place in the castle," I tell her. "The archery range is a close second."

"Archery range?"

"Yes. Do you have any archery experience?"

Her brows furrow. "Does hunting count?"

"You hunt? I'd have expected more ... foraging or something."

A small smile graces her lips, through melancholy. "My father was the hunter. We never lacked meat when he was alive. He taught me, but I have terrible aim. I have terrible depth perception, in general."

Interesting. I walk toward the shelves and brush my fingers along the leather spines. Durvla moves closer, following me and I turn back to her. "Do you have a favorite genre?"

Her brow puckers. "I've only ever read one book."

One book? How nightmarish.

"It's a book of fairy—" Color drains from her face as she leaves the last word hanging in the air. She shakes her head, her curls bouncing. "It's just a children's book," she says hastily.

Fairytales? I tilt my head as her body tenses, her teeth worrying at her lower lip. "Why do you hesitate to say *fairytales*?" I ask.

Durvla stands absolutely still, her defenses up. Briefly, her lips part, then close tightly again.

I exhale. "I've heard that over the years, the rules have gotten stricter, but ..." I walk toward the velvet loungers beside the round table at the center and sit on the arm, crossing my legs.

Durvla inches closer.

"When I was a child, my mother regularly read to me from the *Erleyan Book of Folklore and Fairytales*. We kept it a bit of a silly tradition as I grew older. It's still my favorite book, but also it's—like you said—tales for children. Nothing I'd consider treasonous. There's a difference between that and, say, a book of spells."

Durvla fiddles with her sleeve cuff for a moment before finally speaking up. "Is magic prohibited in Mainland as well? In the Grounds, we don't believe that magic even exists anymore, yet ... People are still apprehended on the accusation. Does magic exist here?"

I laugh. "It depends on what you mean by magic. There are no raids in Mainland, but if anyone is suspected of magical practices, they face the same disciplinary action as Grounders. As for the existence of magic, as far as I've been told, the Purge wiped out all the magical bloodlines a millennium ago. Some people believe that talismans and amulets can still channel the magic that exists"—I wave my hand around in random patterns—"in the universe, I suppose. Theoretically, scrolls, spell books, amulets with distinctive gems, and other things can, for example, allow a lowborn or lesser noble to gain wealth or higher status. Maybe even overthrow the crown. At least, that's the reasoning behind the law."

"But Mages don't exist here, right?" Durvla asks carefully.

"Only in fairytales." I shrug. "Unfortunately," I add with a teasing smirk. I'd love to have the mind reading or divination of a Mage, or any elemental wielding powers.

Durvla barely blinks. I can tell she wants to say something more, but she bites her lip instead.

"The point is: your little fairytale book isn't unlawful."

"You'd think not," she mumbles.

I frown. "What do you mean?"

"I've seen villagers dragged out of their homes because they owned some meaningless object. A milkmaid in my village had her mother taken away because she owned a book similar to mine. She couldn't even *read* it."

That doesn't make sense. "A book of *fairytales?*"

Durvla nods.

"Perhaps you're mistaken. It must've been a spell book."

"It was a book about heroes and mythological creatures. Not a spell in sight. Similar to the one back in my home. My mother used to read me the tale of the Heirs of Agryna all the time. It's my favorite."

My heart stutters. "The Heirs of Agryna?" I echo.

"Yes, it's about—"

"I know what it's about. It's my favorite as well."

We stare at each other, the swell of surprise and curiosity palpable. This woman is a *Grounder*; she's dirt poor, has lived a humble life, endured raids ... and she cherishes the same book that I do. For Rhianu's sake, she has the same *favorite tale* as I do. Meanwhile, her people are being apprehended and hanged for owning a book with children's stories? My mother can't possibly be aware of this. I hop off the arm of the lounger and smooth out my dress, unsure of what else to say on this subject.

I should get to the bottom of this issue. I should go right to Iywan.

Later.

"I brought you here because Ellynne says you seemed excited about it. So ..." I walk toward the shelf and pull out a couple of my other favorite books, trying not to think of what Durvla shared with me. I bring the books back to Durvla and hold them out to her. "For when you're not dressmaking. It can be terribly boring around here. I know that idle time can coax out idle thoughts. And those can be dangerous." So bloody dangerous.

Taking the books, Durvla smiles and thanks me.

Maybe she isn't so daft after all. Just nervous, like Tiernan suggested, or perhaps just coy. I can work with that.

· · ∘ ☽ ☀ ☾ ∘ · ·

Iywan is just closing the door to his study as Callum and I arrive. He turns and flinches as he sees us. "Princess," he says with a bow. "Sorry, I did not see you there. Do you require my attention?"

"Yes, actually. I have a few questions."

His lips pinch tight for a moment, and he nods before opening the door and stepping aside to let me in. The scent of burning wood, wax, parchment, and ink fills the chamber. I don't bother to sit as Iywan steps inside and closes the door behind him.

"Are Grounders being arrested for owning fairytales?"

Iywan's brows dip, his lips tugging down. He runs a hand over his neat, grey braids, and his shoulders slump as he sighs. "Has your new dressmaker been feeding you lies?"

"We've already established that Forayers arrested Durvla for a dress that she made herself. Who's to say that they're not mistakenly arresting Grounder citizens for owning fairytales?"

Iywan scrubs his hand down his dark face. "Princess, you need not worry about such rumors. It's best you focus on marriage. In fact ..." He briskly strides toward his desk and lifts a scroll tied in a ribbon. Approaching me again, he places the scroll in my hand. "A list of suitors for your perusal. I have a meeting with Councilor Jac momentarily. Would it be possible for us to continue this conversation at a later time?"

If it means not having to discuss these suitors, "Yes."

Iywan thanks me and opens the door, allowing me out first. As he bows and walks away, I shove the scroll against Callum's chest. It has been a rather decent day; I'm not ready to ruin it by looking at that godsforsaken list.

Chapter 17
DURVLA

DESPITE THE BEAUTY OF Paramount, I miss my familiar surroundings. I miss being around people who understand me. Here, it's even scarier being under the scrutiny of Carys and her staff.

Back home, I didn't socialize much. When my hearing first began to wane, my mother immediately taught me how to sign. How she'd learned herself, she never told me. But since Osheen was my childhood playmate, he picked up on it at the same time I did. The knowledge of my deafness never went beyond Osheen and Orla.

My ears are ringing again by the time I return to my bedchamber. If I don't try to relax, I'll have an episode. My head is already aching relentlessly. Osheen always knew just what to do when my malady took over. He'd learned from Ma. I can handle most episodes on my own, but sometimes a comforting presence makes all the difference. Osheen would often sit on the ground beside me and take my shaky hands into his. Or rub my back until my world stopped spinning and the nausea eased.

I set the library books down on the side table and sink onto the comfortable bed. For a while, I lie there, trying to clear my mind and relax. But eventually I force myself to get up. There's work to be done.

If I were home right now, I would be spending time with Taig after a hard day of work. Instead, I start working on some swatches with the spun silk from Barr na Cahar, trying to figure out the best size needle to use and the design to stick with. The process is tedious, but there's something calming about it. Before long, my eyes are straining in the diminishing light.

I rise from the bed, walking around the room to light candles and shift around the logs in the fireplace. Then I sit at the desk, drawing a candle closer to the dress design that I've redrawn countless times. Somehow, I have to get an entire gown finished within a month. It's impossible—but impossibility is not an option. The flame from the candle wavers above my paper, casting distorting shadows. An idea strikes.

I know exactly what I need to do.

"I'll ask you one last time," says a gravelly voice. "Where is he?"

Osheen slumps against a boulder on the ground, his hands shackled behind his back. He's a weeping mess, fear radiating off him in nearly tactile waves.

A Forayer draws back his hand and slaps Osheen's face so hard, his head snaps to the side. Osheen's eyes water and his breathing grows ragged. His lips remain firmly shut, his eyes panicked but stubborn, nonetheless.

"Last chance," says the Forayer.

Osheen remains silent. The next slap reverberates throughout the clearing. Osheen spits blood as the Forayer unsheathes a menacing dagger. His eyes widen.

"He's in a trapdoor under the floorboards!"

The Forayer gives Osheen a slow, sinister smile. "Thank you," he says.

Then he drags the dagger across Osheen's throat from ear to ear.

I wake up screaming, my ribs constricting my heart and lungs. Darkness is everywhere, and I fight the sheets that entrap me. Tears stream down my cheeks and I'm shaking so badly that I wrap my arms around my torso in a vain attempt to hold myself together. My skin crawls with astounding unease, and I'm certain my blood has turned to ice.

The nightmare leaves me with the picture of Osheen's gaping neck burned into my mind. I cannot unsee it. I clamber out of bed and head to the fireplace to add more logs, though the fire does nothing to warm me. All the while I can't stop the shaking or the buzzing sensation under my skin. Before the nightmare about Osheen, I dreamed the castle was on fire. Sunlagh, spare me ...

As if the goddess of dreams has ever been merciful to me.

A shadow dances against the wall. *Someone's behind me.* I spin to face the potential assailant, but there's no one. When I turn back to the wall, there are no shadows either. Probably just a trick of the flames.

Or maybe I'm losing my mind.

Cold sweat makes my nightgown cling to my skin. I peel off the drenched garment and take a fresh one from the wardrobe.

Nightmares are a norm for me, but this one has been, by far, the most vivid and certainly the most terrifying. I don't know how long it takes before I can breathe steadily again. I light candles until the room is illuminated enough for me to resume working on Princess Carys's dress. The bed is daunting, even in the light, so I sit at the desk with the spun silk and knitting needles to begin working on the lace motif. It's easier to focus on creating motifs rather than dwell on my overactive subconscious.

I've figured out the appearance I want to aim for, but most of this is going to be freehand. Wherever the stitch takes me, as long as I'm still meeting the measurements, it should be fine. Ideally, it would be better to work a lace design with black fibers in daylight, but I'm not left with many options right now.

I made this choice.

My hands still shake as I work, but I push through.

I have to.

Chapter 18
CARYS

I BOLT AWAKE, RIVULETS of sweat dripping down my back, my heart racing. The sneering face of a former private guard—one before Tiernan and Callum—refuses to leave my mind long after the dream fades away. I can still feel his vice grip around my wrist as he dragged me to my bedchamber, Iywan in pursuit, shouting for him to release me. At thirteen years old, I hadn't understood why someone would want to hurt me because of what he considered to be my parents' misdeeds.

The guard barricaded us in my bedchamber. He threatened to slaughter me if the queen didn't give him whatever had been promised to his family. Even now, I don't understand what had been promised. Thankfully, he never had the chance to do anything beyond bruising my wrists.

Iywan and the Queen's Guard broke down the door and pulled the corrupt guard away. Ellynne was there in the aftermath, before my mother arrived and deemed me brave.

"Nothing happened," my mother repeated over and over. She gently pressed her cool hand to my forehead, and for a while, I convinced myself that I really could forget it all. But all I managed to do was blur the lines between what really happened and what I fabricated in my distressed mind.

My mother ordered his public flogging and execution for the *highest treason*.

I watched. Every moment. And I endured nights riddled by terrible dreams, despite telling myself that he'd deserved all of it.

I press my bare feet into the ground and fight to pull myself out of the past. Standing shakily, I grapple for the long cord beside my bed to pull the house bell.

When I draw back the curtains, the sky is bleeding with the first light of day. My door creaks open. Finally.

"Carys? Early call this morning." Ellynne's voice is still heavy with sleep, her red hair disheveled as though she'd rolled right out of bed and ran here.

I stare at her, wanting to say something—to apologize, maybe—but there's a boulder in my throat. I swallow forcefully.

"Oh, sweet girl," Ellynne says with a poor-dear expression on her face. She pulls her hair back, wrestling it into a messy bun and hurriedly tying a ribbon around it. "Nightmare?"

Sighing, I rub my hand over my face. "Dermot."

Ellynne blanches, her lips a thin line.

Dermot taught me that even personnel considered trustworthy could betray me. A sheen of sweat coats my skin. "I could use a bath."

"I've already called for one to be prepared," Ellynne says gently. "Lowri's supervising. Give them ten minutes, alright?"

Ellynne is always one step ahead of me; I can't imagine what I'd do without her. "I'll be having breakfast with the Grounder girl," I tell Ellynne. "Could you have the kitchens send it over to her bedchamber?"

"*Her* bedchamber?"

I nod.

"Alright. I will. Let me just get a dress out for you," she says. She rummages through my wardrobe, her voice coming faintly from within. "Any dress in particular you'd like to wear today?"

"It doesn't matter." I flop onto my bed and sigh deeply. It's hard to get rid of the uneasy churning in my gut.

"How about this one?" Ellynne holds up a cerulean dress. She lightly presses her fingers to her temple and feigns a dazed expression. "With this dress you will hold all the courage and wisdom required to tackle the day."

I roll my eyes. "That's fine, Ellynne."

Ellynne hangs the dress and begins laying out accessories to match. "Alright, while they work on the bath situation, I'll get the message to the kitchen. I'll be right back."

Anxiety keeps my tongue all tied up. There's a council meeting today. I have so many concerns regarding the realm, so many questions. The reports I get from Alys are vastly different from the renditions that council members present at the table. Then there are the bits of information I recently learned from Durvla … How do those fit in?

A knock comes from my adjoining bath chamber just as Ellynne returns. "Bath's ready!" Lowri calls from behind the door. Her small voice barely makes it through the oak.

I stand as Ellynne holds the door open, and step into the gentle steam of the bath chamber. I unbutton my nightgown and slip the material off my shoulders, stepping out of it so that I'm standing in nothing but my necklace. The rose-scented steam rising from the large tub in the center is inviting, the warmth kissing my skin. But it reminds me of my mother and sadness wraps its arms around me.

The heat of the water is welcome as I submerge seconds after sinking into the tub. Resurfacing, I take a deep breath and lean back against the porcelain with my eyes closed. I need to compose myself.

"Any word about the queen?" I ask, my eyes still closed.

Servants talk amongst each other. They're the ultimate spies—everywhere, but invisible to most. Underestimated.

"No change," says Ellynne. "But think of it as a good thing. It means she's not worse."

"But not any better either."

I stare up at the ceiling, at the painting of a field of wildflowers that my mother commissioned years ago. I keep my focus on the ceiling as a stinging sensation builds behind my eyes. "Leave me," I say. "I need to think. I'll be out momentarily."

I sense their hesitation before Ellynne says, "Alright, we'll be in your chamber. Shout if you need anything."

When the door clicks closed behind them, my tears break free, silently coursing down my cheeks. I have to face my mother again soon. It's becoming harder and harder to deny the decline in her health. Much like the outbreak in Mainland, her sickness is a mystery—same as my father's was—but unlike the outbreak, its onset was gradual, with no cough or rash. It started with a prolonged fever and when the heat left her body, so did much of her strength.

Then the bouts of pain began. Often, she's in excruciating pain for unpredictable amounts of time. Months ago, these moments would come on suddenly and end quickly, with long periods of peace that allowed her to get out of bed and continue with her queenly duties.

Those moments are few and far between lately. The pain lasts longer, and her mind drifts farther and farther away.

No attempted cures have helped.

As her daughter, I can't bear her being in pain.

As her heir, I dread taking her place. I can hardly take care of myself, let alone an entire kingdom.

When the water in the tub starts to cool, I take it as my sign to get out. My pale skin is pink from the heat as I wrap a towel around myself and begin the lengthy process of wringing out my hair. I roll and pile it atop my head before returning to my bedchamber. Lowri lurches to her feet from where she'd been sitting at the table and my tresses tumble down just as dramatically.

Ellynne lounges prone in front of the fireplace, a novel—romance, no doubt—lying open on the rug. "Lowri, you *literally* scared the hair off Carys's head," she says as she gets to her feet and sets the book on my desk.

Lowri giggles. "Apologies, Princess. Did you enjoy your bath?"

I should refrain from responding, lest I say all the wrong things. "No." I roll my eyes at my word that slips free anyway. But luckily, neither of them pushes me to elaborate.

Once I'm dressed, I step out of my bedchamber to where Callum is on guard. "Good morning," he says with a small bow.

I nod to him.

"It's rather early. Do you think Miss Garrick will be awake?"

"We'll see." I'm already walking off, heading toward the dressmaker's bedchamber.

Once again, Durvla doesn't answer the first or second time that I knock. Maybe she's asleep. I push her door open, and she startles from where she's sitting on the edge of the bed, garbed in a rust-colored dress and already hard at work. Very impressive.

"Your Highness," she says, moving to set her knitting needles aside to stand.

I lightly flap my hand at her. "No need to get up. I'd like to see what you're working on."

Callum closes the door softly from the outside as I approach Durvla. She holds up her work, gnawing on her lip as she does so. "This is going to be the bodice."

It doesn't look like much, and certainly not like a bodice … I squint at it, trying to summon my imagination.

Durvla must recognize the incredulity on my face because she smiles and says, "I know it's rather abstract right now. With this sort of thing, you have to trust the process."

"Sounds like my whole life," I mumble.

"Mine too," she says, her smile faltering. She tucks the ball of yarn she's working with into the crook of her elbow and stands, keeping the knitting needle point secured. "May I check the fit? I'm making them in panels, so I just want to be sure that the sizing is adding up correctly."

"Sure." I awkwardly extend my arms out to my sides while Durvla holds the fabric up to my torso and wraps it around to the sides.

"Perfect." Her face lights up. Though she's still been mostly evading eye contact, it's nice to see something other than terror on her face.

I study her work, but I still can't picture it beyond the random stitches somewhat reminiscent of lace.

Durvla sets the *bodice* down and faces me, her posture rigid. The supplies she bought from Barr na Cahar yesterday line one side of her bed.

"Did you sleep with all of this on your bed?" I ask.

"I … didn't get much sleep," she responds.

It seems last night was a restless one for us all.

There's a loud rap on the door and I turn to listen as Callum announces the kitchen servants. "Let them in," I call out.

Durvla's brows scrunch together.

"Private breakfast is great when you don't feel like socializing."

The scent of food hits me as the servants enter, but my stomach is so knotted, I doubt I'll be able to eat. "Set it down on the desk," I tell the women.

"Yes, Your Highness."

"Alright," I say to Durvla. "Let's see what's for breakfast."

Chapter 19
CARYS

A KNOCK ON THE door sounds as I place my diadem atop my head and face Ellynne and Lowri, my lilac dress swishing around me.

"Perfect," they say in unison.

"Princess, may I have a word with you?" Tiernan calls out.

Ellynne and Lowri curtsy and hurry to the door with me in tow. As they slip out, I allow Tiernan in and flash a quick smile at Callum. "Alright, but it has to be brief. I want to visit my mother before the council meeting."

He nods, his face earnest. "Are you prepared to discuss the suitors with the Council? Have you studied the list?"

My face drops as I step back and allow him to close the door, sealing Callum outside. "Tiernan—"

"Trust me, Princess, the last thing I want to do is nag you; you get enough of that. I know it's difficult, but—"

"But *what*?" I fold my arms across my dress, causing the corset to tighten annoyingly. "How would looking at a bloody list help anything?"

"It would make you *knowledgeable*. It will show the Council that you are at least aware of your options, and that you are thinking about it." Tiernan's steady gaze meets me at eye level. "Lord Iywan is very influential. If you don't appear ready to take the throne, the Council will revolt."

My lips curve down, but I remain silent.

"They could make you seem incapable in the eyes of the people. And if the populace, especially the highborns, believe that their princess is not worthy of the throne … there could be an insurrection … Even organized regicide."

For a moment I forget how to breathe, and I quickly push away the memory of the assassin's hands on my neck. It was years ago. My mother wasn't even ill in those days; what if, indeed, more assassins are sent after me if I fail to rise appropriately to my station?

"Fine," I say with a heavy sigh. "I'll look at the bloody list." I wave him off, and he bows before leaving the room. As the door clicks shut, I march toward my desk, plucking the parchment from a small stack of books. It seems to weigh a ton. Slowly, I remove the ribbon and unroll the parchment, taking a deep breath.

Prince Morand of the Kingdom of Caldeon

Odd. Caldeon is a staunch enemy of one of our main allies, Ardall. I scrunch my brows and continue reading.

Prince Odgar of the Kingdom of Uldarvik

Laughter escapes as I imagine a brute of a man with a metal helmet, wooden shield, and furs from head to toe charging into our ballroom with a loud war cry. I clear my throat to cut off the laughter and continue reading.

Lord Bevin, Duke of the Outer Isles

I don't know a thing about this man.

Lord Jamie, Duke of Darragh

My eyes widen. Wynn's *father*, Lord Jamie, is one of my suitors? I grimace and move on to the last name on the list, and perhaps the most confusing of all.

Lord Commander Rheon of Bayenbar

No fancy noble, but certainly a formidable and influential presence in Erleya. Five years ago, Lord Commander Rheon oversaw the most memorable mass flogging in the public square right outside of Paramount's gates—a warning to the rebels. I can still see his eerie indifference as he stood on the scaffold, ordering the mutilation of dozens of people. Rebels, yes, but people, nonetheless. People who fight back against innocents being arrested for owning a nice dress.

I restrain a shudder and chuck the list aside. Every single one of these suitors is awful.

Not a surprise.

My mother is asleep again when I visit her, Callum by my side. Iywan stands at the window, staring off into the distance. He turns to me as soon as I enter, his lips drawn down.

"No change?" I ask softly.

He shakes his head and steeples his fingers together in front of his body, the picture of composure. The tension in his shoulders betrays him. "No change."

I'm rooted to the spot in front of the door. Part of me wants to turn and walk out—I want to pretend that she *is* strong, and awake, and busy with the ins and outs of court life. But I fill my lungs with air and force myself to take a step toward the bed. "I brought her favorite book again," I say, lifting the tome with both hands. "I'll read it to her anyway. If she wakes later, let her know that I was here."

Iywan smiles. "I will." He gives my shoulder a reassuring pat as he passes me, and I'm thrown right back into my childhood. To the time I'd tripped on a loose stone in the garden and fallen, scraping my knee. Iywan had been at my side in seconds, comforting me and even accompanying me to the infirmary to be bandaged. These days, it's easy to forget that side of him.

What happened?

As the door shuts, I pull up a chair close to my mother's bed and set the book on the mattress. Opening to where she'd last fallen asleep, I continue the tale of "The Enchantress Queen."

Enidwen continued to endure eternal days in the Otherworld, barely containing her boredom while craving something greater. She traveled to the Hallowed Hollow and chiseled an azurite from the wall of the cave. With eager anticipation, she awaited the autumn equinox when the Veil was thinner. When she approached Caedmon, there was nothing but love in his eyes. Yet as much as she bore the same love for him, she loved her possibilities even more.

On that day, she plunged a dagger into the heart of her beloved.

From across the Otherworld, growls and snarls arose, the ancient beasts awakening. A rift was torn in the Veil, and Enidwen escaped back to the mortal realm.

Time was very different in the mortal realm. While Enidwen had been in the Otherworld for a few years, her siblings had advanced drastically in age and her parents were long dead. Mortals, she realized, had become even more egotistical, the never-ending rivalry of Magekind versus Ordinaries intensifying. Enidwen traveled through the realm, putting her newfound Otherworldly powers to use—dazzling the masses with spectacular displays of light and magical fanfare. Followers bent a knee to her everywhere she went.

Still, it wasn't enough for Enidwen. She sought to rule the kingdom, to overthrow the fire-wielding king. She stormed the castle, her followers in tow, taking the throne by force.

Other kingdoms rose up against Erleya, but Enidwen couldn't be stopped. She sought ultimate power, poring over ancient texts and hunting for magical talismans to strengthen her ever-increasing powers. She explored runes, symbols, and the dark Underworldly powers of the Fallen Ones—the Underlings within Lugda's realm of the dead.

On the day of the solstice, she stood before the masses, a magnificent crown of fire upon her head, a spear of shadows in hand. She drew runes in the soil, encircling herself as she called out loudly in the Ancient Tongue.

Calling forth the Underling Prince.

The skies turned dark, the sun blood red. The earth rumbled, and ice spider-webbed across the land. Screams arose from far and wide, terror filling the air.

Up from the depths rose not a monster, but a humanoid figure. He stood just outside of the Enchantress's warded circle, golden eyes shining with satisfaction even as vines of darkness kept him bound.

Enidwen dropped onto a knee, bowing her head, her shadowy spear and fiery crown dissipating. "Great Underling Prince," she called. "Grant me unlimited power and I will release you."

A grin spread across the Underling's face, two rows of pointed teeth morphing his perfect humanoid features into something beastly. Yet Enidwen looked into his eyes and saw opportunity. She matched his grin and stood to her feet as the Underling Prince nodded.

"Release me and I shall grant you unlimited power."

I don't have time to finish the story before the council meeting, but we all know how it ends. Enidwen's sacrifice of her own humanity in favor of avarice was said to be the beginning of the end of magic. Ironically, she risked it all for ultimate power, only to lose it not just for herself, but for the kingdom. Other Dark Mages called Basduunai—*death bringers*—were less renowned than her, but equally feared.

Dark Magic instigated a widespread paranoia as deadly as the plague itself. Thus began the Purge that rid the land of any magic. The overwhelming fear of Otherworlders—of faeries and change-lings—led to the banishment of children suspected of being tainted by magic. Deformities and inexplicable illnesses became proof of Otherworld activity.

Then came the mass banishments. Sanctioned by the crown, the raids were meant as a reminder to the "lesser" citizens—a reminder of how Enidwen's actions supposedly sullied the land. Forayers were dispatched to keep people who were different in their place, so that Grounders—as Enidwen allegedly was—wouldn't dare to even *try* to rise to power again.

All because of a *fairytale*.

If the gods were truly still among us, would this be allowed? What would they say?

Damn them all, probably. I'm certain we've already been damned. Did my mother know the kingdom was still such a mess, or did it devolve during the months of her spiraling illness? I rise with the tome in my hands, press a kiss to her forehead, and leave the room as quickly as I can—to get away from the glaringly obvious proof that my ascent to the throne may come faster than anticipated.

Chapter 20
CARYS

SIX PAIRS OF EYES turn to me as I stride into the council chamber in the late morning. The space is spectacularly ornate for someplace where the most boring of affairs occur. Light filters in through the few window panels in the domed ceiling and onto an oval mahogany table at the center, the surface imbued with whorls of gold and bronze. Ten high-backed chairs with cushioned leather surround it. As everyone rushes to stand, their chairs scrape against the varnished terracotta-colored tiles.

I acknowledge the councilors' scattered greetings with a nod. Callum pulls out the chair at the head of the table, and I take my place across from Iywan.

My mother's seat.

Callum stands beside my chair, on guard.

Gods, I hope this meeting doesn't last too long. I've been told that Wynn Odhran, our trades merchant, is scheduled to make a delivery today, and I'd be remiss if I lost the opportunity to see him.

Lady Sessaley, the mistress of ceremonies, smiles from her spot on Iywan's left. Her silvery blond hair is pulled into a topknot so tight it makes *my* head hurt. Closer to my side of the table, Lady Taliesin, the treasurer, runs her fingers through short grey hair. For someone around Iywan's age, her golden-brown skin is uncannily smooth. What's her secret?

"Belhan was just updating us on the situation with the rebels," Iywan says, pulling me from my thoughts.

Ah, the rebels. They're an oddly quiet group aside from the occasional interception of Forayer activity in the Grounds. Their attempts to directly attack Paramount are so scarce I find it hardly worth mentioning.

Belhan turns his beady eyes toward me, his hands steepled across his barrel chest. "Yes, there's unrest in the southeast. Rumors of rebel droves traveling toward our gates have been on the rise. We've already alerted the Royal Brigade of the threat."

I narrow my eyes. "The Royal Brigade? To deal with rebels? Seems a bit … extreme."

"The rebellion isn't just gaining in numbers, Your Highness, but in strength too. They've been attacking with weapons of mass destruction."

"Mass destruction …" I doubt the weapons of a few rebels are a match for the Royal Brigade. "Having the Royal Brigade deal with rebels sounds like a poor allocation of power. What about protecting us from neighboring kingdoms, Ardall in particular?"

"We have a peace treaty with Ardall, Your Highness," Councilor Tomen says.

I turn my attention to the master of foreign affairs, my chin lifted and expression unperturbed. "I am aware of that, Councilor Tomen.

But until months ago, Erleya and Ardall were locked in a three-hundred-day war. Better safe than sorry."

He looks away.

Caldeon, on the other hand, has not attempted to attack our kingdom in decades, but there has been increasing unrest between their kingdom and Ardall. With both kingdoms just a short sail away from the northeastern tip of Erleya, our army has always been vigilant of the possibility of war.

Tomen speaks up again, his cloudy eyes somewhat focused in my general direction. "In the unlikely event that Caldeon or Ardall launches an attack on Erleya, our defense force is formidable enough to spare manpower to protect Paramount from rebel attacks."

"Why not utilize the Forayers rather than the Royal Brigade soldiers to protect against rebel attacks?"

"Mercenaries are complex, Your Highness." Tomen runs his hand over what's left of his white hair and Belhan bobs his head promptly in agreement, his jowls shaking.

"And yet we allow them to abuse their power." The words slip out.

The lines on Belhan's wide, russet forehead deepen. "Forgive me, Princess, but what do you mean by *abuse their power*?"

"I mean Forayers are apprehending innocent civilians in the Grounds for petty misdemeanors. Just recently, a botanist was taken on the suspicion of stealing a dress—from *Ballybaeg*. Under what law is it punishable to sentence her to service as a Veilguard for stealing a garment from another Grounds village?"

My inquiry is met with silence.

"It begs the question: how many more innocents are being snatched from their homes? And what exactly is considered treason? Are we arresting Grounders for owning harmless fairytales? We've all grown up with those books. It's ridiculous to suddenly consider it forbidden." No wonder the rebels want to dismantle the monarchy. I bite my lip to keep from asking more questions. For now.

Belhan's thin lips part for a few heartbeats. My focus darts around the table at the other councilors, hoping to find at least *understanding* on someone's face.

Jac lifts his hand. "The Grounders have been known to disguise books of enchantments as fairytales, Your Highness. Could that be what you're referring to?" His supercilious grin makes me want to shoot an arrow through his pretty face. He notes my glare, and his knuckles scrape across his stubbly jaw. "I will see that it is looked into. If there has been such a case—"

"Are you accusing me of speaking falsehoods, Councilor Jac?"

His umber skin pales. "No, Your Highness."

"Because there *is* such a case and I'm certain there are more I'm unaware of. Something needs to be done about it. How long has it been since there was proof that Mages exist?"

"A millennium, Your Highness." He drums his fingers briefly on the table. "But Grounders are known for finding ways to procure magic through artifacts and—"

"I know that," I snap. "I agree that procuring magic is dangerous and should be punished. But banishing Undesirables and arresting anyone on mere suspicion of using magic is unjustified. Especially when there has been no proof. I've been to the depository after Quarterly Raids. All the confiscated items in there are ordinary. No magic."

Jac lifts a brow as though challenging me. Gods, he's so cocky. I hate that he's also bloody handsome.

"Unfortunately, Princess," Iywan begins. "We cannot demolish centuries of practice in one small council meeting, but we can revisit this discussion at a later time." There's finality in Iywan's voice, and as I draw in a breath to rebut, I think better of it.

I sit back in my seat, simmering. For a while, no one speaks. Someone clears their throat, another coughs.

Then Iywan finally speaks up, his focus on me. "I'd like to discuss the Feast while we have you present, Your Highness."

Of course. I hold back a sigh. "I believe that would be beneficial, Lord Iywan." I glance at the mistress of ceremonies who laces her long fingers together, blue veins standing out on her fair skin. "Shall we start with the most unlikely contenders?" I ask.

Iywan quirks a brow and gestures for me to continue.

"Of the five suitors," I begin, making it clear that I have indeed considered his list. "I am concerned about Prince Morand of Caldeon. Wouldn't that jeopardize our peace treaty with Ardall in a way?"

"In a way," says Iywan, glancing at Tomen briefly. "However, Caldeon has grown significantly more powerful in the wake of Ardall's disease outbreak in the past year."

My brows lower, my head immediately starting to ache while I mull over the ramifications of this. If we form an alliance with Caldeon, it may grant us some protection should Ardall try to infiltrate, but it can also cause a backlash. Ardall may have a weaker army and less power, but they have wealth and a host of arrogance.

"As for Prince Odgar of Uldarvik, he's a … unique choice. Does he know this is a formal event?" My voice sounds strained as I try not to laugh.

"Yes, Your Highness," says Iywan. "The other three suitors are of great noble families. Lord—"

"Bevin, Duke of the Outer Isles," I say, cutting him off. "Lord Jamie, Duke of Darragh." My stomach churns. "And Rheon of Bayenbar, Lord Commander of the Royal Brigade."

Iywan's eyes widen, but he nods. Around the table more expressions of surprise unfold. Good.

"Many wonderful suitors, Lord Iywan. I am excited to meet them all."

In the early afternoon, I catch Paramount's merchant, Wynn, just outside of the wine cellar, his lean arms wrapped around a wooden crate filled with glass bottles. Beside me, Callum's steps falter, but I plow on. Wynn turns toward me, brown eyes alight, his sepia complexion reddening slightly. "Your Highness," he says with a smile and a small bow. "Sir Callum."

Callum nods to him, ice in his glare. "Lordling …" His tone is nothing short of demeaning, a manner reserved for Wynn.

The annoyance on Wynn's face is brief. "It's nice to see you again, Your Highness."

I smile at him. "Is that all the wine you've brought?" I gesture to the crate in his arms.

"No, this is the third one." Wynn nudges the door open with his hip and sets the crate down just inside the cellar.

Carnal need clenches my stomach, but I try to remain casual. "Alys has been eagerly awaiting more honey …"

Wynn smiles warmly. "Yes, she was very happy for … the restock." His gaze lowers to my lips, his last few words delayed as though he'd had to regain his focus.

"Show me the wine stock you've brought." I can't keep the breathiness out of my voice as I step closer to Wynn. I glance sidelong at Callum, addressing him. "Don't let anyone through."

Callum's nod is sharp, his eyes cold, but he turns forward, fully on guard. I step into the cellar, shutting the door behind me.

We're surrounded by hundreds of bottles of wine housed in rows upon rows of shelves. The aroma is nearly as intoxicating as Wynn's lustful gaze and the dimple in his left cheek. Dark stubble has started to grow along the soft curves of his face—he's matured since the last time I saw him. I step toward him, and he loops his arms around me.

But as he leans in to claim my lips, I'm immediately reminded of Lord Jamie of Darragh. They have the same sepia skin tone, brown eyes, and black hair. I turn my head and Wynn's lips land on my cheek. His confusion is evident as he lets his arms fall. "Princess?"

I step back. "The Feast is rapidly approaching."

"I know." He sounds resigned. "How awkward is it that my father will be one of your suitors?"

I glance over my shoulder at him. "*Awkward?*" I laugh with despair. "Sure, let's go with that word choice." He runs his long fingers across my cheek, but my hand catches his mid-motion and he withdraws. Again, confusion crumples his face. I clasp my hands together in front of my body, closing him off. "Thank you for the delivery. Be sure to collect your payment from Lord Iywan."

Wynn blinks at me. In this moment, he looks like the boy I once knew, and not the man only a year younger than me. It takes him a few seconds before he gets the hint and bows to me. "Until next time," he says. I nod at his retreating back.

A flustered sigh escapes me just as the door swings open again.

"Princess? Everything alright?" Callum stands a small distance away, assessing my mood.

I hate it when people do that. "I'm not going to bite," I say, though my tone deceives me.

"I wouldn't object to biting."

It's so unexpected that it startles a laugh from me. I wave him toward me, and he toes the door closed before approaching. Wynn's visit wasn't what I'd anticipated. No, Iywan's choice of suitors ruined that for me. But this … he can't ruin this. Callum regards me with such intensity that my breath hitches.

I'm not sure who makes the first move, but our lips collide, hurried, sloppy, and so very exhilarating. I fumble with his sword belt, until the weapon drops to the floor. The strings of his trousers are next, but he bats my hand away, taking over. My lips part as I start to comment on this newfound boldness from him, but he silences me with another kiss and hoists up my skirt and underskirt. I'm in his arms and pressed against the wall in no time. All thoughts of alliances, betrothals, illnesses, and any responsibilities vanquish. Wrapping my legs around him, I lock my ankles behind his back and fully give in, letting the pleasure numb my mind.

A while later, Callum goes still with a final groan against my shoulder, and it echoes through the cellar. "Hush," I whisper. My lower lip feels swollen from the number of times I've bitten down to silence my own moans. I unwrap myself from around his waist and he sets me down on my feet again. My heart is still racing, and the aftershock of bliss renders my legs useless and trembling. With my hands pressed against Callum's chest, I steady myself. How he's managed to keep both of us upright is a mystery to me.

"Well, that was not quite what I was expecting, but no complaints here," he says breathlessly. He steps back to gather his trousers from around his calves, and I smirk.

I push off the wall to rearrange my underskirts, my eyes on him all the while.

"No affections from the lordling?" he asks.

"I may be marrying his *father*. It's a bit of a turn-off."

Callum schools his features into indifference. I'm aware of his jealousy, but I wish he would wise up and realize that our *arrangement* can be nothing more than what it is.

With a sigh, I straighten my clothes and my hair. I'm still flushed, and Callum doesn't help as he leans in to kiss me. I put up my hand to stop him, and he rights himself again, gathering his sword belt.

The wooden crate of wine that Wynn brought in is right beside us. One crate of many. I walk along the shelves, needing a distraction from everything quickly resurfacing in my mind. How hard would it be to disguise myself and hop into Wynn's wagon? Maybe he's still on the premises. It would get me out of the castle, out of Paramount, away from … everything.

"Princess." Callum's voice tugs me out of my delusions.

"Do you know how old Lord Jamie is?"

Callum is taken aback. "In his forties, I believe."

"That fits," I say with a sigh. I believe Commander Rheon is also in his forties. It's as if Iywan has intentionally lined up men twice my age for my pickings.

Gone is the bliss from moments ago, and I wish I could've just stayed in that moment. Weariness takes hold of my mind, dragging down my mood until I want to crawl into a hole in the earth. It's always the same—the high is immediately followed by a devastating low that makes me question if I've ever truly experienced joy.

"Your Highness?" His forehead is creased with concern. "Are you alright?"

I want to tell him that I'm not alright. That I'm always craving more. *Something* more. That even in the presence of someone I trust, I feel alone. My lips part and the words sit on the tip of my tongue: *I feel nothing.*

I feel everything.

It takes effort to plaster a smile on my face, but I manage. "I'm perfectly fine."

Chapter 21
DURVLA

CARYS'S MORNING CHECK-IN IS brief and uneventful, leaving me with a lot of time to work on her dress. The front panel is halfway done, and as I'm sitting on the floor with yards of purple fabric spread out in front of me, I sense a presence.

Major Kilkenny stands with one hand braced against the doorjamb. I scramble to my feet as though I've been caught doing something illicit. Unsure of the right etiquette, I dip into a curtsy, but my legs are numb from sitting on the floor for so long, and I nearly fall over.

Major Kilkenny presses his lips into a thin line. "You don't have to do that," he says. "I'm not royalty."

My face warms. "Right. You're not guarding Princess Carys this morning?"

His dark eyes search my face, and I resist the urge to press my hands over my cheeks. "Sir Ren is on duty," he says as he steps fully into my room.

I have no clue who Sir Ren is, but before I can ask, he speaks again.

"It's time for your horseback riding lesson."

Horseback riding lessons? I wasn't aware that I would be receiving those.

"Just for an hour and then you can get right back to work."

"Right." I have so many questions, but Major Kilkenny's stony glare robs me of my words. "Uh ..." I tilt my head to the partially cut fabric on the floor before me and then back up at the guard.

He gestures vaguely to my work in progress. "You can wrap things up."

My shoulders relax. "Thank you."

He nods and presses his hand against the doorframe again, his focus drawn to my work. I get back onto my knees and pick up the scissors from the floor. The brand on my left arm has made my dominant hand stiff. If that wasn't enough of a hindrance, now Major Kilkenny's attention sends nervous energy coursing through me. I fight the urge to fuss with the bracelet missing from my wrist and my throat closes up.

I'm so sorry, Ma, for letting them take my bracelet.

I swallow and release a breath before glancing up at Kilkenny. "This ... may take a moment," I admit.

If possible, his stare intensifies. "Try to work faster."

Gods, if only I had the guts to kick him out and slam the door behind him. I blink forcefully and pull all my focus back to the task at hand. Nervous energy aside, I finish cutting and folding the fabric, then place the pieces in a neat stack on my bed. The whole time, I can *feel* the guard observing my every move. As I expect, those calculating dark eyes are still on me when I look up.

"I need to get my shoes on," I say.

He shrugs and makes a subtle gesture with his hands as if to say *so do it.*

It isn't very long before I'm following him through the maze of corridors. It's vaguely familiar—we took the same path the day we headed to Barr na Cahar—but despite my best attempt to keep track of the route, I forget every turn.

We step out of the castle and into the sunlight. The blue sky and a smattering of white clouds are a warm welcome.

Oh, how I wish Taig could play outside on a day such as this. What is he doing right now? My stomach knots. What if his new normal is being in solitude at home all day? I'd had the privilege of mainly working in the comfort of my home, but checking in on Taig in the middle of the day would be hard for Osheen.

My body collides with a solid mass, and I startle. My gaze catches on the collar of Kilkenny's maroon livery, right at my eye level. A silvery scar peeks out from beneath his collar, snaking up the left side of his neck. I snap my focus from his neck up to the scowl on his face and step back quickly, putting space between us. "Apologies."

He folds his arms across his chest, his posture rigid. "If you're going to survive your time here, you need to be more alert. Unless you want to be sent right back to the brig."

I didn't do it on purpose, I want to say. Instead, I nod and continue following him toward the stables. As soon as we enter the building, Ghendor's and Mirren's ears flick our way, their heads swiveling to us shortly after. I swear the black stallion rolls his eyes and Mirren averts hers. I can't blame them. Major Kilkenny steps in front of me and peers into my face. I try not to back away but, gods, he gives the most intense stares.

"We don't have much time," he says. "So, let's skip the part where you're afraid of heights and all of that, yes?"

Oh, certainly. Because it's that simple. I flash him a surely unbelievable smile. "No problem."

We lead the horses out of their stalls and into the open air. Major Kilkenny gestures for me to mount Mirren, and I can't help but pout.

I am not afraid of heights. I am *not* afraid of heights.

I'm *terrified* of heights.

Recalling the way Major Kilkenny had taught me to mount the mare the first time, I swing myself up into her saddle. My heart lodges in my throat as I settle atop her back. I breathe in through my nostrils and out through pursed lips.

Kilkenny rests his hand on my knee and tilts his head, regarding me. "All good?"

"Never better," I grit out as a dull throb starts at the back of my head.

"No fear, right?"

I want to believe that he's trying to be encouraging or to show a modicum of concern. "Right." I rub the back of my head.

Major Kilkenny gets onto Ghendor with annoying ease. "We're going to just take a lap around the grounds, stairs included. Mirren will follow along, but I need you to steer the reins like I showed you when we traveled to Barr na Cahar."

I nod wordlessly.

Major Kilkenny clicks his tongue and nudges Ghendor's sides with his heels. I follow suit. My stomach lurches as Mirren sets off at a walk alongside Ghendor.

Major Kilkenny studies me. "You're not going to faint on me, are you, Garrick?"

"Not if I can help it, Kilkenny." The words slip out before I can filter them. "I mean, *Major* Kilkenny."

To my surprise, Kilkenny only smirks at me. It's so brief that, had I blinked at that moment, I would've missed it. "Good," he says, his face neutral once more.

We set off around the castle grounds, walking the winding pathways that overlook the cliffside down to the striking loch below. It's breathtaking. *Literally*. Beneath me, Mirren is the picture of perfection. She's as good-natured as Kilkenny has bragged. We keep a steady pace, even as the temperature begins to drop, and a gentle breeze sweeps across the bluffs, blowing through Mirren's cream-colored mane and tugging curls from my braids. I lift my hand to push back the coils and the damaged skin around my forearm brand pulls. It's not as painful anymore, but incredibly uncomfortable.

Kilkenny catches my wince. "Everything alright?"

"Yes." There isn't much point in complaining about something that cannot be changed. When I'm deep in my work on Carys's dress, I'm able to ignore this newest bodily nuisance, just as well as I can ignore my frequent headaches.

By the time we return to the stables, I'm a lot more comfortable on horseback. I still have no clue what it has to do with my dressmaking position, but I suppose if ever I need to make another trip to Barr na Cahar, I can do so with greater ease.

"You can use some more practice," Kilkenny says after I dismount.

My chest deflates along with my confidence.

A little muscle in his cheek tics. "But you at least stayed on the path this time and didn't fall into the loch."

My lips tug up in a small smile. "That's something."

He gestures somewhere over his shoulder and the stableboy appears out of nowhere. They exchange a few words too quickly for me to make out before the stableboy leads the horses away.

Kilkenny begins the trek back to the castle and I jog to catch up with him. His angular eyes narrow as he turns to me again, his forehead creased. "Do you have any experience with weapons?"

"Weapons? Like … ?" I motion to his sword, and he nods. "No, not really. I went hunting with my father as a child, but I was never good."

Kilkenny doesn't speak again until we're standing outside of my door. "Well …" His throat bobs as he swallows, and I catch another glimpse of the scar up the left side of his neck before I focus on his lips again. "Have a good day, Garrick," he says.

He leaves before I can even respond.

Chapter 22
CARYS

EARLY THE NEXT MORNING, my alternate guard, Ren, marches alongside me as I make my way to my mother's bedchamber. He doesn't speak much, and while he doesn't resemble Tiernan, with his close-cropped hair that blends into his warm brown skin, and the fine wrinkles across his forehead, he's equally stern. As we enter my mother's room, the bloody apprentice girl—what's her name? Bailey?—is sitting on the bed again.

Iywan steps forward hastily. "Princess, you're early."

My focus sweeps past Iywan to the apprentice girl as she stands with a bowl in hand, like the last time I saw her here. She curtsies to me and offers a smile. "Good day, Your Highness."

My stare lingers on the bowl. "What is in there?"

Bailey's lips part, but she purses them again seconds after. She glances sidelong at Iywan, and he turns to me with resignation.

"I didn't want to worry you, Princess," he says. "Your mother's condition remains unchanged, and the healers believe that perhaps some bloodletting would do her good. That it may get her body to some sort of equilibrium where the medicines could perhaps offer her more relief from her symptoms."

"*Bloodletting?*" My voice sounds shrill even to my own ears.

"Not by cutting, Your Highness," says Brona.

Who does she think she is, speaking out of turn? Heat fills my head and I want to throw something at her. I want to throttle her. With a few long strides, I'm standing beside my mother, my fists clenched at my side to keep from assaulting the healer's apprentice. My mother is paler than ever, and her hair is more silver than blond. Such a drastic change in just one day. It's too bizarre to make any sense.

I lift her cool hand and brush my thumb over her near-translucent skin, over newly formed wrinkles. In just a few days, she's aged significantly. I turn her hand over, palm up, and search her arms for signs of lacerations. There are small, inflamed spots instead that appear more like tiny nicks—like they were made with the very tip of a sharp blade. Or like insect bites …

Brina's words finally make sense in my too-crowded head. *Not by cutting,* she'd said.

"What—?" I make the mistake of peering into the bowl that Brina is still holding. Black, slimy creatures squirm around inside, bloated from the blood they've ingested.

Leeches.

I step away quickly and close my eyes, breathing in through my nose to ward off the nausea.

"It's a less invasive form of bloodletting," the apprentice explains.

I glower at her. "Do *not* speak to me." Thank the gods I don't have the dagger that Tiernan always offers me. I'd love to do some very invasive *bloodletting* on Blair's face right now.

Iywan steps closer to us. "You may leave, Briony. Thank you."

Briony silently curtsies to me and walks off, Ren stepping aside for her to exit. I turn back to my mother as the door opens.

"Briony," I call out, my focus still on my mother's face. Her footsteps halt. "Send Lady Alys."

"Yes, Your Highness."

My mother doesn't stir in the slightest. She doesn't look like Queen Morwenna anymore. "Iywan, I'd like some privacy."

"Yes, Princess."

I sit beside my mother and slide my fingers through her hair. As I pull my hand back, silvery strands come out in clumps as if they were never attached to her scalp. A sob catches in my chest, and I close my eyes, exhaling slowly. Lugda, please give me some more time with her. I'm not ready for a life without her. Nor to be the monarch.

I'm not sure how long I sit there, simply existing with the shell of my mother beside me. The creak of heavy oak draws my attention to the plump figure at the door. Alys strides in, politely nods to Ren and quietly shuts the door behind her before hurrying to my mother's bedside. She stares past me to my mother and frowns. "I just saw her at dawn …" Her voice trails off, her brows drawn together.

My face crumples. "Did you arrange the bloodletting?"

Alys doesn't respond but reaches for my mother's arm and scrutinizes the leech bites. She whispers what I assume is a swear word in her native tongue and shakes her head. "I did not." She places a hand lightly on my mother's forehead, her gaze distant. As I'm about to ask her what she's thinking about, she pulls back her hand with a sharp intake of breath.

My pulse jumps. "What is it? Fever?"

Her face is pinched tight as she stands upright again, idly scratching her cheek. Her focus remains on my mother for a while longer.

"*Alys.*"

"Apologies, dear one. I am just trying to figure this out. It's ... bizarre. I wish I had answers for you. I don't know why Iywan is undermining my authority in this matter. Perhaps he doesn't trust that I have done all that I can and thinks he could command a subordinate to do what I refuse to. Like bloodletting."

I clench my jaw to keep from saying something blatantly unsavory about the *subordinate*. "I don't want that woman near my mother."

Alys nods, her face still pinched.

My attention shifts from my mother's sickly face to Alys's again. "You said you've done all you can ... Is she going to die soon?" My voice comes out flat.

My stomach sinks. I fidget with my amulet and close my eyes as they start to sting.

"I will increase the dosages of her elixirs, and we'll see if any changes happen. We can only wait and see. I'll speak to Iywan about Briony."

Chapter 23
DURVLA

THE WEEK GOES BY in a flurry of knitting, cutting, measuring, sewing, exuberant meals, walks around the castle, horseback riding lessons, and heavenly baths. How can I ever return to Cluain Baile, to the minuscule tub in my tiny home? I want to fetch Taig and smuggle him into the castle. He loves bath time. I can only imagine how much he'd enjoy splashing around in the tubs here. My heart aches every time my thoughts float back to him.

My nights are filled with recurring nightmares in varying degrees of horror. I've dived wholeheartedly into the making of the princess's dress, into my survival here at Paramount. Whenever I allow my mind to be idle, I'm left feeling like my life has been diminished from a greater, more rewarding existence of caring for another human being, to living out a reality that just isn't mine. I feel like an impostor every time I step out of my room in beautiful dresses that don't belong to me. Every time Ellynne and Lowri smile at me in the hallways. Every time I catch myself staring at Major Kilkenny a little too long.

He *is* very easy on the eyes but, by the gods, he is infuriating. Everything he does is for Princess Carys. It's like he doesn't have a mind of his own. Then again it *is* his job, and everything I do is for Princess Carys too, isn't it? Maybe it's just how things are here in the castle. The lives of those who serve the royal family have but one purpose: to serve the royal family.

My head hasn't been hurting as much as it usually does lately. My ears seldom ring, and I've yet to have any episodes. Perhaps the gods figured I have enough to deal with and they've given me a break from my own rebellious body.

I've gotten used to facing the door whenever I'm deep in my work. That way, I'm less startled when someone barges into my room.

I'm sewing one panel of the knitted dress bodice when my door flies open. Princess Carys storms in as though she's on a rampage and Kilkenny stands in the open doorway, his back to us. Princess Carys's ochre eyes are brighter than usual, her brows lowered, her back rigid. "Have you finished?"

I jump to my feet out of respect, but I don't curtsy. She hates that, I've learned. "I ... have not," I admit. "The bodice is nearly complete, though."

She laughs, but the ire on her face only sparks brighter. That's not disturbing at all ...

"The *bodice*," she repeats. "Is that all?"

"It is the most intricate part, the most involved. The lower half is fabric. All I have to do is layer and sew it together, then attach it to the bodice and do the—"

She yawns theatrically and turns on her heels, starting to pace. I follow her steps, tilting my head frequently in an attempt to catch a glimpse of her lips—to catch her words. It isn't until she whirls to face me again that I catch the end of a sentence. "... waste of my time." She closes her eyes and pinches the bridge of her nose, one arm folded across her torso.

The words settle in the pit of my stomach, and heat blooms. A shiver runs down my spine, like ice, countering the heat. I clench my fists, my nails biting into my palms, and for a moment my vision darkens around the edges, around the princess's figure. I want to scream at her. To tell her that *she's* a waste of my time. After all, *I* was the one ripped away from my home, from my family, from the only lifestyle I've ever known, all because of a dress that I'm now being forced to make for *her*.

Kilkenny glances over his shoulder, his eyes widening. He slowly shakes his head as if telling me not to give in to the anger rapidly fueling my body. I inhale deeply and breathe out.

"I gave you my promise," I say to the princess, hoping that my voice sounds as calm as I want it to. "Your dress will be complete before the Feast. That gives me eighteen more days. A lot can get done in eighteen days. It will be worth the time. I swear to Rhianu."

This seems to douse the fire in Princess Carys. Slowly, her posture softens. Her forehead is still creased, and I can tell she wants to yell again, but she doesn't. "And how are you so sure of yourself?" she asks me.

I shrug. "You had faith in me."

The creases in her forehead disappear and her jaw unclenches. She sighs and tips her head back toward the ceiling as if praying to the Mother. Then without another word, she turns on her heels and marches out of the room, tugging the door behind her so that the floor shakes.

I collapse onto the bed and sit there for a while, staring at the door and expecting the princess to make an explosive reappearance. She doesn't, and eventually I sag with relief. My hands are shaking too much to get back to work right away, though eventually I'm able to collect myself and press on. To earn my release from Carys's service. To get back to Taig.

Chapter 24
CARYS

I'M NOT PROUD OF my outburst. Especially when beside me, Tiernan is a mask of disapproving silence. "Say something," I grit out.

"What can I say?"

"Something annoying, no doubt." To my surprise, he chuckles. It's so rare and so surprising that it provokes a brief smile from me.

"I know you're worried about Queen Morwenna's health," he says quietly.

My smile falls. "It's not just her health. It's … everything. I wish she'd wake up so I could talk to her. And I'm frustrated with this impending marriage. It isn't fair. The bloody marriage, the rebellion, the unrest in our neighboring nations, the treaties, alliances, enemies …" I draw in a breath. "I know I've been training for this my whole life, but it's overwhelming in the midst of my mother practically knocking on Lugda's door."

"You're under a lot of pressure," Tiernan agrees.

I'm surprised that he doesn't respond with something stricter, like reminding me that I'm the heir to the throne and I should've known that the responsibility of the nation could fall on my shoulders at any moment.

I scoff. "Pressure is one way to put it. It's more like I'm being held underwater and I'm doing my best not to draw in my last breath. The Council is breathing down my neck, expecting me to be well-versed in being the queen already, but at the same time treating me like I'm a damn child."

"I believe there's one person in the castle who can relate to the pressures of such a deadline and an authority figure looming over her."

I stop walking and fix him with a glower. "You can't possibly be comparing *my* predicament to Durvla's task. She's *lucky* to be here. I'm helping her, if anything. She doesn't have to work for her food, or her clothing, or the roof over her head. And she certainly doesn't have to meet suitors and prepare to choose her … husband." I nearly choke on the last word.

"No," Tiernan says quietly as I start walking again. "But maybe she liked her life before she was taken away from it. I'm just saying that you may want to remember how you feel about these pressures because I'm sure Garrick is feeling it too. She's doing quite well given the short deadline."

"And given that you're sneaking her off to the riding grounds for lessons."

He tenses at my side. Only our footsteps echoing in the corridor fill the void for a moment before he says, "My apologies, Princess. I'd hoped it would help her feel more at home here in Paramount. I did not mean to undermine you."

I chortle. "You don't even try to lie."

"You say that like it's an insult."

I halt my steps and Tiernan follows suit. "Tell me something. Say you had someone else you cared deeply for—hypothetically speaking—would you break the rules for them?"

He hesitates for a moment and then says with disappointing predictability, "The rules exist for the greater good."

I roll my eyes. "That is a disgusting answer. No wonder you don't have a lover."

His jaw twitches slightly, but ever the controlled warrior, he doesn't take the bait.

"Would you break the rules for me?"

"The rules protect you; there's no need to break them."

I groan. "Why must you be so constantly diplomatic? Break a rule every now and then. Drop the formalities. Flirt a little. Durvla is attractive."

He blinks.

"Oh, come on. Those brown doe eyes, the curly hair, the flawless complexion." For Rhianu's sake she's from the Grounds and she has not a blemish in sight.

Is that amusement on his face? He's holding back laughter as he asks, "Doe eyes?"

"You know … those big, innocent eyes. Innocent and maybe a little scared."

"She was taken from her home; it would be strange if she wasn't scared."

"Oh, for fu—come along." I huff and tug on his sleeve. He's impossible.

I'd heard about the horseback riding lessons from Ellynne. It intrigues me. His reasoning is sweet. Could it be that uptight Tiernan Kilkenny actually *cares* about someone who he doesn't have a duty to protect?

Heat hollows out the pit of my stomach. Gods … is that jealousy?

I must grimace because Tiernan slows his pace. "Are you alright?"

"Never better."

Chapter 25
DURVLA

THE HARP AND LUTE *play in harmony, a drum keeping them in time. The Feast attendees dance with the music—the women in stunning dresses swishing with each movement, the men so sharp in their formal attire. Princess Carys sways in rhythm with one of many masked strangers, a smile painted on her face, her eyes the epitome of boredom.*

It's nearly comical.

The music changes to a more upbeat tempo, and dance partners are exchanged. For a moment, Carys is swept up into the arms of a tall and handsome stranger, only to end up in the arms of another. By the end of the song, she's back with the first stranger, his blue eyes peering at her through a black and silver mask. Stepping back, he bows to her. "It's been my honor, Your Highness," he says in an oh-so-familiar voice.

The princess smiles without façade. "Don't go," she says as he turns to walk away.

He halts, confused.

"Remove your mask."

The stranger doesn't hesitate. With a small smile and a nod, he removes his mask.

The princess gazes up at him, and everything within her clenches with eager anticipation. "Callum." Her voice is breathy and laden with surprise.

"Have you chosen your suitor yet?" he asks.

"Oh, yes ... " Her eyes gleam. "It's you, Callum. It's always been you." She launches herself into his arms and he holds her up as their lips meet in a turbulent dance of their own. Callum sets the princess down, but only to scoop her into his arms again, supporting her beneath her knees and her back. He rushes out of the ballroom like their lives depend on it.

Princess Carys doesn't touch the floor until they're in an empty corridor. Callum grasps the neckline of her dress, tearing it with a loud rip and revealing the princess's lack of undergarments beneath.

"I must have you," says Callum, his voice teeming with urgency and lust—

I lurch upright in bed with every desire to run and hide my burning face. Images flash in my mind. Sweaty bodies writhing together, ragged breaths and—oh gods. Even their voices. Loud and clear as if I had the ability to hear. I often hear in dreams fueled by memories— of my parents, birds, babbling brooks. But this ...

I shudder and roll out of bed, ignoring the throbbing in my head and the dizziness that immediately sets in as I rush over to the tankard on my desk. As the lukewarm water slides down my throat, wind whips around my ankles, billowing my nightdress. I march to the window to close it against the draft but ... it's closed?

I'm losing my mind.

The images flash through my mind again. "Out! Out! Out!" I slap my palm against my forehead with each hurried utterance.

I need to get out of this castle; I need to go back to Cluain Baile. I need to finish this dress and wow the princess lest I continue to dissolve into insanity. Swiping my hand over my face, I huff out a breath. I shake my limbs to dispel the tension in my muscles, trying to think of anything other than Princess Carys and Callum having noisy, wild … Sunlagh, blind me. It was absolutely not my place to have *that* dream.

I need to go for a walk.

I grab my dressing gown and toss it over my shoulders. No one should be wandering the corridors at this hour, right? As I step out of my room, I find myself nearly face to face with Kilkenny. I must scream loudly because his hand immediately flies to cover my mouth. My heart hammers wildly in my chest and I push away the impulse to bite his hand.

"What are you doing out here?" he asks as he lowers his hand.

"I was on my way to—"

Ellynne appears, rounding the corner into this corridor. She reels back, a hand clutching her chest, as she mumbles what looks like enough profane words to make a sailor blush. "You scared me!" She's in a frilly nightdress without a dressing gown, her generous curves defined beneath the thin material. Kilkenny averts his gaze, and I wish I could do the same.

For Rhianu's sake. First the dream about the princess, now this awkward encounter with a far-too-scantily clad woman.

I stare at Ellynne's lips, squinting in the dim light as a grin creeps onto her face. "What are you two doing out?"

Both Kilkenny and I exchange bewildered looks and the smirk on Ellynne's lips shoves my mind right back into the dream. My cheeks heat up again. I've never wished so hard that I didn't have to look at someone's face to know what they're saying.

"What are *you* doing out at this hour?" Kilkenny asks Ellynne.

"I'm …" Ellynne glances behind her as though being pursued, then back to us. "I'm on my way to the kitchen for a midnight snack."

Kilkenny stares at her, then something like realization contorts his features. He utters something with disdain that I don't quite make out, then turns to face me. I expect him to say something meaningful. Yet what comes out of his mouth is something about rest. Then he stalks off.

I scowl at his back. Ellynne laughs, pointing between Kilkenny's retreating back and me. "Are you two …"

My eyes flare wide. "Oh, gods no."

Ellynne smirks. "He's a tad sullen, admittedly, but handsome, don't you think?"

That one is hard to deny. *Walk*. I *need* to walk.

Ellynne lays a gentle hand on my shoulder and the dim lighting muddles her words. "… a drink. Come." She starts to walk, heading in the opposite direction of where Kilkenny went. Turning back to me she gestures with her hand. "Come on. A bit of … help … sleep."

My heart lurches; I hate this dim lighting. Even worse, Ellynne links her arm with mine and sets off for toward the kitchen. Being so close makes it even harder for me to catch the movements of her lips when she's talking while facing forward.

She rambles on about something as we make our way to the dining hall, and by the time we step into the unoccupied chamber, I'm almost certain it's glaringly obvious that I haven't heard a word. Is this where my time here ends? Where I get sent to the brig to await my death sentence? But Ellynne only beams at me and relinquishes my arm, holding her hand out to the door that leads to the kitchen.

I suppose she didn't notice after all. Thank the gods.

On one side of the kitchen is an arch of white bricks—the maw of a large wood-burning oven. Tall wooden tables line either side of the room, and the walls are adorned with a plethora of copper pots and pans hanging on hooks.

In this late hour there's no aroma of freshly cooked food, the oven is unlit, but the room is well-illuminated with oil lamps hanging from the ceiling and on the walls. The kitchen is empty save for a woman, her honey blond braid resting between her shoulder blades. She turns to face us as we enter the kitchen, her round eyes growing even wider.

Ellynne says something to her and Eefa grins and utters something about "scrummy leftovers." She chuckles and digs into the large pockets of her apron, producing two apples. "I snagged the last four ... baked with honey ... sweet on their own." She steps forward and holds a bright red apple that is clearly not baked with honey ...

Over the years, I've learned that reading lips is rarely perfect and not always reliable, but context clues and body language can speak louder. It's incredible how many things I've caught that were lost on me before I started losing my hearing—the tiniest tic of the jaw, the briefest wince, the subtle clenching of a fist, and even the way some-one stands in the presence of different people.

I've been in Eefa's vicinity a few times for meals, and I've seen how Carys's posture always changes in her presence—as if she's overcompensating to appear rigid. Around Carys, Eefa is beyond comfortable, daring even, and with a permanent smirk on her lips as though she's keeping an inside joke to herself.

"How goes the dressmaking?" she asks, as if we're old friends.

Unease takes hold of my stomach, and I swallow as I slide my finger awkwardly over my bare wrist. Between the dream, running into Kilkenny, and Ellynne's questions about feelings I don't have for him, I'd almost completely forgotten about my sole purpose here in Paramount. I forgot that I don't belong here. That the very reason for my existence is in Cluain Baile. I need to keep that in mind.

Eefa shifts her attention to Ellynne, asking her something about me.

"Still adjusting to castle life," Ellynne says with a smile.

Eefa grins. "Well, some lemon cake may help. There's only one slice left though. I'll leave the pair of you to fight over that." Then to Ellynne, she asks, "Is Princess Carys awake?"

"Yes, but I wouldn't go to her now if I were you."

"Oh …" Eefa says, but there is no disappointment on her face. Only intrigue.

Clearly, I've missed something.

"Good night, ladies. Enjoy the apples and the lemon cake." She fishes another apple from her pocket, tosses it into the air and catches it before taking a massive bite. She walks off, hips swaying.

Ellynne lets Eefa walk away, then turns back to me, her forehead creased. "I should head back but help yourself to the last slice of lemon cake."

"Alright," I say, trying to hide my confusion. I want to ask her why she's suddenly in such a rush to leave, but I don't bother. "Thank you."

"Sweet dreams, Durvla," she says before rushing off.

Sunlagh, spare me. No more dreams, please.

Chapter 26
CARYS

AFTER WAKING FROM A racy masquerade-themed dream about Callum, I fetched him from his post to bring my fantasies to life. The reality was far better.

"I wish life could always be this simple," I murmur.

Callum gets out of bed and collects his trousers and briefs from the floor. "What do you mean?"

I roll onto my side, resting my head against my palm, my elbow propping me up. I stare at Callum's toned body. "I mean ... this."

"Sex?"

Laughter swells in my chest then dissipates before it can escape. "Well, yes and no." With a sigh, I sit up and scoot back so that I'm leaning against the headboard. "I mean, sometimes I wish I didn't have to answer to advisors and councilors, and the whole damn kingdom. I wish I could … I don't know. Travel the realm or at least see something other than this castle. I wish I was free to fall in love."

Callum goes still, just as he's about to slip his shirt on. "You're in love with me?"

"Don't be daft." I become suddenly interested in the bedcovers, sliding my hand over the duvet. Love is a fickle concept, but perhaps I'm in love with the idea of him. Not that it matters. I lift my head to him again. "It was a hypothetical statement. You know I have other lovers."

To my surprise, he laughs. His body language is relaxed once more.

A series of steady knocks resound outside the door. "Sir Callum Ferrer," Tiernan says firmly.

"Coming, Major Kilkenny!" Callum hears his own unfortunate word choice and cringes, sending me into a fit of laughter.

Now fully dressed, he fastens his sword belt around his waist again and heads to the door. "Before I go," he says, keeping his voice down, "I know you have other trysts, yet when the mood strikes, it's me you usually call for. That must mean something."

I scoff. He's wrong. "You better get back to your post."

It doesn't mean anything, I internally chant to myself. He's wrong. He's so wrong.

Images of roaring infernos burn at the back of my mind as wakefulness pulls me from my dreams in the morning. My amulet is hot—a remnant of my overactive imagination, no doubt.

Gods, I'd rather dream about Callum all night than about untamed flames.

The sun has barely made its appearance, but I lift my book of fairytales from the side table and sit in front of my fireplace. It would be incredible to be a Skinchanger—to morph my features and voice, to become anyone or anything. According to lore, some Skinchangers spent their days as animals, while others made a habit of impersonating other mortals or creating an alter ego.

I find my page and dive into the story of the All-Knowing Skinchanger.

A witch hired an old man to stir her cauldron for a year. Day after day and night after night, the man stirred and stirred and stirred, never asking what lay within. A younger apprentice was hired to assist the old man, but one night, both fell asleep and a passerby, desperate for a drink, consumed the potion within. The passerby obtained almost as much knowledge as even the gods possessed. But he'd doomed himself to being hunted for all eternity by the witch who so desperately wanted this knowledge.

The man became a Skinchanger, disguising himself as a handsome man to distract the witch. But once she became aware of his deception, he transformed into a bird, then—

As I'm about to get to the interesting parts, there's a knock on my door. "Lady Alys is here to see you," Callum calls out.

My brows furrow and I sit up, putting my book aside. "Come in, Alys."

Alys enters, her smile bright against her mahogany skin. How is she so cheerful so early in the morning?

I've brought you something," she says as I get to my feet.

She holds out a small drawstring satchel and I take it. The weight of it, heavier than I expected, settles in the palm of my hand. Pulling the bag open, I peer inside at a clay lid of sorts. "A jar?"

I open the lid and hold the jar up to my nose, inhaling. The scent is familiar—floral notes with something bitter. Fertility suppressant.

"It's your brew, pulverized into a powder," says Alys. "Now you don't have to rely on me bringing it to you. Just one pinch." She pinches the air delicately with her thumb and index finger to demonstrate.

Sealing the jar and the satchel again, I clutch it in both hands and nod.

"You know, Carys," she says. "You have the power to alter your limitations. You don't have to settle."

I stare at her as though she's sprouted another pair of arms. "We both know that's not true. Rules are rules. Laws are laws. It's been that way since the dawn of time. The Council holds the power."

"For now. Change is needed, and it can start with you. Dear one, you break the rules all the time." She smirks.

"Oh, do I? How?"

Laughter shakes some of her salt-and-pepper hair free from the pile atop her head. "Well one example is the very reason I'm ensuring you take that fertility suppressant."

I roll my eyes.

"Two and three: Tiernan and Durvla being in your service."

"I owe that man my life—and have you *seen* him with a sword? As for Durvla, I couldn't stand by and allow a *dressmaker* to be thrown into the Veilguards. That would be a waste of her talent."

"Her talent isn't the only reason you sought to rescue her. You have a greater sense of justice than you give yourself credit for. You have the makings of a queen and the ability to change things for the better."

Silence spans a few moments as I stare at the hearth, sadness settling into my heart. "I don't want to be queen. I don't want to reign over a kingdom that the Council is too stubborn to realize is broken.

SOLACE OF DUSK

I don't want to be motherless." The last word barely makes it past my lips. My jaw tremors, and I press my lips together firmly.

"I know." She mulls over her next words. "Allow yourself to mourn, but then dig deep into that well of inner strength that you don't realize you have. I have every confidence that you will rise higher than you ever have before."

I glower at her, but it doesn't sway her from continuing.

"Even when your lost ones are not physically with you, they stay alive in your heart."

My throat closes up and I fear that if I even so much as swallow, I'll start blubbering.

"Memories can be powerful—both in a negative and a positive way. I know it's tough, but don't run from your memories; reign over them."

It's utter drivel. "I have to prepare for the day," I say dismissively. "I have Audience." Although I already know I'm going to let Iywan take the lead on Audience again so I can go to the archery range. I need to unleash some of this toxic energy.

Alys nods and leaves me in peace, only for Callum to announce Ellynne's arrival. As Ellynne steps into the room, I raise a brow at her. "Yes?"

She smooths her hands over the wide curves of her hips and arches her brow back at me. "I'm here to help you get ready for Audience?"

"Don't bother," I say, waving my hand and stalking toward my bed.

For a short stint, Ellynne is silent. "You have been missing Audience a lot lately. Don't you think—"

"Ellynne, I am not in the mood for a lecture right now. So, either you find something else useful to do or you can leave." I remain facing the bed, not wanting to glimpse Ellynne's reaction. It's a while before the door clicks behind me and I heave a sigh.

Peace, at last.

Chapter 27
DURVLA

RAYS OF SUNLIGHT STREAM through my window and onto my work as I stitch together the back and front panels of the black lace bodice. I leave one side unstitched just in case adjustments need to be made. Losing sleep last night after the Carys-Callum dream at least allowed me to make a lot of progress on the dress.

I can't stop yawning, though. I need a cup of tea before meeting up with the princess, so I don't fall asleep in the middle of breakfast. Rising from the bed, I make my way to the closet and throw on a floral dress with an ivory base and long, slightly puffed sleeves. I slip on my ankle boots, apply some oils gifted to me by Ellynne to my hair, and head out.

As I turn down another corridor, Kilkenny rounds the corner toward me. I stop and nearly head back to my room, but it's too late.

Why do I keep running into this man? It's entirely too early for this. I pinch the cuff of my sleeve, tugging it down as he draws nearer.

With utmost politeness, I say, "Good morning, Major Kilkenny." *Please, keep walking.*

He doesn't. "Out of bed so soon, Garrick?"

"I'm just getting a cup of tea before it's time to meet with Princess Carys."

He folds his arms over his chest, the muscles practically straining against the fabric of his maroon uniform. I avert my gaze, trying to ignore the curiosity of what lies beneath his livery. Gods, this castle is really starting to get to me.

"You shouldn't spend so much time with Ellynne. She's a bad influence," Kilkenny says.

I frown at him. "She's been nothing but kind …" I step to the side, but he mirrors me. Annoyance flares in my chest. "I should get going."

He doesn't budge. "Meet me at the stables at twilight." His gaze is intense.

My eyes widen and I try not to laugh at the pure ridiculousness of his statement. Here he is, telling me that Ellynne is a bad influence and, in the same breath, asking me to meet him in the dark.

"It's pertinent that you also learn to ride at night."

That explanation … is not quite adding up. I hold back a sigh. "I'll be there. Is this also Princess Carys's request?"

"Twilight. Don't forget." Then he steps around me and marches off like the soldier he is, leaving me to continue my quest for tea.

Looking at Princess Carys proves to be more difficult than I'd expected. At least Callum isn't with her, otherwise I'm not entirely sure how I would handle it. The images from last night's dream are so vivid that each time I meet Princess Carys's gaze, I want to cringe.

"What is wrong with you today?" she demands.

I wish I knew. "Just tired," I tell her. "And my fingers are a bit sore." It isn't a lie. She holds the bodice in place against her body while I pin the unsewn side. It fits perfectly, the dark fibers making the foliage motif of the lace appear more abstract. I glance up at her and there's evident uncertainty on her face. "I know it's hard to envision, but …" I consider my next words carefully. "There will be a sheer material underneath since the stitch is so open."

She doesn't respond.

"I'll start on the sleeves later today—same lace motif. Then the lower portion of the dress will be made from purple silk."

Her lips purse with focus as she tries to imagine it.

"It's all coming together. I hope that puts you a little more at ease?"

Her eyes snap to mine, and I recoil slightly. But it's not anger I find in her expression. It's something softer that I can't quite put my finger on. "I appreciate it," she says. "I barged in here like a beast and you laid out a plan for me with the grace of a … queen." She chuckles and I find myself smiling.

"I know what it's like to be weary of the unknown," I tell her. "It's terrifying. I'm sure royal blood doesn't make you immune to fear."

She scoffs. "I wish it did."

I keep the bodice pinned on the side and step around her to remove the pins from the back. As soon as I slide the material off, she spins to face me. "Come to the Feast."

I blink to keep from gawking at her. Surely, I've misunderstood. "Me?"

"There's nobody else here." She makes a point of looking around dramatically. "Lowri, Ellynne, and Callum will be there as well. Tiernan will be my guard for the night—his choice. There are many guests invited; it will be truly something."

Speaking of fear of the unknown ... "That all sounds very intriguing, Princess, but—"

"Don't make me *order* you to attend." There's a coldness in her stare.

I swallow. "After the Feast, am I still allowed to return to my home in Cluain Baile? If you're happy with your dress, that is."

Something shifts in her expression for a brief moment and her shoulders sag, but she says, "Correct. Make the dress of my dreams, come to the Feast, and you may go home. Do we have an accord?"

I smile and nod. "We have an accord." As I lay the bodice out on the bed again, I keep my focus on her. Something in her golden gaze is distant, haunted. "Are you alright, Princess?"

This snaps her out of things. Her long lashes flutter. "Durvla ... can I trust you?"

"Yes." Why does she ask?

"You do seem like the trustworthy type." She smiles, but there's a sadness to it. I wait for her to say more, but she just turns and heads toward the door. If she says anything before stepping out into the corridor, I have no idea. Just as I have no idea what's really on her mind.

As the sun begins to set, I place my work aside and stand from the bed. My legs are stiff, as are my wrists and my incredibly sore fingers. I don't remember when I last had a sip of water or used the commode. I take care of my immediate needs and guzzle down a goblet of water before making my way to the stables. Kilkenny is there with both horses saddled and bridled.

"You're late," he says.

I bite my lower lip to keep from telling him that he didn't give me an actual time. Instead, I pointedly look to the horizon, to the glow of the slumbering sun, the sliver of the crescent moon high in the dark blue sky. Kilkenny taps me impatiently on the shoulder and gestures to Mirren before mounting Ghendor.

Centering myself with a deep breath, I make my customary, graceless climb onto Mirren's back. I've become better at mounting the mare, but gracefulness has never been a strong suit for me.

Kilkenny doesn't say anything, nudging Ghendor into a canter with his inner thighs.

"A man of many words," I mumble under my breath as I follow.

Kilkenny glances over his shoulder at me and I go stiff, making Mirren veer off slightly. Did he hear that? I gently pat Mirren's neck. "Sorry, girl."

Tonight's path is different from the one we usually take, and it's getting darker. I won't be able to read Kilkenny's lips very well.

Great.

He keeps a fast pace and doesn't look back much, so I simply follow along on Mirren.

We end up in what may have once been an open meadow, except there are trimmed hedges creating a zig-zagged pathway of some sort. Kilkenny suddenly brings Ghendor to a halt and swings off the horse, landing adeptly and barely pausing before walking toward me.

Show-off.

I halt Mirren and painstakingly climb down. The ground moves beneath me, so I hold on to her saddle until I regain some semblance of balance.

Kilkenny assesses me before he says, "Right this way." He jerks his head toward the hedges and sets off into them. The pathway is so dark, I can hardly make out my own feet against the grass. Some parts in the terrain crunch beneath my boots, reminiscent of fallen leaves in autumn. It's odd, but I don't stop to figure it out. I remain close to Kilkenny, my heart racing. What if something jumps out at us? A snake? A ... rebel? The princess said there are occasional rebel attacks. I'm tempted to grab his hand so he can't leave me behind.

Kilkenny stops suddenly, his hand flying to the hilt of his sword, and my heart wrings in my chest. I draw in a breath when he relaxes. He glances at me and points down one pathway. It leads to a large clearing—the very center of the maze.

There are a few unlit lanterns on posts bordering the circular clearing, and some sort of small structure at the center. Kilkenny pulls something from his pocket, making his way over to one of the lantern posts. A small ember sparks. He lights each of the lanterns, until the space is illuminated. It's obvious now that the structure at the center is a small stone fountain.

Kilkenny approaches me. Can I scream loud enough for someone to hear if he attacks? My heart is hammering.

Kilkenny holds out his hands, palms up. "Relax, Garrick. I didn't whisk you away to kill you."

To my embarrassment, a sigh of relief whooshes out of me.

He brushes a few dark strands of hair back from his forehead, a brief smirk on his face. It sharpens his cheekbones and makes his eyes dance in a way that's ... not unpleasant?

"I've brought you here to teach you how to defend yourself. You might as well leave Paramount with a few new skills, especially given that you'll be traveling back home and there are plenty of dangerous people out there."

I stare at him, trying to make sense of his words. Does this mean I'll be returning to Cluain Baile without an escort? Can I truly trust this Mainlander?

"The quicker you cooperate, the quicker you can get back to your boring dressmaking."

"It's not boring to me."

I swear he rolls his eyes. "Let's see what those dressmaker hands can do." He gets into a fighting stance. "Hit me."

"Excuse me?"

"Hit. Me." He makes a fist and waves it around.

"I'm not going to *hit* you. I don't want to hit anyone."

He reaches out and grasps my left hand, balling it into a fist.

He's noticed that I'm left-handed? That's … observant.

"Make sure that your thumb is never tucked into your hand like this." He folds his thumb in, hiding it in his own palm. "If you strike like this, you'll break your thumb."

There have been a lot of confusing moments since the night I was taken from my home, but this one is rising higher on the list. I'm convinced this man is unhinged. "I cannot afford to hurt my hand. I have a very important dress to make."

His expression is flat. "Well, aren't we high and mighty?"

My jaw slackens.

"Hit me."

I shake my head firmly.

"I'm sure you have a lot of frustrations to get out. I represent a lot of what this place is. I keep taking you away from the work that you must do to secure your freedom. I answer to the princess, who is forcing your hand, and to the very people who sanctioned your arrest. In fact, I have once personally enforced the banishment of Undesirables." He pauses, eyes narrowed on me. "What good are Undesirables for any—"

A chill rushes through me before I see red and swing. Kilkenny's on the ground before I even register what's happened. My chest heaves and my pulse roars in my ears, hair rising on the back of my neck. My hands tingle. Too much dressmaking, probably. Too little sleep. Too much frustration.

Kilkenny jumps to his feet and stares down at me so intensely that I fear he'll hit *me*.

"I-I'm sorry," I stutter, taking a step back. "I didn't even feel … I didn't realize …" I splay my fingers before my face and stare at them, perplexed. Kilkenny reaches out and takes my left hand in his.

"Did that hurt?" he asks, gently turning my hand over.

My heart is still racing as I yank my hand from him. "No."

"What did you feel?"

I felt anger! What does he expect? I don't bother to respond; I only stare at him, my fists clenched as though I'm physically holding on to the last strand of control. He couldn't have meant those things. Could he? Most likely he was just goading me on, trying to provoke the very reaction I gave him. I'm ashamed I took the bait.

Kilkenny rubs his cheek and then scratches the back of his neck. The awkward moment stretches on and on with Kilkenny staring at me like I'm a puzzle to be solved. Then at last he exhales, and his stance relaxes. "I didn't mean what I said about Undesirables. I did enforce it because I had to, but that was in the past."

My forehead creases and I shift slightly on my feet.

"Change of plans. Tonight, we'll do some meditation; everyone needs to center themselves sometimes. Especially when you work in this place." He waves vaguely in the direction of the castle. "Tomorrow, more self-defense."

Chapter 28
DURVLA

NEARLY A FORTNIGHT GOES by, filled with days of dressmaking and evenings with various lessons from Kilkenny. The horseback riding lessons precede self-defense and meditation sessions. He's as careful as can be, vigilant of my *valuable hands*, as he so mockingly puts it. He insists that meditation is as important as learning to protect myself—*mental strength boosts physical strength and may help steady those newborn foal legs*, he'd said. As suspicious as I am about Killjoy Kilkenny's insistence on teaching me these things, they've become a surprisingly welcome distraction.

Doing something other than dressmaking keeps me from worrying too much about Taig and Osheen. About Osheen's family. It keeps me from wallowing in the increasingly vivid nightmares that sap my energy on an almost nightly basis.

I'd take another lewd dream any day over the ones filled with fire and omens, demons, and darkness. On a good night, I dream of warmer shores, sunshine, and sand beneath my toes. I dream of lush forests and deep blue oceans. Of sailing. Or flying. Clearly my subconscious is fed by my desire to get out of this place.

I use it as a driving force to complete Princess Carys's dress, and I manage to balance a rapidly growing social life within the palace. My time with Princess Carys varies as the breakfast consultations grow shorter, but also less daunting.

It's hard to believe that I've been here for nearly a month. Brick by brick, my reservations about Mainlanders—at least *these* Mainlanders—are torn down. I've grown accustomed to the way everyone speaks and lipreading is easier. I find myself able to relax a little more, and my fear of being discovered as an Undesirable is pushed to the back of my mind.

Ellynne is an absolute sweetheart, consistently attentive, and so very open about her love life. Ostanha be damned, she's open about *everyone's* love life—everyone's but Carys's. She's made it her mission to ensure everyone finds time for *fun*, as she puts it—as if she's the god of love herself.

Lowri, on the other hand, is willing to speak when addressed, but otherwise reserved and secretive. While Ellynne is the picture of punctuality and never late to any summons, despite whose bed she's in—and she makes a point to tell us—Lowri is the opposite. Always running late, always profusely apologetic.

Even Eefa has become a daily part of my life, often saving a slice of lemon cake for me. She's overtly flirtatious with Carys, while Callum secretly worships the ground Carys walks on. Whether Carys sees that, I'm not sure. It likely doesn't matter, since she's to be married to a nobleman of high standing or another royal. Still, the way Callum looks at her is heartwarming, yet heartbreaking.

Kilkenny is … Kilkenny. Too confusing to dwell on.

As much as I want to return to Cluain Baile, to my sweet boy, I know I will miss these surprisingly lovely people.

Who would have imagined that I'd come to actually like Mainlanders? Even more surprising, who would've imagined they'd like *me*?

Five days before the Feast, by some divine intervention, all I have left to do is embellish the bodice of Princess Carys's dress with tiny gold beads. I'm rather proud of the dress. I hope the princess will love it.

As if I've summoned her, Princess Carys waltzes into my room. "Is it done?" she asks, but this time there's no anger or hurried aggression directed at me. Only eagerness.

I beam at her. "Just a few more finishing touches, but yes."

She comes to an abrupt stop, her eyes wide. "*Yes?*"

"I'm just sewing on a few more beads and that's it. Do you want to try it on?"

"Is that even a question?" She walks farther into my room and pulls the string of the call bell.

I tear my focus away from it to Princess Carys. "I'm going to focus fully on this last bit for a moment, so I may not hear you. Just … one moment. Is that alright?"

"Yes, yes, go on."

"Thank you." I smile and pick up another bead, threading it onto my needle and securing it by sliding the needle into a stitch on the bodice. Meanwhile, the princess is pacing back and forth like a predator on the prowl. It's distracting, but I force myself to add a few more beads until I'm satisfied with the appearance. At last, I secure the final bead, sever the thread, and stick the needle into my pincushion before announcing, "Finished!"

At that moment, Ellynne strides in. "Is it dress fitting time?" she asks excitedly.

Princess Carys turns to her and responds in a way that makes Ellynne grin even wider. Something else is asked of her and Ellynne glances over her shoulder before saying, "... kitchen a moment ago ... started without her though."

It's hard to make out all her words from the small distance, but I assume they're talking about Lowri.

"Wonderful," says Princess Carys, turning her back as Ellynne approaches. She pulls her dark, golden-streaked braid over her shoulder so that it settles against her hip.

"Have you ever cut your hair?" I blurt out, my nervousness dissolving my filter. I immediately regret it when two sets of eyes gawk at me. I shrink back into myself. "Sorry if that's too personal ..."

"It's not," says Princess Carys. "And yes. Once or twice in my life, but I can't exactly remember when."

"It's beautiful. I've never seen dark hair with streaks like that."

"It runs in the family. And I wouldn't have been able to take care of this on my own. Ellynne is incredible."

Ellynne is busy unbuttoning the back of the dress the princess is currently wearing, so I don't make out her response, but the princess laughs. Ellynne makes quick work of removing the gown and corset. By the time Princess Carys is down to her gossamer chemise, Lowri slips into the room and practically runs to Ellynne's side.

"I've sewn some extra fabric into the underlayer of the bodice, so you won't need the chemise," I tell Carys. "But you can keep it on for now just for—"

And the chemise is off. Tossed into Lowri's hands like it's no big deal. Lowri giggles and sets it aside with the rest of the princess's clothes.

My face must be red because the very naked, very unabashed Princess Carys smiles with slow amusement, "Durvla, are you blushing?"

I nearly trip over my feet as I approach.

Carys's cheeky grin expands. "You don't have tits of your own?"

The other two laugh, and I force a smile onto my face.

"For the love of Rhianu, Durvla," says Carys. "People have been dressing me since I was a child. I'm not ashamed. And Ellynne would roam the corridors naked as a wee babe if we allowed it."

"Clothing is so restrictive." Ellynne shrugs.

They laugh and I relax into my smile.

"Lowri was like you not too long ago," she says. "She was briefly the wife to a stuffy old duke before joining my service."

Lowri nods shyly. At nineteen, she's more than old enough to have been a wife, but it still surprises me. She smiles, but it doesn't make it to her eyes.

The princess waves and I pull my gaze back to her. "Remember me?" she asks.

My pulse quickens. "Right," I say past the tightness in my throat. "I'll just … hand this over and let you ladies handle the dressing. Please be careful." Gods, what if it rips, or the beads fall off, or it unravels completely?

What if she hates it?

With trembling hands, I place the dress in Ellynne's arms and half-watch as she and Lowri help Princess Carys into it. Part of me cringes at the speed with which Ellynne pulls it up over Princess Carys's narrow hips, the lace stretching. I bite my lip so hard that it stings. "Careful," I murmur.

Ellynne glances at me, nodding in understanding. I hold my breath and count until dizziness presses into my awareness. Until I've made it to nearly forty-five and haven't exhaled. When I do, it all comes out in a rush.

Then Ellynne and Lowri step away and the three of us stare at Princess Carys in her finished gown. The fit is perfect, tapered at her tiny waist, extending subtly at her hips and then cascading downward. The bodice hugs her torso, the black lace extending from the waist and overlaying the top half of the deep purple skirt in valleys and peaks. The lace on the décolletage curves over her petite breasts, showing just a bit of cleavage without being overly revealing. The back of the dress dips downward in a wide V that ends at her waist, leaving her back mostly exposed.

Princess Carys's freckles stand out against her already pale face as she blanches. "What?" she asks as we stare at her.

Ellynne steps forward and I only make out one word: *stunning*.

Lowri bobs her head enthusiastically in agreement.

Lifting the skirts, Princess Carys hurries to the floor-length mirror. The other two ladies follow while I remain rooted to the spot. *Deep breaths*, I remind myself. I close my eyes, gathering my composure. I finally convince myself to move as Princess Carys steps back from the mirror in apparent shock. She edges forward again and leans closer as I approach. She blinks once. Twice. She turns her head slowly to face me.

"Durvla …" She says. "Durvla, Durvla, Durvla, I knew you'd come through for me. I knew it. I *knew* it! This is bloody brilliant. Incredible!" She turns and spots the low back of her dress in the mirror. Her jaw drops. "Oh, my gods, I'm going to knock them all dead! Their heads will explode! Durvla, I *adore* this dress!"

I turn her words over in my head again and again.

She adores the dress! My tension finally dissipates, though now I'm shaking, relief and excitement coursing through me.

My smile spreads so wide, my cheeks twitch in protest. "Is it the dress of your dreams?" I ask.

Princess Carys grins. "More than I could've ever dreamed. Look at this! Damn all the gods above and below. *You* are a goddess, Durvla."

I'm so surprised at the statement that laughter bubbles out of me. If I were coordinated enough, I'd do a happy dance right now. Instead, I stand there like a fool.

Princess Carys steps toward me. Is she going to hug me? Her hands raise, her body leans in, but she stiffens and lays a hand on my shoulder instead. "You've gone above and beyond, Durvla. I owe you."

Chapter 29
CARYS

ONE MOMENT I'M SOARING sky-high, and the next I'm plummeting back down to reality. Moments after I'm dressed in my regular attire again, a knock on the door brings a summons to my mother's chamber. Tiernan and I practically run across the castle, and I barge into my mother's bedchamber, expecting the worst.

Instead, she's sitting up in bed, wide awake.

I nearly collapse, relief and surprise washing over me. "Mum ..." It comes out as a pant as I try to catch my breath.

"My sweet cariad," she says. Her voice is hoarse, her words languid, but I couldn't be happier. Beside her, Alys is perched on a chair pulled close to the bed. Iywan is nowhere in sight.

Everything about this situation is so odd. I stride toward my mother and take her pleasantly warm hand in mine. Weariness may have dulled the vibrance in her eyes, but they're lucid, nonetheless. "How ... ?" I glance at Alys for a moment, then back at my mother.

"We don't have much time," my mother says. "Even now I can feel the drowsiness looming over me."

My shoulders droop. This isn't permanent?

"Listen to me, cariad. Don't let that book of fairytales I gave you out of your possession."

"Never," I say, but I'm perplexed she's chosen to talk about fiction when this is the first time we've spoken in weeks. "Mother, I'm so happy to see you so wide awake."

She smiles and reaches a shaky hand to caress my cheek. A moment later, her hand falls heavily away. She blinks slowly. "Before sleep takes me again, I need you to remember something of the utmost importance."

I tilt my head at her. "What is it?"

"I need you to remember what happened to your brother."

My face crumbles, that familiar inexplicable guilt and unease clouding my mind. "Mother, you never told me what happened to Aneirin. How can I remember?"

"Because you were *there*," she says. Her words are slower.

Alys's face is strangely neutral, as though she doesn't want to give anything away.

"I wasn't," I remind my mother. "It wasn't until I woke up the morning after his death that I found out he was gone. Remember?"

"You ... were ... Think ... about it." The rise and fall of her chest becomes more prolonged, more prominent. Her gaze dims as she slips back into the prison of her deteriorating mind.

"Mum, stay with me, please. I need to know. Were you also there? Can you tell me?"

No response.

I turn my focus to Alys, silently demanding that she does something. With slight hesitation, she puts her hand over my mother's. Her eyes close as if she needs to focus, and my mother's flutter open.

Her breath rasping, my mother says, "You were so young. So very fragile, but so very powerful. My little fireball." She chuckles.

She's always described me as her fireball, her feisty fighter, but never as fragile. It throws me off for a moment. "Fragile?"

Her eyes are closed now, but she responds. "You have such a bleeding heart, cariad. You couldn't help it. You needed to learn to control it. I should've taught you. The necklace was the best I could think of …"

My hand moves to my amulet. I straighten and try my best not to look at my mother as though she's gone completely mad. "I'll take care of the necklace, Mum. Always. I promise."

Her eyes flutter opened again. "I'm sorry I took your memory. You would have been distraught. And if anyone else had found out … It would've meant your death. Perhaps even mine."

Magdin's tits. What is she talking about?

"I was too afraid to be brave for you, so you have to find that courage yourself."

"Afraid of what? Mother, I'm trying to understand, but…"

She smiles sadly at me. "Afraid that if you let yourself remember, you would be vulnerable. But vulnerability does *not* diminish your strength, Carys. I gave you that necklace after your brother's death to give you a sense of solace. But it's only a dampener—it does not control you. Only you can do that."

Dear gods, she's completely incoherent. A fresh wave of guilt joins the cacophony of emotions clawing at me. My shoulders tense and I press my lips firmly together, begging my patience not to unravel. For so long, I've been desperate to have a conversation with her, to lay out the hundreds of unanswered questions that have piled up in my mind. And now, she can only speak in riddles. Now, I have even more unanswered questions.

My heart breaks all over again.

"Talk to me, cariad."

"I—" The words flee from me and my eyes sting. I reach for her hand, my own trembling. "I want you to get better," I say, and my voice is barely louder than a whisper.

Her eyes flutter closed. "You're not listening." Her words aren't gentle anymore, nor is the grip of her hand on mine.

My chest tightens and I feel like a child being disciplined. My mind spirals back to an image:

I'm five years old again, weeping in a corner. My mother, so much younger than she is now, is the picture of serenity as she kneels before me. "I know it feels overwhelming," she says. "This will help." She slips the necklace over my head and the pendant settles heavily against my chest, instantly placating me.

I blink as I fall back into myself. The memory was so vivid that, for a moment, I'm befuddled by the woman, sixteen years later, withering away before me. "Mum?"

"Still here, my sweet child," she says. "I have made many regrettable blunders. But never forget how much I love you. I've only ever wanted to protect you."

I nod, tears brimming. This is too much like a farewell. It's too painful to bear. I worry at my lower lip before saying, "Please, don't go." My voice comes out thick with tears.

A moment later, her head lolls, and Alys jumps to her feet as my heart tumbles into my stomach. Leaning close to check her breathing, her fingers lightly resting on her throat, Alys says, "Just asleep."

I release a sigh of relief.

"Help me lay her down again."

I nod and we get my mother onto her back once more. I stare down at her, zipping the pendant back and forth along the chain of my necklace. I should be the one in that bed, losing my mind, losing my life. Not her. This kingdom needs *her*. She would know what to do about the rebellion, about the questionable choices of the Forayers and the leniency they're given. About Iywan and the bloody Council.

How am I supposed to get the Council and Iywan to take me seriously when they consider me but a mere child? Iywan was the most incredible advisor to my mother. Together, they were a force to be reckoned with. He respected her as the queen and his friend, but he can't see beyond the child he still thinks I am.

Beyond the child who can't control herself.

When my father died, Iywan was there for me. When my mother's time comes, I fear it won't be the same.

"Carys." Alys's voice is quiet. I'd almost forgotten she was there.

I startle, my mind reeling back. "How did you … ? Did you do something to make her lucid?"

"It's unfortunately temporary," Alys says.

"Why temporary?" I snap.

"Her body is failing. All treatments right now are like putting a bandage on a festering wound. I'm truly sorry, dear one."

Failing. Festering wound. My stomach curdles. "Look at me and tell me there's absolutely no hope." My voice trembles even as I try to sound brave.

Those grey, weary eyes of Alys's brim with tears and my heart fractures. Alys's posture straightens and her lips form a line.

Her silence is loud enough.

Indebted to Durvla for not only making my dress but always being so patient with me, I send word to Barr na Cahar to have a dress made for her. Ellynne helps with sizing estimates and specifications. Durvla is going to look better than any noble.

My mother's state remains unchanged, yet the palace becomes busy with preparations for the Feast. Decorators come in and out of the castle, foreign foods are imported, and various guests take up residence in our visitors' quarters. It's a welcome distraction from my nightly unrest.

My staff put on their best professional behavior—except for Eefa whose advances nearly earn her a trip to my bed. Callum doesn't hide the disappointment on his face, and for the first time, guilt convinces me to turn Eefa away. I need to talk to him when this Feast is over. To both of them. I need to reduce the distractions in my life—become queenlier, I suppose.

After all, I'll be betrothed shortly after the Feast.

· · ◦ ☽ ☀ ☾ ◦ · ·

There is fire everywhere. *It billows out from beneath the door even as I slam it shut behind me. I tear off down the palace corridor. "Help!" I cry out, the smoke triggering a violent fit of coughing. "Please! Anybody!" Fear fills me as surely as smoke and ash fill my lungs.*

A beam crashes from the ceiling, cutting off my only escape. The wood splinters, embers and ash flying. I back away, my forearm over my nose and mouth. I cough and cough until my throat is raw, until I can't stop wheezing. Collapsing to my knees, I stare helplessly as the flames grow larger, black smoke obstructing everything around me.

A book materializes on the ground in front of me, and as I reach for it, the symbol of the sun on the cover glows brighter than the flames. As quickly as it appears, it vanishes.

"Don't fear the flames," a familiar voice says. "Reach out." My mother's voice?

The flames close in on me, and my eyes dart around, my vision blurring. "Mother?" I cry, but there's no one there.

"Reach out, cariad."

The flames are so near now that the heat stings my skin. The silhouette of a feminine form seems to appear in the fire directly in front of me. Plumes of smoke circle around her. Then in an instant, the silhouette disappears again.

I shut my eyes, holding my breath, ready to face my death as the flames blast toward me—

I'm catapulted into awareness in a mess of gasps and endless coughing. The taste of ash remains in my mouth, my throat raw. Sweat coats my skin, and my amulet is searing hot against my chest. This same bloody nightmare again! How many times has that been this week alone?

Eventually, the coughing subsides, and I stumble over to ring for Ellynne and Lowri.

I need a cool bath and a goblet of wine or three.

Chapter 30
DURVLA

WITH THE DRESS FINALLY off my plate, I can breathe a little easier. Even if I awoke this morning from a nightmare full of flames.

Choosing not to dwell on the strangely real fear that lingered from the dream, I begin packing for my return to Cluain Baile. Having gotten permission to take whatever I want, I pack the plainest dresses—I shouldn't take a lot of fancy attire—some underclothing, a woolen coat to keep me warm, and some fabric. These new clothes will give me time to make Taig new clothing. I'm sure he's grown in the time I've been here.

One month … It's felt like a lifetime. So much has happened. But soon, I'll be able to reclaim my identity. To live in the familiar comfort of my own home, in my own village, with my own people.

I'm too excited to be confined to my room, so I take to wandering the castle. Each step is more eager than the next, until I'm standing in front of the grand entrance to the royal library. I have just four more days here, and I can't leave without taking advantage of this opportunity.

Yanking the doors open, I hurry in and nearly jump out of my skin when I spot someone else standing there. The young woman whips her head around so quickly that her blond braid hits her in the face, and she flinches. She shuts the book in her hand and grins at me. "Durvla! You startled me!"

Eefa. "My apologies. I didn't expect anyone to be in here. I didn't mean to barge in like that."

Eefa laughs and hugs the book to her chest as she approaches me, hips swaying. "I've heard you're leaving us after the Feast. Such a pity. I've grown quite fond of you." She pouts, but something in her large eyes isn't quite sad. They almost seem to challenge me. "It's great here, you know. I didn't grow up in the castle, but I could never go back."

That piques my interest. "Are you also from the Grounds?"

"Worse. I'm from Darragh, west of here."

Worse?

She throws her head back and laughs like it's the funniest thing ever. I'm torn between laughing along falsely or just staring at her. It ends up being a strange mix of both.

"So, you're …"

"The daughter of a noble. La. Di. Da." She sighs heavily and twirls one finger in the air. "There was no freedom in my household. Always 'elbows off the table, Eefa. Straighten your back—you're not a troll, Eefa. Lower your voice; shouting is unbecoming of a lady, Eefa.' Thank the gods for my apprenticeship with Master Steffan, who happened to be the head cook here. I couldn't believe it when I was given the opportunity to work in *Paramount*. It's been an absolute dream come true."

People in Darragh are clearly thankless and entitled. Eefa, at least. "I'm glad your dream came true," I say. Hopefully my voice doesn't come out as flat as I feel it does.

"If you play things well here, you can rise in the rankings, save your wages, and acquire enough wealth to live out your elderly days on a large estate of your own. Imagine having servants doing *your* bidding. With your skill, that is *absolutely* possible. Mark my words, Durvla. I hope the same for myself. I'll be saving my wages once I supersede Master Steffan."

"Is ... that happening soon?"

"Eventually." She twirls the loose end of her braid around her finger and smiles coquettishly. "Anyway, I must return to the kitchen. Nice to see you. I hope you decide to stay with us."

She walks away, and I resist the urge to roll my eyes. If Eefa thinks that living in a wealthy village in Mainland was terrible, she would've never survived life in the Grounds. Though, admittedly, her life in Darragh sounded void of love while mine was full of love even in the midst of hardships.

Once Eefa leaves, I stride toward the very back of the library, through the archway and along a dusty row of nondescript books. The strangest sensation reverberates in my body as I home in on one of the leather spines closest to the wall. Four symbols glow along the spine, but when I blink, there's nothing there. A trick of the light, I suppose. Or too little sleep.

The floor vibrates slightly and I whirl to find Princess Carys leaning heavily against the door. My heart leaps as I move quickly back through the archway and closer to Carys. Her face is contorted, her chest heaving with forceful breaths.

The door shakes very slightly in rhythm behind her, and Carys shouts something in response, her hands flying to cover her ears against whoever is pounding on the door. Is she being chased or something?

As her entire body starts to crumble, her gaze locks on me. She stiffens for the briefest moment before folding in on herself, sliding down to the floor with her forearms in front of her face, her fists in her hair.

I recognize her struggle.

I've been the one huddled on the floor, lost in the labyrinth of unrelenting panic, desperate for relief. It's so uncomfortably familiar that it takes me a split second to get my legs moving toward her. I gently touch the back of her hand, and she pulls away so hard that her hand slams into the door behind her. Pain flashes across her face and she swears, rubbing her knuckles.

I hold up my own hands in surrender. "I just want to help. What can I do?"

Her chest heaves, tears streak down her reddened cheeks, and I stand there like a fool, completely useless. I gather my skirts and sit carefully beside Carys. I don't touch her or speak to her—I just sit there, existing in her space.

She pulls her knees up to her chest and her shoulders shake with sobs.

Behind us, the door thuds three times against our backs. Someone is knocking. My guess is that it's Kilkenny. "I'm here with the princess," I call out. Maybe not the smartest thing to say. "It's me, Durvla." I wince at the even more worthless phrase, but the knocking subsides.

Carys is still sobbing, and I hesitate before resting my hand on her back lightly. "I am here if you want to talk."

She doesn't react, but she doesn't pull away either. I'm at a loss for how to calm her down. By memory, I start reciting one of my favorite stories from the book we both love. Sometimes telling myself these tales has helped me when I've been in such a state.

"Osha was the weakest of them all," I begin, and there's a brief pause in her tremulous breathing beneath my hand. I continue. "Born fragile, she was prone to illness. Her bones easily fractured, and her stomach often rebelled. Osha showed little aptitude for magic unlike her siblings and cousins who were incredibly powerful. No one dared to spar with her in fear of snapping her bones, and they teased her for her delicate fingers emitting only tiny tendrils of light during wielding practice. But what she lacked in physical strength, she made up for in spirit."

Carys lifts her head, and her gaze finds mine. Her face is still a splotchy mess of tears and snot. Wiping the sleeve of her dress across her face, she says, "Osha is my favorite."

I smile at her. "Mine too."

She closes her eyes and slumps back against the door, her face tilted up slightly toward the ceiling. I remain silent for a moment, letting her gather her composure.

"Do you want to talk about whatever's bothering you?"

She gnaws on her lower lip and the weariness on her face increases tenfold. I regret asking.

"You don't have to—"

"My mother is dying. The whole nation is going to mourn their queen, but I am going to lose the only person who has always loved me for all that I am. Volatile emotions and all."

The queen is dying? I'm aware that she is ill but ... I stifle the surprise and focus on the ache of sympathy for Carys. "I'm sorry." I hesitate. "Has someone called you volatile?"

She sighs. "Who hasn't? They're not wrong, but aside from Alys, everyone dances around the subject. I know there is something *different* about me. I'm aware that sometimes I'm not the easiest person to put up with. Gods, I can barely put up with *myself* at times." Her eyes flick up with annoyance. "I could use Osha's cloaking abilities. It would be remarkable to put up a force field and block out the rest of the world."

I can't help but chuckle. "I've never heard a more relatable statement." I would love to be a Lightweaver. I would put a force field around Cluain Baile, destroy the fears that lie in the shadows, block out the evil Forayers. My sweet Taig and all my people would have freedom.

If only such powers still existed.

Princess Carys tilts her face into my line of view, and I startle. I wince as blood rushes to my cheeks. "Apologies, Princess."

She raises a brow, mild amusement creeping into her features. "You are such a daydreamer, Durvla. And drop the formalities. I believe we've moved past that now." She gestures to herself in a dramatic, downward sweep of her hand.

A small smile buds on my face, and I nod before my lips tug down again. "I have episodes too," I say. Two different types of episodes, or whatever other euphemisms that have been used to diminish the sheer magnitude of the experiences. One is physical, and the other deeply rooted in my mind. "It's awful being at the mercy of your own mind and body, isn't it?"

Carys's eyes are wide as she nods. "Gods, yes."

"Also, I am very sorry about your mother. I know what it's like to lose a parent. Both parents."

Compassion softens her face, and she says, "Condolences."

"It happened a couple of years ago. I've learned to cope."

"Does it still hurt?"

A plea fills her wide eyes, but the truth is that it hurts to some degree every day. Sometimes I want to tell Ma about my day or ask her for advice, and when I remember that I can't, it wounds me all over again. I slowly nod and the tiny bit of hope burns away from her.

She inhales slowly, then with the next exhale, she paints a mask of calm on her face. "Well," she says. "I suppose I'll have to learn how to cope too."

"You will," I assure her. "Just think about all the people who will rely on you. That's what keeps me going." I had Taig to keep me going after Ma's passing.

Color drains from her face as she wets her lips. "People often say 'listen to your heart,' but how does one do that when they don't know what their heart wants?" Pain is evident in her gaze despite the smile she deliberately forces onto her lips. "Every bloody day I'm confronted with so many feelings that I don't know what to make of them. I don't know what's a farce and what's truth. Underreaction or overreaction? Euphoria or despair? I can't even decipher between love and lust, hurt and anger. It all feels like one giant cauldron of emotion soup."

Images of her and Callum flash in my mind and, along with it, so many emotions. "You're conflicted about Sir Callum." My words slip out, unbidden, and I flinch as if Carys is about to strike me.

Her immaculate brows raise, her lips pursed. For the briefest moment, I expect a flare of her temper, but the tension in her jaw loosens and she very slowly pushes loose strands of her raven hair back from her face.

Say something.

"I'm … that was out of line. My apologies, Car—"

"Explain yourself."

Bewilderment competes with my rising pulse, my sweaty palms. My hand moves toward where my bracelet once circled my wrist before I remember it's no longer there. Shakily, I slide my sweaty hand over my sleeve.

Carys's brows are raised. "How are you so sure that I'm conflicted about Callum?"

It just came to me. An inkling that is oddly like a memory. But I can't say that without sounding mental. "I've seen the looks exchanged between the pair of you." I choose my words *very* carefully. "Sir Callum stares at you constantly."

"He's my guard."

"Yes, but the look in his eyes isn't obligation. It's ... adoration."

She goes still, her mind calculating. "Go on," she says after a pause.

My teeth graze my lower lip for a moment, and I inhale deeply. "When you look at him, it's ... flirtatious, playful. You do seem to care for him, but you're not sure if it goes beyond that ..."

A laugh bubbles out of her, taking me by surprise. I blink and my anxiety unfurls. She rubs her hands over her face and mutters something before turning her gaze to me again. "You're an even better oracle than Ellynne thinks she is."

I smile—I've heard Ellynne's *visions*.

"Callum is ... tantalizing," she says.

I was expecting her to say something profound, so when she finishes the sentence, a snort bursts out of me, drawing laughter from Carys. I cover my mouth, embarrassed by what was no doubt the most unladylike sound ever.

Carys continues, unbothered. "Have you *seen* that man? Those blue eyes, that jawline, the blond hair, and all those rippling muscles." She tilts her head back against the door and laughs. I can't resist smiling at the sight.

The sorrow is hidden for now, replaced with joviality that warms me all over. I have a sense of having helped her. That I've made the tiniest difference in someone's life—or day, at least.

"So, what about you, Durvla?"

I frown. "*What* about me?"

"Do you have anyone you're fond of? A certain broody guard perhaps?"

Not her too ... "No," I say far too quickly.

Her eyes sparkle. "I knew it!"

"No, no, I—"

A series of knocks reverberate through the door behind us, and I all but jump out of my skin.

Carys huffs out a harsh breath. "Magdin's tits! Keep your knickers on!" She gets to her feet—I follow far less gracefully—and yanks the door open.

Kilkenny stands there, a fist raised in midair. He lowers his hand, the agitation on his face replaced with his typical mask of indifference. His focus darts between Carys and me and he asks, "Is everything alright?"

"No," Carys says. "But Durvla helped me calm myself. For now." She smiles softly.

Something in Kilkenny's eyes softens as they settle on me. There is no stoic indifference left.

"Let's go," says Carys, starting down the hallway.

Kilkenny hangs back for a moment, giving me a subtle nod.

He then lifts his hand and *signs* "thank you," before leaving me behind with my mouth gaping open.

Chapter 31
DURVLA

I'M GOING TO BE arrested—clearly Kilkenny knows that I'm an Undesirable. He admitted that he'd enforced the sanctioned banishment of Undesirables. It isn't until the next day that I encounter him alone. He's waiting atop Ghendor as I arrive at the stables. I have so many questions burning in my mind as I clamber onto Mirren. But Kilkenny takes off without a word.

There's an incessant dull ache in my head today, the dizziness and nausea creeping in behind it, but I manage to keep up with his pace as he takes a path that's familiar now. We arrive at the hedge maze and walk to the clearing without exchanging a word.

We stand face to face, the fountain flowing beside us.

"Ask your question," he signs, and my heart races.

So, I didn't imagine it! "You can *sign*?" I ask aloud.

"*That's* the first question you choose to ask?"

I track the movements of his hands and his lips. He's a little slower, translating his words very literally rather than more concise signs. Still, he is surprisingly fluent. He's going to report me and they're going to banish me to the Wastelands. After all of this! I'm not going back home. It's over. Black spots and waves of darkness tunnel my vision. The hair on the back of my neck rises, and that annoying tingle in my fingers returns.

"Find your center!" Kilkenny motions.

I almost can't believe what I'm seeing, or that he's telling me to control myself when everything I've worked so hard to achieve is rapidly unfurling. For so long, I've hidden this part of me. I've worked my rear off learning how to read lips, resisting the urge to sign instead of speaking as it became increasingly difficult for me to fathom what my own words sound like. My entire life has been shrouded in secrecy.

Pain swells in my head and chest and I realize that I've been holding my breath. It's like I've forgotten how to breathe.

"Deep breaths. Find your center, like we've practiced in meditation. Your secret is safe with me. Knight's honor." Kilkenny's hands move urgently, though some of his translations aren't exactly correct. Still, it's comprehendible.

The words throw a blanket over my rising fears, but anxiety still fights for dominance.

For a few heartbeats, I inhale and exhale slowly. "How do you know how to sign?" I ask when I can breathe again without having to think about it.

"I said I'd keep your secrets, Garrick. I didn't say I'd tell you mine."

I glower at him and press my lips together to keep the hostility inside my head.

"We're going to work on sparring tonight since your sacred princess-dressmaking-hands are free."

I puff out my chest as I sign my spoken words: "Haven't you heard? I'm leaving tomorrow after the Feast. I'm going back to Cluain Baile. You're not obligated to teach me anything anymore."

His brows disappear beneath the dark hair falling onto his face, the few silver strands standing out. "Then what do you have to lose with one last lesson before you leave?" He gestures to his face and goads me on. "*Hit me.*"

My lips tug down. He obviously hasn't reported my deafness or my ailment to anyone, and he's continued to go out of his way for these lessons. I'm certain he should be catching up on rest when not on duty; I don't understand why he's chosen to help me.

I exhale and get into a fighting stance like he's shown me many times before. Then I go in for a strike.

My heart is still racing from my lesson with Kilkenny—I never imagined I would come to enjoy the inexplicable lessons. But now, bathed and dressed in fresh clothing, I'm buzzing with disquiet. My chamber feels awkward now that I've completed Carys's dress. With the Feast not until tomorrow and my return to Cluain Baile quickly approaching, my mind is a nonstop tumble of what-ifs and the very real question of what now. My hands itch for something to do, so I fight to find a comfortable position in bed and dive into an epic adventure novel I borrowed from the library.

My door flies open and Carys strides in like a woman on a mission, her gold and raven tresses billowing out behind her, pale cheeks flushed, golden eyes ablaze. Behind her, Kilkenny gives me a semi-apologetic look. By the time I focus on Carys, she's already said whatever she had to say and turns to walk back out of the room.

"No time to explain," Kilkenny signs.

I flip the book over on the bed to save my page and get to my feet. Without the traction from my boots, I slip from the sudden shift in position and nearly fall over.

"Meet us at her room," Kilkenny motions before taking off after Carys.

As quickly as I can, I lace on my boots before rushing after them. By the time I arrive at Carys's quarters, she and Kilkenny are already inside. I freeze in the doorway.

Carys's room looks as though it was in the path of a tempest. "Great Lierwen and Rhianu ..." I mumble under my breath.

Except I must've spoken rather loudly because Kilkenny's gaze snaps to mine and I step back. I take in the overturned chair, the sheets and drapes on the bare floor. The plush rug has been rolled back and stands upright against one of the posts of Carys's bed. Stationery is strewn all over the floor and Lowri is shuffling pages back into order and placing them atop a disastrous desk. Ellynne stands near the fireplace, trying to talk Carys down as the princess paces endlessly.

Kilkenny approaches me. "You got through to her in the library somehow. Can you ... ?" He nods his head toward her.

Kilkenny steps aside as Carys suddenly rushes toward me, a wild look on her face. "Can you fix this shit pile excuse for a bedchamber?"

I blink, unsure of how to react.

"Godsdamned useless Grounder." She throws up her hands and turns away from me.

Resentment constricts my throat, and I swallow tightly around it as Kilkenny fixes me with a look that says *be calm*. This is not the Carys I got to know yesterday in the library.

Volatile emotions, she'd mentioned. Emotion soup. "What do you want me to fix?" I blurt as she resumes pacing, her fingers speared into her hair.

She spins to me, her long hair flying behind her. "This mess." I note the way her face contorts, the way her throat bobs and her chest heaves—the word snagging on a sob. In those two words, there's so much anger, frustration, confusion … fear. She's speaking of something deeper than the literal mess around us.

"Alright. Maybe we can start by putting up a force field."

Kilkenny's brows dip, as do Ellynne's. Carys just stares indifferently at me, but she swipes her hand across an escaped tear on her cheek.

"You know, like Osha the Lightweaver?" I try again.

She continues to stare at me, but there's a stillness to her now that wasn't there a moment ago.

I turn to Kilkenny. "Do you mind if I maybe speak with Princess Carys alone?" What am I saying? My palms grow clammy at this possibility. I've handled meltdowns from Taig before, but he's a tiny five-year-old and Carys is not only taller than I am, but intimidating too.

Kilkenny frowns, cautious. But he nods and turns to Ellynne and Lowri. He says something to them and they hurry out of the room, Kilkenny a little slower. Casting one last look over his shoulder, he closes the door behind himself.

I need to distract Carys. She'd wanted to know more about me before Kilkenny interrupted in the library. I may be grasping for straws, but …

"I know relationships can feel fickle. You could have many things in common with someone, maybe even trust them, but they're outside of who you are, and it's so difficult to know what's going on inside someone's mind. What their true intentions are."

Her fists are clenched at her sides, her body rigid.

"I'm from the Grounds. Across the bridge. A very different lifestyle. Yet, you and I can bond over things like books. Dresses. Food."

She doesn't move a muscle, her focus on the floor.

I need to play into her curiosity about me. What did she want to know? I release a breath and my cheeks burn prematurely. "You asked me if I was fond of someone," I say. "The truth is, romantically, I'm not. I've never felt that … special something that people speak of. No sparks. No racing heart or sweaty palms. No butterflies in my stomach. No fantasies …"

Her fists unclench and her body slowly relaxes. She lifts her head, but it's clear she has no clue what I'm talking about.

"The love stories in the book of fairytales are all sort of similar, aren't they? Enidwen and Caedmon—well, alright maybe not that one. Osha and … what was his name again?" I know his name, but what I don't know is where Carys is mentally right now.

"James," she says.

"Right."

"Maeve and Catriona," she adds.

I nod. "Sam and—"

"Donegal." She smiles as if proud about completing my sentence, but there's still something unsettled about the smile. With a heavy sigh, she sinks down to the floor, pushing her curtain of hair out of her face and over her shoulders as she crisscrosses her legs beneath her dress.

I sit in front of her, mirroring her position. "So many great romances in Erleyan history."

She gawks at me. "It's *fictional*."

"I'm not entirely convinced that romance *isn't* purely fiction. At least for me."

For a while, she stares down at the tiles, her long fingers tracing the lines in the floor design. When she glances up at me, she appears less frazzled and more like the Carys I've gotten to know. "So, you've never been attracted to *anyone*?" she asks.

My shoulders sag with relief; there she is. There is that lucid spark. I shake my head.

"So, then you've never …" Her eyes widen, her brows hidden by her disheveled hair.

Heat blooms in my cheeks but, again, I shake my head. Then I shrug.

The corner of her mouth lifts very subtly as if she's too exhausted to muster a full smile. "Don't be embarrassed. If you want it, I hope the perfect moment and the perfect lover finds you."

I smile, warmed by her sincerity. "Thank you, Carys."

A while later, I usher an exhausted Carys to bed and open the door. Lowri is no longer there, but both Kilkenny and Ellynne stand behind Carys's door like a pair of concerned parents. I gesture toward the bed and shrug. "I can help tidy up," I offer.

Ellynne smiles and nods gratefully. "Much appreciated," she says.

Afterward, *I'm* exhausted and retire to my own bed for a much-needed nap. Just three more days and I get to go home.

Chapter 32
CARYS

THE EVENTS FROM HOURS before rush back to me as the clock chimes six times and sunlight trickles into my bedchamber. My body is heavy, weary, and try as I may, I cannot banish the memory of my behavior from my mind. These incidences are happening more frequently, and no amount of *meditation*, even with Alys's guidance, can help me control them. First the spiral, then the rage.

I know what's next, and I fear the crash that's poised above me like a dagger.

Blinking, I survey my bedchamber. Someone has cleaned up the godsawful mess I made. I don't even know what happened, exactly. One moment, I was contemplating changing my drapery, the next I was in a stranglehold of fury.

The Feast is almost upon us, meaning Durvla's departure is almost upon me. I don't want her to go; I selfishly procrastinate, putting off the necessary discussion with Iywan. Her talent is wasted in a region specializing in agriculture and wool harvesting. She's a greater asset here.

It doesn't escape me that all my friends are in my service or service to the crown. It's an obligation. Perhaps it's the same for Durvla. She is kind, patient and controlled, creative and logical—everything I'm not. Yet, I cannot figure out if she's only kind because soon she can walk away from this godsforsaken palace.

Stop wallowing, an inner voice tells me.

I jump, chilled to the bone.

You don't need friends.

But I do. Don't I? … Gods, am I arguing with myself?

To distract myself from my spiraling mind, I leave my bedchamber, and Sir Ren offers me a tight-lipped smile. In silence, we make our way to the kitchen. The rest of the staff is on break, and Eefa's perceptive gaze settles on me as I step into the kitchen. She knows exactly the kind of mind numbing I need as I tell Ren to stand guard outside the door.

His voice reaches my ears through the roar of my eager pulse while Eefa's lips are on my neck, her hand grazing my thigh beneath my dress and chemise. We spring apart as a hunched older woman, who I recognize by face only, waddles into the kitchen. Taken aback, the woman places one hand on the counter for balance and dips into a shallow curtsy.

Beside me, Eefa is grinning like a fool. My heartrate refuses to slow down, competing with my mind as it assaults me with a plethora of negative thoughts, though none have any discernible origin. Without bothering to say anything to either of the women, I sweep out of the kitchen, flanked by Ren who, thankfully, asks no questions.

I don't stop walking until I'm standing in the infirmary, tears stinging my eyes. Alys rushes to my side, worry etched into her plump face. "Carys?" she asks. "What's amiss, dear one?"

"I don't know," I choke out as I glance around. There's no sign of Briony, thank the gods.

"Tell me what you see," she says.

I know this routine well enough, but somehow, I can never remember it on my own. Not lately, at least. "You," I say.

"I'll accept that. What do you hear?"

I listen and there's a gentle flap of the white curtain as wind blows through the window. "The curtain." I draw in a breath. "I feel my feet in my shoes, the floor beneath. I taste nothing at the moment. I smell ... something herbal."

"What a surprise in an infirmary, hmm?" she asks sarcastically.

I smile weakly.

"Well done," says Alys. "Lie down. Let me make you a cup of tea."

On Alys's suggestion, I leave the confines of the castle to get some fresh air in the late afternoon. Back on duty, Callum silently follows me outside. We step out of the stuffy palace and into the cooling air beneath the lavender and orange sky. As we walk farther from the castle and through the floral archway of the garden, Callum draws his sword with a *shiiing* that startles me more than the large man who appears in our path.

The stranger is even taller than Callum, with coppery skin and thick, dark blond curls tumbling onto his broad shoulders. Sapphire eyes with a sunburst of brown settle on me. On my diadem.

My heart races.

He steps back, lowering his head. A bronze pin—diamond-shaped with an X intersecting it, a triangular blue-green labradorite gemstone at its center— shimmers on his chest. The royal symbol of Uldarvik.

I hold my hand up to Callum and he lowers his sword.

"Apologies, Your Highness," says the stranger. "I did not mean to frighten you." His warm, resonant voice washes over me, his accent thick and melodic.

Callum hesitates but sheathes his sword.

The Uldaran man is clad in leather, a tattoo along his left jawline, peeking out from beneath his short-cropped beard.

"It's an antler," he says, and I tear my lingering gaze from the inked design in his flesh.

"I didn't mean to stare," I say, lifting my chin despite the fire in my cheeks.

A low laugh rumbles in his chest. There's something so at ease about him. His posture has a certain sureness ... or perhaps arrogance.

"You must be Prince Odgar," I say.

His ocean eyes sparkle, crinkling at the sides. "Yes."

"You're early."

The corner of his full lips quirk up. "Indeed. The god of the sea had mercy on our travels. It's an honor to finally be in your presence, Princess Carys."

"The honor is mine." My words are rehearsed, automatic, but his tone is genuine.

Prince Odgar steps aside, getting out of the way so I can continue my walk, but I don't move. He isn't at all like I'd imagined. I'd expected an uncouth brute. The tip of a battle-ax peeks over his shoulder, and it makes me smile. Maybe not an uncouth brute, but he's armed and without a sentry by his side.

Warrior Prince.

"What brings you out here, Prince Odgar?"

"The fresh air," he says. He lifts his face into the breeze that blows through the garden. "I hold no love for the indoors."

"I assume you spend the majority of your days ... on the ocean?"

A wistful look crosses his face. "I wish." He glances toward the sky then turns back to me.

Another low, mellow voice rings out from beyond the bushes, prattling off in rapid Uldaran. The words are as lively as a jaunty bard song. A man with a peachy complexion and a crooked nose steps into view, his thick, dark brows raising. "Apologies," he says in the common tongue when he spots Callum and me. He's about Callum's height, with gentle brown eyes that belie the hard cut of his square jaw. With a bow, he says, "Forgive my insolence, Your Highness; I was admiring the beautiful view of the lake." His accent is clipped, the vowels spoken with amplified precision.

My brows furrow. "You are not from Uldarvik."

"We stole Seth from Ardall," Odgar says with a playful smirk. "Or rather my sister stole his heart and Uldarvik grew on him."

The man, Seth, has the integrity to appear bashful. I don't bother to pry more information from either of them. Beside me, Callum's hard focus doesn't waver from Odgar. Suddenly, I feel short among these three handsome men towering over me.

I clear my throat. "Well, Prince Odgar. I hope you enjoy your stay at the Fortress on the Mount."

"Oh, I am certain I will. Thank you for your hospitality. I will see you soon." He bows once more, as does Seth, then they step around me to head toward the castle.

I stare at their retreating backs, at the axe strapped across Odgar's and the sword across Seth's, before they disappear behind the castle doors. Callum is straight-faced and I remain unmoving.

Definitely not what I'd expected. Maybe my suitors won't be so bad after all.

On the night before the Feast, I rouse from yet another heart-racing nightmare, Aneirin's name on my lips, my skin and amulet so hot to the touch that I might as well be on fire. I blame my mother triggering my memories of him. It's ironic since she says she took away my memory, whatever that means.

With my heart hammering, I throw a robe on over my nightgown and hurry out of my bedchamber. I nearly collide with Tiernan, who is on my service tonight so he can rest during the day and be ready to guard me at the Feast.

He turns to me, brows pinched together. "Is something the matter?"

"Everything is the matter." My voice wavers and I wipe sweat from my brow with the back of my hand. "I need a glass of wine."

He doesn't question me further, even as his gaze very briefly skims over my attire. He doesn't approve of me walking around in my sleepwear, but he nods and walks alongside me. Only the sounds of his boots and my bare feet against the floor echo in the corridors. As we walk into the dining hall, it's not just Eefa there, but also Durvla, sitting across the table from her.

Durvla's spine straightens when she sees me, but her face is drawn and exhausted. Eefa glances over her shoulder at me, a salacious glint in her gaze.

I avoid her gaze and focus on Durvla, channeling the level-headedness that I lack. "Looks like everybody is in need of wine," I say with a smirk.

Empty plates sit in front of them.

"Oh, did I miss the cake?" I pout.

"There's still more," says Eefa, standing from the table. "Let me grab you a slice and a goblet of wine."

My stomach is at odds with itself, between the nightmare I cannot remember and the fact that in less than twenty-four hours, I'll be meeting my suitors.

"On second thought, just the wine, please," I interject.

Eefa smiles and uncorks the wine with a pop that echoes in the empty, otherwise quiet dining hall. "And for you, Major Kilkenny?" she asks, turning his way.

He sets a no-nonsense gaze on her, and she giggles.

"I thought I'd try," she says with a shrug. She winks at him, but he doesn't react.

My head swivels back and forth between Durvla and Tiernan. My stomach curdles for many reasons. Gods, I hate the jealousy that rises in me like a tide at any given moment, for no purpose other than to be there. I have zero romantic interest in Tiernan, and yet … I hate that he may have an interest in someone other than me.

Our relationship was forged five years ago when he saved my life. I'm uncomfortable in my own skin as I recall the sacrifice he made for me. He could've lost his own life. He's been an unwavering boulder in many storms throughout the years. He's been kind and patient, even though I constantly tease him for being broody and a stickler for the rules. If he has feelings for Durvla, I should be happy for him.

Just like I should be willing to let Durvla go for the sake of her own happiness.

"Carys?" Eefa's standing beside me with a goblet of wine outstretched.

"Right," I say, clearing my throat as I take the goblet. I intend to just sip the liquid, but it's gone within seconds. I plop into a chair and demand a refill. I don't stop drinking until my mind slows down, even as Tiernan protests each goblet. My limbs grow heavier, until I am warm, sleepy, and blissfully unbothered.

"I shhhgotooo my shamber," I say, bracing my hands on the table to stand. I turn the words over in my head and chortle. Am I slurring my words? "I mean ... my *shamber* ..." Concern draws Durvla's brows close, but Eefa laughs along with me.

"Princess, I think you've had enough," says Tiernan, suddenly at my side. He grasps my arm, and I pull back.

"Unhand me, you brute. Just because you shaved my lie does not make me mine—yours."

There's a mixture of amusement and worry on his face. He presses his lips together.

"Do you find me funny, Sir Killian?" I frown. "That's not your name. I know your name. The knight who prefers Major." I sing the last phrase.

"Come on. Up you get," he says. He turns toward Durvla. "Would you mind helping me get the princess back to bed?"

Then suddenly Durvla's at my side. It takes a bit of hoisting to get me out of my chair, and even then, my legs are like pudding. We start to move, but it is more like I'm being dragged. "This is *not* the way to fleet a princess," I protest. My tongue betrays me with each word. "I can walk by my own." I tug my hand away and stagger several steps forward before Tiernan catches me. "My hero. Again."

Durvla and Tiernan continue half dragging me to my bedchamber in silence.

"Do you regret the ar— the aaar—the *a-rrow*? Fugin 'ells, that word's hard to say!"

Deep lines form in Tiernan's forehead. "That was years ago. And you are *drunk*."

"*I* don't get drunk. *You're* drunk!" My legs give out and I squeal, but Tiernan scoops me into his arms. I rest my head against his shoulder. "Teran, I don't want Durvla to go. She's very lovely."

Tiernan keeps his focus ahead as he walks. *Rude.* I put my hand on his head and force it toward me. His brows shoot toward his hairline.

"Your eyes are also very lovely. If we get married, our looks will be shildren." I frown. Not what I meant to say. At all. "I mean our shildren will be—"

"Princess, with all due respect, you should stop talking."

"I make the commands around here, *Major*." I salute.

He smirks and keeps walking. I grow sleepier with each step until my back sinks into a soft surface. I lay against my pillows and caress my sheet. Durvla appears out of nowhere. "Oh, hello! Where have you been?"

She smiles at me. "By your side the whole time."

"Oh, you sweet dove." I pat her hand. For a moment, I close my eyes, but they fly open again of their own volition. "Broody knight?" I call out. "Where are you, broody knight?"

Tiernan looms over me. "Yes, Princess?"

"Good night." I pat his face and he flinches so hard that it makes me laugh. The bed welcomes me like a giant hug and tugs me into the most peaceful sleep I've had in ages.

Chapter 33
DURVLA

IT TAKES ALL MY restraint not to burst out laughing when Carys unknowingly slaps Kilkenny's face. I'm sure she intended to give him a gentle pat, but the assault is so satisfying that I want to thank the intoxicated woman.

"Thank you for the help," Kilkenny says as he closes the door to Carys's room.

I smile and shrug. It wasn't a big deal. "May I ask … What did Carys mean when she called you *the knight who prefers Major?*"

Kilkenny's jaw works, then at last, he says, "I was a soldier in the Royal Brigade, and I worked hard for that title. I chose not to drop it in favor of *Sir* when I became a knight."

I draw in a breath to ask about the arrow, but Kilkenny shakes his head.

"No more questions. Dawn is in a few hours and tomorrow is a big day. Get some rest."

"Yes, Major Killjoy," I mumble, the words slipping out as I turn to walk away.

I freeze, my pulse picking up. I force myself to face Kilkenny, ready to apologize.

A half smile tugs at one corner of his lips. "Did you just call me 'Major Killjoy'?"

Should I lie? "Yes ..." So much for that.

Kilkenny's tongue trails over his lower lip, clearly trying to staunch the temptation to laugh. I catch myself staring as his tongue retreats and his lips form words ... Words that don't register in my head. Maybe I shouldn't have had even that one goblet of wine.

His hand rests on my shoulder, and I fall back into my senses. "Sorry, what?"

"Go to sleep," says Kilkenny. "I might be a killjoy, but if you don't get some rest, the title will transfer to you come morning."

I nod and press my lips together before retreating to my room as quickly as possible.

·· o ☽ ☀ ☾ o ··

"I won't ask again," says a voice that grates against my senses, throwing my heart into a chaotic rhythm. I'm in a dark room with a single torch against the wall. There is no warmth, and below my bare feet is raw stone. Before me are two figures. It takes a while for the image to clear, but I soon recognize Kilkenny. He's bound to a chair, a figure towering over him, their broad back partially blocking my view of Kilkenny's face. But it's Kilkenny in the chair, no doubt.

That scratchy voice reaches my ears again. "How long have you—"

But the rest of his words are garbled as Kilkenny's focus snaps to mine from across the room. His face is bloody and bruised, his lip split and swollen. When he speaks, his voice comes out as a strangled whisper, hoarse and heavy. "Garrick." It's almost a growl.

The figure in front of him raises a hand, and something glints in the torchlight before the whole scene begins to tilt at unnatural angles, forcing me to close my eyes against the nauseating dizziness—

I awake with a scream as searing pain travels from behind my left ear down to my collarbone.

The pain is so intense that bright light dances before my face for a moment. I clutch my neck as ragged breaths force their way through my clenched teeth.

The room materializes around me again as the pain slowly melts away. I release my neck and stare at my hands, expecting blood. Disoriented, I scramble out of bed, tripping over my feet and landing heavily on the ground, my hands taking the brunt of the fall. When everything is steadier, I launch myself to my feet, lighting a candle and bringing it to the mirror to stare at my reflection.

I search my neck desperately for signs of injury, but the pain is gone, and there is no wound. Sunlagh, spare me. These dreams ... My nightgown is drenched again, and as I search for a new one, I mull over the dream.

Kilkenny.

I can't make sense of what was happening. He was bound and someone was torturing him for reasons I don't know. And the pain ... The image of the scar on Kilkenny's neck comes to my memory. It must be a coincidence. *Must be.* It's just my mind trying to make sense of something I know nothing about.

Dressed in a fresh nightgown, I crawl back into bed and wait patiently for sleep to find me again.

· · ◦ ☽ ☀ ☾ ◦ · ·

My shoulder is jostled gently and, after a month in this place, it doesn't startle me as much as it annoys me. I force my eyes open. Ellynne's way-too-cheery grin and red hair is painfully bright in the sunlight that filters in through the windows.

My head is throbbing. I didn't have much wine last night—I'm sure Carys had enough for all of us. The headache starts at the base of my skull and radiates to my ears, leaving them with that uncomfortable, full sensation that I haven't experienced in a while. The headache has been building for days, but of course, on the day of the Feast it decides to up the ante.

I send up a prayer to Ehlach for the pain not to worsen—for the possibility of an episode to stay away. I just need to get through the day. Then I can go home. I can do this.

"Our darling daydreamer," says Ellynne, using the same term that Carys has used before.

I groan and rub my head.

"Don't be so forlorn. Tonight, you get to attend the Feast as a guest, off duty. You can dance with whomever you want, flirt with whomever you want." Her eyelids lower, a smirk playing on her lips as she says, "Bed whoever you want."

Much to my surprise, I don't even blush. Clearly, I've become desensitized. Ellynne's head snaps toward the door and I follow her gaze. She turns back to me with a question on her face and I mimic her expression. "Shall I let your knight in shining armor in?"

My head tilts as I try to make sense of her words. Knight in shining— Oh! "I—"

"Enter!" Ellynne yells.

I have all but one second to yank the covers over my body as the door opens. The amusement on Ellynne's face is undeniable, and I glare at her as she walks away, her shoulders shaking with laughter. She says something to Kilkenny that I can't make out before she steps out of the room.

Kilkenny turns to me, and I instantly blanch as I remember the vivid nightmare. He keeps his distance for a moment, also pale, even as the door shuts behind him. He steps just a little closer to sign. "I'm on my way to the infirmary. Princess Carys needs"—he fingerspells the next word—"a *wormwood* tincture. I thought you'd like to come along?"

I want so much to tell him about the nightmare. The scar on his neck is barely visible from where I am, but it's clear in my mind. The sheet is clutched in my fists, pressed up against my chin by now to conceal the thin material of my nightgown. "Why do you want me to come along?" I ask.

"I know what pain looks like. And you've been rubbing your head for days."

This gives me pause. "You're ... very intuitive ..."

"It's my job," he says with a shrug. For a moment, he stares at me as if he wants to say something more. "Our head healer is the best in Mainland," he motions after a while.

His sign for "head" healer is literal, incorrect. I bite back a smile, and he lifts a brow.

"What?" he asks.

Keeping the sheet clutched to my chest with one hand, I sign with the other. "Not *head* healer. *Expert* healer."

He repeats the motion.

"Unless she only heals heads ..."

Unamused, he continues what he'd been saying before. "Our expert healer can have a look at you and perhaps give you something to help with the pain. I'll step outside before you choke yourself with the sheet."

Is that a smirk on his lips? My shoulders relax a little.

"Make haste, please," he motions. He turns before I can respond.

I heave a sigh. What a demanding pain in the rear. I swing my legs over the side of the bed and press my feet against the floor, making sure that I can bear weight before standing. My vision swims and I release a slow breath, closing my eyes and counting to ten, willing my body to cooperate with me.

Taig, Finn, Osheen, Orla and Granny ... I'll be with them all again soon. If I can just make it through today. Opening my eyes, I put one foot in front of the other, slow at first, until moving becomes natural again. I pull on the forest green linen dress that I'd worn to Barr na Cahar, cinching the bodice laces tight and tying them in a neat bow. Then, standing before the mirror, I braid my hair, tying a bow on the end that rests above my shoulder blades. I'll miss these clothes.

When I step out of the room, Kilkenny's gaze sweeps over my figure, and heat floods my face. Tiny crinkles form at the corners of his eyes and the ghost of a smile plays around his lips. He doesn't turn away.

"What?" I ask at last.

"You wore that dress when we went to Barr na Cahar."

"Yes ..."

"The ladies around here don't tend to re-wear things. At least not for quite some time."

Oh, to be wealthy. "Well ..." I brush my hands over the skirt. "I like this dress." I pick a stray thread off my sleeve as we stand in awkward wordlessness. "So, are we going?"

"Right," he says. "Yes. Come on."

I take one step and suddenly the floor is flying up toward my face. A solid force wraps around my middle, holding firmly until I stop flailing my arms for balance. I'm pressed against Kilkenny's rigid body, his arm still around my abdomen, and heat blooms everywhere in my body. My breath hitches as I try to dissect the embarrassment from … whatever else has my heart racing.

I clear my throat. "You can let go now."

His hand drops away, and I turn to face him, lifting my gaze to his.

"Still a newborn foal," he says, grinning in such a cocky way that I wish we were in a self-defense session. Just so I'd have a valid excuse to hit him.

When I'm finally steady again, we set off for the infirmary. "Why are *you* fetching the tincture. That doesn't seem quite in your list of duties."

"Ellynne went to make sure that the heaviest sleeper in the palace woke up—"

I glare at him.

"—and Lowri was sent to get the tincture, but she's wary of the infirmary, so I volunteered to go in her stead." Even as we walk briskly, he angles his face to mine, ensuring that I can easily read his lips. The action is not lost on me—the small, kind gesture leaves me oddly reassured, almost like I'm in the comfort of my own home. I stare at his lips, drawn to the soft curve that diminishes the harsh angles of his jawline.

I nod, trying to force rational thought back into my head. I *really* need to get out of this place. "Why is Lowri wary of the infirmary?"

He shrugs. "That's none of my business or yours."

I huff out a breath, and my head continues to throb. As I rub at the spot, I remember Kilkenny's words and let my hand drop, focusing on keeping up with him instead.

We arrive at the infirmary, and a host of aromas infiltrate my senses as we step into the pristine room. There are a couple of other healers focused on their own tasks, but a familiar face approaches, a bright smile dominating her dark features. It's the healer who'd tended to me when I was held prisoner. Instinctively, I press my hand against the branding beneath my sleeve. A month later, it no longer hurts, but I always avoid looking at it, evading the fear that the mere sight of it brings back to the surface.

"Hello again," she says with a smile. She extends her hand, clasping my forearm in greeting. "Alys," she says, reminding me of her name.

"Durvla," I say, giving her forearm a squeeze before letting go and stepping back. "Thank you again."

"No thanks needed at all, sweetling." Her gaze briefly roams my face before she turns back to Kilkenny. "Let me guess, you're here for a tincture for Carys."

He nods. "Also, Garrick is too stubborn or foolish to admit it, but she's been enduring headaches. Will the same tincture work for her?"

I bristle, narrowing my eyes at him. Too stubborn or foolish? I turn to Alys just as she shakes her head disapprovingly at Kilkenny, but he doesn't falter.

Alys turns a concerned face to me again. "Do you have a headache right now?"

"Yes, but it's manageable." Headaches are a part of my existence more often than not. I'm so used to it, I'm more likely to notice when it's absent.

Alys lays a hand gently on my shoulder for a few seconds before heading to her workstation. There are assorted containers of colorful liquids and powders in racks against the walls and lining the counters. Dried herbs and flowers hang from iron brackets anchored to the walls, and rows of clean linen are neatly arranged on wooden shelving.

I barely have the chance to blink before Alys returns with two tiny amber glass vials. She hands one to Kilkenny and one to me. "One gulp," she says, her steady gaze on mine. "It won't taste pleasant, but it'll do the trick."

The vial in the palm of my hand feels strangely illicit. I've never had anything to help with the pain before—most medicinal herbs are dispatched to Mainland, and there are others in my village, particularly the elderly, who need what's left of our stock far more than I do. I force my lips into a smile as I face Alys again. "Thank you."

As we head back toward the sleeping quarters, Kilkenny glances at me every now and then, lost in thought about something.

"Aren't you supposed to be sleeping in preparation for tonight?" I ask to redirect his mind.

He waves his hand dismissively.

"Do you *ever* sleep?"

His expression is sharp enough to cut metal. "Of course I sleep."

It seems whenever he's not on duty guarding Carys, he's still on duty.

"You care about her a lot, don't you?"

More cold glares from Kilkenny. "The princess requires a lot of care."

"That's not what I'm asking," I mumble.

He slows down. "I know what you're asking, but the answer remains the same."

You're impossible. I stop in the middle of the corridor, second guessing my directions. I should get breakfast and get ready for whatever is thrown at me before the Feast. I voice my thoughts aloud to Kilkenny and he nods in agreement.

"I'll head to bed, then," he says, starting to walk backward away from me. "Don't let that tincture go to waste. It's not the time to be a martyr. You need to be at your best for tonight."

I slide my thumb over the small cork of the vial as I watch his retreating back. A tincture to cure my headache. Unbelievable … Taking deep breath, uncork the vial. One gulp, Alys had said.

It's still enough to make me nearly gag as the bitterness hits my tongue.

Water. I need water. I've never made it to the kitchen so quickly. Eefa swivels in my direction as I rush in.

"Good morning," she says, a smile on her face. "Eggs?"

"Water, please." The bitterness remains on my tongue, but sure enough, my headache is already starting to fade. I stand perfectly still, trying to figure out if this is a figment of my imagination—if it's that simple to alleviate something that has left me in tears so often.

A cup of water appears in my line of vision, and I startle.

"Are you alright?" Eefa asks, cocking her head at me.

"Yes. Thank you." The water washes the bitterness away and I hand the cup back to Eefa. The headache is more of a background nuisance than an overwhelming pain. I have a suspicion it'll be completely gone soon.

"Are you ready for the Feast?" Eefa asks.

"Ready as I'll ever be. What about you?"

"Oh, I'll be working. All hands on deck in the kitchen tonight." She appears unbothered about it, pleased in fact. But then she adds, "I'm looking forward to it. It's wildly more exciting than the norm." Her smile certainly verifies her words. "So, about those eggs?"

"Yes, please."

"Bacon? Bread?"

"Sounds heavenly." Who knows when I'll get bacon next.

She winks and disappears behind a set of doors.

A while later, I'm savoring one of my last breakfasts in the palace when I sense an approaching presence. I raise my head as Carys lumbers into the room with Callum at her side. One of the other kitchen servants drops into a deep curtsy, then hurries off to the kitchen. Carys stares me down, fiddling with the amulet against her chest as she plops gracelessly into the seat across from me. "You look way too chipper," she says.

"Me?"

"You just cannot wait to leave me, can you?"

My spine stiffens. There's no humor in her eyes. Instead, there's a hint of genuine hurt and annoyance.

"It's not that …"

"Then what is it? The palace isn't large enough for you? The food not good enough? Your bedchamber not to your liking?"

"No …"

"Then what is it?" The demand is clear on her face.

"I miss my family," I blurt.

She slumps in her chair, her focus zeroed in on my face. A moment passes between us, and she slowly says, "Your family is dead."

It might as well be a physical slap. I dig my teeth into my lower lip and breathe out slowly. "My best friend and his family. We've been close since childhood." He's the only one who knows all my secrets.

She huffs out a breath and drops her face into her open hands. A servant appears with a tray of food—an even grander spread than my own. Carys lifts her head and stares at the food, not even acknowledging the servant who stands by, waiting for some sort of validation.

Carys lifts a slice of bacon. It's dark around the edges and stands upright in front of her face. She scrutinizes it in simmering silence before dropping onto the plate, disgust on her face. "Get me one that doesn't look like it caught fire," she demands. "In fact, take the whole thing away." She flicks her fingers toward the plate as if shooing it away.

Everything about her is off today. She's a cornered animal, wounded and more than willing to lash out at anyone. Once the servant is gone, I eat my own bacon slice to keep myself from speaking out of turn. Carys pinches the bridge of her freckled nose and closes her eyes.

"Do you want to talk?" I ask.

Her amber gaze flicks to mine and I bristle. "Nothing to talk about," she says. "No point. You're leaving tomorrow, right? No need to pretend that we're friends."

Ouch. "I'd like to think that we are … Just because I'm going back to Cluain Baile doesn't mean that our friendship has to end." What am I talking about? "I will be eternally grateful for the opportunity you gave me. For saving my life, really."

She laughs without humor. "Saved your life … No, Durvla, I saved my own arse." She heaves a sigh of epic proportions. "I'm going to miss you and your daydreaming."

My lips curve up hesitantly. "I'll miss you, too." The truth of it takes me by surprise. Maybe in another circumstance, we really could be friends.

"When I get married," she says. "Will you make my dress?"

The question catches me off guard and I burst into laughter. I nod. "Yes," I say. "Maybe give me more than one month next time?"

She chuckles. "We'll see."

Chapter 34
CARYS

FEAST DAY IS HERE at last, and the confines of the castle walls are especially suffocating today. After breakfast with Durvla, I face the mirror far longer than necessary. My hair falls loose down my back, zero effort, but I wear one of my best diadems—meant to clearly announce my station as the future queen—and an ornate gown of ivory and gold. Ignoring the confusion on Ellynne's and Lowri's faces, I hurry toward my wardrobe and remove my quiver filled with arrows, slinging it onto my back over my constricting dress and corset.

Ellynne makes a sound of protest and sighs heavily. "That dress is not for— Do you even *have* a lesson today?"

"I just need some air," I say, lifting the comforting weight of my bow into my hands. "Take the rest of the day off."

"I'll come with you," she responds.

My head whips toward her, my brows raised. "You loathe the outdoors."

Lowri nods, mirroring my surprise.

"And?" Ellynne winks at me and I smile.

As we step into the corridor, Lowri takes her leave and Ellynne beams up at Callum whose eyes dart between the two of us and the bow in my hand.

"To the archery range?" he asks.

"Good guess, Callum!" Ellynne chirps, and Callum sheepishly smirks at her.

There are far too many people in the castle, and as we stride through the corridors, my cheek begins to twitch from the forced, constant smiling. We pause more often than I'd like to greet the occasional lord or lady. Finally, we step out of the castle and my lungs inflate for what feels like the first time in ages.

The sweet scent of roses is a far cry from the comfort I'd hoped for, so I pick up the pace, Ellynne barely keeping up. We move through the garden, past the summerhouse, and across the small covered bridge to the other side of the castle grounds.

Deep laughter reaches my ears, and I come to such an abrupt halt that Callum's steps falter. Ellynne catches up, breathing heavily. "Damn, Carys. I didn't expect such physical exertion."

My focus remains straight ahead at the tall hedges as a high-pitched whistle followed by a hollow *thunk* snaps me to attention. In my peripheral vision, Callum's hand moves to his sword, but I hold my hand out as laughter reaches us through the hedges.

"Alright, how about best out of nine?" says Seth.

I step forward through the arched trellis and onto the range as Odgar hands his bow back to Seth.

Immediately, Seth spots me and bows. "Greetings, Your Highness."

"Hello, Seth."

Odgar spins face me. "What a lovely surprise." He lowers his head a fraction, his sun-kissed curls falling loose in front of his face, and I return the gesture. "You shoot?" he asks, a brow cocked.

"Perhaps." A soft smile touches my lips. "How about some friendly competition?"

He smirks. "Alright? Name the conditions."

I look toward the far right of the archery range where there are dummies made of straw and fabric set up to match the human body. Jerking my chin toward that area, I say, "Follow me."

"You've got it, Princess."

Beside me, Ellynne is grinning like a fool as we make our way closer to the dummies. The wind sweeps through the clearing, whipping my dress around my calves as I gesture toward the nearest dummy, forty paces ahead. "Are you up for the challenge, Prince Odgar?"

A sparkle of amusement settles on his face. "Absolutely."

Seth presses his lips together as they fight to curve into a smile.

I step away from everyone and nock my arrow, the bloody corset fighting against me. Working through the restriction and adjusting my stance, I draw the fletching back toward my cheek, the bowstring singing as I release the arrow. It zips through the air, finding its home in the center of the dummy's makeshift heart. A fresh arrow already between my fingers, I march toward the next shooting point, nock, draw, and release. Twice more in rapid succession, I hit the remaining targets, aiming for a different point each time. The fourth and last arrow transpierces the straw body of the dummy and spears into the ground.

I march back toward the others. Ellynne's uncertainly chewing on her lower lip, Seth is failing to keep a straight face, Callum's brow is raised, and Odgar focuses on the dummies for a while longer before turning toward me. "Top points for effort and confidence," he says. "But you missed at least three times."

I smirk at him. "Heart. Eyeball. Gut. Cock." I jab my finger toward each of the dummies in the distance as I speak.

Seth whistles a sliding note and Odgar's raucous laughter follows. It fills me with an unexpected warmth and my cheeks twitch, fighting the wide smile that stretches across my face. "Alright, Princess. You win," Odgar says through his laughter.

I squint at him. "How are you so certain?"

"Because he's rubbish with archery," Seth says. He yowls as Odgar jabs him in the ribs and I flinch. That *had* to hurt.

I stare up at Odgar. "You took on a challenge knowing that you're rubbish at it?"

"What's a *challenge* if it isn't difficult?" His sunburst eyes settle on me with such intensity that I find myself unable to turn away. The brown of his irises melding into the blue is almost golden in the sunlight.

I blink to hopefully break the charm and force myself to speak. "You have to at least *try*." I extend my bow to him. "It's my lucky bow. Maybe it'll bring you some good fortune."

He smiles, his white teeth flashing through his neatly trimmed beard. As he takes the bow from me, his fingers brush mine and it sends a jolt straight into the pit of my stomach, warming me to the core. I release my grip so quickly that Odgar tilts his head at me, a question carving a line between his brows. But there's something knowing, something mischievous, in his stare. I lick my suddenly dry lips, and he chuckles as if we've shared some private joke.

"Are you going to shoot or what?"

"Are you going to hand me an arrow or what?" The amusement on his face is undeniable.

"I never said the arrows were lucky, now did I?"

He chortles. "You win again, Princess." He holds his hand out to Seth who places an arrow in his palm. Odgar takes the same path I did, each of his arrows hardly coming close to mine. The last that he intentionally aims at the ground, doesn't even make it across the field. He returns to us and sketches a playful bow.

And I giggle. *Giggle.* Like an infatuated maiden. Magdin's tits ...

Beside me, Ellynne's mouth falls open, and I want to jab her in the ribs just as Odgar did to Seth.

"Well," I say to Odgar, "like your friend said, you're rubbish."

"Dreadfully so." There is barely any space between us when he holds the bow up. This time, when I take it back from him, I make sure our hands don't touch. Odgar winks almost imperceptibly as I extend the bow out to Callum. When Callum doesn't take it, I turn and catch him also staring at Odgar. His knuckles are white on his sword hilt, his jaw tight.

I clear my throat, and Callum jumps before taking the bow with a quiet apology.

"Thank you for entertaining my challenge, Prince Odgar," I say. "It was ... pleasant."

He grins. "I pride myself on bringing pleasure." As he winks again, Ellynne makes a choking sound beside me.

I thrust my arm through hers, linking our elbows and tugging her back the way we came as she loses the battle to keep her laughter at bay. The sound of Odgar's own glee follows us as Callum catches up. I don't stop walking even as tears of merriment streak down Ellynne's pink cheeks. "Apologies, Carys. But that was a good one."

I bite my lip to keep from joining in her delight. Callum's sullenness at my side helps sober me as we make our way back to the castle and the reality of tonight's Feast ahead of us.

Chapter 35
DURVLA

A WOMAN CROUCHES BEFORE *a young Carys, a pained expression on her fair face, a golden crown settled atop her head. "Cariad, deep breaths," she says. "You're going to burn the whole palace down."*

Something jostles my shoulder, and I flinch, but the picture before me doesn't change, nor do I wake up. I am dreaming, aren't I?

The woman stands, and the image of young Carys fades to nothing. I recoil. What in the name of the gods is happening? The blond woman's eyes widen, her jaw going slack. "It's you," she says, and I glance around, but there's no one else here.

"Òr fìor-basduun ..." Awe is written all over her face as she rambles off more words in a language that sounds both familiar and strange.

I stare at her brown eyes that look into my very soul. It sends a shiver through me. She's suddenly directly in front of me, grasping my hand, and it feels ... so real.

I've got to wake up.

Another jostle to my shoulder and my surroundings wavers as though I'm viewing everything underwater.

"Not yet," the woman says. "Stay a moment." Her face is so warm and so wrought with emotion. Before me, her features morph, changing from that young queen from years ago to an older version of herself. "Don't be afraid," she says. "Everything is going to be alright." She lifts a delicate hand to my face and cups my cheek. It's both warm and cool at the same time. "Deep breaths. You're going to wake up now. Keep breathing."

My brows draw together but I nod and follow her deep breathing. In slowly, out slowly. In. Out.

A stinging sensation tears the fabric of my dream. The world before me crumbles away, along with the queen, leaving behind … my bedchamber.

My eyes fly open, my chest heaving. I crawl back against the bed blinking rapidly. Deep breaths. In. Out. In … My arm smarts and I rub at it, finding Ellynne's concerned face hovering over me.

"… me a scare," she says. I only make out half of her words. She's sitting on the edge of the bed beside me. "Sorry I had to pinch you."

That explains the pain. My mind stumbles over the strange and eerily familiar words uttered by the queen in my dreams. Perhaps I've read in the book of fairytales before? Goose bumps prickle my skin, and I force myself to face Ellynne again.

"—t've been one hell of a nightmare. Or a daymare, I suppose."

"Something like that," I mumble. I push unruly curls from my face and glance around. Beside me lies the book I'd been reading. It hadn't been my intention to fall asleep. One look toward the window tells me that it's already evening. I've been out for hours. That's what I get for going to bed so late last night.

"Don't panic," says Ellynne. "You still have time. We'd better get started though. We have our work cut out for us." She reaches out and lifts a limp curl from my forehead before dropping it.

I frown at her. "Shouldn't you also be getting dressed? What about Carys?"

She waves her hand dismissively. "I'm an old hand at that—and don't you dare make a comment about my age."

A giggle tumbles from me. "I won't. Besides, you can't be that old?"

"Thirty. But I've been doing this for a while. I'll be in my dress, hair done, makeup complete in no time. And currently, Carys is visiting the queen." She smiles at me. "I know I absolutely reek of royalty, but don't forget I'm a mere servant—Carys's personal servant, yes, but still a servant. Not much is expected of my attire."

"You know she doesn't see you as a *mere servant*."

She smiles and there's a trace of sadness in her eyes. "Maybe Carys doesn't, but everyone else does."

I go still for a moment, pondering her words. "But if that's true for you, what makes me any different?"

"*You* created the dress of her dreams and gave her the confidence that she lacked for this Feast. The suitors are guests of honor, but you are *her* guest of honor. You must dress and act the part. You might have a lot of attention and questions coming your way tonight. Who knows, maybe you'll even get a job in a noble's household. Or perhaps a job in Ballybaeg? You wouldn't be too far from your home and your loved ones, but you could still supply wearables for Mainland and earn your keep."

It sounds tempting, but impossible. There's Taig. There's my comfortable life at home. I crave the tedium right now.

My last bath in Paramount Castle is divine, and I savor every moment. When it's over, I sit at my desk in my chemise while Ellynne works her oiled fingers through my curls. Lowri stands within my view, rummaging in the large pocket of the apron over her blue linen dress. She holds up a thick green ribbon for Ellynne, then lowers it. No seal of approval, I assume. Lowri fishes a long, silver clip from her apron pocket. A moment later, she smiles.

There's the seal of approval.

After my hair has been tugged repeatedly, Ellynne dips a square of muslin cloth into a small container and rubs rouge over my cheeks. "Carys was right. You do have flawless skin. I'm jealous," she says. She chuckles and I smile back at her. "One more touch." She holds up a small paintbrush. "A little color on your lips. Just a little."

I nod and sit still as she applies the color to my lips.

"There," she says. "All done."

My face is … heavy. Blinking is uncomfortable and when I move my lips, they're slightly stiff.

Ellynne laughs. "You'll get used to it. Come." She nudges my shoulder, prompting me to stand while Lowri fetches a garment bag that is hanging on a hook near the door. Lowri lays the bag on the bed and pulls out an emerald gown.

My legs gravitate toward Lowri as I try to take in the details of the dress, but she drapes it over her arm, cutting off my view. I swear that I only blink before Ellynne and Lowri have me fully dressed. Then I'm staring at my reflection, at the cinched waist and the voluminous skirt made with layers upon layers of fabric. The outer skirt is made from silk and shimmers subtly in the light with each motion I make.

My hair is pinned up with loose curls falling here and there, the silver clip shining against my dark strands, soft coils framing my face. My rouged cheeks appear to have a healthy glow, my lips dark red and plumper.

I don't recognize myself and the ladies gush over me as though I were royalty myself.

"It's too much," I catch myself saying. I fumble with the edge of my long sleeve.

"It might be *too much* for a certain someone." Ellynne winks.

Her meaning isn't lost on me, but I don't crack a smile. I'm too busy trying to find myself in my reflection, but it's more like I'm masquerading in costume at a festival. Or worse, that I've given in to this dressmaker persona. It would be amazing to stay here. Away from worries, from having to find my next meal or having more responsibilities. Guilt churns in my stomach, and I have to tear my focus away from the unrecognizable young woman in the mirror.

Taking a steadying breath, I step back and summon the most genuine smile I can. "Thank you," I say to Ellynne and Lowri.

I'm surrounded by men and women dressed in an array of colors. I've never seen so much vibrance in one gathering. The atmosphere is cheerful and carefree. The ballroom is immense. Several chandeliers hang from the high, domed ceiling, the crystals iridescent in the candlelight. A large square of lacquered wood makes up the dancefloor in the middle of the ornate tiles that cover the rest of the banquet hall's floor.

Long oak tables border the ballroom, white candles hanging over them, illuminating the golden plates with pristine napkins folded neatly in front of each seat. Garlands of green foliage add to the ivory lace runners that decorate every table.

On a dais near the dancefloor, a small string ensemble plays, accompanied by a couple percussionists, and their jovial music thuds through me. Ellynne is with Carys, expected to help her to the very last moment before her grand entrance. Mercifully, Lowri remains beside me, but she's constantly fidgeting and does nothing to soothe my hammering heart. I am more than happy to stand here, statue still, the entire Feast—walking in these heels feels like walking on slick stepping stones.

I wipe my sweaty palms on my dress and clasp my hands together. It grows more awkward by the moment, standing on the sidelines, trying to make myself invisible. Beside me, Lowri is doing the same. She's in a cornflower blue dress that makes her azure eyes stand out.

"Have you been to one of these Feasts before?" I ask her, trying to make conversation and diffuse our nerves.

She smiles painfully and shakes her head. "I've only been here for about eleven months. I arrived shortly after last year's Feast. So, I just missed it."

"So, we're both new to this."

She giggles and nods again, her head swiveling around the large space, taking in the sight of the nobles mingling. Her gaze falls on the large clock over the double-door entrance on one side of the ballroom. Her impatience is palpable, and I can relate. I can't wait for the Feast to be over so I can go home.

I can already feel little Taig in my arms.

Once I'm home, I'm keeping an even lower profile. No more dressmaker Durvla. I am an older sister, a caregiver. A botanist. As grand as Ellynne's plan for me was, I have no intention of leaving the comfort of my home again. I've had my share of adventure.

"—being the help is that no one really pays attention," says Lowri.

I blink, having missed half of what she'd said. But I smile back at her.

"It works in my favor because I'm terrible at making conversation," she adds.

I grin. "Me too. With strangers at least."

"Oh, gods, same," she says. "Strangers are the worst. One never knows what to expect of them."

My response is on the tip of my tongue as everyone's attention is suddenly drawn away from their own doings. All eyes gravitate toward one area, and I follow, facing the top of the grand, winding staircase overlooking the ballroom. There stands Carys, a picture of royalty. A magnificent picture in startling black and deep purple, contrasting the bright colors that are customary of these Feasts, apparently. I can *feel* the collective gasp that travels through the room.

I take in the black lace bodice and sleeves I'd so painstakingly worked on, the subtle dip of the decolletage—no one has seen how low the back of her dress plummets. My palms grow slick. What if the dress falls short? Figuratively speaking … I hope.

Her hair has been miraculously wrangled into twists and complicated braids, pinned efficiently, impressively to the back of her head. One would never know that her hair usually hangs freely well below her bottom. A beautiful tiara of gold with shimmering gems rests atop her head.

She's met in the center of the staircase by a wiry man with umber skin and grey hair braided in neat rows. He's dressed in a formal robe, burnt orange with copper thread embroidery on the collar and down the button panels. Carys smiles at him and takes his hand, continuing the journey down the stairs. He's clearly important enough to escort Carys, but my attention snaps to the guard not far from them. A knight, with gems shimmering in his golden armor. I recognize his stride before I take in his dark hair, slicked back into a tight ponytail at the nape of his neck. No strands fall over his forehead as they often do, and his face is stony, giving away nothing.

Kilkenny.

The suit of armor is beautiful, but I can imagine him seething beneath that cold mask of indifference.

Lowri waves to me, excusing herself to go to the toilet. I smile and tell her that I'll see her later. If I get the chance before I head home.

Carys is in the ballroom for all of ten seconds before she's flocked by many attendees. People stand by to greet her, waiting their turn, bowing to her. Carys twirls for a gaggle of young women fawning over her dress. The skirts swish around her and it's mesmerizing. The gold beads on her bodice catch the light and glimmer with her movement.

I'm filled with a sense of pride that almost makes my harrowing experience of being forced from my home worth it. I wish Osheen and Orla could see my handiwork. I wish I had a painting of this moment to hang on my wall back home. I hope I never forget the hard work that paid off.

The festivities proceed, and Carys dances with various suitors. Ellynne appears at my side, and I nearly fall over from the surprise.

"I feel like you've been standing in this very spot all night."

She's stunning in a red dress that hugs her curves, the color rivaling her hair. She's chosen to leave it unbound, loose waves framing her face and cascading over her shoulders. Her makeup is far from subtle, but it suits her.

"I have," I admit. "You look beautiful, by the way."

"I think the word you're looking for is *ravishing*, sweetheart."

This time I can't bite back the laughter. "So, are you trying to impress anyone in particular or … ?"

"Hmm, not so much *impress* as *torment*," she says with a wicked gleam in her eyes. "He's already mine. I just want to remind him of what he has."

I giggle. "Who is he?"

"His name is Vaughn. He's one of the royal healers." She points out a man with dark, slightly thinning hair and a green suit. He isn't particularly handsome, but Ellynne's face says otherwise. I can't help but smile. Ellynne ... in love? Unexpected, honestly, but incredibly heartwarming.

"Well, shouldn't you go dance with him?"

She raises a brow and lowers her head, as though she's whispering to me. "Will you be alright here?"

"Yes, of course."

She smiles. "Sorry that your knight in shining armor is on duty tonight. Plenty of other victims though."

Victims. I huff out a laugh. "Go to your beau."

She grins at me and nods before walking off. Vaughn's face lights up as though no other woman exists besides Ellynne. She greets him with an embrace and a tender kiss. My focus gravitates toward the dance floor again. Carys dances with a huge man with a braid of dark blond hair. She doesn't appear as annoyed as I expected. Instead, she laughs freely at something he says.

Kilkenny's never far from Carys, even as she moves about the dance floor. There are other knights scattered around the ballroom, though none are in such extravagant armor as his. I admire the armor of the other knights one by one, and when I turn back to Kilkenny, he's watching me.

I must be mistaken, though. He wouldn't dare to take his eyes off Carys, would he?

Intrigued, I take a few steps as if I'm heading toward the refreshments table, and his head swivels, following me.

My lips curve into a smile and his attention snaps back to Carys ... who, to his surprise, has moved on to another part of the dance floor with her massive partner. Kilkenny hurries toward her, and I can't hold back my laughter. It draws the attention of someone nearby.

No, not just someone. The man in the fancy robes.

He starts toward me, and my pulse quickens as I spot a pin over his heart with the emblem of Erleyan royalty. This must be the Hand of the Queen who I have heard so much about. Gods, I hope I haven't offended him by laughing.

"Good evening," he says. "Nice to finally meet you in person, Miss Garrick." His brown eyes regard me, and he offers a slow nod. "I'm Lord Iywan Maddock. My apologies for not going out of my way to introduce myself sooner. I take it you have enjoyed your stay at Paramount?"

"Good evening, Lord Iywan. I have, thank you."

"How are you enjoying your first Feast?"

"It's very exciting and everyone looks so lovely."

He chuckles. "Everyone cleans up pretty well, I'd say." There's something accusatory in his gaze as he studies my attire. My skin prickles. "You must have made Her Highness quite content to earn that dress."

"I suppose I have," I say, more unease crawling beneath my skin.

"So, I see."

I move my hand toward my sleeve to fiddle with the bracelet that I'd forgotten no longer lives on my wrist, and as I search for Carys on the dance floor, her sudden absence surprises me. I turn back to Lord Iywan. I want so much to excuse myself from this uncomfortable interaction, but he hasn't dismissed me.

Please dismiss me.

"Impressive work on the princess's dress," he tells me. "A ... bold choice going with such dark colors rather than one more suited for a royal maiden."

I resist laughing at his *maiden* statement.

"I ..." All words elude me. I'm not sure what to say. That the princess *wanted* something bold?

Iywan leans in a bit closer, sizing me up. "You ... ?" There's something mocking on his face.

I run my fingers along my empty wrist again. *Say something, Durvla.*

An arm loops through mine, and though I startle, the flash of a red dress beside me quells my nerves.

"The princess has requested the presence of Miss Garrick. My apologies, Lord Iywan. Excuse us." She nods to him, and he nods back, his jaw clenched.

Ellynne whisks me away and doesn't speak until we're halfway across the ballroom. She releases my arm. "You looked like you needed some rescuing," she says.

I huff out a relieved laugh. "Yes. Thank you."

"I know Lord Iywan can be … intense." She shrugs. "Come. Let's get you a glass of wine."

Wine sounds great. I follow her to the refreshment table, and she lifts a crystal wine flute from among the others, handing it to me. Just a sip. I have to prepare for my travel back to the Grounds tomorrow morning. I have no intention of nursing a hangover as well.

Chapter 36
CARYS

MOMENTS BEFORE THE FEAST, I seriously considered locking myself in my bedchamber. Surprisingly, Alys never made an appearance beforehand, but thank the gods for Ellynne coaxing me out of my nervous stupor. Because of her, I manage to put on my best future-heir face and make my grand entrance when expected.

There are even more people than I imagined. As I descend the stairs, everyone gapes in wonder. I'm swarmed by admirers as soon as I touch the floor. Everyone is stunned by Durvla's handiwork. I take joy in the yearning glances, and even more joy in the silent disapproval from nobles who need to get off their bloody high horses.

While the food is still being prepared, I'm faced with my suitors one by one. They're all an absolute bore.

Prince Morand of Caldeon reeks of every flower in existence—as if he *bathed* in cologne before stepping onto the dance floor. I greet him by sneezing, and he responds to it by speaking in rapid Caldeon and flamboyantly whipping out an elaborate handkerchief from his breast pocket. We proceed to dance, and he's the embodiment of a horse competing in dressage. I get away from him as quickly as I can.

Lord Bevin of the Outer Isles is probably Ellynne's age and paler than the bloodsucking *Dearg Due* of folklore. But rather than fangs, Lord Bevin is missing two godsdamned teeth, front and center. I'd have preferred it if they *were* fangs because I cannot, for the life of me, stop gawking at the gap as we dance. I reflexively jerk my head away every time he speaks and his tongue snakes through the gap, tossing spittle onto my face. My impatience has long escorted my conduct to the exit, so I excuse myself with a painful smile and a curtsy.

Only to collide with bloody Lord Jamie.

As I dance with the Duke of Darragh, my stomach is in knots. He's basically an older version of Wynn—same tan skin, same smile, same gentle mannerisms. It's disturbing. My face is no doubt red as I avert my gaze constantly and shove away lewd thoughts of everything I've done with his son.

I'm ready to call it quits when a low voice sounds from behind me. "May I interpose?"

Jamie stares up somewhere past me before bowing and making a swift retreat. Prince Odgar takes his place. Like me, he's in dark colors. A black suit with what appears to be leather peeking out from beneath his collar. Four neat braids are attached to his scalp down the center of his head, the sides shaven to reveal multiple whorls and symbols inked into his flesh. I stare at them as he gives a slight bow.

He steps into my space, one hand clasping mine, the other going around my waist. His callused fingers brush against the valley of open lace at the small of my back. I shiver, but it has nothing to do with the roughness of his skin.

"You seemed bored with your dance partner," Odgar tells me.

"Absolutely." I grin at him. "Was it that obvious?"

He twirls me seamlessly, and when I face him again, his rugged smile makes my stomach take a silly little dip. "Painfully so," he says.

"Well, that's unfortunate." We glide across the dance floor. Odgar is unexpectedly light on his feet. "I thought you'd have stepped on my feet about a thousand times by now."

He grins. "There's more to me than meets the eye, Princess."

Obviously … "Don't tell me the Warrior Prince of Uldarvik takes dancing lessons."

His face lights up mischievously. "Fine, then I won't tell you."

I squint at him, and he winks. I swear my skin heats.

Clearing my throat, I reach up to pinch the leather that's peeking out from under his collar. "Tell me this, then," I say. "Are you wearing armor beneath your formal attire?"

He barks out a laugh so sudden and loud that it draws the attention of people around us. Odgar clearly doesn't care. "I'm always in armor, Princess."

"*Always?* Even while you sleep?"

He spins me out and back in again. "Even while I sleep."

I raise a brow, dubious. Then a playful smile turns up one corner of my lips. "Certainly not while you bathe?"

He grins at me. "You're just trying to think of me naked."

I let my eyes roam his broad chest. "I will neither admit to nor deny that statement."

He dips me and I yelp, making him chuckle. I hold on to him, afraid he'd let me fall to the floor, but he sweeps me up into his arms again and across the dance floor. "You will be more than welcomed in Uldarvik if ever you decide to step out of this castle, Princess."

"Call me Carys," I say.

"Carys." His deep voice reverberates in my chest, and the way my name sounds rolling off his tongue makes my skin tingle with delight.

My lips part to request that he repeat my name—purely to ensure that he says it correctly, *of course*—but Tiernan rushes from wherever he was standing to where we are now. Seconds later, he focuses somewhere in the distance, and I follow his line of sight to … Durvla.

She's leaving tomorrow, and I had Tiernan remain on duty tonight rather than give him the night off. Granted, he didn't *want* the night off, but I should've insisted.

"Excuse me for a moment," I tell Odgar. "I need to have a word with my sentry."

Odgar flourishes, bowing so deeply that the leather armor beneath his shirt creaks. "I'll be waiting, Raven Princess," he says.

I hesitate for a moment, questioning the nickname. But then I roll my eyes, even as a smile creeps onto my face. I stride toward Tiernan. "Major Kilkenny?"

He bows slightly to me. "Your Highness."

"You're dismissed for the night."

He blinks rapidly. "I'm—I don't … what?"

I can't recall ever seeing him at such a loss for words. "Dismissed," I repeat. "You're officially off duty for the night. Change out of your armor and come back. As a *guest*."

He balks, battling internally. After a moment, he asks, "Is that an order, Your Highness?"

I scoff at him. "If that'll get you to shut up and get out of that damn armor, then yes. Also, I have one more order, and it's nonnegotiable."

Chapter 37
DURVLA

ROASTED POTATOES, MUTTON, AND hearty gravy are piled onto my plate, courtesy of Ellynne. As much as I want to dig right in, it's already impossible to keep track of the chatter around the table without having to look down to attend to my plate. My head swivels left and right, trying to take in as much as I can, trying to respond appropriately as needed. Ellynne introduces me to Vaughn, and he introduces me to someone else. Lips move rapidly, laughter ensues, and I find myself utterly lost in an overwhelming sea of conversations that simply wash over my head like turbulent waves.

My shoulders are tight, my stomach knotted up as I fear missing words that should be obvious—as I fear being outed on the night right before my freedom.

As the night draws on, the Feast attendees move back and forth between partaking in the foods and gracing the dance floor. Ellynne is whisked off to the dance floor by Vaughn at one point, while I sip from the same glass of wine I've had since escaping Iywan's scrutiny.

I'm dangerously close to dozing off, my chin in my palm, my elbow against the table, when something touches my shoulder. My head snaps to the side, my vision wavering. I blink over my shoulder at whoever is hovering behind me and meet captivating onyx eyes.

"Apologies for scaring you, Miss Garrick," Kilkenny says formally. He doesn't so much as crack a smile, but he holds his hand out to me, palm up. "May I have this dance?"

The discomfort that has been sitting in my chest all night starts to unfurl. Briefly. My brows knit together. At Carys's table, a different knight stands behind her. "Weren't you …" I slowly pull my focus back to Kilkenny.

He nods, his hand still extended to me. "Yes, I was," he says. "And now I'm here. Am I going to have to stand here all night with my hand out?"

"No. Sorry." His warm hand wraps around mine and he pulls me to my feet. He doesn't move right away, waiting until I steady myself. He's in a light blue suit with gold trimming along the cuffs, hem, and button panels of his long jacket. The shirt underneath is crisp white, matching the stockings beneath his knee-length trousers, which do absolutely nothing to hide his powerful calves.

I'm about to tease him about wearing stockings, but as my gaze trails back up to his face, his own lazily sweeps over me, absorbing every detail of my dress and hair. My face heats from the approval written all over his countenance. For a moment, his chill demeanor is gone, and his lips part as though he intends to say something, to compliment me perhaps, but then he turns forward and starts, gently tugging me along.

The moment dissipates

"Wait!" I call out.

He stops. "What's the matter?"

"I can't dance. Newborn foal legs, remember? To make matters worse, I'm wearing these." I lift a foot out from under the dress, displaying the ridiculous heels Ellynne forced me into.

There's the tiniest hint of amusement in his eyes and a ghost of a smile on his lips. "Be that as it may, Princess Carys ordered a dance."

My heart drops into my stomach and, before I can filter my actions, I tug my hand out of Kilkenny's.

He has the audacity to look confused. "Is there a problem?"

"Yes." I turn to march away, but Kilkenny lays a hand on my shoulder again. I shrug it off only for him to gently catch my wrist. There's an inexplicable emotion heavy on my chest. "I'm going back to my seat."

"You're being melodramatic, Garrick. Find your center, for Rhianu's sake. There are people looking."

Sure enough, I've drawn some attention. My face heats.

Kilkenny releases my wrist and extends his hand, a peace offering. As much as I want to just walk away from the man who's dancing with me simply because he's been ordered to, I have to make a good impression.

Why do I care about his intentions anyway?

"Found your center?" he asks.

"Yes." My teeth are clenched in what I know is not nearly a convincing enough smile. I take his hand and follow him onto the dance floor.

He places a hand on my waist, and I stiffen. I'm still standing there firmly when Kilkenny takes my left hand and places it on his shoulder. He pauses, focused on me. Then he huffs and takes my right hand. "Do you need me to move your legs as well, Garrick?"

"No, I don't need you to move my legs, Killjoy."

He smirks. "Perhaps take some of that attitude and put it into actually dancing."

"I told you I don't know how to dance."

"Not a problem. I've got you." There is so much certainty in his eyes that I almost believe him. He starts to move, and I follow along, the epitome of awkward gracelessness. I go left when he goes right, I sway when I should stand still. Kilkenny's face is pulled tight, but his gaze shimmers with amusement. When I trip over my own feet and crash against him, the inconsistent rhythm of restrained laughter vibrates through his body.

He steadies me and says, "You weren't exaggerating." But there is nothing insulting in his expression. His smile is even … friendly. For once. It stifles the offense that was quickly rising up.

"Told you," I say, offering him a smile that is strangely foreign on my face.

We start to move again, the triple rhythm of the upbeat waltz pulsating beneath my feet, and *again* I stumble into Kilkenny. He holds me against him, and something hard presses into my hip, making me go absolutely still as blood rushes to my face.

"Tell me that's a dagger," I say. A small crease forms between his brows. Confusion plays over his features for a moment before color blooms across his cheeks.

Tiernan Kilkenny is actually *blushing*.

"It *is* a dagger," he says. I lean back as he lifts the lapel of his suit jacket, revealing a hilt peeking out.

"Oh." *Lugda, take me.*

"Don't flatter yourself, Garrick," he says.

I narrow my eyes at him.

We resume dancing, and I start to get the hang of it, even if I'm relying on his guidance for every step. The song ends, and a slower waltz begins. I step out of Kilkenny's hold.

"There, that should make Carys happy. I'll head back to my seat."
I smile tightly and turn to leave the dance floor, but Kilkenny catches
my wrist and pulls me back toward him. Quickly, he places both my
arms over his shoulders and leans in, effectively capturing me as his
hands rest on my waist.

"One more dance?" There's a silent plea on his face that I can't
resist. I nod, giving in. He leans in close, his lips brushing against
my ear as he says, "*You're braver than you give yourself credit for. Keep that
fighting spirit, always.*"

His voice is a soothing baritone, like warm honey, enveloping me
in a cocoon of safety and familiarity.

"*Whatever happens, keep being brave. Don't break,*" he adds with an
intensity I've never heard before.

Heard ... Wait a minute ...

I blink once. Twice. Thrice. I try to step back, bewildered, but his
hands tighten on my waist. I heard him.

I.

Heard.

Him.

As if he's inside my mind. He still has me trapped, propelling
my heartrate even faster. I shove my arms down between our bodies,
slackening his grip, then duck out from his grasp. Just as he taught me.

I hoist up the hem of my dress and dash toward the lower ballroom entrance.

My feet scream at me from the level of torture I've put them
through tonight. I don't stop running, even as I draw odd stares from
those in my vicinity, until I'm in the mercifully empty corridor. Panic
surges through me. I have to get away from this Feast, from this
castle, from the man or whatever he is who spoke to me *in my head.*

He's a Mage ... who can read thoughts. Like from the fairytales.
Can it be true?

Does Carys know?

Of course she doesn't know! If she knew, he wouldn't be her guard. He wouldn't even be working in this palace. A hand clamps around my forearm, and I turn, my left fist flying toward Kilkenny's face. I hit his open palm instead and seethe over the smile that plays on his lips.

"Good one," he says. "If you'd actually *meant* to hit me, you would've."

"Get away from me!" I take a giant step backward, moving further down the empty corridor.

He holds up his hands. "Center, Garrick. Find your damn center or you'll blow both of our covers."

"What are you talking about?" I'm walking backward rapidly but Kilkenny follows.

"I can't explain, but I need you to listen to me."

"Get. Away. From. Me."

"Garrick."

I'm still walking backward, holding my hands up to keep him at bay. My family, my entire village, for so long we've been blamed for using magic. We've been persecuted for owning fairytale books because of the ridiculous fear that Paramount has against magic users—who have been considered extinct for years now. Yet, here is an actual *Mage*, straight out of the fairytales, right under their noses.

"I'm not a monster," Kilkenny signs. "I'm no different than you. Haven't you wondered about your dreams? Like *my* dream that you happened to walk right into?"

My blood freezes in my veins. *His* dream?

"Those aren't ordinary dreams."

I stare at his hands as I continue slowly backing away, so focused on them that I trip over my own feet. My arms windmill wildly as the ceiling comes into view. I'm falling backward, and then Kilkenny has his arms around my waist, setting me upright again. I squirm to get free of his grip.

"*Stop fighting me, Garrick,*" he says into my mind.

I shudder. "Stop that!" My hands move sharply.

"Then stop fighting me!" he motions, just as sharp.

His words are so casual that I want to send my fist flying at his face again. I clench my hands at my side.

"Give me just one minute." He starts urgently searching his pockets and pulls something from one of them at last. He takes my hand, places the small item in my palm, and closes my fingers over it.

I search Kilkenny's face, but he's as stoic as ever. "Put it on."

I open my hand to a leather band with ...

My gaze snaps up to Kilkenny's. "How did you—?"

"I have my ways," he says. "Now put it on. I know I haven't earned your trust, but I need you to trust me on this. I'll explain everything later."

I stare at my bracelet, at the gift bestowed upon me by my mother so long ago, the gift that was confiscated from me when I arrived in this place. The image of the bracelet blurs before the tears slip down my face. My chest is tight as I start to put the bracelet on, and my hands are shaking so hard that the ends keep slipping from my fingers. Kilkenny's hand closes over mine and he takes the bracelet. He secures it onto my wrist and takes a step back, giving me space.

A stillness comes over me, but it doesn't bring me peace. It's as though I'm being smothered, an invisible force pressing against my body.

"I know," Kilkenny says. He glances around and then takes my hand. "Come," he says, then he begins marching down the hallway.

I follow behind him numbly, having to focus on my breathing, trying to push away the strange, illogical despair that fills me.

I'm not sure where we're going until we enter a familiar corridor, the vacant pathway to my door. I step into the room and stand there, gawking at my shaky hands. It's like my energy has been sapped and I have the urge to crawl into bed and sleep for a few days.

"I feel …" I blink up at Kilkenny.

"I know." Sympathy softens his otherwise sharp features. He lifts a hand to my face, his thumb stroking over my cheek, wiping away a tear that I didn't even know was there. "Your bracelet is a dampener." He lifts my hand so that it's eye level. "Within it, there's an element imbued with a rune that prevents elemental wielding. Or it can stop the wearer's powers from manifesting if they haven't before."

Elemental wielding? I yank my hand from his grasp. "You've lost your mind. There's no such thing as elemental wielding." I know my voice is breathy.

My mind is racing. Dampener. Powers. Magic. Laughter escapes me and I clap my hands over my mouth. Bursts of giggles continue to erupt through my fingers. My hands are useless at quelling the outburst, so I let them fall, the laughter spiraling even more out of control. As Kilkenny opens his mouth to say something, the floor beneath us quakes.

My laughter is cut off.

Pictures fall from the walls, crashing onto the floor, and I'm launched into Kilkenny's arms. He staggers into the door and presses his back against it, his arms around me protectively as the shelf of wool and fabric shakes and throws materials onto the floor.

"What's happening?" I yell.

At last, the tremors beneath us stop, and Kilkenny releases me from his arms. "Explosions," he signs. "I have to get out there, but don't leave this chamber. Lock your door." He stares intently into my eyes before my gaze falls to his lips. "Please do not be stubborn about this, Garrick. For your own good."

I nod hastily, my heart racing, my ears starting to ring.

Kilkenny turns to open the door, but I grab his hand. He spins back to me, confusion breaking through the urgency on his face.

"Be careful," I tell him.

He nods and runs off, shutting the door behind him. I lock the door just as everything shakes again, though not as aggressively as before. I hope Carys, Ellynne, and Lowri have gotten to safety.

I hope that Tiernan stays safe.

Chapter 38
DURVLA

I'M ON EDGE AS I pace my bedchamber—not *mine* for much longer. I'm stuck in my own world without anyone to tell me what's going on. I've since changed out of my ballgown and into a lightweight slate blue dress with loose sleeves. My bare feet throb as badly as my head does, but I can't sit down. I can't quell the unease inside me or the suffocating stillness that filled me after I put the bracelet on.

I've tried convincing myself that it's all a coincidence. I've worn this bracelet for as long as I can remember. There's no way that it was a dampener or whatever Kilkenny called it. There's no way that I'm ... like *him*.

I can't get the sound of his voice out of my head. It was both entrancing and disturbing. I want to believe that it was some kind of trick—that it wasn't *magic*—but I can't remember when last I heard anything with such clarity.

You're braver than you give yourself credit for, he'd told me. *Keep being brave. Don't break.*

I laugh at the memory of it. Brave. Right. I'm anything but brave. All I want to do is go home and not have to deal with princesses and sewing and overly flirtatious cooks and servants. Not to mention explosions.

Stalking toward the window, I draw back my curtains and glance out. Thick, grey smoke billows against the midnight sky. My chest tightens as there's a sudden tremor behind me. I turn quickly—my door has been broken down by a royal guard in maroon. Two brig guards in charcoal livery storm in, one holding a set of iron manacles.

Not again.

My heart starts to beat in triple time and my head lightens. The soldiers march toward me, and I back away, hitting the windowsill.

"Durvla Garrick," says one guard. "You stand accused of treason by the decree of Her Majesty Queen Morwenna Meredyth, the Good."

Treason? Has Kilkenny finally exposed me as an Undesirable? Did they discover that my bracelet was a dampener? That I have … magical dreams?

Whatever the guard says next, I cannot decipher behind the black spots waxing and waning in my vision. The room feels smaller than the crawl space where we've kept Taig hidden during raids. The air is too dense to breathe.

I barely feel the soldiers latch the manacles onto my wrists. My limbs grow heavier as they tug me out of the room, my feet stumbling along numbly. My pulse rushes in my temples, sweat cooling on the back of my neck as the soldier continues to haul me away from my freedom. I was almost home. *Almost.*

But treason is a death sentence.

A fresh wave of dizziness hits me like a swift kick.

They're going to hang me. I'll never see Taig or Osheen or anyone back home again. My breaths come in fast puffs. I gulp down air as my vision spots until I'm rendered sightless.

The floor rushes up toward me with no return.

· · ◦ ☽ ☀ ☾ ◦ · ·

I come to with a gasp for air, jolting upward against something hard. Pain blossoms in my wrists, and my head hammers painfully. An image of a large figure swims in my bleary vision as I try to focus.

A pair of mismatched eyes, one clouded and scarred stares back at me. "Welcome back," says the soldier woman. Sergeant Angharad.

No …

I look around frantically at my surroundings. A single lamp barely illuminates the room; the walls are dark stone and the floor unfinished. I'm in a chair, my hands manacled behind my back. I tug against them but the metal bites into my skin and I swallow a gasp of pain.

"Answer truthfully and you'll be released from this room," says Sergeant Angharad.

I turn her words over in my mind. Released from *this room* … I'm not going home, am I?

"Do we have an understanding?" Angharad asks.

I nod, my chest heaving, tightening painfully.

"Have you ever consorted with faeries or any being from the Otherworld?"

I almost bark out a laugh. "No."

"Have you harbored an Undesirable or covered for someone who has?"

"No." Gods, I hope my voice sounds steady.

She leans in, her eyes narrowed, and my heart is ready to break through my ribs. "Are you sure?" she asks me.

"Yes."

She doesn't turn away from me, but she shouts, "Bring them in!"

Spittle lands on my face, and I want desperately to wipe it away. The shackles bite into my skin as I move my hands, and I remember that I'm bound. The room brightens slightly from the oil lamps beyond the door as it opens. In a flourish, Cadet Bronn marches in, his pale, bald head shining in the flames. My cheek immediately smarts with phantom pain as I remember when he struck me weeks ago. He's tugging a chain attached to manacles on the wrists of a taller man.

The prisoner's auburn hair glints in the lanternlight. His face is bruised and scratched, a trail of blood congealing on his broken nose and down his chin.

Panic surges within me and his name rushes out along with the air in my lungs. "Osheen!"

"Durvla," he says. "I'm so so—"

Cadet Bronn sinks his fist into Osheen's stomach and Osheen drops to his knees, his body shaking with violent coughing. I yank against my chains, thrashing my body even as the chair goes off kilter.

Angharad grabs the arms of the chair, shoving it back onto all four legs. "I'm going to ask you one last time," she says. "Have you ever harbored an Undesirable?"

Heat floods my veins. "Where is my brother?"

Angharad straightens and steps aside as Bronn hoists Osheen to his feet.

"Where is he?" I repeat to Osheen.

There is pain all over his bloodstained face. "I don't know! We got separated."

An icy fist squeezes my heart with unrelenting force.

Another soldier grabs Osheen, hauling him away as Cadet Bronn marches toward me. My stomach churns, pinpricks racing across my skin. I blink as black spots fill my vision. One moment Osheen is there, the next he's gone from my sight. *Again. No …*

More black spots. My head swims. Lungs constricting. The soldiers tug me out of the room.

If Taig is here … all alone. Gods …

Dinner churns in my stomach and dizziness renders me intermittently blind as the soldiers drag me along.

I was *so* close to going home. So close.

Pain erupts through my knees as I'm flung onto the rough stone floor of a prison cell. I scramble to my feet and run toward the cell gate just as it closes shut and a guard locks it. Grabbing the bars, I shake them with all my might, the manacles chafing my wrists. I throw my shoulder into the bars and cry out when pain shoots down my arm.

Sobs tear through my throat, even as I scream to be released. Even as I beg them with all my heart and soul to let me see my brother. My Taig.

My energy dwindles, and I throw my shoulder against the bars one last time before dropping to the floor like a rag doll. I squeeze my eyes shut against the image of Osheen, bloodied and battered. My stomach roils at the memory of that dream—his throat split from ear to ear.

At least he's alive, but he's been taken, along with Taig, and I have no clue where.

Not that it matters. There's nothing I can do about it.

With a grunt of frustration, I pound my fists against the ground and suck in a sharp breath when pain flares in my hands as well.

Don't break.

Find your center, Garrick.

A huff of despairing laughter rushes out of me, Kilkenny's words lingering in my mind. I've managed to survive a month in Paramount, under the constant scrutiny of Mainlanders. I've made friends and even a home here. Perhaps the others will find out that I'm down here and vouch for me. Perhaps they'll help me find Taig.

Deep breaths. In. Out. In … Out. I close my eyes as my tears continue to flow. I sit, breathing slowly, letting the heat and tumultuousness flow from my body and the physical pain pour in.

Everything hurts but I won't break. I *have* to stay strong for Taig.

Chapter 39
CARYS

"Major Kilkenny requests an audience with Your Highness," Callum calls from behind the door.

"Let him in!" I jump to my feet from my bed where I've been restlessly awaiting news since being whisked away from the ballroom.

Back in his maroon livery, Tiernan rushes into my bedchamber. "Carys," he says breathlessly. Beads of sweat cling to his forehead, and his eyes are wide and frantic.

I've never seen him this flustered, and the sight of the ordinarily calm and collected Tiernan in this state twists my gut.

"I wish I could explain everything, but Alys was arrested just before the Feast," he says. "For treason."

The blood rushes from my face, and I step back.

"Durvla was arrested shortly after. They're both in the brig, both on the docket to be hanged come morning."

"No, no, no, no—" I take another step back, but my knees give out, my arse plopping onto the bed. I press my palms against my eyes. This can't be happening. *Please tell me this is another nightmare.*

"Carys, we have to act fast."

I drop my hands. "What the fuck can *I* do?"

"Save them."

I jump to my feet, staring him down. He makes it sound so easy. I'd gotten Durvla out of the brig by sheer luck last time.

"It wasn't luck when you saved Durvla."

I blink at him—it's as if he read my mind.

"You are the heir to the throne and the queen is unable to make decisions. *You* speak on her behalf. You can pardon Alys and Durvla. You have that power."

"You're wrong. Iywan holds the power. The fucking Council holds the power! All decisions go through them."

"The brig guards don't know that."

We stand there for a moment, face to face, tense silence drawing out between us, then I say, "What would you have me do? Storm into the brig with a quiver of arrows and a bow at the ready? Shoot the guards and break out Durvla and Alys?"

"Order their release. They need to get far away from here. Alys knows where they can go. All you have to do is give them the opportunity."

"But—"

"Durvla is deaf. And—"

I hold my hand up, silencing him. Durvla? Deaf? I stare at Tiernan, ready to tell him he's wrong, but it explains so much about the odd interactions I've had with her. "She can read lips," I say aloud. Tiernan nods. "I see ..." A pang of guilt strikes me for all the times I lost my patience with her.

"She also has a brother who's been identified as an Undesirable. Only five years old. They were going to banish him to the Wastelands and hang Durvla for harboring him."

My stomach clenches. So that's why Durvla was so eager to get back home. She had a little brother to look after. And I was planning to demand that she stay here ...

"You said they *were* going to banish him? Does that mean they aren't anymore?"

"He was rescued. The Forayers were ambushed on the way to Paramount and quite a few captives were rescued. Durvla's friend who's been looking after her brother in her absence wasn't so lucky. He's in the brig right now."

"Let me guess, also sentenced to be hanged tomorrow."

Tiernan nods and everything I'd eaten during the Feast churns in my stomach. I breathe in slowly through my nose and gulp.

"Alright," I groan, smoothing my hair back from my face. I march toward my desk. "If the gods start listening now, that would be wonderful."

Tiernan makes an odd sound between a laugh and a despairing groan. I push aside the pressing guilt and terror weighing on my limbs and start writing.

· · ◦ ☽ ☀ ☾ ◦ · ·

Rubble is strewn around the entrance to the brig, and the air is thick with smoke. I cough and try not to inhale too deeply as we stand at the top of the dark, stony stairs that lead down to the levels below the castle. The groundskeepers, under the watch of the guards, are steadfastly trying to repair the gaping hole in the brick wall.

"Careful," Tiernan mumbles as we turn sideways to walk down the stairs littered with more debris.

The rebels had apparently blown a hole in the wall adjacent to the stairs leading down to the prison cells. They'd ambushed the guards and managed to break several prisoners out before reinforcements from our forces flooded in and put an end to it.

I'm still in my ballgown, my diadem firmly on my head once more. I expect a host of guards at the entrance to the brig, but there are just two standing watch. I guess the others were dispatched to the outside where the attack had occurred.

"Your Highness," the guards murmur, bowing to me as I stand before them with my chin raised.

A large, unsettling woman steps forward. One of her eyes is unseeing, but her stare has the intensity of two fully functioning eyes. She bows to me. "Sergeant Angharad at your service, Your Highness. What brings you here?"

I present a rolled paper with a wax seal to her, and she breaks the seal to read what's within.

"There has been a mistake," I tell her. "Lady Alys Pritchard and Miss Durvla Garrick are loyal staff in my service. There has been no treason committed. Only a misunderstanding. Release them and no further disciplinary action will be taken."

My heart is racing as Sergeant Angharad reads the ordinance that I hurriedly scribbled. The paper is official royal letterhead, but the seal is not quite an official seal. Beside me, Tiernan stands resolute, his hand on the pommel of the sword against his hip.

Sergeant Angharad stares at Tiernan for a moment, and his own glare challenges her. I glance between the two of them, but neither of their faces gives away anything. The guard then steps toward the brig door and opens it. I lock my knees to keep from going limp with relief. "Right this way, Your Highness," she says.

Her strides are long and purposeful, but I keep up with them despite the heels on my feet. The stench and the cries of despair are overwhelming, tugging on my heart and turning my stomach, but I trod on as though unbothered.

This rescue mission is rather easy so far. It's surprising given that Durvla was arrested for hiding her brother, a child who was deemed Undesirable. Worthless. Dispensable. My stomach roils.

We walk past a cell with a tall fellow standing with his forehead pressed against the cell closure. His knuckles are white from the grip he has on the bars. He suddenly pushes off the bars and stands upright as he sees me, but I keep walking. Next to him is Alys. She's sitting on the floor, appearing otherwise undisturbed. When she sees me, a smile lights up her face.

"Princess," she says, getting to her feet. "I knew you'd come through for us."

I keep my features stony, not wanting to give away my utter relief and happiness. Not in front of Sergeant Angharad. "Release her," I say.

The guard nods and yanks a set of iron keys off her belt, opening the gate. As Alys steps out, she curtsies to me and smiles. I do a quick sweep of her figure—she doesn't seem too physically hurt.

We walk a few more cells down and find Durvla sitting on the ground, her arms looped tightly around her legs, her face buried in her knees. "Durvla," I call, but she doesn't move. Gods, I was an idiot for never realizing that she's deaf.

Tiernan draws his sword, and for a horrifying moment I fear he'd do something outrageous, but he simply raps the sword against the bars a couple of times. The clanging echoes loudly through the brig, and Durvla's head flies up. Her stare is unfocused for a moment, but she finally blinks at us. Her face is bruised and so wrought with heartbreak.

"Open the cell," I tell the guard.

"Yes, Your Highness."

Angharad opens the cell, and I step in, crouching in front of Durvla. She squints at me as though I'm unrecognizable. "Shall we get out of here?" I ask.

Her confusion is not lost on me, but I smile to assure her that this isn't a trick.

"The Feast is over. I believe we had a deal?" I try again.

That does the trick, but as she stands, she's so unstable that she has to clutch the bars. It's as if she's forgotten how to walk. I cast an accusatory glance at Sergeant Angharad. "What did you all do to her?"

"Nothing, Your Highness. Just an interrogation."

It doesn't look like *nothing*. I sigh and put an arm around Durvla. Alys joins me on the other side, and together we walk her out of the cell.

"You can let go, Princess," says Tiernan. "I'll hold her up."

I nod and let go, Tiernan taking my place.

"Durvla?" a hoarse voice calls. It's the man in the cell beside Alys's. Durvla doesn't react to his call, of course. I'm suddenly impressed that she managed to conceal her deafness these past weeks.

The bloke calls out to her again and again. His voice breaks under the weight of his desperation, his remorse, as he begs us to talk to her. To apologize. To tell her that he tried his best. His voice claws at my heart. I turn and walk back to him, standing directly in front of his cell. Tears drench his face, joining in the cuts and bruises and the blood, but he quits his hollering and stands straighter.

"You must be Durvla's friend," I whisper.

He nods.

"What is your name?"

"Osheen Oakley." His voice is rough, as though he hasn't had anything to drink in ages.

"Osheen Oakley," I repeat, committing the name to memory. "I cannot get you out of here right now, but I will find a way to break you out."

He nods again, his eyes wide, but I've never seen a man so distraught. I have to find a way to get him out before he's hanged. Somehow.

Chapter 40
CARYS

TIERNAN AND ALYS NAVIGATE the tunnels beneath Paramount as though they've done so a hundred times before. It's a long trek, and Tiernan ends up carrying a disoriented Durvla until, at last, we resurface and stride across the grounds to the stables. A chestnut horse and a shiny black steed await us, packs strapped across each of their backs. The scrawny, blond stableboy smiles and, when Tiernan dismisses him, walks away as though it's just another casual day. A cool breeze billows around us, and heavy clouds illuminated by the waning gibbous moon race by.

Tiernan gently sets Durvla on her feet again. "Remember everything I taught you," he tells her. "Alys will go with you."

Durvla doesn't respond, and Tiernan is still supporting her weight.

My chest aches. "This is ridiculous. She cannot ride a horse in this condition."

Tiernan puts an arm awkwardly around Durvla as she leans into him, her stare vacant. Alys presses a hand to Durvla's upper back with an intensity I've only seen on her face when she's dealing with my mother. A moment later, her hand falls away from Durvla and her focus shifts back and forth between the packs on either horse.

Alys. My confidant, my second mother in a way. She has been a better advisor than Iywan could ever be.

Tiernan saved my life. He's been a stickler for law and order ... until now. He's skilled in all sorts of weaponry, and he has the ruthlessness expected of a Royal Brigade soldier. Without him, I'm not sure whether Durvla and Alys will make it very far, even under the cover of night, and I'll be damned if I help them run from the cauldron right into the fire.

My chest tightens and my eyes sting, but I inhale deeply and hold steadfast as best as I can. Swallowing around my narrowing throat, I fix my eyes on Tiernan. "Go with them," I force myself to say before I change my mind. Before I lose the courage.

His brows draw together. "But Princess—"

"That's an order, Major Kilkenny."

His lips curve into a half smile. "I think I've proven tonight that I don't always follow orders."

Something between a scoff and laugh escapes me, and tears well. "Don't make this harder than it needs to be, Tiernan."

"Carys, there's more you need to know. Pertinent information that could—"

I squeeze his shoulder, shutting him up. "Thank you for your years of service. Now, get them to safety."

His lips part, then close again. "It's been my honor, Princess." He stares at me as if he has more to say, but in the end, he only says, "You're going to make an incredible queen when the time comes."

I choke back a sob and wave him away. "Hurry before some-one comes."

He nods and helps Durvla onto the horse. She's so disoriented that I'm surprised she's able to do much to help herself at all.

Alys tugs me into her arms before I can turn to her, hugging me so tightly that I can't breathe until she lets go. "Dear one," she says, brushing tears off my cheeks with her fingertips. She wraps her arms around me again, lighter this time, and whispers, "I've left a letter for you in the infirmary. There's a vial labelled 'Belladonna' with one of the *L*'s capitalized. It's subtle so you may have to look closely. Break the vial and you'll find a message."

I pull back, frowning as I try to dissect her words.

"Do not tell a soul. Read the note in your chamber and then burn it."

My heart lurches, but I nod.

"Don't run from your memories; reign over them."

There's that line again. I nod again and this time, I'm the one who throws my arms around Alys. "Thank you for everything. Now leave, all of you."

Tiernan sits atop the black stallion now, Durvla in front of him, still discombobulated. I pat her knee as Alys gets onto the mare. I smile tearfully at Durvla. "It's a shame to lose my best dressmaker," I say.

To my surprise, a smile touches her lips as well. "I'd like to think you've gained a friend."

Her words pull at my heart, and my throat swells with tears. Dammit, I need to hold it together. I can only nod as I step back. "Go."

Everything feels wrong as two of the most important people in my life ride away, perhaps forever. Paramount won't be the same without them.

I won't be the same without them.

· · ∘ ☽ ☀ ☾ ∘ · ·

After watching Alys, Tiernan, and Durvla ride away, I return to the castle and hurry straight to my bedchambers. I find Ellynne already there, but she doesn't argue when I dismiss her. Knowing nothing about Osheen Oakley other than his name and relation to Durvla, writing him a pardoning notice is a challenge. It takes me longer than I expected, but I manage.

As soon as I step out of my chamber, I'm approached by Queen's Guards—their black sashes and emblems proudly identifying them. My breath catches as I shove the notice into the pocket of my dress.

"Apologies, Your Highness," says a short woman with a peachy complexion and eyes as dark as Tiernan's. "We've been asked to escort you to the council chamber for an emergency meeting."

My heart plummets, but I nod. With each step, my pulse beats faster, and I have to fight to keep the muscles in my face relaxed. A multitude of people are packed into the concourse, everyone still in their bright Feast attire. The cacophony of voices grates on my senses and I force myself not to slam my hands over my ears and run in the opposite direction.

With the Queen's Guards skirting me, people keep their distance, but there is a sickening amount of genuflecting and greetings that I acknowledge with all the politeness I can muster. We move through the packed forecourt, between the ornate pillars, and into the private west side of the castle. Stepping past the corridor to my mother's room, we take the stairwell up to the council chamber.

From outside the door, panicked voices rise and fall. The Feast food roils in my stomach and my steps falter. As a guard opens the door to the council chamber, I step inside. Iywan paces the front of the space while the other councilors—with the exception of Lady Taliesin who sits with her arms folded—shout at each other.

"Where in Lugda's hells were the brig guards?" Belhan squeaks, his jowls shaking.

I would've laughed at his tone had my heart not jumped into my own throat. Taliesin smirks, her arms still crossed. Who'd have thought the treasurer had a sense of humor?

Iywan continues pacing as if Belhan hadn't *squeaked*.

"Forget the brig guards. Where were the other soldiers?" another voice booms. Tomen's hazy gaze remains pinned on Iywan. "Those rebels should not have gotten beyond the gate!"

Iywan whips his head toward Tomen, and spots me still standing in the open doorway. He stops pacing as everyone goes silent. Sessaley, Taliesin, Jac, Tomen, and Belhan all turn in my direction, and I suppress the urge to step back.

"Your Highness," Iywan says, his tone suddenly light. "Apologies for our behavior."

"That's alright, Lord Iywan. Tonight was frightening. We all have every right to be in a bit of a panic." My pulse pounds in my temples, but the words flow effortlessly. Alys would be proud.

Iywan's face is stony despite his tone, though the other councilors visibly relax, and Tomen sinks into his seat again. I take my place in my mother's seat—it never becomes easier—and steeple my fingers atop the table.

"Tonight was a disgrace," Iywan says. "Several prisoners escaped from the brig including our own head healer who was found guilty of treason for concealing important information from the crown."

He lumped Alys with the escapees, yet he doesn't mention Durvla ... That can't be a coincidence. Does he also know that I played a part in their *escape*? Somehow, I manage to keep my face utterly still, even as shivers slide down my spine.

Iywan eases himself into his seat. "Tonight was one of the largest and most anticipated events in Erleya. It's unacceptable that the rebels were able to get beyond our fortified gates. We will be questioning the brig guards and the other soldiers within the Paramount encampments."

Ask about the Veilguards, my inner voice says, and my back jolts straight.

My brows dip. "What about the Veilguards?"

Iywan scratches his neck and releases a slow breath. "What of them, Princess? They guard Fiada Purlieu, not the brig."

Something within me insists on knowing more, but I ignore the voice in my head and convince my facial muscles to relax.

"At present, we need to keep up appearances. I've offered the diplomats and our guests of honor a longer stay here at the castle. While the rebels are still at large, it would be best for everyone's safety."

Great.

"I've asked the cooks to have some fresh baked goods delivered to our guests," Lady Sessaley chimes in. Silver beads glitter on the bodice of her lilac gown, rivaling the silvery strands of hair that fall in gentle waves over her shoulders.

"That's a wonderful idea, Lady Sessaley," I say.

Iywan clears his throat. "We have dispatched Forayers to take care of the miscreants who escaped."

I swallow hard. "Lord Iywan, kindly have someone bring me a list of every prisoner who escaped tonight."

Iywan blinks rapidly. "Yes, Princess." He shifts in his seat and clasps his hands together atop the table. "How do you propose we handle the attendees still present?"

He expects me to deflect my duties, but not tonight. My heart hiccups. I am not afraid of speaking publicly, but it's odd to be perceived as *the* authority. Yet I remember my mother telling me that in tough times, a great morale booster was always when the leader offered comforting words. "I will be more than happy to make a statement in the concourse, Lord Iywan," I say. "Then we will reconvene in a few days' time when things have simmered down. For now, let us keep our guests happy, yes?"

The councilors agree.

I swallow, so many questions swimming through my mind. Iywan didn't specifically mention Durvla or Tiernan. But the cold stare he has pinned on me says he is very aware of more than he's letting on. I slip my hands beneath the table and smooth them over my skirts. "Thank you all for being level-headed in these frightening times," I say. "The Feast was a wonderful event regardless. We should keep that in the forefront of our guests' minds and not the nasty aftermath. I will be sure to make an announcement shortly."

The councilors murmur various things and Iywan's lip twitches. I'm not sure whether he intends to smile or what. But he nods, stony faced, and I rise from my seat.

The Queen's Guards escort me back the way we came, and as I arrive in the loud concourse that's still packed with far too many people, I point my guards in the direction of the small marble dais between two massive pillars. One of the guards pounds a staff three times against the floor, and the din gradually falls to a semblance of quietude. A person here or there coughs and it echoes in the hall.

"Greetings, one and all!" I project. Gods, I hope years of countless oration lessons come back to memory. I smile at the replies tossed my way. "Tonight, I am filled with gratitude for your presence here in the Fortress on the Mount. The Feast was ... *thrilling*, if I do say so myself."

Quiet laughter totters through the room, and I beam at the hundreds of faces before me.

"We are all safe and sound and very well fed, are we not?"

Murmurs of agreement.

"On top of it all, we look absolutely stunning!"

More laughter, more murmurs of agreement and other pleasant mutterings.

"I am proud of our resilience, and I hope you all enjoy the excellent service and, yes, more delectable food at Paramount Castle. This
small hiccup just means that we get to enjoy the festivities a tad longer.
Tomorrow, the sun rises again and so shall we all."

"So shall we all!" the crowd echoes.

"Enjoy your stay!" I shout over applause and gleeful chatter.

I exhale as I step off the small platform. Nearby, Iywan's arms
are folded tightly across his fancy robes. I'm hardly able to gauge his
expression before the Queen's Guards flank me again.

"To your bedchamber?" the woman guard asks.

"Yes, indeed," I respond.

When I finally arrive at my room, a lanky guard with brown skin
and short-cropped hair is already standing at my door. I blink as
Ren's dark eyes settle on my face. He bows deeply. "Welcome back,
Your Highness."

My throat is too tight, so I simply smile, nod dismissively to the
Queen's Guards, and step into my room as Ren holds the door open
for me. As soon as I'm inside, I ring for Ellynne and Lowri.

Once I'm bathed and changed into my nightgown, Ellynne and Lowri
take their leave, and I climb into bed. Moments later, a knock on the
door is followed by Ren calling out to me, "There is a scroll here for
your perusal, Your Highness."

A frown tugs at my lips for a moment before I figure out what Ren is referring to. I leap out of bed and run toward the door, grabbing my dressing gown to throw over my nightwear. As I pull the door open, Ren extends a rolled parchment to me.

I open it in front of him. *Many* names are listed including Alys Pritchard, Durvla Garrick and, after much searching, Osheen Oakley. My heart skips a beat. That doesn't make any sense. There were two explosions only and that was during the Feast. How could he have escaped?

As I reroll the scroll I stare up at Ren. "Do you know the details of tonight's rebel attack?"

Ren's dark brows draw close, and he turns away for a moment. When he nods, I step aside, allowing him to enter my bedchamber. The door closes softly behind him and he remains rigid, a soldier at full attention.

"You are a man of few words, Sir Ren, but I get the inkling that you know a lot more than you disclose. I am trying to be the best ruler I can be, but with the Council and my own advisor constantly leaving me in the dark ..." I breathe out harshly and pace for a moment. Turning back to him, I step close enough that he draws in a breath but doesn't exhale.

His dark brown eyes focus on my face, every muscle frozen. "A renowned rebel sympathizer by the name of Kenna Gallagher was apprehended. There was to be a hanging held in the square, but somehow rebels appeared just below the Paramount plateau and broke through the brig walls with explosives."

My jaw goes slack. "What do you mean *appeared?*"

Ren shrugs. "I've been told it was like ... magic, Your Highness." His voice wavers, then trails off.

"That's preposterous."

"I would say the same." He gnaws on his lip. "There have been a lot of odd happenings, Princess."

He could say that again.

My lips part, the question on the tip of my tongue, but I close my mouth forcefully. Ren raises a brow, and I scrub my hand over my face. With a harsh exhalation I tap the scroll against my open palm.

Ask, my inner voice prompts.

"Do you know anything about the Veilguards?"

I swear redness spreads up his neck. He clears his throat but doesn't say anything.

"*Sir Ren.*" My voice comes out sharp and so authoritative that I surprise even myself.

"Your Highness, I took a vow. I cannot."

I step closer to him, and he turns his face down to the ground. "Alright," he says tightly. "Alright." He breathes deep, his chest sinking in on the exhale as he lifts his head. "There are no Veilguards."

My stomach drops. "What?" Surely, he must be delusional.

"The Veil was opened here at Paramount about a thousand years ago, right? But it's been inactive for centuries. No magic. No monsters. All just ... myth by now. So those who were traditionally conscripted for what used to be the Veilguards are ... redistributed."

My entire forehead hurts from frowning.

A muscle twitches in Ren's cheek for a moment before he speaks again. "There are other clandestine positions within the Royal Brigade unknown even to us. But it's all rumored. Some say they're sent to guard another Veil elsewhere. Some believe they're dispatched to the Wastelands, not for banishment but, well ... to keep the banished away. Some say they're simply ..." He makes a line across his throat with his finger.

I blink at him, my jaw dropping.

"But again, it's all rumored." He raises his hands as though pleading innocence. "I have said far too much, and again, I've taken a vow—"

"Ren, I promise I won't say a thing. Thank you."

Chapter 41
DURVLA

TAIG IS ALIVE. ALYS overheard a few guards back in the brig: Rebels ambushed the Forayers escorting prison wagons to Paramount. Taig and a few others had been rescued, but Osheen had not. It was shortly before the attack on the brig and my arrest. Osheen hadn't known a thing about Taig's fate.

Leaving Paramount was surprisingly easy with a knight in tow; no one at the gate suspected a thing—I'm certain they'll pay for that. Leaving Osheen behind feels wrong, but after Carys had already put her name on the line to ensure our escape, it was too risky.

Hours later, as we ride into Barr na Cahar, heavy drops beat upon the cobblestones, and our horses dash through intermittent puddles. We stop just on the outside of the city, in an area thick with bushes, as the rain subsides.

"We can't stay still for long," Kilkenny says after he helps me down from Ghendor.

The stallion huffs like he's happy to be rid of our weight on his back. I can't blame him.

My fingers are numb from the cold rain, matching my emotions. I nod at Kilkenny and rub my hands together, trying to get some sensation back into them after we all take turns relieving ourselves in the bushes and mount our horses again. As we set off once more, my head reels as the events of the past few hours catch up with me, coursing through my body like poison. I start to shiver, uncontrolled; so much so that Tiernan halts Ghendor, and Alys does the same with Mirren.

We dismount again, and for the life of me, I can't stop the quaking that rattles my body or the nausea that makes my mouth water unpleasantly.

Kilkenny puts an arm around me. "What's happening to her?"

I stare at his mouth. The question isn't for me, and I miss whatever Alys says in response, but the two escort me off the main road to sit on the wet grass. More water soaks into my clothing, though I'm already drenched anyway—we all are—and I regret having taken my shoes off back at the palace.

Alys crouches in front of me. "You're in shock." Her signs are gentle. Maybe nothing should surprise me by now, but I blink and stare at her hands as though I've never seen signed language before. "You're just coming down from a lot of heightened emotions."

A short burst of humorless laughter escapes me.

Kilkenny starts to say something, when suddenly he draws his sword as he jumps to his feet. My heart hammers in my chest, but there's no way I can stand right now. Alys does it for me, facing another traveler who dismounts a drenched brown horse in the middle of the cobblestone road.

For a moment, I fear that we've been caught. Already! But as the figure walks toward us, I recognize the auburn hair, darkened by rainwater, sticking to his bruised face.

"I'm Durvla's friend from Cluain Baile," he swiftly motions to Kilkenny and Alys.

Kilkenny stares him down, as if memorizing the signed words, but he doesn't put his sword away.

I stare at Osheen, and emotion slowly resurfaces through my numb state. I struggle to my feet and take awkward steps toward my oldest friend. My most trusted companion, the one who's always been there for me. The one who risked everything to look after the person who means the most to me in this unjust kingdom.

Then I'm running, and Osheen is running toward me. I throw myself into his arms with the little strength I have left, and he wraps his around me, his chin resting atop my head. His chest rumbles slightly as he says something.

I step out of his embrace at last and ask, "How did you get away so soon?"

"The princess," he says with a pained smile. "She promised she'd find a way to set me free. I don't know how she did it, but she managed as soon as you all left."

True laughter escapes me now. "That's brilliant!"

Kilkenny, however, appears dubious. He sheathes his sword and asks, "How is that possible?"

Osheen shrugs his broad shoulders. "She just ... let me out."

"How do we know we can trust you?" Kilkenny asks.

I frown at him. "This is *Osheen*," I say, as though it means something to this soldier-turned-knight-turned-accomplice. "I'd trust him with my *life*. With my brother's life." I feel my voice break and a fresh wave of sadness washes over Osheen's bruised face.

Osheen digs into his pocket and pulls something out. "She told me to show you this." He holds up a small, circular jewelry piece with a sunburst on one end. A decorative wristlet.

Kilkenny steps closer, squinting at it. Then he straightens, his lips pursed, and his head tilted. "That *is* Carys's," he signs at last. "She used to wear it a lot more a few years ago." He wrinkles his brow as he angles his face to Osheen again. "She *gave* this to you?"

Osheen nods.

"Keep it safe. Maybe we can return it to her someday," Kilkenny tells Osheen. He looks at me in particular, signing as he speaks to everyone else. "I'm sure Lord Iywan isn't going to be happy when he discovers us all missing. I know how we can throw anyone off our scent, but we need to get back on the road."

Osheen scratches his chin then slips the wristlet into his pocket before running his palms over his trousers. I'm equally daunted knowing that there may be forces after us.

Kilkenny gestures widely to get my attention, then signs, "Alright, clan. Let's go find Taig."

Chapter 42
CARYS

IN THE MORNING, I'M able to make it to the infirmary. It's suspiciously empty, especially as I've asked Callum to wait outside of the chamber for me. But it gives me the opportunity to peruse the shelves for the vial that Alys instructed me to take. I lift each vial, one at a time, reading the names on them. St. John's Wort, Chamomile, Patchouli, Belladonna—this one is written correctly—Henbane, Hemlock, Lavender, Wormwood, Mint … and, at last, BelLadonna. *Found you.*

I slip the vial into my pocket just as the door shuts behind me, and I jump so hard that my shoulder nudges the shelf, a few vials falling out and shattering on the floor. "Shit," I mumble. I turn to the healer who's just walked in. Bloody Briony … I wish I could throw a vial of Belladonna at her.

"Your Highness," she says sweetly, curtsying. "I'm sorry, but Lady Alys isn't here."

"I know," I say. "I just came to get something for a headache."

"Oh, let me get that for—"

"No need. I've gotten what I came for. You may"—I'm already heading to the door—"get back to whatever it is you need to do."

She curtsies again. "Thank you, Your Highness." Her overly sweet voice grates on my nerves, but I smile tightly at her and walk out of the infirmary, joining Callum.

"Got your tincture?" he asks.

"I did."

Once back at my bedchamber, I head to the balcony and fish the vial out of my pocket. It's tiny, fitting in the palm of my hand, so I have no clue how Alys claims to have left a letter in it. Smash it, she'd said. So, I do, dropping it onto the floor of my balcony.

The glass breaks, leaving behind a rolled parchment that is too large to have been inside the tiny vial. My eyes must be deceiving me ... I crouch and wrap my hands around the parchment. It is real, full-sized. My heart stutters in my chest.

With shaky hands, I open the parchment and smile at Alys's beautiful, elaborate penmanship.

Dearest Carys,

I cannot apologize enough for telling you all of this through written word. I waited for the right moment but ran out of time faster than anticipated. Your mother thought it was important that you remembered certain details on your own, and I regret not disobeying her requests because there is so much that you need to know.

My dear, magic does exist. Mages are not extinct. They are hiding in plain sight. As history often repeats itself, there are forces at work, attempting to purge our people from this realm.

I pause. *Our* people?

Your mother's illness is incurable. I believe if it were not for whatever potion or enchantment is keeping her alive, she would have passed from this realm. I am not sure why they're keeping her alive, but it may be because they've somehow discovered her powers. Luckily, they don't seem to know about yours.

What?

Someone in the fortress may be able detect magic. For that reason, you need to be very careful. The amulet around your neck is a power dampener and may be keeping you shielded. As much as your mother wanted you to remove it, don't. I've taught you grounding in hopes that I could eventually help you learn to control your flamewielding, but we never got the chance. I am very sorry for that.

Images flash in my mind. The space around me burning, my mother's hand on mine, quelling the fire within. My breath catches in my throat, and I swallow thickly. Icy dread snakes down my spine. It can't be … I hurriedly absorb the last paragraphs of Alys's letter.

I wish I could explain more, but this is the best I can tell you for now. As for your marriage,

K. V. MEADOWS

choose someone outside of Erleya. Someone less likely to give in to Iywan and the Council's ways. If you fall into danger, speak to Angharad, the brig guard. She'll know how to get you out of there, but it would have to be a last resort.

Dear one, dark times are upon us, but you can be the light.

With unyielding love,
Elviera A.

My blood runs cold, and my hand flies to the amulet around my neck. It warms to my touch as it always does.

Because I have damn flames coursing through my veins.

It should be farfetched, but deep down, I know it's true. The air becomes too thin, my breathing too quick. I stride back into my chamber and toward the fireplace. Moments later, the paper curls and disintegrates in the fire, burning all evidence of Alys's words.

Remember what happened to Aneirin. My mother's voice plays in my head.

My mind reels, and I'm five years old again.

"Toss me a sword!" I yell to Aneirin.

He chuckles, the sound deep in his chest. I wasn't used to his deep voice just yet, but he was getting older. Occasionally, it still cracked, but I hated that he was growing up and leaving me behind to be treated like a weak little girl. "What?" he asks.

"Toss me a sword, come on!"

He tosses me a wooden play sword.

I jump aside and let it clatter to the floor. Annoyance burns through me as I stare at him. "A real sword."

"Why on earth would you want a real sword, sweet sister?"

I hold my head up proudly. "Because I'm going to be a warrior."

Aneirin laughs again. "You most certainly will not. You will be a queen."

I march toward him, rage flaring. "Take that back!" I shove him as hard as I can, my hands connecting with his middle, but he barely budges.

He holds his sword out, his arms wide open, afraid he'll accidentally hurt me. Or more likely, that I'll hurt myself. "Are you having big feelings again?"

Big feelings—it was a patronizing euphemism for my mood swings. "I am not!"

He regards me as though I'm a wounded pet in need of tending to. "Are you cross with me, then?"

It's not him in particular that I'm cross with. It's the conversations I've overheard: the talks of my future marriages, strangers plotting my betrothals to outsiders. It's my tutors insisting that I learn embroidery and harp, and that I ride sidesaddle in a stupid dress. It's the pressure to be a perfect, demure princess who wouldn't be able to defend myself against Dark Mages and Shadow Wielders like the heroes in my book.

Instead, I'm only allowed to watch my brother as he trains. He's the best in the fortress. So fearless. So fearsome. I want to be just like him. I want to feel strong and fearless and fearsome. Not weak and angry and sad all the time. Not useless.

I snatch the sword from him, ready for him to take me seriously, ready to prove I'm a worthy adversary. But the sword is heavier than I anticipated and though I grasp the hilt with both hands, the blade dives forward, pulling me with its weight. I nearly lose my balance, but I manage to right myself.

I beam at Aneirin with pride, and he laughs. Laughs! His head thrown back, the free, taunting sound fills the training room. The sound infiltrates my mind. Heat prickles my skin.

My brother, who I adore and admire more than anyone else, doesn't take me seriously.

I'm sick of it!

"Enough!" I scream. With all the pent-up emotions of the entire day, I throw my arms out, pitching the sword.

Flames burst from my hands, a wide sweeping arc consuming everything and sending me flying backward.

The last thing I remember is Aneirin screaming in agony.

I find myself on the floor of my bedchamber, plopped back into my present reality. My body trembles with the effort to expel the memories along with the contents of my stomach, and I dig my nails into the floor as I dry heave uncontrollably.

The realization tears at my heart, guilt and revulsion clawing up my throat. I retch again and dissolve into sobs that I can't stop.

I can't breathe.

I can't breathe.

I can't—

A series of knocks from the door sound in my ear, and it's so urgent, I'm certain it's not the first time they've knocked. A voice calls to me, distant through the roar of my pulse in my ears. Then there's an arm around me and Ellynne's soothing voice. "Carys, what is it? Are you hurt?"

I lift my face to Ellynne's, and my sight is so blurry that I can only make out her fiery hair.

Fiery ...

I pull away from her and scurry back on my arse, my chest heaving. "No," is all I can grind out.

She holds her hands up. She's harmless, only wanting to help. "Talk to me."

What can I possibly say to her? That I'm an abomination? A monster? That I killed my brother and that I'm a danger to everyone around me?

"Let me just ... give you a hug or something. You look a fright."

Unable to respond, I stare at her. But her arms wrap around me again, her hand gently rubbing my back. "Whatever it is, you can tell me. Did someone hurt you? Is it Callum? Eefa? I'll gut the bastards."

In another time, I would've laughed. But I just shake my head. "No," I say, my voice sounding raw. "It's me. It's always been me."

Chapter 43
DURVLA

EVERYTHING THAT I'VE EVER known has been a lie. Not only do Mages like Kilkenny exist, but so do Wielders who can bend the elements. I can't fathom a human truly shooting flames or lightning from their hand—such occurrences are the things of myths and legends. Yet Kilkenny can speak into my mind, and Alys can mend wounds and some illnesses with the touch of her hand.

Osheen had gone bone white when Alys mended his broken nose, and even whiter when I told him that I also had powers. I choose to ride with him rather than Kilkenny anyway. We've been friends for as long as I can remember—I *should* feel more comfortable with him. Riding with him should be the more natural thing to do.

Still, the image of his horrified face lingers in my mind. It doesn't help that my own powers are a mystery to me; Kilkenny and Alys aren't willing to divulge the details until we're in a safe place.

As if this all isn't mind-jarring enough, both Alys and Kilkenny are involved in the rebellion in some way. Another thing they won't discuss until we're sure no one can overhear us.

We gallop through the torrential downpour, our horses' hooves sluicing through the mud as we flee Mainland. My heart constricts as we ride far away from the friends I've made—farther from my home in Cluain Baile and toward the unguarded bridge on the western side of Erleya. We cross the bridge, riding into the Grounds, staying just outside the borders of Fiada Purlieu. Apparently, not many people would dare to wander so close to the Veil to the Otherworld.

My body is a discordance of aches and muddled thoughts as I'm the last to dismount, clambering off Osheen's horse, Ffion. Everything buzzes within me, as though we're still fiercely riding across the land, even as the forest ground sucks my feet into the mud. I have to pull my knees up ridiculously high with each step as I make my way toward a large, mossy boulder nestled between two thick tree trunks.

Kilkenny, Alys, and Osheen also have to regain their footing after riding without rest for so long. They all stretch stiffly before Kilkenny finally speaks up.

"We cannot stay for too long," he signs. "But we should rest for a little while."

Kilkenny's plan is to ride along the coast as far as the forest will take us before we're forced back to civilization. Hopefully it's enough to throw any Forayers off our trail and buy us some time before making our way to his hometown in Dubh Carrig.

"I'm going to make sure no one's followed us," he says, focused on me. "How is that dampener treating you?"

I glance down at the leather bracelet around my wrist. I'd almost forgotten about it. "Fine," I say as I scoot backward on the mossy rock and pull my knees to my chest. My soaked clothes stick to my body, sending shivers of cold through me that make my teeth chatter. A throbbing pain on one side of my head and face slowly makes its way to the forefront, besting every other ache within me. Nausea roils my stomach, and I swallow hard.

Kilkenny stares at me, concern etched between his brows. "Even though you're wearing the dampener again … let me know if anything changes, yes?" he signs.

I nod numbly. In my attempt to stop shivering, I prop my chin atop my knees and squeeze my arms even tighter around my legs. Kilkenny hesitates for a moment, rooted to his spot before he turns to walk away.

Osheen approaches me, running his fingers through his damp hair and spraying water onto my face. I wince and he immediately apologizes. "How are you faring?" he signs. "I mean … you have magic … Do you feel any different?"

Yes. "No."

"That's … good."

Then why are you being so awkward about it?

I inhale shakily, afraid to open fresh wounds when I've only just calmed from the storm of emotions—finding out that Taig was captured, then rescued, and somewhere on the road to safety. Hopefully. But I have to know. I tentatively sign, "After the Forayers took me away … what happened next?"

Osheen's shoulders tense, rising slightly. "I had to tell Ma and Granny about Taig."

My stomach drops. It isn't necessarily a surprise, but after so many years of keeping my brother's existence a secret—even from the people who'd taken me under their wings—it just feels … odd. "I understand," I sign.

"I didn't know how else to make it work. I stayed at your place—with your home empty, no one complained about me claiming it—and

Ma brought over food as often as she could. Granny stayed with Taig while I was out in the fields where Finn accompanied me."

My heart swells with relief. Taig had someone with him at all times? It's ... unfathomable. Amazing. And my sweet Finn. It's good to know that he's alright. "I'm grateful. How did they react when you told them about Taig?"

"Granny seemed unsurprised, and Ma was ... well ... not the happiest that you'd kept it from them. She says they would've dropped everything to help."

Annoyance leaks into my gratitude, leaving me bewildered. "I don't regret keeping him hidden. It was for the best." I gesture at our surroundings, my hands trembling from the cold. *"This* is what I was trying to prevent. I never wanted to put you or your family in danger."

"They're fine, Durvla."

"You were almost hanged! They could've suffered the same fate." They still can. I shove the nausea away.

His brows pinch together, his face tensing. At last, he unclenches his jaw, relaxing his face. "I don't want to argue."

I clasp my numb hands together.

Osheen has been the person I've trusted more than anyone else in the world. Since my parents' passing, at least. He's put his life on the line for Taig, for me. He's been caught and it was my fault.

A chill rises within me, threading along my arms, only to abruptly end. I let out a huff of air, my throat closing, my head flaring with pain. As I press my palm to my forehead, Osheen takes a step toward me, his arm outstretched.

Then he seems to reconsider.

"Do you feel an episode coming?" he signs. His struggle to hide his panic is painfully obvious.

I look at him with one eye closed, wincing. "No ..." I motion. This is different. Maybe it has something to do with the dampener. I blink and open both eyes, resisting the urge to squint as I stare down at my bracelet. "I'm fine," I mumble aloud to Osheen, my focus still on the dampener.

He gently waves his hand to draw my attention, and I turn to him, waiting for him to say something. After a tense moment of wordlessness, he signs, "If we find Taig, the three of us ... we should flee Erleya. Build a life together elsewhere."

I blink at him, combing through his words in my mind. *Flee Erleya?* "*If?*" I ask aloud. Perhaps too loudly, because Alys glances over from where she's been stroking Mirren's ecru mane. I turn to Osheen again, returning to silent signing. "There's no *if*. We are *going* to find Taig." And then I intend to stay put; I am already tired of fleeing.

"It's good to have hope but ..."

I press my tongue against the roof of my mouth to keep from saying something hurtful to the man who's looked after Taig in my absence. Until he was caught, of course. But this whole fantasy he has of us fleeing Erleya together is not my desire. I don't know what will come next once I find Taig. We're ultimately heading toward a place where the rebels dwell; only the gods know what will come of that.

I fiddle with the leather of my bracelet, running my finger over it. My mother gave me this bracelet when I was very young and made sure I understood that it was not to be taken off. I've never questioned it. Never had to. I've always assumed it was valuable, and she feared that I'd lose it.

Who would've thought that she feared I'd lose *control?*

For three days, we lie low in the forests close to the Veil, before we set off toward Dubh Carrig. The foliage seems sparse even for spring—the pine trees appear emaciated, oaks and other deciduous trees barely blooming. Strange …

One week drags by—forest turns to flatlands, dirt roads replace brick roads then morph into winding, grassy pathways. We ride through rolling green hills with majestic black mountains all around us.

I tug my fur-lined cape, stolen from a clothesline, tighter around my neck. A cold gust of wind sweeps into the valley, and I tighten my arms around Osheen's middle, pressing my face against his back. Kilkenny rides along beside us and I swear there's a flash of something like discontentment across his face.

He becomes increasingly broody the closer we get to his child-hood home in Dubh Carrig. It's the only true stop we have planned on the way to the rebellion base in the Verge. I'm unsettled, but I keep my mind on the thought of wrapping my arms around Taig again.

Overhead, thick, dark clouds roll through the dimming sky. A surprisingly decent road stretches out before us and soon, we're walking between rows of brick houses, workshops, and forges. The scents of metal and smoke cling to the air. Beside us, Kilkenny sits even straighter in Ghendor's saddle. He glances sidelong at me, his face drawn.

"Welcome to Dubh Carrig," he signs.

All the houses in this valley are built identically—one story of crude black brick and gambrel roofs of stone and steel. The homes blend into the backdrop of the black hills surrounding the village. Still, they each have a touch of something unique.

Kilkenny dismounts Ghendor as drizzle chills my skin. The cottage before us has a door with a knocker welded into the shape of a bull's head. Massive horns curl out from either side, and there's a ring through its nose.

My legs and rump are sore from the last ten days of nearly constant riding, my back aches, and my first few steps on the gravel walkway are unsteady. Alys and Osheen appear similarly afflicted, but Kilkenny—of course—appears unbothered.

He smiles at the knocker as we approach. "We've always called my sister bull-headed," he signs.

The pride that briefly gleams through his mask when he speaks about his sister is touching. The only thing he's told us about her before now is that, at twenty, she's seven years his junior.

Raindrops begin to seep into my cape and a gale whips curls around my face as Kilkenny grabs the bull's nose ring and raps it three times against the door. Moments later, the door swings in and a petite young woman stands in the doorway, her very presence rivaling the storm brewing out here.

Her eyes are dark in the candlelight, angular and slender like Kilkenny's, but deeper set. She shares his high cheekbones, but unlike the warm undertone of his complexion, hers is like moonlight. Her straight hair falls to her shoulders, colored muted blue from her roots, then darkening to deep brown from midway to tips. Something like recognition crosses her face and she steps forward, not even flinching when the intensifying rain showers down on her.

"Tiernan?" she asks.

Kilkenny swallows and nods, his throat working as if he wants to say something but doesn't know what. "Hi, Cloda," he says at last. He starts to smile, hesitantly.

Then his head snaps to the side from the force of a slap.

Chapter 44
DURVLA

THE PETITE WOMAN'S HAND is still raised, rings on her middle finger, index, and thumb. That slap *had* to hurt. I fear she's about to go in for another slap when Kilkenny steps back and puts his hands up to block her onslaught. The young woman squints at him and then at the rest of us as though she's only just noticed our presence. There's no remorse on her face, only ire. She tucks her hair back, revealing several small, metallic rings around the outer shell of her ears. As Kilkenny presses his hand to his reddening cheek, the woman folds her arms over her chest.

"Alright," he says at last, the tension pulling even tighter between him and the young woman. "May we come in?"

"No." There's nothing on her face nor in her body language that suggests she'll change her mind.

"Cloda," Kilkenny says.

"I go by Chiyoko now."

Kilkenny's brows are high, but he nods. "Chiyoko," he says. He turns and fingerspells her name for me.

Chiyoko's eyes widen, lips slightly parted.

Kilkenny introduces Osheen, Alys, and me to Chiyoko as well. I'm touched that he's picked up on the unique signs we use for our names. "They all escaped the brig under Paramount. We're heading to the Verge for sanctuary."

The ire in Chiyoko's eyes melts into curiosity. She unfolds her arms and lets them fall to her sides. After one last glance at each of us, she steps aside to let us in. I sigh with relief as we enter the warmth of the humble dwelling. After more than a week on the road, this cottage feels as extravagant as the castle.

A small fireplace, a few threadbare armchairs, and a shaggy woven carpet over a terribly scratched wooden floor make up the cozy room. A woman with straight grey hair down to the nape of her neck steps into the space, a hand behind her back. Eyes identical to Chiyoko's analyze the scene, and as they settle on Kilkenny, it takes a moment before recognition takes hold. Her hand flies to her gaping mouth and her chest expands with a deep breath.

"Hello, Mam," Kilkenny says with a wavering smile followed by a small, respectful bow.

Despite her short stature, his mother closes the gap between them with four long strides and wraps her slender arms around him tightly. When she pulls away, her hands rest on his shoulders as she peers up at him, eyes brimming with tears. The hilt of a dagger peeks out from the back of her trouser waistband, and my heart lurches at the realization that this woman could've probably killed us on sight if she wanted to.

She turns to Alys, and they greet each other with warm familiarity, a swift hug and a kiss on each cheek. Osheen and I observe from a short distance, the space between us annoyingly tense. Kilkenny and his mother approach us before I have time to dwell on my relationship with Osheen, and Kilkenny introduces us. "This is my mam, Haruka."

"Welcome," Haruka gestures. "Please forgive my signing. I'm a little out of practice."

I smile at her. "No need to apologize. I appreciate even the effort."

"I know how lonely it can be." She pauses, then continues motioning as she recalls the signs from memory. "My father was deaf before he died. Chiyo took a very long time to speak but she learned some signs from my father. He learned from a friend. So that's how we communicated for a while. Only within our home, of course."

Of course.

"Where's Da?" Kilkenny asks.

Haruka frowns. "Currently far away in Ballygort. On a special assignment. I'm afraid you'll miss him."

Kilkenny's shoulders sag.

We all take turns changing out of our wet clothing, and a while later, as I return to the sitting room from the bathing chamber, Kilkenny is still there talking to Haruka. He glances at me over his shoulder, his face unreadable as usual.

I have so many questions. About this stop, his family dynamic, my powers, his … But I don't have the energy. My sore body sinks into one of the worn armchairs. If I never ride a horse again, it'd be great, but I remind myself that this comfort is only temporary.

As I lean back against the cushion, I catch Kilkenny's gaze on me again, a crease forming between his brows. "All good?" he signs.

I barely have the energy to lift my arms, so I risk a worsening headache and nod gently. I've forgotten to take the tincture, but I'm not leaving this seat.

The concern disappears from his face, and he turns back to Haruka, says something, then heads toward the bathing chamber.

The next thing I know, someone is nudging my shoulder. It's Chiyoko, a steaming cup in her hands. Behind her, Alys is spreading out blankets on the floor. "I've brought you some chamomile tea," says Chiyoko. She sets it down on a small circular accent table beside the chair.

"Thank you." I sit upright.

"You're welcome. So, are you *fully* deaf?"

The question comes out of nowhere, but there is only curiosity on her face, no ill intent. "I am," I reply.

"Were you born deaf?"

"No. I fell severely ill when I was thirteen and it left me with an ailment that's grown worse over the last … decade. Hearing loss was part of it. At first, sounds slowly faded, then they just ceased to exist."

Kilkenny walks back into the sitting room in only a loose tunic and trousers. The sleeves are rolled back, leaving his powerful forearms exposed for a second before he tugs the fabric over an inked design on his skin. His feet are bare, his hair still damp and unbound, falling to just above his shoulders where a towel is draped. He still hasn't shaved the facial hair that's grown over the eleven days of travel, but the look works for him. I do a doubletake. I've only ever seen him in his guard livery or riding gear. There's something oddly … intimate about seeing him this way.

I am compelled to turn away, but at the same time, I don't want to.

Chiyoko tilts her head back into my range of vision. I startle but she doesn't react. "Is that why you were in the brig?"

I frown at her, having lost track of our conversation. Kilkenny crosses behind her, heading toward Alys to help with the bedding.

"Don't they normally send Undesirables to the Wastelands?" Chiyoko asks me.

Kilkenny's head snaps to her, and he shouts something—her name, I believe.

She regards him briefly before turning back to me, ensuring that I can read her lips. "Relax, Tiernan, I'm just stating it as *they* see it."

"That doesn't mean you have to use the term."

I stare at his hands and then at Chiyoko as she rolls her eyes so hard that I half expect them to pop out of her head.

Kilkenny huffs out a breath and stalks away, trading places with Alys.

"Sorry to eavesdrop," Alys signs. She lowers herself into the armchair perpendicular to the one I'm in and angles herself to me so I can see her hands without effort. "I know we're short on time, but I can try to lessen your headache and dizziness for longer than the tincture can. If you'd like that, of course."

Chiyoko gives me a pointed look that clearly says, *that sounds amazing,* but for some reason, my gut twists. The younger woman smiles and walks off, giving us privacy.

I turn to Alys again and lift my hands, hesitating. "You … can do that?"

"With an ailment like yours, it isn't as simple as healing a headache that doesn't have a long-term cause. I'm so sorry you've endured this for a decade now." There's compassion on her face. "It would take many long sessions over a few days to pause your symptoms for a while. But one session will at least give you a day of no headaches or dizziness. I'm not sure about your balance, but with less dizziness …"

It's probably nonsensical to say no to a quick session, but it feels wrong to say yes. Taig has had so many challenges, yet there's no magical *pause* for his struggles. Tears sting my eyes.

Alys tilts her head, a gentle smile on her full lips. "You don't have to say yes," she motions. "But think about it. No pressure."

I force a smile onto my face. "Thank you, Alys."

Chapter 45
DURVLA

BY DAYLIGHT, THE WHOLE household gathers in the small kitchen. I sit with my hands enveloping a mug of hot tea, Kilkenny across the table from me, and Alys and Haruka on either side. Chiyoko leans back against the counter, her hands busy with a small metal figurine and a paintbrush. Osheen stands a short distance from her, his focus drifting to the work in her hands every now and then.

It's bizarre being among so many with varying degrees of sign knowledge, but heartwarming as well. Haruka and Chiyoko are fairly decent, though they don't sign consistently. Kilkenny has become increasingly fluent and makes an effort to always sign for my understanding. Alys has mentioned having plenty of practice with patients in the safety of their homes. And there's Osheen who knows nearly as much as I do.

Haruka waves her hand to get my attention, and I draw my focus to her. "So, what exactly brings you all here?" she asks, signing as she glances around the table. "Or rather, how did the three of you end up in the brig?"

"Garrick was apprehended from her home on suspicion of theft," Kilkenny answers. "She'd made a dress—"

He stops speaking abruptly and his attention shifts to Chiyoko. "Could you let her speak for herself?" Chiyoko asks irritably.

I'm mildly tickled. "No, it's fine," I tell her, but Kilkenny remains speechless. "Well, alright … It was Quarterly Raid night, and the For-ayers found a dress I'd been working on." A dress I'll never see again. Sadness tugs at me, but I push it away. "They assumed it was stolen, but somehow Princess Carys got her hands on it and recruited me from the brig to be her dressmaker. I made her Feast dress."

Chiyoko's jaw drops. "You made her *Feast dress?*"

I smile and nod.

"You, a Grounder, made a dress for one of the most important events of *Mainland.* And the princess's dress, nonetheless! Bloody impressive!"

My smile widens, a tiny bud of pride loosening the tightness in my chest. "Thank you."

She nods and turns her attention back to her work, dipping the small paintbrush into a little container on the counter and making precise strokes on her metal statuette.

"Alright, so what about Osheen?" asks Haruka.

We bring her up to speed on the events that led up to both our arrests, including Alys's—for which she was given no reason other than treason, no elaboration. Haruka turns to me, curious. "So Tiernan tells me you're a Dreamwalker."

I glance at Kilkenny. "So he says, but I don't know how it works."

"You can enter the dreams of others," says Haruka. "See what they see, feel what they feel. For someone who's not been able to practice and hone their powers, it's natural to not be able to control it just yet."

Carys and Callum pop into my mind, and I immediately force the imagery away and focus on what Haruka is saying.

"A practiced Dreamwalker can also interact with the person dreaming, and sometimes, influence their dreams. It's called dream-weaving. There are also certain Mages able to distort another person's dreamscape or even what they see while they're awake."

Gods … that's terrifying. And so wrong.

"Have you had any strange experiences with dreams lately? When you weren't wearing the dampener?" Haruka asks.

Clearly, Kilkenny or Alys already caught her up on the bizarre magic things.

Again, I push away the vulgar Callum-Carys dream and the menacing Kilkenny dream. I glance at him, and he averts his gaze. My heart sinks.

Haruka is still waiting for a response, so I clear my throat. "Apologies, yes … Well, I often can hear in my dreams, which is already strange. But when I dreamt about Queen Morwenna, the Good, she said something directly to me."

"What did she say?" Alys asks.

"I'm not sure. Something in a different language. Somewhat familiar, like I've heard it before, but I didn't understand it."

The three around the table exchange expressions of an unspoken understanding between them. I shift uneasily in my seat. Osheen appears as confused as I feel, while Chiyoko sets her paintbrush and statuette down before leaning in attentively.

I wipe my clammy hands on my trousers before asking, "Should I be concerned?" Disquiet prickles my skin.

Haruka smiles a tad hesitantly. "No. It has just been ages since any of us met a Dreamwalker."

A tiny huff of nervous laughter slips past my lips. "Until the night of the Feast, I thought magic was just folklore. Everyone in my village believes that magic can only exist through objects. I thought Mages were purged from Erleya centuries ago."

"That's what most believe," says Haruka. "And, on the surface, it does appear that way. But look around." She smiles and sweeps her hand in a circle.

"I thought powers were inherited. Neither of my parents had powers, as far as I know."

Chiyoko steps closer, leaning her forearms against the back of the chair where her mother sits. "Sometimes it skips a generation ... or a person," she says. "Like me. Both of our parents are Mages of different powers and Tiernan is an Amalgam; he got powers from each of our parents. It's like he took both powers for himself and left me Ordinary. Selfish bastard since birth, obviously." She smirks bitterly.

Pain flashes across Kilkenny's face for a heartbeat, but he presses his lips together and doesn't face his sister.

"Wait, powers from each parent?" I regard Kilkenny as if I'm seeing him for the first time. I can still remember the sound of his voice in my head.

"It's rare," he says with a pained smile. "My da is a Mimic, so he can wield the power of another Wielder in the vicinity—like flamewielding and galemaking—but not mind magics like sorcery, skinchanging or ... well, dreamwalking." He shrugs. "Healing, I can to some degree. I haven't had a lot of chances to practice and test the extent of my powers, but I can heal decently, thanks to Alys."

She smiles warmly at him.

"And from Mam's blood, I'm a Mind Whisperer."

I gnaw on my lip. "What about Dark Mages? Are *they* myth or also real?"

Haruka, Kilkenny, and Alys say three different things, and I rub my temples, overwhelmed. They all look at each other, then Alys says, "They are real, but magic isn't black and white. I suppose the most famous Dark Mages in Erleyan history were the Basduunai."

That word sounds familiar. Chiyoko returns to her previous spot and picks up her work again, even as she seems to be listening to her mother's words.

"Basduunai were Mages of ancient and dark magic," Haruka says. "The name is literally translated from the old language as 'death bringer.' In the past, before magic was endangered, Basduunai were feared and usually executed if found. The Basduunai who chose to stay in hiding and suppress their dark abilities often went mad because of it. So that particular set of magical abilities has been extinct for at least a thousand years. Probably for the best, because the most well-known Basduun became corrupted by her own powers and sought illicit magic—opening portals and dabbling in the things of worlds beyond ours. She nearly destroyed our realm as we know it before she was banished."

My head buzzes with theories. "She sounds like the Enchantress Queen Enidwen from my fairytale book." The statement slips out.

Alys and Haruka nod. "The very one," says Haruka.

I don't remember the terms Basduun or Basduunai mentioned at any point in the book of fairytales. But who could forget Enidwen? The enchantress was mad enough to release a prince of the Underworld.

Haruka tells us that Enidwen was a Grounder and the catalyst for the Purge and continued banishments. That the royals used Enidwen's actions as an excuse to oppress Grounders, to instill the fear of magic in all generations. Even at the expense of targeting *Undesirables*—we're just scapegoats in the grand scheme of things.

"They think they can keep us down. If only they knew just how organized the rebellion is." She grins.

The tale of the Enchantress Queen is real. Gods above and below ... To have lived in a time when such dark magic existed sounds horrifying. No wonder the crown goes to such extremes to keep magic away. Have they any idea that it still exists?

Haruka drums her slender fingers on the table. "One more question about your dreamwalking: aside from the queen addressing you, what else happened?"

The details are beginning to grow fuzzy by now, but I pull what I can remember to the forefront of my mind. "The queen was younger in the beginning of the dream, and she was with a young Carys. She told Carys that she'd burn the castle down."

Haruka's eyes widen, and Alys says, "Carys is a Flamewielder."

My jaw practically hits the table, as does Haruka's. I glance at Osheen whose face has gone as white as a wraith.

"She wasn't aware," Alys continues. "But she should be by now. I left her a note."

"A *note*?" Haruka blinks rapidly at Alys. "You left her a *note*? Elviera!"

Her shoulders hunch. "I know."

"When did you discover that she had powers?" Haruka asks. "How has it been kept a secret?"

I would like to know the same.

"Morwenna told me about a year ago. It's complicated."

Complicated ... I press my hand over my mouth to keep nervous laughter from escaping. The heir to the throne has magical wielding abilities. And terrifying ones at that.

"When Carys was a child, she lost control of her powers, and the results were catastrophic. So, Morwenna manipulated her memories and runed an amulet to make a dampener. I tried to convince Morwenna to talk to Carys about it several times, but she insisted it was important that Carys figure it out on her own, and that if it was forced upon her unnaturally, it would cause her to lose control again.

"Carys can be unpredictable, impulsive, but she's learning to deal with it. I've tried to teach her grounding and give her some tips on meditation to help her calm down in times of turmoil, and she has done well, but I'm afraid the pressure of taking the throne is causing a flare-up."

Poor Carys ...

Alys lowers her head a moment, rubbing the spot above her brows before glancing up again with a sigh. "Iywan is up to *something*. Morwenna has been ailing for some time, but most recently, when I tried to feel for what ails her, it was ... tainted. Whatever Iywan and the new healer's apprentice are doing involves something that feels like *dark* healing magic. Unhealing. They're keeping her in a sort of limbo; keeping her alive, albeit asleep. For what purpose, I'm unsure. But I believe that if Carys's power manifests, they'll let the queen perish, but they'll also keep Carys's powers hidden from everyone else."

"What makes you say that?" Kilkenny asks.

Alys shrugs. "Iywan once cared very much for the queen and, by extension, for Carys. But he's since begun caring more about impressions—about the royal titles, rather than the people who hold them. He wants Erleya to be seen as perfect. The last thing he would want is for word to get out that the heir apparent is a Wielder. Especially a *Flamewielder*. It would shatter the façade of the Purge and all that the kingdom has continued to do to ensure that magic does not become a reality again."

My mind buzzes with more and more questions, all itching to spill free from my lips. I take a shaky sip of my tea and then set my cup down again. No one speaks for quite some time, everyone deep in thought.

Then, thankfully, Haruka speaks up. "Durvla needs to be trained. Her powers would be a great asset to the rebellion."

My back goes rigid. That's a change in subject. Me, an asset to the rebellion? Before Paramount, I had never even heard of the rebellion.

"Tiernan, would you be able to train her to weaponize her abilities?"

"It's up to Durvla," says Kilkenny.

Osheen tenses; it isn't feasible with his whole running away fantasy.

Then everyone's attention is on me. I swallow hard. "I—"

"You don't have to decide now," Kilkenny says. "The rebellion is complex. It's not what people expect it to be. Rather than rising up against the crown directly, the rebellion aims to make the kingdom as safe for everyone as possible. Alys has been a covert rebel for years, my parents as well—my mother provides weapons, not just to the Royal Brigade, but to the Verge fighters and rebels outside of the Verge as well. My father travels, assisting with rescues, setting up contact points and safe houses throughout Erleya. I've never been to the Verge, but Alys has."

Alys smiles.

"I've also never actively been part of the rebellion myself, and I was *raised* by rebels." Kilkenny turns to his mother. "We can't expect Durvla to make such a huge decision on a whim. She could also live peacefully in the Verge. After all, the Verge offers sanctuary to those that seek it." He glances at Alys. "Right?"

I lean in expectant, and Alys nods.

Releasing a breath, I sit back in my seat, but I find myself unable to remain still. I have no desire to fight in a rebellion I barely know a thing about, but being able to remain in the Verge, living a quiet, boring life with Taig? That sounds … unbelievable. I sip my tea wordlessly to keep from saying any of that aloud.

Haruka heaves a sigh. "Fair enough." She's silent for a while, then she says, "You all should stay for the festival today. You can leave again under the cover of dark while the festivities are still ongoing."

Behind her, Osheen shifts on his feet, his lips pursed. Each stop may mean that there's a stronger chance of the Forayers catching up to us, so I understand his anxiety. I turn my gaze back to Haruka, my brows furrowed. It has been a month since the beginning of spring, so there shouldn't be one of the big festivals.

"It's the festival of Damarlach, our patron goddess," Haruka says with a smile.

The goddess of war and blacksmithing. That makes sense for Dubh Carrig.

"It's lots of fun," says Chiyoko. "There are fighting and black-smithing competitions, art contests, and a lot of people dress up as warriors. One big pissing contest for who has the best metalworking skills, honestly, but it's my favorite." She's animated as she speaks, face lighting up. "Basically, you have no choice but to say yes to the invitation," she adds.

I glance at Alys and Kilkenny. Alys smiles and shrugs while Kilkenny huffs a sigh and scrubs his hand down his face. "I guess we're going to the festival," he says.

Chapter 46
CARYS

THE WATER LEVEL IN the loch is particularly high after all the rain we've had. Usually, all the trees have bloomed by now, leaving the surroundings at Paramount washed in the colors of spring, but many are still surprisingly bare.

After over a week, my days are equally bare without Alys, Tiernan, and Durvla.

Bitterness coats my tongue. My mother, and even Alys, withheld so much from me. Gods, I'm destructive enough without wielding. I heave a sigh and lean against the balustrade, drinking in the fresh air.

The sisters join me in my bedchamber around noon, attempting to cheer me up with card games and Ellynne's special brand of fortune telling. "Ah," she says, not even showing me the card she holds in front of her face. "You will fall in love with a handsome brute, get married, and have very blond children with eyes like fire."

At that, I burst into tears.

Unabashed, ugly, forceful tears. Lowri jumps as if I've startled her and Ellynne drops the cards, reaching out to place her hand over mine. "I'm sorry," she says. "I didn't mean to upset you."

Lowri snatches up the bottle of wine sitting on the table and fills my goblet. She's not even finished pouring before I snatch the goblet from beneath the stream of wine and gulp it down. Lowri scrambles in her pockets for a rag to mop up the mess left behind while I dissolve into an equally messy fit of tearful hiccups.

"I know you miss them," Ellynne says gently. "But we're here for you. Aren't we, Lowri?"

Lowri bobs her head, agreeable as always even as she mops up the wine on the table. I should be grateful for what I still have, but it's so damn hard to find joy when there's a black cloud above me, waiting to rain down some unknown terror.

· · ◦ ☽ ☀ ☾ ◦ · ·

The aroma of something sweet and buttery greets me as I step into the dining hall. But before I can make a beeline for the kitchen, I catch a glimpse of a broad figure sitting with their back to the table, hunched over something. My shoes clack loudly on the floor as I come to a stop and Callum grumbles something under his breath that I don't quite make out.

The figure lifts his head, a bearded face turning my way, the braid down the center of his head like warm brass the chandelier light. I take in the immediate glint that rises into the man's eyes and the easy smile that spreads across his full lips. "Hello, Carys," Odgar's resonant voice greets me.

An odd, warming sensation expands in my chest.

"I was hoping to run into you," he says.

He shifts as if to stand but I gently hold my hand up. My steps are quick as I make my way toward where his chair is awkwardly turned away from the table. In his lap is a fuzzy ball of grey-flecked ivory spinning fiber. His right hand holds a thick wooden needle with one end of the fiber through the large eye, and in his left is a swatch of what appears to be knitted fabric.

I stop midstride, doing a double take from his face to his hands then back again. "You're ... *knitting*?" My voice comes out embarrassingly high.

Odgar shrugs his broad shoulders, chuckling softly. "Nalbinding. It's similar."

I will my mouth closed and fix my face into a hopefully unperturbed expression. This warrior prince is sitting in a public space, casually engaging in a domestic hobby. I bite back the bark of laughter that threatens to escape. As I grasp the back of a chair to turn it, Callum steps forward.

"Allow me, Princess!" he says hurriedly. I step away, briefly catching a glimpse of his pinched expression as he turns the chair for me.

"Thank you, Callum." I sit and Callum steps aside, his jaw set firmly.

Odgar sets his *nalbinding* behind him on the table and turns, his full attention on me.

"I'd expected you to have already departed," I tell him. I quickly glance at the clock on the wall then back to Odgar.

His smile is endearingly crooked when it reappears, and I stare at his lips for a heartbeat longer than necessary.

"I am actually setting sail soon," he says. "I wanted to say goodbye first, but I didn't want to summon you if you were busy."

I start to gnaw on my lip but force myself to stop. "Prince Odgar ..." I start formally.

His posture straightens, and he leans toward me very slightly.

My gaze skims over the tattoos on one shaven side of his head, then down to those captivating sunburst eyes of his. "About the attack during the Feast. I hope that doesn't completely shatter the prospect of a possible union. Should you be my chosen suitor and should you ... agree."

I'm not sure what I expected from him, but it wasn't laughter. It echoes through the dining hall with an almost musical quality. My heart drops and I clench my hands in my lap, fighting the desire to fidget while he doesn't even bother to regain his composure.

"Erleyans are so concerned with appearance," Odgar says.

I unclasp my hands and wrinkle my nose, leaning back. "Pardon me?" I shift my focus to the clock again, then back to Odgar.

A smile graces Odgar's lips once more, and he lowers his head, shaking it slightly. When he raises his head again, his expression is adamant, yet gentle. I practically melt into a puddle.

"I would love to get to know you better," he says. "Outside of the"—he waves his large hands around—"air of perfection you're forced to hold on to."

My brows furrow.

"The rebel attack hasn't scared me off. I would love to be your chosen suitor." He leans in closer, and my breath hitches. "Between you and me, my competition was ... underwhelming." He grins before leaning back, calmly assessing me.

My traitorous lips quirk up into a smile of their own volition. "From where I was standing, it was *over*whelming. I almost lost an eye or a toe a few times."

"Gods, who was that scraggy little man prancing like a reindeer?"

I press my hand over my mouth as another bloody *giggle* escapes me.

"See? Appearances," he says with a smirk, reaching out to gently lower my hand. My skin warms. "What's wrong with laughing aloud, Raven Princess?"

I let out a forceful sigh.

"Now that's more like it. A raw, unhindered reaction. Something *real*."

"Gods," I mutter with feigned exasperation. I glance sidelong at Callum whose jaw is clenched so tightly, I fear he'll break his teeth. Turning to Odgar again, I say, "I believe the prancing reindeer was Prince Morand of Caldeon. Thank you for rescuing me."

He smiles almost leisurely, and I find myself wishing for his easy-going nature. "Any time, Princess," he says.

"How on earth can you remain so calm and collected? Even when the explosions happened, you barely flinched."

He shrugs a broad shoulder. "I was raised a warrior, as are many Uldarans. I am not afraid of death. Nor am I of fate."

A shiver flitters across my skin, his words replaying in my mind. "Odgar, this may sound strange but … may I ask you a few questions about Uldarvik?"

His smile widens. "Please do."

For a while, I ask whatever comes to mind, taking mental notes as he responds with ease and proficiency. When I'm out of questions, the silence draws attention to the clock ticking away. I swear inwardly. Odgar stands, extending a large hand to me, his sleeves rolled back, revealing more ink against his copper skin.

"You've looked at the clock several times now. I imagine you have someplace to be?" he asks. His voice draws me back to his face, to the braid peeking over his shoulder, brassy blond curls escaping it.

"Unfortunately, I do." I slip my hand into his, and he gently pulls me to my feet.

His lips lightly brush the back of my hand, and my heart gives an unnecessarily hard *thump*. Godsdamned … His sparkling gaze finds mine. My lips part, but emit no words.

The sound of footsteps cuts through the silence, and I tug my hand away, putting space between us.

Iywan stands in the doorway of the dining hall. He quickly covers his pinched expression with a smile, his voice hollow as he says, "Good afternoon, Your Highnesses." He bows so deeply that I quirk a brow.

"Good afternoon, Lord Iywan. I was just bidding Princess Carys farewell. Many thanks for your hospitality on behalf of me and my right-hand man. He is out enjoying the garden as we speak. I will be sure to tell King Freyr about your wonderful Feast and the lovely Princess Carys." Odgar's tone has changed from friendly to formal, but his body language remains relaxed. I envy him.

"I am glad to hear it," says Iywan. "I heard there are sweets in the kitchen. I hope you will take some for your travels."

"How could I decline such a delicious offer?" Odgar rocks back on his feet, beaming at Iywan.

Iywan chuckles but, again, it sounds hollow. He bows once more, says a quick goodbye, and leaves. My brows furrow, and I remain staring at the spot where Iywan stood a moment ago. Had he truly come in here for sweets, or did he somehow learn of my whereabouts and came to investigate?

It's likely the latter.

I turn back to Odgar, finding it in me to smile at him once more. "Safe travels. I hope we'll meet again."

"May fate bring us back together, Raven Princess," Odgar replies with a small dip of his head.

I turn to walk away, and Callum follows along. The council meeting starts soon, I never got anything to eat in the end, but I need to gather my composure and mentally prepare. As we walk back toward my bedchamber, Callum is rigid at my side.

"For the gods' sake, Callum. Speak your mind."

"Do you truly see yourself marrying someone like Odgar?" he asks.

"Yes," I say automatically. I chance a glance at Callum, his throat bobbing as he swallows.

"He may make you happy." His voice sounds strained, but he has the grace to fake a smile.

I nod and take a deep breath. "Perhaps."

Mentally repeating everything I learned from Odgar, I step into the council chamber, prepared to make my case. Only Iywan and Jac are present, but moments after I take my seat, the other councilors arrive. "Welcome," Iywan says. "Most of our guests have departed. So, without further ado, we must discuss the matter of Princess Carys's marriage." He turns to everyone except for me as he continues. "Because of the rising unrest of the rebels in Erleya, Councilor Tomen has advised that it would be in our best interest to keep our ties within our kingdom rather than form a foreign alliance."

I lurch forward in my chair, my palms flat against the table. "*What?*"

All heads turn to me except for the master of foreign affairs. I want to yank out what's left of Tomen's white hair and shove it down his throat. He steeples his hands on the table and keeps his cloudy eyes on Iywan, who continues.

"The attack was unfortunately timed with our foreign diplomats present. No one wants to ally with a nation that cannot even control their own citizens. It makes us look as though we're on the brink of total anarchy."

My mouth falls open, but I immediately press my lips firmly together until they start to go numb. I move my hands to my lap, clenching them to hopefully stop them from trembling. I want to protest, but I don't want to lose my temper. "What are you proposing, Lord Iywan?" I ask as calmly as possible.

"Your betrothal to Lord Commander of the Royal Brigade— Rheon of Bayenbar."

Fucking hells. My mouth opens and closes again. I swallow, praying to keep my composure. "Lord Iywan, I have a different proposal."

Jac leans back in his seat, amusement playing across his dark face. Gods, he is infuriating. Iywan draws himself up in his chair, cold challenge on his face while Tomen and Belhan simply blink at me.

"Odgar Erlingson, prince of Uldarvik."

Iywan's exhales slowly and the annoyance on his face melts into contempt. Meanwhile, Sessaley looks intrigued and, as always, Taliesin is indifferent.

"Prince Odgar has informed me that he would gladly accept my proposal should he be chosen. His brother, the king of Uldarvik, already gives his blessing. Uldarvik will be a strong ally. They are excellent in the export of fish and timber, and they are a robust agricultural kingdom. Given the state of the growing blight in Erleya, it would be beneficial for us to be united with a land abundant in thriving crops, particularly oats, barley, and rye. They are also rich in iron ore, silver, and copper."

I glance at Taliesin, but her dark eyes are half-lidded, her fingers drumming silently on the table. I want to shake her; she's useless.

I sigh and continue. "Should our armed forces require more weaponry, Uldarvik's cannon production is notable. You speak of your concern about the unrest from the rebels, Lord Iywan, Councilor Tomen, but Uldarans aren't intimidated by that. A large fraction of their population is born and raised to be fighters. They have shieldmaidens and fearless warriors. They are brave and fiercely loyal. My marriage to Prince Odgar would be exactly what is needed for the kingdom. A *strong* union. In manpower, in trade goods. Prince Odgar is kind and intelligent. Our people will adore him."

The silent tension is so thick that the air is suffocating. My hands shake even more where they're hidden beneath the table, and I wait with apprehension for *anyone* to say something.

"It's too risky," Iywan says at last. "These are trying times for Erleya. A foreign union is out of the question. Lord Commander Rheon Odhran has been the superior officer for decades. He has been a part of the Royal Brigade as a soldier for even longer. He charges all divisions and is revered not just by soldiers, but civilians. His long-standing, renowned presence in Erleya is just what the people need. With your impending transition to reigning monarch, Prince Odgar would offer no such familiar comfort to the masses, I'm afraid."

"Long-standing, renowned presence? Revered? I think the word you're looking for is *feared*. Lord Commander Rheon orchestrated a public flogging five years ago!"

"Careful, Princess," he says, his voice tight. "That public display was justified and sanctioned by Queen Morwenna."

I sink back in my chair, my entire body trembling as I fight not to scream at Iywan. Tomen's hazy stare is on me as well this time, his gaunt face giving away nothing.

"Given the circumstances," Iywan continues. "The commander is your best option in the interest of Erleya."

Heat crawls over my skin and floods my chest. My chair scrapes unpleasantly against the floor as I shove my seat back and rise, slamming my hands on the table. "Meeting adjourned. Everybody out!"

The clock on the wall ticks loudly for a few seconds before barrel-chested Belhan slowly pushes his own chair back. He's followed by Tomen, then a progressive trickle of the other councilors taking their leave. Each member bows quickly as they walk past me before retreating with mumbled farewells. My amulet is uncomfortably warm against my chest—a sensation I've always blamed on my own emotions rather than … well, magic.

Iywan pushes himself slowly from his seat once the chamber plunges into silence behind the closed door. Callum is frozen at my side.

Resisting the urge to fiddle with my necklace, I clench my fists at my side. "I am the heir to the throne," I say calmly. "I make the final decision in this. *You* said that from the beginning when we went into this whole suitor thing. Why in Lugda's hells are you repealing my choice?"

He doesn't so much as blink. "You said it yourself, Princess. You are the *heir* to the throne. You have not come into full power. I am your advisor and final decision-maker in your mother's stead while she is still very much alive."

"She is *hardly* alive!" My voice quivers and I cringe inwardly.

Something like pain briefly crosses Iywan's face, but he blinks and it's gone.

"You once cared about her. You once cared about *me*. I don't understand what happened! I don't understand why we're always at odds now at the time where I most need you to actually be on my side."

His eyes glisten with tears, but he takes a steadying breath and his face hardens. "I am trying to get her spoiled daughter to understand—"

"*Spoiled?*"

"You cannot be trusted to make decisions that affect this entire kingdom." His voice is surprisingly brazen, his tone clipped. "You are reckless, juvenile, and lacking decorum. You strut around here, cavorting with your servants like an entitled brat, bedding whomever you please, whenever and *wherever* you please."

Color blooms on my face.

"You're delusional to think that nobody can see how utterly flawed you are."

My chest tightens at not just his words, but the coldness in his voice.

"I hate to shove the truth down your throat, child, but everyone knows you cannot control your emotions, nor what you do with your body. Even with your *guard* who is supposed to keep you in line."

Callum bristles beside me.

I push my shoulders back rather than shrink away in shame. "Don't call me a child." My voice trembles, but I maintain a cool tone. "I am a woman of twenty-one and soon to be the queen, whether you like it or not. My behavior aside, I have a right to choose my future husband, and you have no right to speak to me the way you just did in front of the Council or the way you're doing now, for that matter."

To my surprise, he doesn't retaliate right away. He folds his arms across his scrawny chest and says, "Then don't *act* like a child, Your Highness."

The formal address is mocking, and I bite the inside of my cheek to keep from giving him a piece of my mind.

"Tell me, Princess, if you weren't attracted to Prince Odgar, would he still be your choice?" Disdain drips from his voice.

I blink at him.

"You say that you're the future queen and a woman grown. That you care about this kingdom. But rather than think with your *head*, you choose to go on a whim, based on an attraction. Tell me honestly, is allying with Prince Odgar any better than allying with Prince Morand? Caldeon has much to offer as well. Yet, you didn't waltz in here and tell me all about its exports."

I try to imagine my life with the overly energetic, cologne-reeking Prince Morand who spits when he speaks. To keep from facing Iywan directly, I stare down at the table. *Am* I making foolish decisions just because I like Odgar? I keep my head down even as Iywan speaks up again, my pulse thrumming in my temples and muddling my hearing.

"You chose the wrong suitor after I trusted you," Iywan says. "So now, it's in *my* hands. You will be marrying Lord Commander Rheon. End of discussion."

There's a heavy *thud*, and when I glance up again, Iywan is gone. I'm left in the empty council chamber with Callum. He spins to me. "I swear I've never told anyone."

My chest is too tight, my breath growing thready. Anyone could've told Iywan about my bedding habits. Ellynne, Lowri, Eefa, Wynn ... even Callum. My legs grow unsteady, forcing me back into the seat as I fight to get air into my reluctant lungs.

"Carys ... What can I do?" Callum asks. He steps closer, but I shove my hand toward him.

"Don't ..." I fight down shallow breaths between gritted out words. My heart is sure to pound out of my chest. "Space. Give me space."

I don't know who I can trust at all anymore.

Chapter 47
DURVLA

I GAPE AT MYSELF in the mirror. I'm out of my depth in an ankle-length, midnight blue dress with translucent long sleeves. An impressively forged *something* that I can only describe as a literal *breastplate* encases my upper torso, stopping just above my soft midriff. My waist is cinched with a thick leather belt that rests against my hips. The light material of the dress and the accessories accentuate the curves that I've always been determined to hide.

For the hundredth time, I tug closed the slit that comes up to the middle of my thigh.

Chiyoko grins and fiddles with the thin silver chains interwoven in the braids that Alys helped put into my hair. The intricacy of it has me questioning Chiyoko's lack of magic.

I can only stare at my reflection in the mirror, at my kohl-lined eyes, subtle compared to Chiyoko's generous application to her own.

Her makeup gives her a fierce appearance ... even as she steps back and applauds with the overenthusiasm of a toddler.

"What a work of art!" she exclaims. "And you look stunning! Like a ..." She hesitates, deep in thought. "Warrior ... ?" She fingerspells the word she doesn't know: queen.

I laugh lightly and supply the sign.

Chiyoko repeats the sign, laughing as well. "You look like a warrior queen." Her eyes twinkle. "Alright, one last thing." She grabs another belt from her table of supplies and kneels.

"What are you—?" My words are cut off by a yelp that escapes me as she binds the belt tightly around my thigh.

Chiyoko glances up at me with a smirk. "You've lived for a decade with debilitating headaches, and you can't handle a dagger sheath on your thigh?"

Her words startle laughter from me. So bold, but so true. Until I realize what she's actually said. "Did you say a dagger sheath?"

Chiyoko stands and produces a dagger out of nowhere. She holds it by the tip and flips it, catching it by the pommel, and I flinch. "Relax," she says. It won't hurt you. It's not like you have to use it." She slides it into the sheath now buckled to my thigh, and I once again tug the slit of the delicate dress closed. "Oy, don't hide my handywork," Chiyoko scolds.

I pout at her, and she steps back, admiring me like I'm her masterpiece.

She's dressed in skin-tight leather from head to toe, with a wildly elaborate breastplate that's certainly more artistic than it is protective. There are metal bracers on her forearms, and tall boots that stop just below her knees. She is every bit formidable. Her blue and brown hair is pulled back into a short ponytail and secured with a silver circle hairpin in the shape of a raven's wings.

"You look like someone I wouldn't mess with," I say, and she grins.

"Good. Let's get out there, then." She grabs the small metal statue she'd been working on last night: a little highland cow with a painted crown of flowers across its head. It would make a lovely toy for a child, if the horns weren't pointed.

Everyone else already left a while ago, but Chiyoko was determined to complete my ensemble before we headed out.

When we arrived last night, there was hardly anyone around. Now, the streets are filled with villagers of all ages dressed in colorful costumes or warrior gear. Children run by with play swords and hobby horses, one running into me. The small girl stops and tips her face up to me with large brown eyes that remind me of Taig's. "You look *pretty*!" she exclaims, shoving curly blond hair out of her face.

I manage a smile, swallowing. "Thank you. So do you."

She twirls in her leather skirt and armor until a little boy taps her on the shoulder, then they run off to join the others.

Chiyoko nudges me with her shoulder. "You alright?" she asks.

I lift my hands for a moment, nearly forgetting that we're in public again. No more signing. I smile and nod.

The village has been transformed, decorated with metal statues that glimmer in the afternoon sunlight, coats of armor, and humanoid figures made of hay.

Osheen appears, dressed in leathers with a bow and quiver. I'm reminded of his hunting skills, which far surpass mine and always will. His eyes widen as he takes in my ensemble. "Wow," he says.

"You can say that again," Chiyoko agrees.

"It suits you." The smile returns to his face.

I glance back and forth between the two until Osheen's last comment brings me pause. I raise a brow at him. The outfit is edgy, fearsome, and sensual—everything I'm not. My mouth remains shut.

The festival is vivacious and filled with more activities than I could even handle. We spectate a few terrifying swordfights. Plenty of blood is drawn but no lives are taken, thank Rhianu. It's all in good fun. Chiyoko wins an art competition with her highland cow statue and flaunts her ribbon to everyone that comes close.

Chiyoko introduces Osheen and I to an array of foods typical of Dubh Carrig. Osheen gorges himself on roasted pork, white pudding, and a spicy potato stew that is the most delicious stew to have ever graced my tongue. I want to smuggle a pot of it into my pack.

Alys and Haruka join us, bringing along pieces of delicious currant cakes wrapped in cloth for us to munch on. The spices explode on my tongue, and I hum in pleasure. It beats Eefa's lemon cake by a landslide.

By the time the sun begins to sink below the mountains, my belly is full, my soul refreshed. A massive bonfire is lit in the center of the village, smoke billowing into the darkening sky, energetic embers jumping off the main inferno. A ghost of anxiety settles into the pit of my stomach. It's almost time for us to leave.

And I still haven't seen Kilkenny.

His absence leaves me surprisingly unsettled. Maybe I've just gotten used to his broody presence nearby in the past few weeks.

Chiyoko links her arm with mine and tugs me toward the bonfire. With each step, the bass of the drums booms heavier in my chest, the rhythm lively and captivating. The dancers cast wavery shadows as they move about. There's drinking, clapping, and stomping. A far livelier occasion than even the Feast at Paramount. As the music continues to resound in my chest, I can't help but bob my head in time with the rhythm as adults and children alike dance around the roaring flames.

Despite the merriment, an ache is building in my head. It's been a long day, and my feet are getting sore, so I find a seat on a thick log. Osheen sits beside me as Chiyoko runs off, disappearing into the crowd.

With a smile, Osheen bumps his shoulder lightly against mine and says, "Are we alright, you and I?"

Returning his smile, I nod. "We're alright. We just have some reacquainting to do."

"I can work with that."

Chiyoko reappears, shoving a cool mug of ale into my hand before yanking Osheen off the log. He resists, but she's deceptively strong and yanks him up and toward the crowd of dancers. Osheen cranes his neck to look back at me, a desperate plea for help written all over his face. With a grin, I wave innocently and quickly sign one-handed, *"Have fun."*

He points to me, making a playful threat, but I only shrug and sip the ale.

Chiyoko exudes exhilarating energy as she does a jig around Osheen, one hand on her hip, the other in the air. Her legs move with impressive speed in tempo, up and down, back and forth. She jumps and twirls and sways her hips, her movements as free and assured as the bright smile on her face. All the while, Osheen stands there, straighter than an iron rod, clearly not knowing what to do with himself.

His face turns progressively redder in the firelight, matching his hair, as Chiyoko grabs his hands and swings them around in an attempt to get him to move. I can't stop the laughter that swells in my chest and slips past my lips. The sight is so absolutely chaotic and so wonderful.

The heat of the flames, the crowd gathered, the music thumping in my chest … Like a rock, Taig drops into my thoughts. His sweet face leaves me almost breathless. I've had so much fun today and I have no idea how Taig is managing. I pray that he's safe and sound, that the rebels who rescued him made it to the Verge. That they know how to take care of him and how to handle him. My chest constricts.

It is so wrong to be in this merry setting without him by my side. I'd love to see the awe on his little face. But now … Is he scared?

Confused? Does he miss me? Does he even *remember* me? The heaviness in my chest grows and I rub my hand against my collarbone. I need to put some distance between me and this scene.

I set my mug of ale down and massage my throbbing temples. As soon as I get to my feet, I run into one of the hundreds of people clad in black. The man grabs my arms to steady me, and once I right myself, I take in the leather armor, the series of laces and belts strapped across his torso and hips, and the sword hilts peeking over each of his shoulders.

Kilkenny.

The top half of his hair is pulled back into a bun, and he's shaved the beard that grew over the past week, taking about ten years off his age despite his silver streaks. I can't stop the smile that spreads across my face.

"Always crashing into me," Kilkenny says once he lets go of me. There's a faint spark of amusement in his eyes, though something changes as he takes in every detail of my attire. His focus lingers on the dagger strapped to my thigh.

The tips of my ears burn. I pinch the slit of the dress, and his face lifts to mine.

"That dagger isn't going to do," he says.

A surprised laugh breaks away from me. "Killjoy …"

His lips twitch and he shrugs a shoulder. The leather armor he wears tightens across his chest from the movement, and I'm drawn to it for a heartbeat too long. He plucks a dagger from his hip. "Switch."

My brows snap together. "Why?"

"Because that dagger's not right for you." He holds out his open palm, revealing a blade. This one is slightly shorter and sleeker than the dagger I'm wearing, and the hilt is bound in alternating stripes of green and dark brown leather.

I fold my arms across my chest, the movement awkward thanks to the decorative breastplate. Gods, I can't wait to get out of this outfit. "What's wrong with the dagger I'm wearing?"

He sighs. "Nothing, Garrick, but I made this one especially for you."

My heart hiccups and I blink at him. He *made* that one for me?

Kilkenny moves his outstretched palm closer to me. When I still don't move, he takes it upon himself to confiscate my dagger and replace it with his. The tiniest shiver thrums through me as his fingers brush against my thigh.

It's just a chill from the wind.

Even if the trees aren't moving …

My head throbs and I wince, rubbing at a painful spot on my forehead. Concern replaces the undecipherable expression on Kilkenny's face. "Don't worry," I tell him. "It's just—"

"A lot?" He gestures to our surroundings and I nod. "Come," he says, nodding his head toward the grassy path as he tucks Chiyoko's dagger away somewhere in his leather vest.

I have half a mind to refuse, to ask him where he's been all day. But instead, I follow along wordlessly. The overwhelming thudding of the drums gradually diminishes, and the small seed of anxiety in my chest dissolves the farther we get from the bonfire.

We take a path through a small copse of trees to a winding grassy trail. We're moving uphill … steeply … My shoulders tense, matching the tightness in my stomach, but I continue walking. Narrow trees line the ascending route, the leaves not as full as they should be by now. Through the sparse leaves, the edge of the mountain is visible, uncomfortably close. We could fall to our deaths if dizziness ambushes me.

My heart seizes and I stop abruptly.

Kilkenny regards me, signing now that we're alone. "What is it?"

"I'm afraid of heights, remember?"

He presses his lips together for a moment and holds his hand out to me. "I won't let you fall, Garrick. I promise." I don't take his hand, so he closes his fist gently and opens it again, urging me.

I sigh and reluctantly slip my hand into his, ignoring the little flip of my stomach. We continue our trek up the mountain, and as the trees make way, we're left with wide open land overlooking the valley below. My head reels and I shut my eyes. Kilkenny gives my hand a squeeze and nudges me with his shoulder. I open my eyes and take a deep breath.

"The likelihood of falling is low," says Kilkenny. "I spent a lot of my childhood here. It has the best view in the village. Look." He nods up toward the sky where bright stars twinkle between ribbons of midnight blue and deep purple. Below are beautiful mountain ranges surrounding a large river. At least if we fall, we'll fall in water, right? Too bad I can't swim.

Kilkenny releases my hand. "See, you're braver than you think. Don't let your fears break you."

Don't break. I step back. "You knew …"

"Knew what?"

"Back in Paramount. The horseback-riding lessons, self-defense, meditation … At the Feast, you told me not to break. And then the rebel attack happened, and my imprisonment … you knew."

There's the slightest indication of guilt on his face. "I knew that Alys had been arrested; I wasn't sure what would happen next." I try to stop frowning at him, but it must fail because he quickly adds, "I wouldn't lie to you."

I sigh. "Tell me about my powers then. The whole truth."

He pulls in a breath to speak, but his head flicks to the left and then back to me, alarm on his face. "Something's happening down there. People are screaming."

My stomach lurches.

"Stay close." He takes my hand again and we bolt.

Rushing down the mountain proves to be way harder than the climb. I nearly twist my ankle too many times, but soon we're back on even ground. An acrid scent tickles my nose as people run by. Panic is all around us, and in the distance, red-orange flames flare and billow, throwing thick, black smoke into the air. Those aren't just torches; houses are burning.

Fear climbs up my throat.

"Forayers," Kilkenny says. "Get back to the house. The horses are already saddled. You just need to grab our packs from the sitting room."

I nod frantically, and just as I'm about to run off, Kilkenny catches my arm. "If none of us show up and the Forayers are getting closer, use your intuition and *run*. Don't stop until you put as much distance as possible between yourself and here."

I shake my head. "I'm not leaving without everyone."

He pauses, then sighs heavily. "Alright, go."

I run as fast as I can, my lungs screaming at me. I nearly get lost on the way to the house, but when I get there, Chiyoko and Osheen are exiting, our packs in their arms.

"The horses are waiting in the back," Osheen says.

"Where are Alys and Haruka?" I ask.

"I don't know," says Chiyoko. "But if the Forayers happen to be here for you lot, they'll know to look here. We need to leave."

That was our fear when we considered coming here in the first place, but no time to dwell on that. Osheen and I race toward the back of the house where the saddled horses are waiting. Alys and Haruka come jogging into view. Kilkenny isn't far behind them, and my body relaxes with relief.

Everything happens so fast. Chiyoko rushes right past Kilkenny and leverages herself onto Osheen's horse. Haruka and Kilkenny both protest. There's a brief flurry of hand signing for my sake, but it's incoherent, and I give up on trying to follow anyone's line of conversation. At the end of it all, Chiyoko says, "I'm going!" Stubbornness etches every angle of her face.

Kilkenny huffs out a breath and helps me up onto Ghendor's back before I could figure out what to do next. Confusion crosses Osheen's face, but he mounts Ffion, sitting right behind Chiyoko.

Kilkenny hugs his mother tightly, exchanging some words with her before turning to his sister. Then I awkwardly scoot back to let him climb into the saddle. I *feel* his disgruntled groan from Chiyoko's insistence. He makes sure everyone is set, then, glancing over his shoulder at me, he says, "Hang on to me, Garrick."

I barely have a chance to react before Ghendor takes off at a gallop. I wind my arms around Kilkenny's waist, avoiding his sword sheaths, and press my head against the spot right above where they intersect. We ride like mad, the wind tearing through the ridiculous slit in my dress and chilling me. I dare to look back at what we're leaving behind, and my heart constricts in my chest.

Dubh Carrig is burning.

Chapter 48
CARYS

WITH ALL THE COURAGE I can summon, I march to Iywan's study, Callum's steady footsteps beside me. "Are you certain you're ready to confront him again?" Callum whispers as we round the corner, slipping past a couple of servants carrying trays.

"No, but I must," I whisper back.

As we arrive at Iywan's study door, I pause at the sound of an unfamiliar feminine voice inside. Beside me, Callum draws in a breath to question me, but I press my finger to my lips, and he swallows his words. With caution, I lean my ear against the sturdy oak door, focusing intensely. "It cannot be done, my lord," says the alto voice. "We've tried everything. We've even attempted to imbue an already runed crystal, but it isn't stable enough on its own."

"What do you mean *on its own*?" Iywan asks.

"The blood needs a live tether, likely close by. On its own, it's too weak. It can maybe get a person through the wards temporarily, but it cannot break them down completely, and it certainly will not be successful in the summoning you seek."

"But she *is* alive. We've ensured it. If we get her to the ward …"

"Her Majesty is too weak; The amount of power needed would kill her in no time. You need a live, healthy Mage, and a powerful one at that. It doesn't have to be the queen."

My blood runs cold.

Wards, imbuing crystals, blood magic? Hells, what am I hearing?

"It has to be royal blood, but her heir has never shown any signs of magic. She's painfully Ordinary, and quite frankly that's probably for the best."

I hold my breath, grateful that no one can hear my heart.

Iywan continues. "It's time for the contingency."

"I'm afraid the contingency is implausible, my lord," the other voice says.

"Try anyway." Iywan's tone leaves no room for argument. "*Find them.* You're dismissed."

My pulse scurries as I grab Callum's arm and steer him away from the door, practically running back around the corner toward my bed-chamber so we're out of sight when Iywan's cohort leaves the study.

It isn't until we're near my own door that Callum asks, "What did you hear?"

My throat works, but no words come out. I can hardly wrap my mind around what I've heard. They're trying to *draw magic* from my mother's blood? If Iywan finds out that I also possess magic … A shudder runs through me.

I stare up at Callum, apprehension pulsating through me. "Have you heard anything strange lately? Like from the other guards?"

"No." He shakes his head, confusion written on his face.

I frown and retreat into my bedchamber. What is Iywan trying to do by bringing down wards? Magical wards protect things. Like the ones that have kept the Veil closed through history, that the Veilguards have traditionally guarded.

Bringing down the wards would mean … opening the Veil?

My stomach squirms. That can't be it. Why would Iywan want to open the Veil?

Callum is called away to a brief meeting later in the afternoon—regarding stepping into Tiernan's leadership role—and Ren stands in his place. My body and mind *refuse* to settle down, so I head to the garden in hopes of stilling my mind for just a moment, but not even the fresh air helps. A steady thrum of uneasy energy pulses through my veins as a never-ending barrage of scenarios poison my mind.

A month ago, my biggest issue was choosing a suitor. Then fighting to step into my mother's role.

I am the heir to the throne, godsdammit, yet Iywan holds so much power, so much influence over the Council.

My stomach churns as I rack my mind for solutions.

Do I confront Iywan? How far would he go to keep his clandestine meeting a secret? And what does Lord Commander Rheon have to do with any of this?

I've been standing on the cobblestone pathway of the garden, staring at a pitiful rosebush that's reluctant to bloom.

I should have more concern for the kingdom, but my own plight has me in a chokehold.

What exactly does Iywan gain from his outlandish plans? What exactly *are* his outlandish plans?

"Carys," a familiar voice says.

I spin away from the rose bush and come face to face with Eefa.

She's in a simple brown linen dress without an apron. Even her honey blond hair is unbound from its usual braid, cascading over her shoulders and onto the full swell of her breasts. A cheeky smirk plays on her lips, and need immediately replaces the nervous churning in my stomach.

I should walk away. Right now. I should just turn and—

"Are you off duty?" I hear myself ask.

"Yes." She smiles. "Unless … you need something?"

Just off the cobblestone pathway, barely a few paces from me, Ren is staring off into nothingness. I appreciate his façade of not eavesdropping.

"I need plenty," I say. I glance sidelong at Ren before turning to head inside. Eefa doesn't ask any questions—she simply follows along, falling into step at my side opposite Ren.

I've never made it to my bedchamber so quickly, and as soon as Ren shuts the door behind Eefa and I, the little control I have crumbles, crushing any fighting embers of logic beneath its rubble. Eefa's even more adept than Callum when it comes to removing my corset, and it's on the floor in no time, along with the rest of my clothes and her overdress. We're a tangle of tongues and limbs, breathing heavily when we finally crash into my bed.

In no time, Eefa's expert fingers have me writhing. But as I cry out in bliss, my mind tumbles in a freefall, guilt smothering the ecstasy. I shouldn't be doing this right now—I should be figuring things out. I should be fighting to get to the bottom of things. Maybe Iywan is right; maybe I *am* just a spoiled child.

The door flies open with a bang, and I lurch upright, my heart in my throat, tugging the sheets over my body. It gets caught under Eefa and only partially covers me.

Callum's eyes are frantic as he yanks his arm from Ren, who apparently tried to stop him from barging in.

The words come flying out of my mouth before I can filter them. "Fucking hells, Callum!"

He steps back, blinking rapidly as he registers the scene before him. "I—"

"You *what*?!"

Suddenly, he can't face me. "I thought … I heard … Apologies, Your Highness."

The formal address somehow makes my stomach turn over. Beside me, Eefa is shaking with restrained laughter. I grumble a string of expletives as she settles down beside me, her legs crisscrossed. She's in her shift and I am as naked as the day I was born.

Not that it's anything Callum hasn't seen.

"Why don't you join us, Sir Callum?" Eefa asks.

Both our heads whip toward her.

She laughs lightly and holds her hands up in surrender. "I was only kidding. You aren't my type, pretty boy." She winks at Callum, and he turns the brightest shade of red.

"That's it. Both of you, leave!"

I don't have to say it twice. Callum salutes and marches out of the bedchamber. The deepest ache fills the hollow of my chest. I rub at the spot and hop out of the bed, grabbing Eefa's dress from the floor and tossing it at her.

My aching heart begins to pound as though it intends to leave my chest cavity. I grab my dressing robe and throw it on over my shoulders before storming out to my terrace. Gooseflesh creeps along my skin. I dig my fingers into the cool balustrade to keep myself from leaping off the balcony.

To avoid the temptation of a definite escape.

Gods, what is wrong with me? What is *wrong with me*? The tears come hot and fast as I bend and press my forehead to the stone surface. Alright, I have to stop this. I need to compose myself.

My gaze sweeps across the loch and the castle grounds. I draw my focus down to the coldness seeping into my bare feet. The air smells of stone and freshwater and foliage—of the outdoors. Birds chirp mockingly somewhere nearby, and the taste of something sweet and citrusy lingers on my lips from Eefa's heedless kisses.

With a slow exhalation, I stop my mind from spiraling and chant all the senses aloud to myself over and over. "Loch. Cold. Outdoors. Birds. Citrus."

Oh, Alys. I'm sorry for all the times I resisted your coaching. But thank you.

"Loch. Cold. Outdoors. Birds. Citrus."

The first thing I need to do is start taking back my power as heir apparent. I need to show Iywan and everyone within the castle that I am capable of taking charge.

Tomorrow.

Chapter 49
DURVLA

WE RIDE LIKE MAD until we can't any longer. I'm hardly able to wrap my mind around the devastating shift that the night has taken. How many villagers of Dubh Carrig are without a roof over their heads tonight? How many have been left to tend to their injured or mourn their dead?

Because of us.

My chest aches from holding back tears as we ride. My returning headache and sore body are nothing compared to the sinking guilt. I hope Haruka is alright. Gods, after her hospitality and her wealth of information—I can't imagine how worried Kilkenny and Chiyoko must be.

Hours later, we finally dismount in a desolate valley beside a small river. We're on the ground for all of five seconds before Kilkenny reels on Chiyoko as she approaches.

"What in Lugda's hells were you thinking?" he asks.

She frowns up at him, arms akimbo. Kilkenny is a man of average height, but Chiyoko's petite stature makes him appear much taller. "Oh, come off it," she says.

I squint, hardly able to make out the movements of their lips in the sparse light from the waxing crescent moon. Alys and Osheen lead the horses away, leaving me with a free escape route, but I find myself unable to move.

"I'm not going to … little mission," Chiyoko says to Kilkenny. "… can use the extra help."

"Little mission?" Kilkenny holds up his palm, a small ball of light forming there, illuminating the small space between him and Chiyoko.

It's incredible. Startling, but incredible. Yet, Chiyoko doesn't even blink.

"You think this is a game?" Kilkenny continues. "Those Forayers back there are seeking to *execute* us. They burned down our village to find us. Do you understand that? Why on earth would you intentionally put yourself in danger? You're smarter than that!"

"How would you know how smart I am? You've been gone for ten years!"

"Chiyoko, lower your voice."

She certainly does not—the muscles in her neck strain as she continues, as though she's shouting now. "You never so much as sent one letter until you left the Royal Brigade. We thought you were dead, Tiernan!" Her face is red, and Kilkenny's body is rigid.

Osheen and Alys keep their distance.

"When you were knighted and sent us your first letter, we thought you'd visit. Or that you'd at least have the decency to send another letter after that. Now you just show up after all this time and expect … what? What did you expect from me, Sir Tiernan?"

The title makes him flinch. For a while, there's nothing but visible tension buzzing between the siblings. Then Kilkenny says, "I can't explain ... Not right now."

Chiyoko's shoulders droop, her body deflating. She stares at Kilkenny for a while before storming off. Kilkenny clenches his fist, and the magical light goes out. He doesn't move from where he stands for some time. Neither do I.

Eventually, we all take care of any immediate needs in the bushes and change out of our festival outfits. We even risk sitting down for a moment. With a heavy, achy head, I move toward the riverbank to refill my waterskin. My body is unsteady, exhaustion seeping into my muscles and numbing my emotions. The world wavers before me as I stand by the river, and I fear for a moment that an episode is looming near.

Alys appears at my side. "How are you feeling, sweetling?" she signs, gently placing a hand on my shoulder.

"Fine." The practiced lie slips out and Alys purses her lips and raises her brows with incredulity. "And ... you can feel exactly how I'm feeling right now, can't you?" I ask with a sheepish grin.

Alys smiles and nods. "Indeed." She pulls a vial from the pocket of her trousers and slips it into my hand. "At least this will help the headache."

"Thank you, Alys." I uncork the bottle and swallow down the tincture before handing the vial back to her.

She pockets the empty bottle again and faces Kilkenny where he's seated a small distance away, tossing pebbles absentmindedly into the river. She calls to him. "How much longer before we should leave?"

Kilkenny rubs his face and then gestures, "Less than half an hour. Then we need to find someplace with more coverage."

Easier said than done.

Rolling his shoulders a few times as if he needs to shake the tension off, he approaches me. "If you're to learn how to use your powers, we need a baseline. Would you be open to sleeping without your dampener at night? That way we can get a better idea of how your dreamwalking works."

The idea makes my chest tighten, but I say, "Alright …"

"*Alright?* Do you understand the weight of this situation?"

I frown at him, the sudden switch startling me. "Of course, I do but—"

"I don't think you do."

Don't take your anger toward Chiyoko out on me, I want to say to him. But I swallow the words and scowl at him. As he inhales to speak again, Alys's hand appears on his shoulder.

"Tiernan," she says. She releases her grip as his face hardens.

"Coddling Garrick isn't going to help her, Alys. She's going to be in danger if—"

"You need to cool down," she says, holding his gaze. "Now." There's no anger on her face at all, and she signs with such gentleness, despite the heaviness behind her words, that I bet her tone is soothing as well.

Kilkenny huffs and laces his fingers atop his head as he walks off.

Chapter 50
CARYS

THE CONVERSATION I OVERHEARD last night replays incessantly in my mind. Directly confronting Iywan about it is too risky, but I somehow need to get more clarity on his plans.

"Carys?" Ellynne's face appears over my shoulder in the mirror.

"I'm alright," I assure her. I stare at my reflection—at the pale pink off-the-shoulder dress with wide, flowy sleeves, a voluminous skirt, and a short train that trails behind me when I walk. I normally wouldn't dare to wear this dress, wary of Iywan's disapproval about my bare shoulders and visible cleavage. But today I don't give a damn. Over the top, I don an ivory cape of velvet. Ellynne places one of my favorite diadems atop my head—the simple gold piece with opals that glint with movement.

I draw in a shuddery breath and turn, my dress and cape swaying heavily against me. "How do I look?" I ask.

The sisters utter a multitude of praises.

Liars. The internal voice is accompanied by an odd pang in my chest.

I suck in a breath and nod to the ladies before heading for the door.

Ren bows to me as I exit my bedchamber. "Where to, Your Highness?" he asks.

Gods, I miss Tiernan. He wouldn't have had to ask that question; my appearance would be enough to clue him in. And the dress I'm wearing can barely hold a candle to the Feast dress Durvla made me. I would've loved for her to make me more dresses—hells, I would've loved to get to know her better. I wasted such precious time being … egotistical. I straighten my posture and refocus on Ren. "To the throne room," I say with the most poise I can.

Together, we make our way through the corridors. I half expect him to lecture me about something the way Tiernan always did, but Ren is silent. It does nothing to pacify that infuriating pang in my chest that keeps reappearing.

The throne room is through the concourse, in the opposite direction of my mother's bedchamber. Outside of the room, a large crowd has gathered, a queue leading up to the archway. A pair of Queen's Guards, their black sashes standing out against their maroon livery, guard the archway where a large marble statue of the sun goddess, Agryna, stands.

"Look, it's the princess," someone calls out.

A flurry of bows and blessings make my heart hammer in my chest. I keep my focus on the statue of Agryna as I draw closer to the throne room entrance.

The marble figure wears a flowy dress, and a spherical shape with wavy metal details extending from it sits behind the figure's head, representing the sun.

My hand flies to the necklace at my chest and I clutch the warm pendant. Agryna's blessing … I nearly laugh. Wielding powers that murdered my brother … Thank you, Agryna for this bloody *blessing*.

"Your Highness," Ren says beside me, and I startle.

I swear under my breath. "Just paying my respects to the goddess," I say. I incline my head to the statue, all the while wishing that the gods still walked among us so I could have a word with this particular one. "Alright, let's go."

The guards step aside, and we waltz into the throne room where the domed ceiling is decorated with various sun paintings. Two statues, one of the Mother, Rhianu, and the other of the Father, Lugda, stand on either side of the room. Right now, I don't feel like the gods are on my side, but I resist scowling at the statues and instead glower at the man who sits on the throne.

Get your scrawny arse off my mother's throne, I want to say. I bite the inside of my cheek briefly to stop the words from flying out.

An older couple stands a few feet from the steps where the throne sits, their arms around each other. They're in the middle of a tragic story of sorts when our echoing footsteps cut off the man's narration. The couple turns to Ren and I, and, noticing my crown, they immediately genuflect. I paint a subtle smile on my face and nod politely.

"Welcome to the Fortress on the Mount," I say.

"Thank you, Your Highness." They speak in tandem.

Behind them, Iywan's dark hands grip the intricately carved arms of the throne before he pushes himself to stand. He takes in my attire, from my diadem down to my shoes, his brows raised. But he's practiced at concealing his emotions, and with an air of arrogance, he bows to me. "It is a pleasant surprise to have you here, Your Highness."

"Thank you, Lord Iywan for attending to our fine citizens in my absence. I will take it from here."

He bows again and gingerly makes his way down the red velvet-lined steps while I wait at the bottom. There are but four steps up to the throne, but each is weightier than the last. Ren stands beside me as I take my seat. My pulse quickens, and I press my feet against the floor, my hands gripping the arms of the throne that is far too large and menacing. But Tiernan would be proud of me, as would Alys.

"As you were," I say to the couple, and they begin telling me about the sickness that destroyed their families. Their adult daughter contracted a fever and very swiftly developed a cough. She began having fits and then lost the ability to breathe all together. Their infant granddaughter followed shortly after, but no one else in the household contracted the disease.

In the remaining hours of Audience, I listen to various citizens recount more of the same. Stories of the outbreak, of food shortages, and blight. Tradesmen between the Grounds and Mainland report crops perishing inexplicably or simply refusing to grow. Brooks are drying up, water levels sinking. Animals are struggling to thrive. I'm horrified that I didn't know the full extent of these issues.

What is the point of a Council if the issues that are actually plaguing our people are not being handled? Just as how the issues of the Forayers' overeagerness to apprehend Grounders unjustly have been swept beneath the rug. The councilmen are insufferable, and the councilwomen hardly speak up—typical. Things cannot continue this way.

It's time that I made some changes.

Time to take back the crown.

"More." I inch my wine goblet toward Eefa, who stands on the opposite end of the dining table. Hours ago, I was ready to take on an entire army—now, for no purpose that I can pinpoint, I feel as empty as my wine glass. Red liquid flows from her bottle into my cup.

"You should take it easy," Ellynne says from the chair beside me.

Eefa pouts. "Oh, but I find intoxicated Carys so titillating!"

I peer at her over the rim of the cup as I take a swig. Many scandalous promises shine in her eyes. I set the wine glass down. "Lord Iywan is aware of my ... activities," I drawl. "So, it ends now." I intend to sound sure and firm, but my voice comes out deflated. It matches my sentiments.

Eefa exhales dramatically. "Oh, pity."

Honestly, she doesn't appear too bothered, but that's Eefa. I have no doubt she has many other lovers. She leans over the back of the dining chair across from me, bracing her forearms on it. "I take it Lord Iywan is giving you a hard time about your choice in suitors?"

My gut twists. "I don't want to talk about it."

Ellynne reaches over and rubs my back gently; the gesture makes my eyes burn and my chest tighten. "I need to go," I say to no one in particular.

I'm up before either Eefa or Ellynne can say anything, and Callum follows along as I practically jog out of the dining hall.

We make it to my bedchamber in record time, and as I'm about to walk in, Callum grasps my arm, but I yank it away. He regards me with such tranquility that the fight is snuffed out of me. "I'm concerned about you," Callum says.

Laughter sputters out of me. "Of course you are. Who isn't? Callum, I'm so tired. I—"

"Maybe we should step inside?"

I sigh softly, gesturing to the door. Together, we enter my bedchamber, and I'm hit with a surge of more longing than I know how to handle. Normally, Callum entering the inner sanctum of my bedchamber is simple, but now I can only stare up at him, my eyes prickling with tears.

"Car—"

My hands act on their own accord, shoving him against the door. With fistfuls of his livery, I yank him down to my level and press my lips against his. He resists, pulling his head back slightly. I don't know what comes over me, but I bite down. It's not driven by passion, but something else. Something blistering and enraged and so very confused.

Callum pulls away with a sharp gasp, lifting a hand to his lower lip where blood blooms.

I step back, my hands over my mouth. "I didn't mean— I just ..." I turn to walk away but Callum grabs my hand, pulling me close.

"I did once say that I wasn't opposed to biting, didn't I?" he asks me, the corner of his lips quirking up.

I smirk at him. "Yes, but I'm sure you didn't mean for me to bite you like some rabid hound."

He lowers his forehead against mine, and it's so tender that my heart aches to the point where I can't breathe. He cares so much for me, and I ... I'm just perplexed. It's too much. I turn away from him. "Leave."

He doesn't move right away, but before I can shout at him, the door shuts behind me. I start to pace, fiddling with my amulet until a knock startles me.

"It's me."

Ellynne. I don't respond, but that doesn't stop her from barging in.

"Please talk to me," she says quietly when the door shuts behind her.

A solitary tear rolls down my cheek, and I swat it away as I continue pacing.

"Carys."

"Please, just go away." I hate how small my voice sounds.

Ellynne nods, but the question remains on her face. "Alright. But I will be back later. You just need a hot bath and rest. Tomorrow is a new day. Nighttime brings out the worst in us, but with the dawn comes new perspectives."

Abruptly, I stop pacing and reel on her. *"Go. Away!"*

She blinks quickly, but then she bobs a small curtsy and retreats.

The door closes behind her and I allow the tears to fall. I cannot trust her. I cannot trust anyone. I need to figure things out myself— there is no one else to help me clean up this mess. Not my mother, not Alys, not Tiernan. Not Callum, Ellynne, Lowri, or Eefa. *Certainly* not Iywan or the councilors.

Audience was one small step, but it solves nothing. I need to expose Iywan to the Council. But with my history, will that only make it look as though I've finally lost my mind?

I fear I'll have to risk it.

Chapter 51
DURVLA

AS WE RIDE ACROSS the contours of the land, my arms wrapped around Kilkenny's waist, I desperately want to stop to admire the stars above. There is a vibrant blend of colors that I've never seen in the night sky before. I want so much to dismount Ghendor and lay in the grass. To just take some time to breathe, admire the constellations, connect the dots, sleep ...

I'm exhausted; long gone is the satisfied fullness and joviality of the Festival of Damarlach. My heart contracts at the memory of Dubh Carrig up in flames. I can't get the image out of my head.

Durvla needs to be trained. Her powers would be a great asset to the rebellion. Haruka's words echo in my mind. Me, a great asset to the rebellion? It's laughable. On a daily basis, I trip over my own two feet, I'm susceptible to dizziness and headaches ... Until two weeks ago, I had no idea that magic even still existed, let alone that *I* had magic. I highly doubt that I can hone my powers to be any use to the rebellion, anyway.

Unwittingly, my arms tighten around Kilkenny's middle, and he tenses in response. I immediately loosen my grip and prepare to apologize, but he just keeps riding. He never looks back, nor reacts further. He's been generally speechless since the scene back at our riverside stop hours ago. I can't blame him after the chewing out his sister gave him.

Why didn't he write to his family all those years? Especially with knightly privilege, he should've been free to write to them and even to visit them. Yet he didn't. There is so often a faraway look on his face, as though he's living in some distant past or an even more distant future. He seldom smiles, seldom jokes, seldom reveals much of anything.

He perplexes me.

The dagger he made for me is suddenly heavy against my thigh. I don't know how to use it, and I can't fathom taking a life, anyway. Hopefully, there will never come a time when I'll have to.

In the dark, it's hard to make out the changes in the landscape, but we've not seen a house for some time, and there are no trees or dense shrubbery for refuge. The air grows cooler and my eyelids heavier. But at last, we make it to a town with scattered houses, and Chiyoko suggests that we stop at a stable.

Kilkenny dismounts and enters the stable, returning a moment later. "There's water and hay and a couple of goats, so we'll need to leave before the farmhands or owners arrive in the morning."

That's good enough for all of us. We're worn out. I would sleep on a rock formation at this point. As I dismount, my knees nearly give out and I can't walk straight for a while. Alys sets a glowing ball of light from her hands in a glass lantern hanging against a wall, illuminating the stable where two brown goats gawk at us uneasily from the corner.

At least they aren't aggressive, because none of us have the energy for that. We spread out our bedrolls over the hay, and Kilkenny approaches his sister. I hold my breath, certain he is going to instigate another argument, but he speaks to her in a calm manner. Chiyoko nods, a hint of a smile flickering across her stubborn face.

I squint at Kilkenny's hands in the darkness as he waves me over. We step closer to the magically lit lantern to better see each other. Nervous energy surrounds him, his leather vest rippling across his chest as he pulls in a deep breath. "I shouldn't have approached you the way I did earlier. My apologies," he signs silently.

His apology is so unusual for the Kilkenny that I've come to know over the past few weeks, I can only stare at him.

"I did, however, mean what I said about you needing to train."

Typical.

"I know it's scary, but we need to know. You need to know the extent of your dreamwalking. It's a very rare power that a lot of people don't fully understand. So, there will be a lot of figuring it out. Once we get to the Verge, there will be people with more experience that might be able to help. But for now, it will only do you a disservice to leave you with no idea at all of how to control your gift."

My chest tightens and I force myself to take a steadying breath. "Alright. So, you want me to remove the bracelet now?"

"Yes. If we don't find any answers tonight, we'll take a different approach tomorrow. One step at a time."

It certainly can't be that simple, but I nod. "Thank you, by the way. For admitting that you were in the wrong."

His lips curl up into a semblance of a smile. "Don't get used to it, Garrick."

A little band of anxiety wraps around my heart again as I lift my wrist and stare at the bracelet. It's incredible that this little, seemingly valueless trinket holds so much strength. I flip my hand over and untie the bracelet from my inner wrist. As soon as it's off, my knees buckle as an overwhelming force surges through my body, pulsing through my veins, buzzing beneath my skin. My vision blurs, and Kilkenny grasps my upper arms.

"Breathe." He inhales exaggeratedly, demonstrating.

I inhale and exhale deeply until my head clears and the unease slowly melts away. When that soldier had ordered the removal of my bracelet back in Paramount, the sensations had been overwhelming, but at the time I'd blamed it only on my emotions.

Kilkenny's expression is assessing. "How do you feel?"

I roll my shoulders, trying to shake the unease from my body. "Strange."

"Put the dampener in your pack so it's away from you completely for the night. I don't want it to interfere."

"Alright." I stifle a yawn behind my hand.

"Sleep." It's not a question, but he doesn't have to tell me twice.

I slip my bracelet into my bag before heading over to my bedroll between Osheen and Alys, with Chiyoko across from me. "I'm going to talk to Tiernan," Chiyoko signs. "We have some catching up to do."

The sentiment warms my heart. "Good luck."

Alys and Osheen still regard me. "All good?" Alys asks, her focus moving to my bare wrist.

"I'm anxious." Admitting it aloud makes me even more worried. Especially with Osheen looking at me as though I'll erupt at any moment.

Carys stands on the deck of a ship, her hand lightly grasping the railing while a gentle ocean breeze blows through her curtain of raven hair. Her face is lifted to

the blue sky, the rays of the sun bringing out the golden streaks in her hair. The scattering of freckles across her nose and cheeks extends across her sun-kissed skin.

There's a swell of happiness in her chest, a sense of freedom and hope.

Holding on to the mast, I watch from a distance, and it's all so eerily … real. I glance around. There are only wide-open waters, no land on the horizon. But Carys doesn't care. She turns and I hold my breath, but her gaze slides right past me. Her back is to the railing when a monstrous wave rises up, up, up. Horror drains Carys's already pale complexion as she turns, the same cold terror invading my own body. I grasp the mast, but it isn't enough to keep me safe when the wave comes crashing down—

I awake with a gasp, coughing and sputtering, my lungs reluctant to expand. Firm hands grasp my shoulders, yanking me back into the present. I frantically gauge my surroundings, squinting in the bit of sunshine that fills the stable. There's no ocean. No boat. No Carys. But it's a while before I stop coughing and find my breath again.

"I dreamt something," I choke out.

Kilkenny's eyes widen. "Tell me," he signs.

I continue speaking, the words rushing out of me. "Carys. She was on a boat of some sort. She just stood there. But she looked … happy. Until a wave sunk the ship."

He sits back on his heels and stares at me as though I'm a puzzle to be solved. "She's always dreamt of sailing far away from Erleya," he motions as he speaks. "Sounds like a good dream turned into a nightmare."

I'm not sure what to make of that. It's nothing like the dream I had of the queen. It's more like … that *other* dream, but with an added nightmare element. My cheeks redden and I glance around, but everyone's busy getting ready to set off again. I return to signing silently. "I had another dream of Carys before. Back in Paramount."

He waits and my cheeks heat. It must be evident, because his brows rise.

"Gods … I can't believe I'm going to admit this …" Maybe it's not even important, and then I'll have made a fool of myself.

"Now you *have* to tell me."

I sigh. "It was the night when you caught me going for a late walk in the castle. I had a not-so-innocent dream of Carys and Callum … you know." I wince. "I'm certain it was her dream about Callum because there is no way I could've … heard … gods, don't make me spell this out."

His puzzled expression lingers, then his brows dart up again and he straightens. "Oh. Are you saying that you dreamt of—"

I can only nod, the flush crawling up my neck. I try to read his face. His jaw is set but his eyes twinkle.

"How much did you—"

"It was rather vivid."

Slowly, Kilkenny's mask starts to fracture, his lips working to remain tightly shut. He suddenly turns his face away from me, but the moment the laughter breaks free, his shoulders shake, and he holds a fist against his mouth.

"Oy!" I exclaim. I shove my hand against his shoulder, and he faces me again, but that amusement is far from gone. "It's not funny!"

We draw the attention of the others, particularly Chiyoko who intentionally steps closer to listen in.

I stare at Kilkenny's lips as he says, "You're … you're absolutely right." But he can't rein in his amusement and the wide smile remains. He scrubs his hand over his face and his chest expands with a deep inhalation. When he exhales again, he tries to school his features, but it only leads to more laughter.

"Stop!" I tell him, but for some reason, I can't help but join in. His genuine laughter is refreshing. His whole face lights up endearingly, his disposition relaxes. The man before me is not Sir Tiernan, not Major

Kilkenny. Just … Tiernan Kilkenny. His laughter simmers down to an occasional chuckle. There is no pretense, no angst, no sadness.

I wish I could do something to keep that smile there forever.

"Apologies," he says, sobering, and I want so much to tell him not to stop smiling. "We'd better get going. Don't want you to have more lewd dreams."

My jaw drops. Is he teasing me?

"Durvla's having lewd dreams?" Chiyoko asks. "Oh-ho-ho do tell! Who was it with? Don't tell me it was with this sorry bastard." She jabs her thumb toward Kilkenny.

Still crouched in front of me and not even flinching from Chiyoko's insult, Kilkenny winks at me, and I'm sure my *entire* body flushes. He stands and walks away, leaving me to deal with Chiyoko. I get to my feet and wait for my head to clear. Chiyoko remains, grinning at me. "So …"

"I didn't have a lewd dream … this time."

Chiyoko dissolves into laughter. "You've dreamwalked into people's sex dreams?"

Now Osheen is blushing, and I want the earth to swallow me whole. Alys comes to my rescue, playfully nudging Chiyoko's arm. "Chiyo, she can't help which dreams she walks into yet. Don't tease." Alys gives my shoulder a little squeeze before heading off to her horse.

Chiyoko walks backward, still grinning at me. Then she signs, "I still want details."

I hold back a chuckle.

Of course, I'm the last to get ready. I rinse my face and mouth with a bit of water from my waterskin. Osheen joins me, gently bumping his shoulder against mine. "What was that about?" he asks.

"Nothing." I don't know why I lie to him, but there was something about that dream. It was more than just the context that bothered me—it was the intrusion. So wrong in so many ways.

I don't want this power. To be privy to people's innermost desires.

My laughter from moments ago completely dies now. Though as I glance over at Kilkenny, sheathing his swords again, I'm reminded of *his* laughter, and a small smile returns to my face.

Chapter 52
CARYS

THE SUN HAS BARELY risen when I awake from my dream, but like Ellynne said last night, it's a new day with a new perspective. Once I'd cooled down, I'd summoned her and Lowri and asked Ellynne to read my fortune—as close to an apology as I could muster.

As I sit back against my headboard and stretch, I catch a bit of red on the edge of my vision and I startle. I'd forgotten that Ellynne had refused to leave me alone last night. She's sprawled out on the bed beside me, her bright curls tumbling over my pillow, her mouth gaping open. I slip discretely out of bed and pad over to my wardrobe. I put on a sky blue dress that fastens at the front, strap ivory shoes onto my feet and practically tiptoe to my door.

My hand barely rests on the knob when Ellynne's groggy voice comes from behind me. "Trying to sneak off?"

I wince and glance over my shoulder as Ellynne slowly sits up, her hair beyond unruly.

She lazily smooths her hands over her waves, a scowl on her face. "Oh, like you look much better when you first wake."

I've never seen her quite so fresh from slumber—her cattiness makes me grin. Since Ellynne braided my hair before I slept, it's been spared the same fate as hers. "I'm going to visit the queen," I say.

Ellynne hops off the bed and strides toward me. "Not looking like that, you aren't." The stubborn pucker of her lips tells me there will be no arguing with her.

Twenty minutes later, my hair is rebraided and rolled into a crown as Sir Ren and I step into my mother's bedchamber. My stomach lurches as Iywan turns toward me. Once again, Briony is there. She stands with a sweet smile and curtsies to me, as usual. She doesn't say a word, however, and she's out of the chamber before I can even move from where I stand.

The fairytale book is hugged to my chest—perhaps more truth than fable. I still can't believe it. Iywan doesn't look away from me, and I'm chilled by the detachment in his expression.

"The queen needs her rest," he says to me at last.

A dozen brash responses flow through my mind, but I ignore him and make my way toward the queen. "Good morning, mother." I channel my unease into the tome clutched in my hands, but I manage to keep my voice calm somehow. "Ready to continue our story?"

Iywan turns toward the window, and I settle on the bed beside my mother. She's asleep, her hair nearly fully silver, her face haggard and ashen. My heart constricts in my chest, and I swallow thickly as I open the book to the last page I'd read her.

"Where were we?" I ask softly. It's awkward reading to her with Iywan here, but I'm not going to let him intimidate me out of the one thing I have left with my mother. I will deal with him later. "So,

Enidwen summoned the prince of the Underworld, and when he smiles, it's bloody terrifying."

By heart, Enidwen recited the enchantment that she had so often rehearsed to release the Underling Prince from his bonds and be granted her greatest desire. The sun grew black in the sky, the earth froze over, and a tempest-like gust of shadows rose from the depths, swirling around Enidwen relentlessly. Enidwen was ecstatic, eager to receive ultimate power. She envisioned destroying armies, claiming thrones, claiming nations, raising an empire. She saw the realm bowing down before her, she saw the people's adoration of her. No more weak Enidwen. No more useless bride of an Otherworlder. She would be the Enchantress Empress.

No, the Enchantress *Goddess*.

Her laughter filled the air, but soon she realized that the power pouring into her was tainted. It wasn't her own.

No, the Underling Prince now stood before her, that jagged-toothed grin too close to her face.

Enidwen's laughter was choked off as the Underling Prince wrapped a bony hand around her throat. "My eternal thanks for releasing me," he said. "Now you are mine."

The Underling Prince squeezed Enidwen's neck until her world faded to nothingness. When Enidwen awoke again, she assumed the Underling Prince was gone. But no … she could hear his taunting voice inside of her. He pushed his way into her memories, her desires, her very being. Enidwen clasped her hands over her head and screamed until she was hoarse, until she could no longer fight the intrusion, until there was nothing left of her own mind.

She'd fallen for the prince's trap, wanting power for selfish reasons, for desiring it more than life itself. Her body was the perfect vessel for the Prince of the Underworld.

The now-possessed Evil Enchantress Queen rose up from her haunches and unleashed her terror upon the realm. Hope was lost until the Heirs of Dusk and Embers appeared. Within the solace of dusk—

Wait a minute … I stop reading and stare at the page. That can't be right. The Heirs of Dusk and Embers? Solace of dusk? My fingers crawl over the words. I've read this tale countless times before and it's always said *the Heirs of Agryna*. The Heirs of Agryna rose up against the Enchantress Queen and defeated her while cloaked in the light of the chosen. It's the same tale that both Durvla and I have always favored—the one where the Lightweavers saved the realm.

I flip through the pages. This is the same book I've always read, isn't it? The heavy pages thud as I flip to the front, seeking the first page where *Carys Meredyth fa Rhodri* and the word *translated* had been written in beautiful calligraphy from the time my mother first gave the book to me.

My name is still there, as it's always been, but the words *prime edition* sits below it.

This isn't my original book.

What does prime edition even mean? I search my mother's unresponsive face, desperate for the answers I know she can't give. As I turn to an earlier page in the book, Iywan appears in my peripheral vision, staring down at it before I can close it. My pulse quickens.

"You were reading *that*?" he asks.

My brows draw together, and I scrutinize the words on the page again. "Yes … ?"

"When did you learn to read the Ancient Tongue?"

"I ..." Staring down at the page again, I frown. Slowly, the symbols morph and I recoil; it's definitely not the common tongue. How is it possible that I never noticed? I slam the book shut. "I have to go," I say, jumping to my feet.

To my surprise, Iywan doesn't stop me as I rush out, my heart hammering. My heels thud against the ground as I run through the corridors, ignoring Ren's calls even as he keeps up with my rapid footfalls. I'm winded by the time I get to my bedchamber and slam the door in Ren's face without a word to him.

Dropping the book onto my desk, I step away from it and stare. What next? It'll burst into flames? I'm not sure what to expect of it anymore. How could I have been reading a different *language* without realizing it?

Pressing the heels of my hands against my eyes, I pace back and forth, trying to remember the details of when I was given the book. I was probably five years old, and the book definitely had *translated* written on it where *prime edition* now exists. I'd read the book so often and so frequently that the pages began to wear, and the binding loosened. It was only a year ago that my mother—

Wait, I remember my mother had taken the book and sent it away to be repaired. Nothing had appeared different except for the front and back cover that had been replaced with nondescript leather. How could I have never noticed that she had replaced the entire book? How can I read in a language I didn't even know existed?

When my mother had given me the new book, she'd made me read a passage aloud to her. She'd stared at me hopefully as I read and had beamed as if it was my first time ever reading. *You're a natural,* she'd said, and I never thought much of it.

Heirs of Agryna.

Heirs of Dusk and Embers.

If one is a translation of the other, are they synonymous?

Gods help me.

·· ∘ ☽ ☀ ☾ ∘ ··

I'm still flipping through pages of my fairytale book when the sun sets. I sit on the floor in front of my fireplace, combing through page after page for any other discrepancies. In the translation that I had, Shadow Wielders practiced dark magic and were vanquished by the Lightweavers. But in this version, the Shadow Wielders fought along-side the Lightweavers.

Once again, everything I've been told is a lie.

I want to march into my mother's bedchamber and force her wake, to demand that she explain things to me. Like how I can read the Ancient Tongue without even noticing. Why she intentionally replaced my book and didn't bother to tell me. Just as she didn't bother to tell me about my own powers—or her powers for that matter.

I slam the tome shut and rise with it, slipping it under my bed, although I've walked around the palace with it fully on display plenty of times. Now it feels like something that should've been kept secret. I need to know more. I need to figure things out.

I need to get to the library.

·· ∘ ☽ ☀ ☾ ∘ ··

Thousands of books stand before me—shelves upon shelves from the floor to the top of the ornate domed ceiling ... I'm suddenly struck with just how daunting this search would be. Where do I start? What am I even searching for? I fiddle with my amulet, turning in a slow circle in the royal library.

Walk, says a voice within me, sending a shiver down my spine.

A strange sensation draws me toward the very back of the library, through the archway that leads to the historical archives. I approach a shelf of plain leather spines.

"Now what?" I ask aloud, as though my own internal voice would respond.

Silence.

Gods, I hate silence. I zip my amulet along the necklace as I walk down the row of books. Dust coats the shelves, as though no one has dared to venture this far for quite some time. I make it to the wall, and as I'm about to turn to walk back down the row of shelves, one book in particular catches my attention. As I stare at it, four glowing symbols materialize: a singular spiral, three whorls, a cross within a circle, and a triquetra. The symbols fade away as I reach for the book.

I remove the book carefully and stare at the title: *The Book of Agryna*. The symbol of the goddess is inked into the front cover. I trace my fingers over the beautifully engraved whorls within the sun, the wavy rays radiating off the center.

It's exactly like my necklace. I press my hand against my pendant before taking the book to one of the two velvet armchairs in the main chamber and sinking into the comfortable cushions. The book is thin, but the text—written in the Ancient Tongue—is tiny. There's a lot more information here than I expected from such a small book, beginning with a short history of Agryna in the days when the old gods and goddesses roamed the mortal realm.

Agryna is the patron goddess of the royal house of Erleya— my ancestors on my father's side. I flip through the pages, searching for something—but *what?* There are references to shadows and dusk quite often, used almost interchangeably. The sun casts shadows.

Dusk comes after sunset, just before nightfall. Under the cover of dusk and shadows, there is protection and relief from the heat of Agryna's rays.

Solace of dusk ... ? Like from the book of fairytales. Is it connected somehow?

From the beginning of time, Agryna and Ehlach, sister and brother deities, worked to maintain perfect balance. Day and night. Fire and shadow ... Embers and dusk.

The Heirs of Dusk and Embers.

In ancient times, there were priests and priestesses of Agryna. They not only worshipped the goddess, but also possessed magical powers, gifts bestowed upon them by Agryna. Namely flamewielding and lightweaving. They spoke in the Ancient Tongue and documented many prophecies in sacred texts. Which ... my moronic ancestor later destroyed when he sought to eradicate magic from the kingdom.

I suppose Enidwen's tale isn't fictional either.

I thumb through the book, skimming over texts of the Veil being forced open and the sun and moon *falling* from the sky, setting off an eternal winter and never-ending darkness.

My hands slicken with perspiration, gooseflesh breaking out over my arms and the back of my neck. I roll my shoulders to loosen them, wipe my hands on my dress one at a time, then flip to the back of the book where there are handwritten notes. A list of references.

```
**The Song of Moonlight (prophecy). Banishment of
Enidwen. The Beginning of the Purge. Lugda's hells (and
the secret prison). Caiolair's Champion.
```

Then there is an underlined note scrawled on the bottom of the page:

Caiolair foretold the fall of the old gods in 1024
After Purge. It will begin with the rise—

The corner of the page is ripped out along with the rest of the text. How convenient.

My entire body goes cold. 1024 After Purge. That's … next year. And … *fall of the gods*? No one's seen proof of the gods in ages. The name *Caiolair* doesn't ring a bell to me, not from any fairytales nor word of mouth. Yet it's here twice on one page.

"Carys?" Callum calls. I jump so hard that I nearly fall out of the chair.

"Yes, Callum?" I ask, an edge to my voice.

"Everything alright? You've been in here for a while." He steps in, shutting the door behind him before approaching.

My head is light, my breath shallow as I pinch the bridge of my nose. I press my feet against the floor to keep myself rooted in this moment. Slowly, I loosen my grip on the book and gently set it on the table before lifting my face to Callum's. "I need you to help me find something. Please." I'm on my feet, already hurrying back toward the dusty shelves. "*The Song of Moonlight. Banishment of Enidwen* … Something about Caiolair."

Callum's quick footfalls trail me. "I don't understand," he whispers, closer than I'd expected. I spin to face him and my back hits the shelves, sending a pang through me. He grasps my upper arms and pulls me away from the shelves, closer to him.

It takes effort to inhale and release the breath. "I don't understand either."

Still holding me away from the shelves, he tilts his head slightly.

"I can't explain, but I need to find these other books. *Song of Moonlight. Enidwen's*—" All the titles flee my mind, my body unsure how to handle his proximity in the midst of this situation. "Oh for …" I push my hand against his chest to put some space between us and point beyond the shelves with my free hand. "It's in the book I set down on the table. *The Book of Agryna.*"

Callum leans in, his brows drawn together as he presses his hand over mine where it's still against his chest. "Alright. I'll get the book, and we'll figure this out." His tone is gentle and hushed.

My legs turn wobbly, and I sag against him for a moment. Pulling in a slow, tremulous breath, I stand upright again and clear my throat. "Thank you, Callum."

Once Callum gets *The Book of Agryna* for our reference, we begin an intense search for the books listed. Shelf after shelf, book after book—we search and search until my head aches, until my vision begins to blur. When every book title has been checked, we collapse onto the armchairs.

There are a thousand questions written all over Callum's face, none of which I can answer, because I'm equally befuddled, but I need to figure it out. Iywan wants to open the Veil … just as Enidwen had. *Everyone's* life may be in danger.

Chapter 53
DURVLA

A RIVER WINDS AND dips and eventually gives way to a trickling creek as the land levels out, and wide pastures stretch before us. We ride past a herd of fluffy cows, and Chiyo moos aggressively at them, forming horns atop her head with her fingers before waving as if they'd wave back. It tugs laughter from all of us. She is wildly unpredictable and couldn't care less about keeping up appearances, much unlike her brother.

We stop by the river to fill our waterskins and allow the horses to drink again. Along the banks is an unruly growth of vibrant yellow flowers, though several patches are dull in color, the stems limp and hanging over the water. Still others are completely brown and withered. I move toward the plants, crouching. As soon as I touch one of the limp flowers, it falls off the stem. Another falls apart in the palm of my hand.

It's similar to what I encountered in the greenhouse shortly before I was taken from Cluain Baile. Osheen crouches beside me, a question on his face. "What's going on?" he asks.

I extend my hand with the dying petals and sign with my free hand, "This isn't the first time I've seen this. The plants in our greenhouse were dying. Even though they'd had the best care. I hadn't thought much of it then, but along the way, I've noticed some other foliage that appears … blighted."

Osheen's lips tug down. "Mam says they never grew back," he signs. "And the crops have been sparser than usual this year."

The others join us, equally curious. We catch them up on our discussion and Chiyoko says, "What are the odds that it's just a coincidence?"

I shrug my shoulder and drop the petals at last, dusting my hands off on my trousers as I stand. "Perhaps invasive insects?" I suggest, but deep down I suspect there is something else responsible. I just can't fathom what.

We soon mount our horses again—as much as I need to train my powers, it's more important that we stay ahead of the Forayers.

Training is delayed.

We've been traveling for over two weeks since fleeing from Paramount, and I realize that I don't know much about my travel companions. As we refill our waterskins in a small brook and give our horses a chance to rehydrate, Kilkenny's sleeve slips back, and I catch a glimpse of the ink on his inner forearm. He firmly tugs his sleeve down again. There's no point in trying to pretend that I wasn't staring, so I apologize. "I never noticed until back in Dubh Carrig that you have a tattoo."

"I've made sure to keep it hidden."

The same way I've made sure to keep the brand mark on my arm hidden. I cork my waterskin again and reattach it to my belt as I stand. It's no surprise that he doesn't want to talk about his tattoo—he rarely wants to talk about himself. I remember his words back in Paramount: *I said I'd keep your secrets, Garrick. I didn't say I'd tell you mine.* I know where I stand in the exchange of information, so I offer him a tight smile and turn to leave, but he waves to keep my attention.

Trying to feign nonchalance, I stand still and wait silently.

"When I was first conscripted, they branded me," he signs.

My hand involuntarily moves to my forearm, where my own brand remains.

"When I started working with Alys, she noticed the scars and offered to tattoo over them." He pulls back his sleeve and shows me the symbol inked into his skin. The tattoo extends from his wrist to his inner elbow, and I can't help but smile at the almost predictable symbol he's chosen.

"A sword. How fitting." I smile at him.

He shrugs and one corner of his lips tilts up in a little smirk.

I suppose tattooing over the scars on his neck would've been too hard to conceal.

Chiyo and Osheen, who have been conspicuously eavesdropping, come closer to get a better look at Kilkenny's tattoo. Chiyo grins at her brother, the apples of her cheeks and her nose flushed despite Alys healing her sunburn multiple times. "Daring," she says. "I like it." She regards her brother with a newfound respect. Her blue and brown hair is pulled back into two low buns, and her multiple earrings glint in the sunlight.

Kilkenny tugs his sleeve down again, and my smile fades as I remember the sear of the branding stick marring my own skin. Even now, I can almost smell my singeing flesh … I must wince because Kilkenny's face grows heavy with worry. "Are you in pain?" he signs.

I release my arm where I'm clutching it across my torso and coax a smile to my face. "No pain. Just …" I glance at Alys who nods knowingly. "I was also branded when I was brought to Paramount."

Kilkenny's shoulders tense. He reaches for my left arm but pauses. "May I?"

Nodding, I watch as he unbuttons and rolls back the sleeve of my tunic. The burn has healed, leaving behind an unsightly scar in a gruesome semblance of the royal insignia. It's a mix of dark brown and tan, and my skin is slightly raised in some parts, pulled too tightly in others.

Chiyo has her hand over her mouth, her eyes wide, and Osheen is no less shocked. Somehow it never dawned on me that they haven't seen the brand before.

"Durvla, I had no idea they did that to you. I'm so sorry," Osheen signs.

Kilkenny continues to hold my arm with one hand while his fingers lightly trace the outside of the scar. His touch sends a shiver through me and it's surprisingly not unpleasant. There's a degree of anger etched into his face despite his tender motions. He turns to Alys, "Is it too late to completely heal this?"

"She already did," I say. "Well, she did what she could without looking suspicious, I assume."

Regret ghosts across Alys's face. "I sped up the natural healing process. I wish the circumstances had been different, so I could've healed it completely. I'm sorry, sweetling."

"It's fine, Alys." I peer down at my arm again as Kilkenny starts to roll my sleeve back down.

His eyes are steely when they meet mine. "Who branded you?"

"One of the guards in the brig." I dig into the recesses of my mind. "I think his name is Bronn."

A spark of rage flashes on his face. "If he ever crosses my path, he'll regret ever having laid a hand on you."

My stomach does a somersault as his eyes promise violence.

Violence for *my* sake.

Confusion nestles just beneath something that oddly resembles appreciation. I've somehow forgotten that I need to exhale, and when I do, I tear my gaze from his to find Chiyo staring at me.

"What?" I ask.

"Maybe Alys can tattoo over your branding as well."

My brows rise.

"Maybe knitting needles. Or a spool of thread and a needle." She laughs, and it tugs a smile from me. Kilkenny's mood remains solemn.

"Wait until we get to the Verge," Alys motions. "My husband is an even better tattoo artist." She winks.

"You have a husband?" Osheen speaks at the same time I do. Neither Chiyo nor Kilkenny are surprised, though.

Alys laughs and nods. "Oh yes," she says. "But that's a tale for another stop."

Chapter 54
DURVLA

AFTER ANOTHER WEEK ON the road, the village of Glinrew surprises us with a vibrant open market. The dirt roads are strewn with a multitude of vendors and villagers, the air thick with assorted aromas. My legs can't decide whether to be grateful for the break from horseback or provoked by having to walk. At least we've managed to stay ahead of the Forayers—there hasn't been any sign of them lately.

We reluctantly leave our horses at a stable, and Alys generously tips the stable hands. Walking through the streets, we're among vendors selling textiles and produce, wood crafts, and metalwork. I walk between Alys and Kilkenny with Osheen and Chiyo a few paces ahead. They're chatting, as usual, Chiyo nudging Osheen with her elbow and laughing at something he says in response. Something tugs in my chest. I used to have that sort of easygoing relationship with him.

"So, your husband is a rebel," I say to Alys, hoping to distract myself.

Alys smiles, tugging loose waves of her thick salt-and-pepper hair beneath the colorful headscarf she wears. I focus on her mouth, back to fully relying on lipreading. "Yes. He's second-in-command, in fact."

I stare at her, wide-eyed. I want to ask so much more about the rebellion and the chain of command. But more importantly, I want to learn about Alys and her family. "How long have you two been apart?"

"I last saw him very briefly probably a year ago. We met up in Darragh for a night. He was a tradesman from Moicriach but has been in the Verge for about seven years by now."

"*Seven years?*"

Alys nods. "Yes, about as long as I've been the head healer at Paramount. Before that, we lived in Moicriach and then Darragh ... With our daughter."

I stop walking. "You have a daughter, too? How old? And how long have you and your husband been married? Too many questions?"

Alys laughs. "She's twenty-six. A woman grown by now. My husband and I were together when I gave birth, then we separated. We didn't reconcile until Ava was about ten years old, but we've been thick as thieves since then. Being away from them is hard, but necessary. When we can, we exchange notes via enchanted parchment."

I hope that my next words come out as quietly as I intend. "*Enchanted parchment?*"

Alys smiles and nods.

Gods, there's so much I don't know about magic. "Alys, you must be the greatest spy of all time."

She laughs.

"The name that Haruka called you: Elviera ... Is that your real name?"

"My birth name, rather. When I moved here as a child, I took up a new name to fit in with my friends. At this stage in my life, I'm as much Alys as I am Elviera."

"Where were you born?"

"Balghero. It's a land far south of Erleya. My parents were from even farther away. To the east. My grandparents and the generations before lived a nomadic life, but my parents decided to settle in this new land. I'm so very glad they did, as I got to meet all of you." She smiles and winks at me, and my lips curve up.

"Do you miss Balghero?" I ask her.

"Sometimes."

Ahead of us, Chiyo grabs Osheen's hand and drags him to a vendor selling weapons. Beside me, Kilkenny follows his sister's movements. His jaw is set, his body rigid. We pause, but Osheen glances back at us from where Chiyo is chatting animatedly with the blacksmith. He gestures vaguely and mouths something that I can't make out.

Kilkenny faces me. "He says we can go on without them."

I'm not sure if it's a good idea to separate, but we've already agreed to meet up at the stables before nightfall if we do lose track of each other.

Not long after we've separated from Osheen and Chiyo, my stomach sinks with a sudden thought. We left Carys all alone with powers that she doesn't know how to control. I'm at least with people who understand what it's like to possess an ability that could literally get me killed, and it's still terrifying for me. My body begins to thrum with nervous energy, my hands tingling.

Kilkenny gives me a questioning look, but I turn to Alys again. "Does your husband also have powers?" I ask her as we follow the dirt road around a bend that leads to yet more vendors.

"No, he's Ordinary, but absolutely extraordinary if you ask me."

I can't help but giggle at the enamored glaze that comes over her face. "Extraordinary in looks or personality or both?" I ask with a grin.

She laughs. "Both."

Her smile remains, but the faraway look on her face is one I've seen before. I just can't pinpoint it.

We walk a bit further, moving through the crowds and past various vendors. "What's your husband's name?" I ask Alys.

"Dayfyd," she says with that dreamy expression again.

I giggle. "Alright, now you *have* to tell me what he looks like, because I can tell you're picturing him."

She laughs freely, her teeth bright against her smooth mahogany skin. "He's very handsome. His eyes are a gorgeous hazel green. I remember so clearly when I first met him, I was lost in his eyes. It turns out, he was lost in mine." She smiles sadly, but then something catches her attention. A stall with colorful fabrics like the scarf she has tied around her hair. "Those are stunning. You lovelies go ahead. I can use a new scarf." She winks at me and walks toward the stall.

As I turn my attention back to the path, a delicious aroma wafts into my nostrils, making my mouth water. My stomach gurgles, and Kilkenny glances at me with an arched brow. "Hungry?"

I hadn't noticed it until now but … "Starving."

He nods to a stall up ahead where little wisps of smoke rise into the air. The aroma grows stronger as we approach a stand where a man with tanned skin and white hair turns some kind of brown meat on a stick over a fire. Beef, by the scent. My stomach growls again as Kilkenny has a chat with the man.

There are so many people here, both shoppers and tradesmen alike. Chiyo and Osheen are nowhere in sight, but we all know where to meet each other later. Happening upon this market was a godsend— something so comfortingly typical to distract us from the fact that we're running for our lives. We can't stay here long, but with so many people here, it would be hard for Forayers to find us in the crowd.

Though, that didn't work out so well for the villagers of Dubh Carrig … My stomach twists uncomfortably.

Kilkenny gently nudges me before handing me a skewer of meat. I take it, and steam wafts off the charred beef. The aroma is sinfully delicious, and I lick my lips, restraining myself from biting right into it and burning my mouth. Kilkenny, however, has no such restraint. Before I know it, he's huffing and puffing and fanning at his mouth. I burst into laughter, and he fixes me with a stare that only makes me laugh more.

Alys catches up with us. "That looks delicious … What happened to you?" She smiles as she points to Kilkenny and lifts her brows in a question.

"Kilkenny was too impatient to wait for his meat to cool," I explain.

Alys chuckles and digs coins out of her pocket to pay the vendor for her own chunk of beef. "Those sellers I found are from my homeland, Balghero, so we're just having a chat," she says. "I'll meet up with you all later, alright?"

"Alright." Kilkenny responds at the same time as I do.

It's a little uncomfortable meandering through the market after being continuously on the run for over a week. I keep catching myself glancing around for signs of danger.

Kilkenny isn't any less paranoid, his shoulders tense as he blows on the meat and takes another bite. He glances at me. "Eat."

I blow on my own beef before taking a cautious bite. It's still hot, but so packed with flavor that it's worth the pain. "Delicious," I mumble around the mouthful.

Kilkenny nods in agreement and takes another bite. "Do you have a favorite food?" he asks me after he finishes his bite.

I purse my lips. *Do I?* "Osheen's grandmother makes the most delicious sourdough bread. Even more delicious than the bread at Paramount."

"That sounds impressive."

"It is. And what about you? What's your favorite food?"

"Spicy beef stew."

"Oh, I had some during the festival. It is delicious."

He nods and rips off another hunk of meat with his teeth. No palace manners to be found, and it somehow makes me smile. I don't realize that I'm staring at him until his brows lower and he slows his pace even more. "What is it?" he asks, concern etched into his forehead.

"Oh. Nothing." I shake my head. We turn onto a grassy pathway. This one is lined on either side with tents and semi-covered stands. "It's just … You're so different than you were back in Paramount."

He turns forward, stoic Kilkenny once again. As though I called his palace personality back into being.

"I mean that I like seeing you be more natural. In Paramount, you hardly ever smiled. *Truly* smiled. Or laughed. I thought you were nothing but arrogant and intimidating back there."

His brows lift. "Arrogant, I'll accept, but intimidating?"

I shrug. "Well, you did force me to hit you by taunting me."

He smirks and it's every bit arrogant, but it makes me laugh lightly. I munch on my meat skewer as we continue our leisurely pace. There are so many scents—perfumes, soaps, flowers, that the meat starts to taste a bit questionable. I look around, hoping to find ale or something to wash down the food.

Kilkenny eyes the meat in my hand and when he directly faces me again, he asks, "Are you going to finish that?" His skewer is empty now. I hand mine to him—there's still quite a bit of meat left.

A smile blooms across his face and his eyes grow small again. It's a genuine smile that warms my heart and makes my stomach flip pleasantly. I stop moving again as we make it through the pathway and into a small clearing surrounded by shrubs. "Dead end," he says, unbothered.

We may be in the worst of situations, but in this very moment, it's all distant. Kilkenny's expression is tender. Stubble has grown along his jawline again, and it looks good on him. I find myself staring at it, then at his lips as he says, "Everything alright?"

"No." I nod upward to the ribbons of color in the sky that preset the sun's nightly descent. Soon, we'll have to set off again. "Reality calls."

"I know." Kilkenny's hands hang down at his side, the two now-empty skewers clutched in one hand.

"In another time, another circumstance, I think you and me would've gotten on very well." I smile, but his face drops slightly.

"You don't think we get on very well right now?"

"Well … we do."

He steps closer and I'm forced to stare at his mouth. "What would've been different in other circumstances?"

"Well …" My breath catches in my chest, and I step back a little. In other circumstances, I would admit that he's so very handsome, so kind deep down, yet so afraid to show it. Something changed him; something he didn't want to discuss with his sister right away. "Why didn't you write more to your family after you were knighted?" I ask. "Why didn't you visit them?"

His face crumbles and he steps back as though I've dealt a physical blow.

I regret asking. "Never mind. You don't have to answer. We should get going, to meet the others." I start to walk away but his warm hand gently closes around my arm. Slowly, I turn back to him.

Regret is painted on his face. "Becoming part of the Royal Brigade means essentially relinquishing your original family. The brothers and sisters of the Royal Brigade become the only family that matter. We're trained to consider each other thicker than blood. We're put into so many life-and-death situations where we rely on each other that we do form unbreakable bonds. I, however, rose through the ranks so quickly, I barely had a chance to form such bonds. Most of my subordinates were either jealous or intimidated by me. So, I mostly kept to myself. Until I met Maura."

The tear that clings to his lashes sinks my heart. He exhales slowly, turning away from me for a moment before continuing. "Maura was fierce, never jealous or intimidated by me. Her parents were also rebels, and she had dreams of escaping from the Royal Brigade and running away to the Verge. Just ... the three of us."

My heart stops beating for a moment. "Three?"

Kilkenny nods. "Obviously, children had never been part of our plan—we were both diligently taking our fertility suppressants. So, when Maura found out that she was with child, she declared that it was fate. Her terror turned into excitement though, while I remained scared shitless." He smiles but there's no light in it. "We were scheduled to be stationed at Paramount for a couple of weeks for recuperation and a small training collaboration with the Forayers, and Maura thought it was the perfect opportunity for us to escape."

My head is still reeling around Kilkenny having a lover and a child on the way, once upon a time.

"I was in the infirmary chatting with Alys—I knew her as a friend of my mam, and she was aware of our ploy to get out of Mainland—when Carys wandered in. Alys had told me once before that Carys would someday be important to the rebel movement, and maybe it just stuck with me ... But that's when rebels stormed the infirmary."

I raise a brow.

"I'd been left in the dark. I would've never expected Maura to execute a plan behind my back. But she snuck rebels into the castle with the intention of killing Carys."

"Damn ..." I mumble.

"Indeed." He sighs and scrubs his hand down his face. "Carys's guard was immediately shot down by an arrow, and I remembered thinking, *she's just sixteen*. She might've been the heir, but she'd done nothing wrong. The next arrow that flew her way … I dove in front of it. Absolute chaos broke out, and the next thing I knew …"

His throat bobs as he swallows. He turns his face toward the sky and his breathing grows uneven until he focuses on me again. "Maura didn't make it. I'd like to think that the arrow in her heart killed her immediately … Because the next arrow struck her in the abdomen."

My stomach clenches so painfully that I press my hand to it. "I'm so sorry."

He waves my sympathy away. "It's been five years."

"That doesn't mean it hurts any less."

His eyes are fraught with so much pain that tears come to my own. I hesitate for the briefest moment before I slowly wrap my arms around his middle, my palms flat against his upper back and my head pressed against the hollow of his neck. I feel him swallow again, feel his breath shudder before he rests his chin gently atop my head, his arms closing loosely around me. I'm swept up in a tide of sadness for him.

I don't know how long we stand there, but our surroundings begin to dim. I unwrap my arms and peer up at him.

"Thank you," he says.

I shrug and smile gently. "We all need a hug sometimes."

He sighs heavily and turns his face to the sky again. I catch a glimpse of that scar on his neck. That dream I had back in Paramount …. I want to ask him about it, but perhaps now is not the time.

Kilkenny looks down at me again. "We should get going. Find the others." He extends his hand to me, and my lips curve up as I slide my hand into his. Now my stomach flips for a very different reason. I try not to dwell on the sensation as we take the path back the way we came. Things are too complex to give in to feelings. At the end of this journey, we'll likely be going our separate ways—me remaining in sanctuary, and Tiernan off to be a hero, I'm sure.

Chapter 55
DURVLA

CHIYO BOUGHT ME A new dagger belt at the market, and I adjust it around my waist. Chiyo's full name is Cloda Chiyoko Kilkenny, but it dawns on me that I don't know her brother's full name after almost two months since meeting him. He walks beside me, leading Ghendor by the reins, and I glance at him with curiosity.

"Do you have another name like Chiyo?" I ask.

He blinks at me for a moment, but then signs, "I do."

I watch him expectantly, and a tiny smile buds on his lips.

"Itaru," he says, fingerspelling it slowly.

"That's lovely." I smile at him, and he shrugs. We fall back into comfortable silence for a while longer. My legs are like lead, but my rump is sore from riding. There's no winning.

Alys, Chiyo, and Osheen are engaged in conversation up ahead, with Kilkenny having volunteered to bring up the rear. He glances at me, signing one-handed. "Tell me about Taig,"

A pang settles in my chest, but I exhale slowly and will it away. Today has been a day of memories for sure. For Kilkenny, for Alys, and now for me apparently. "He's an incredible little boy." I'm warmed by the memory of his goofy smile. "He was just a baby when we noticed that he was different. It didn't make us love him any less, though. If anything, we loved him even more. He doesn't talk. Not yet anyway."

What if he said his first words, and I missed them?

"He loves soft things and hates loud noises. Ironic since ... you know." I point to my ears and Kilkenny chuckles and nods.

"How did you all keep him hidden for so long?"

"Trap door," I sign with a shrug. "Osheen helped us create it for him." Osheen glances back from where he's walking alongside Chiyo. He smiles softly at me, and I smile back. We've all dismounted our horses to give them a break from our weight. Soon we hope to find someplace suitable to rest for the night. "No one else has really taken care of him. Well, aside from Osheen's family when I was apprehended. He can be a challenge."

"If it makes you feel any better, Alys tells me that the Verge is a paradise for those with ailments and differences."

Alys looks back at us, signing, "Everyone is welcome in the Verge." She wears a different headscarf now, wrapped around the front of her hair and woven through a thick braid down her back. "Ordinary, magical, different, typical, healthy, ailed ..."

That sounds divine, yet I can't quite fathom it. The world we live in hates differences— differences are seen as weaknesses. "Sounds perfect for a magical woman with an ailment," I motion with a small smile.

"Let's stop here," Kilkenny says, coming to a halt. We're under a few trees in a small clearing. We've already ventured off the main path, so it would offer us some coverage.

Kilkenny stalks off with Ghendor after handing me a bedroll, and Osheen approaches with something like hope written all over his face. But he turns to Alys instead of me. I tilt my head into his view, and I'm not prepared for the question he asks. I stare in shock as he asks without signing, "Can you fix her? Can you make her normal again?"

Heat claws into my chest, and Kilkenny whirls toward us from where he's standing. *Can you fix her? Make her normal again?* What's worse is that Osheen asked as if I'm not standing right here.

He blanches, glancing between the three of us as he notes our stares. Chiyo turns our way as she struggles to unload the bedrolls from their horse, Ffion. Kilkenny now stands near me, his unsettling glower boring a hole into Osheen.

"I ... didn't mean that," Osheen says.

I cross my arms over my tightening chest. "What *did* you mean then?"

"I meant if Alys could *cure* you. Your deafness. Don't you want that fixed?"

"She doesn't need curing or fixing," Kilkenny says before I can. "She isn't *broken*. Make yourself useful and go help my sister with your bedrolls."

Osheen's lips part a few times as though he wants to say something. He turns to me as if for help, but I can only frown at him.

Is that what he thinks about me? That I'm broken?

"Durvla, I only meant ... Alys is a healer, and if she can make your life a little easier. It'll help ... it'll help all of us."

Chiyo appears, placing her small hand on his shoulder. "Mate, your foot is halfway down your throat. Quit prattling already." She shoves a bedroll into his arms as I turn to storm off.

I take only a few steps before he rests a heavy hand on my shoulder. I whirl to face him, shoving his hand off and ignoring the dizziness from the sudden movement. "Can't talk to you now," I sign sharply. "Give me space."

He draws in a small breath and rubs a fist over his heart—"*Sorry,*"—before he walks away. Darkness swirls around the edges of my vision, and I shut my eyes.

Something cool presses against the back of my fist and I unclench it to take the cool waterskin offered to me. "Drink," Kilkenny says. "Then rest."

I nod, but I meet Osheen's gaze across the clearing. He thinks I'm broken. After all this time. After everything we've been through together. His father's death, my parents' deaths, health issues, Taig, struggling to put food on our tables, raids ... Still, I never wanted to appear like someone who couldn't handle things; this is why I never liked asking for help.

Hurt by yet another crack chiseled into our fragile friendship, I try to swallow the cool water around the lump in my throat and then wordlessly retire to my bedroll for the night.

Carys is standing on the shore of the loch, staring out into the vast water. Beneath my feet, the grass is cool and slightly damp. A gentle breeze blows through my curls and through Carys's unbound hair, which sways below her knees. The glint of the setting sun reflects off the golden strands in her raven hair as she stoops to remove her shoes.

She's in a simple charcoal-colored gown. She stands and toes off her shoes, nudging them aside with her bare foot. Sadness and hopelessness roll over me in waves that are almost nauseating. I clutch my stomach as Carys steps into the cold water. She bites back a yelp, and the sting of the cold water catches me as well. Another step. Then another.

Carys is submerged up to her waist as my heart hammers erratically in my chest. I gravitate toward the loch against my will. There's a pull from the water, luring me in, promising peace. Behind me looms the Fortress on the Mount, but it's ominous. Dark. It promises nothing but misery and torture.

As I turn back toward the loch, Carys is slowly sinking into the dark water. "Carys!" I hear myself scream, and I clap my hands over my ears. The scream echoes, and Carys stands upright, splashing water as she does so.

She whirls toward me and blinks. Just ... blinks. As if she's unable to register anything. When she speaks, her voice comes out whispered and broken. "Durvla ..."

"Carys, come out of the water."

Her internal struggle is visible, but she slowly makes her way to shore again. She's shivering, drenched up to her shoulders. Wrapping her arms around her torso, she regards me with confusion. "How are you ... ?"

I shrug my shoulders. "It's ... a dream." I glance around, hugging my arms across my torso as well. "Your dream."

"I don't understand."

"I'm ... a Dreamwalker, apparently."

She takes my hand. Hers is cold and wet, much like her neutral expression. "Are you alright?" I ask her.

"No." She's shivering now, and I'm sure it's not just from the cold. She starts rambling about Iywan working with someone to possibly open the Veil at Fiada Purlieu. That the fairytale book she's been reading is in an extinct, ancient language, and that there's a prophecy that has something to do with the goddess Agryna.

Her words muddle up my mind, but I pull my focus to her and force myself to commit what she says to memory.

Pausing, she takes a deep breath and fiddles with her amulet. "I'm a Flamewielder, Durvla." She huffs out an uncertain laugh, and I smile at her.

"I know."

"This is madness."

"And apparently our new reality."

"I need to somehow stop Iywan's bizarre plan and keep him from marrying me off to Rheon. That man …" She visibly shudders. "I—"

My body prickles and things start to fade on the horizon. Behind me, the castle is also beginning to fade. "Our time's running out."

She squeezes my hand tightly. "Don't go."

"Garrick!" The voice catches me off guard, but it's not Carys who speaks.

I blink at Carys. "I'm sorry," I tell her. "But listen."

"For the love of Damarlach. Garrick! Open your eyes. We have to go." Kilkenny's voice in my mind.

My shoulder is jostled, and I'm almost pulled out of the dreamscape, but I hang on to Carys's hand.

"Don't do anything rash. You'll figure things out. You can do this."

"I'm not sure I can."

"Wake! Up!"

"I believe you can," I say. "Just as you believed I could knit you an entire dress in a month."

She smiles and squeezes my hand even tighter but the world around us is fading rapidly.

I try to ground myself in this dreamscape but it's no use. It's like grabbing on to air. "Be brave," I tell her, echoing the words Kilkenny has said to me more than once. "Don't break."

"OPEN YOUR EYES—!"

I awake with a gasp, squinting against the small ray of sunlight that shines through the trees. Alys and Osheen are frantically tacking up the horses while Chiyo and Kilkenny fend off three men clad in ragged clothing and leather. Another man lays unmoving nearby.

I scramble to my feet, my heart in my throat, my head spinning, as the scene unfolds before me. I'm rooted in my spot, unable to make my feet move. Kilkenny is quick and light on his feet, matching each strike of the assailant's sword, swing for swing, jab for jab. That man goes down quickly.

Chiyo slings a small, sharp weapon toward a gaunt ruffian off to her side, and it slices across his thigh, darkening his stained trousers with crimson. She draws two daggers as the man screams and wildly brandishes his sword.

Alys shouts something, gesturing from off to my right. Before I know it, Osheen is tugging me toward Ghendor and hoisting me up into the saddle. Cold prickles at the back of my neck, and a bizarre buzzing sensation flares up beneath my skin. I clench my fists and try to will myself calm again. Kilkenny glances over his shoulder at me, his brows raised in a question.

The buzzing under my skin becomes nearly unbearable, and suddenly Kilkenny's voice is in my head. *"Put the bracelet on."*

I jump so hard at the sound of his voice that I nearly fall off Ghendor, but I rummage around in the saddle bag and grab the bracelet, quickly fastening it to my wrist. I breathe through the sudden shift in my body as my powers are silenced.

I'm focused on Kilkenny as he sheaths his sword over his back and wraps his arms around his attacker's neck from behind. The man struggles, his face turning bright red, then blue, as he flails and swats at Kilkenny's arm.

Chiyo is *fast,* dodging the brawny assailant again and again, a delighted grin lighting up her face. She's *playing* with the man, goading him on, taunting him as she ducks and weaves, twists, and spins. She makes it look easy—graceful. A lethal dance.

Kilkenny gives her an aggravated look and shouts something at her. She rolls her eyes, and as the brawny attacker swings again, she ducks. The man Kilkenny is holding stops struggling, his face purple, and Kilkenny drops him as Chiyo flings her dagger into the brawny attacker's chest. The man drops like a rock.

I didn't even lift a finger, but I feel like I've been running for miles.

"Let's go," Kilkenny says, hurrying toward Ghendor while I try to ignore the dead bodies we're leaving behind.

My heart is still racing as Kilkenny mounts Ghendor, but it slowly calms as his arm encircles me. As we gallop out of the clearing, Kilkenny's voice is loud in my head once more.

We really need to work on you controlling your powers.

Hours later, green mountains loom to our right, and there's a massive body of water far up ahead. The azure sky fights for visibility through dense white clouds, but the sun is warm enough that I shed my cloak as soon as Kilkenny helps me dismount Ghendor.

"I spoke to Carys in a dream last night," I blurt as soon as my feet touch the ground.

His eyes widen, intrigue washing over his features. The interest spreads to the rest of the group as Kilkenny asks, "Did she speak back?"

"She did."

Osheen can hardly face me as I glance at everyone. His words from last night hit me hard all over again. *Can you fix her?* I feel even smaller, as if standing here in the mountains doesn't already heighten my vulnerability enough.

Shoving down the rising hurt, I focus on describing the dream to everyone, not sparing any part in case even the smallest detail turns out to be important.

"It's not a surprise she can read the Ancient Tongue," Alys says, thankfully snapping me out of my woes. "It's in her blood."

I wait for an explanation.

"The royal family were descendants of Agryna's Chosen, or the Heirs of Embers, as some call them."

Again, right out of my fairytale book.

"Carys's late father, King Rhodri showed no manifestation of powers, nor did the king before him, but in the years before,

Agryna's Chosen were Flamewielders and Lightweavers. Some were even oracles."

"She did mention something about there being a prophecy."

"Prophecies are complicated. Sometimes they're translated so often that the entire meaning changes or they're just interpreted incorrectly." There's weight to her words.

"Do you know the prophecy that Carys might be referring to?"

Alys nods, her plump face solemn. "Something about the daughter of Agryna and Ehlach restoring balance. Some translations replace Agryna with Sunlagh, I believe."

Sun. Moon. Dreams. It makes sense how they may interlock.

"Has anyone theorized who this *daughter* is?" Chiyo asks. "Is it symbolic or literal?"

"Prophecies are always symbolic. The problem is that people take it literally and lives are destroyed." She bites her lip and shakes her head. "We should get going again. It's too open here."

She's right. But Kilkenny's face is contorted in deep thought; he doesn't respond.

Although Mages aren't beings of myth as I once believed, to fathom that this prophecy is real, and that Carys is somehow connected to it, is bizarre. Yet a shudder shakes my core, a weight settling in my chest as I replay everything I've been told regarding Carys's situation. I press my fingers to my lips to keep from inappropriately bursting into laughter. Breathing out slowly through my nostrils, I rise to set off with the others again.

Chapter 56
CARYS

Last night, Durvla visited me in my dreams. This morning, my eyelids are heavy as I wake up, my body heavier. It sinks into the bed as if there's nothing beneath me, and my chest aches for reasons I'm unable to confront.

But I must get up. Today is a council meeting, and I'll be damned if I allow Iywan and the councilors to continue to dictate my moves.

I'm a jittery mess sitting in my vanity chair as Ellynne plaits my hair and Lowri pours me a goblet of wine.

"Not too much," Ellynne says firmly to her sister.

Lowri eases up on the pouring, and I scowl at Ellynne even though she can't see my face.

"You ought to have your wits about you when you meet with the Council, don't you think?"

I have to swallow more forcefully than usual to get the wine past the lump in my throat. "Part of me wants to drink until I pass out, and then I won't have to attend the meeting."

Lowri pulls up a chair to sit closer. "What are you going to say?" she asks me.

"I haven't a clue," I sigh.

There's sympathy etched into Lowri's face. "You … could rehearse with us? There's still time."

I decline her offer and sip my wine.

"I'm going to accidentally stab your scalp with this pin if you keep moving," Ellynne says.

My leg is jostling up and down of its own volition, so I press the heel of my foot down to stop the incessant motion. The little courage I have is slipping through my fingers. "I don't want to go to this damn meeting. What's the point? They don't listen to me."

I want to go back to sleep. I want to talk to Durvla again. Too bad I have no clue how this whole dreamwalking thing works. But was the first time in a long time that I've had even a semblance of hope. My hand moves to my necklace, clutching the amulet like a lifeline. Sometimes I want to yank it off my neck and set fire to my bedchamber while I'm locked inside it.

Then I can avoid this loathsome palace life.

"Princess …" Lowri's voice is soft, but it snaps me out of my thoughts, nonetheless. "Why are you crying?"

"I'm not …" I touch my fingers to my cheeks, and they come away wet. I swipe the tears away and drop my face into my hands.

Ellynne's grasp on my hair releases and her voice comes from in front of me suddenly. "You have a lot going on, I know," she says gently. "And also … I miss them too."

I open my eyes, and I hate that a trickle of tears escapes. I swipe at my cheek again.

"It's perfectly normal to miss your friends when they're no longer with you. Especially when it's so sudden and when there is so much going on. It's alright to let yourself feel it all in here." She points vaguely behind me. "But you'll have to walk into that council chamber like the warrior princess you are and show them that *you* are the heir to the throne, *not* Iywan."

Lowri's expression mimics my uncertainty. As perfect as Ellynne's words are, I'm just so tired.

"Carys." Ellynne's tone is firm, determination on her face. "You can do this. Heart of a warrior remember?"

I nod, although I certainly *cannot* do this.

Ellynne pulls a handkerchief from her pocket and hands it to me. "Now wipe those tears and stop messing up my makeup." She winks at me, and I choke out a small laugh as I dab at my face. "I'm going to have to start all over now. What a mess."

I laugh even harder, the tightness in my chest loosening a bit. It lasts all of three seconds before my mind starts reeling again.

My chest aches as my breathing grows faster, and Ellynne leans over me, her hands firmly on my shoulders. "Heart of a warrior."

I gulp down air and nod. Tucking the amulet into my high neckline, I rub my clammy hands over the skirt of my dress and pull in a breath. "Alright." My voice comes out whispered, and I clear my throat.

Lowri reaches across to pour a little more wine into my goblet. Ellynne protests, but Lowri says, "Just a little more. She needs it."

It's such a bold move for her that I can't resist chuckling. "Thank you." I take the goblet from her and sip it slowly while Ellynne shakes her head at me with disapproval.

I'm barely finished drinking before Ellynne takes the goblet away. "Let's get rid of the evidence of your tears. No more wine."

$\cdot \cdot \circ \, \underset{\sim}{\text{)}} \, \underset{\text{☀}}{\text{☀}} \, \underset{\sim}{\text{(}} \, \circ \cdot \cdot$

The council chamber is empty save for Iywan standing there with his fingers laced together in front of his body. I halt, Callum beside me, having switched his shift with Ren today. As much as I try to keep the confusion off my face, I know it's more than evident.

Iywan offers me a polite smile. "Apologies for the late notice, Princess. But the meeting is canceled today."

Relief and dread wrestle for dominance within me. It doesn't help that I'm already nauseated. "Why?" I force myself to say.

"None of the council members were able to be present today."

I wait, but he offers no further explanation. He only squints at me.

"I will find out what your plan is, Iywan." My voice sounds annoyingly breathless, my hands shaking as I clasp them together.

Iywan grinds his teeth together then unclenches his jaw. "I know not what you speak of, Princess."

My lips part, everything I've learned about magic and what I've overheard from Iywan set to tumble free.

Don't, says a voice in my head. *Patience.*

I snap my mouth shut, wincing as the amulet burns against my skin.

"You know exactly what I speak of," I say.

Iywan sneers and my heart jumps. "They'll never believe a thing you say," he says. "They'll never believe the princess who has always been volatile and unstable, coddled by her royal parents and protected like a fragile gem within the castle walls. Who do you think they trust more? The fickle, pampered royal who drinks in excess and beds anything with two legs, who has hardly ever taken the time to listen to citizens in Audience? Or *me*, the queen's loyal advisor who has been there for them when you refused? Wake up, Princess. You are nothing without me bolstering your credibility."

A tremor starts from within me and spreads to my limbs until my arms start to tingle. My eyes prickle, a knot tangling my insides. Turning, I practically run toward the door.

"By all means, Princess, tell everyone what you *know*." Iywan's voice sounds far too amused before the door shuts behind Callum and me.

"Princess?" Callum calls, keeping up with my panicked steps.

"We're going to my mother."

He nods. My mind is reeling as we hurry toward my mother's bedchamber. It does nothing to help chase away the dizziness that's slowly creeping up on me. I'm too overcome. I need to head back to my bedchamber and just lie down for a while. But first, I need to figure things out. When my mother was awake and lucid, she claimed she'd taken away my memories. What sort of powers does my mother have that she could take my memories away?

"Princess?" Callum calls again.

I stand rooted to the spot, unable to move as piles of information flood my mind. Maybe my mother's a Mind Whisperer ... Though I've never heard her speak into my mind, unless I was ... dreaming.

I have no clue how any of this all works, but I'm grasping at straws. I need one last moment with my mother. I need her advice. I need *her*.

"*Carys.*"

I blink at Callum, then gesture in the direction that we had been going.

He couldn't look more confused or worried, but I don't have time to put his mind at ease. Soon, we approach my mother's bedchamber where more maroon-clad guards than usual stand directly in front of her door. I wait, expecting them to step aside as they always do, but no one makes even the slightest shift.

"Step aside." The command in my voice is deceptive.

"Apologies, Your Highness. We've been given instructions not to let anyone through," one of the guards speaks up.

"I am Princess Carys Meredyth fa Rhodri, daughter of Morwenna, heir to the throne." Gods, when last did I have to drop my entire title. It's so exuberant, so unnecessary.

"The command came from Queen Morwenna, the Good, Your Highness."

I bark out a laugh. "Lord Iywan does not speak for the queen. *I* do." This has his name written all over it.

"Your Highness, it was not Lord Iywan. It's the queen's request."

What in Rhianu's name?

He bows deeply, as if that would make me forget everything. As I'm about to demand they let me in, there's a knock on the door from the inside, and Briony steps out. The guards close the gap again as soon as she's through.

"Oh!" Briony holds a hand over her chest as though I've surprised her. The other hand clutches a bowl. "I didn't see you there, Princess. My apologies. The queen is not in the condition to have visitors."

I glower at the bowl of leeches. "Whatever you and Iywan have planned is not going to work. Now get out of my way, all of you." I sound less regal by the moment, but my patience is hanging by a thread.

"I don't know what you're referring to, Your Highness." Her sugary voice makes me want to slap her across her plain face and break her little upturned nose.

"Don't play the fool with me, Briony. Get out of my way." I shove past her and start to shove past the door. Something changes in Briony's eyes.

"Sir Callum," she says. "Escort the princess back to her bedchamber."

My head snaps to Callum, and I burst out laughing. "Callum does not take orders from you. Who do you think you are?"

Briony smiles and steps toward me, placing a hand on my shoulder. Pain lances up my arm and I yelp. Callum yanks Briony off me while I'm whimpering and clutching my shoulder. What in the gods … What is happening?

"Your Highness," says Lord Iywan. "What seems to be the problem?"

I don't even know when he arrived. I'm still reeling from the sudden pain in my shoulder.

"Your mother has requested no visitors. And that includes you. My hands are tied."

I turn to each person one at a time. Is this a nightmare or has everyone gone absolutely mental? "My mother couldn't possibly give such a command because she is *unconscious*," I say loudly.

Iywan stands tensely, his shoulders squared. "Princess, before you say something else slanderous about the monarch of this nation, I would suggest that you retire to your bedchamber for the night."

Slanderous? My jaw slackens. "What now? You'll accuse me of treason?"

Callum doesn't hesitate this time. He places his hand on the small of my back and steers me away from the chaos.

I have no words. I barely have thoughts.

My head is even woozier as we trek back across the castle. A servant rushes by, and I call out to her. "Yes, Your Highness," she says, dropping into a curtsy with a tray held firmly in her hands.

"Send Ellynne and Lowri to my bedchamber."

"Yes, Your Highness." Another curtsy and she's off.

Once we're standing in front of my door, Callum turns to me. "Carys …" His eyes are wide, and his voice unsteady. His fear is unmistakable, almost suffocating. "Something strange is going on."

"No shit, Callum." I say louder than I mean to. "This is … mutiny, right?"

"If we were on a ship, yes."

I grunt in frustration.

"I'll be out here."

With another grunt, I step into my room and Callum shuts the door. I yank *The Book of Agryna* and the *Erleyan Book of Folklore and Fairytales* out from beneath my bed and place them atop the mattress. I have both open in front of me as Ellynne and Lowri barge through the door without even so much as an announcement.

"What happened?" Ellynne demands.

"I couldn't even begin to explain," I mumble as I trace a passage of sacred texts. Even though it is written in the Ancient Tongue, some sentences are out of sequence, and some have dubious word choices. As though whoever wrote it was not as well-versed in the Ancient Tongue.

The bed sinks as Ellynne crawls onto it from the other side and settles in beside me. "Callum says that the Queen's Guards turned on you?"

I pinch the bridge of my nose and exhale slowly. "Yes." My voice is not nearly as tense as I am. I glance up briefly at the sisters. "I'm not sure what's happening. I think Iywan is trying to overthrow me. They're all claiming that the queen ordered that no one, including me, enters her bedchamber. Which is impossible, because she has been unconscious for weeks and she wouldn't say no to visits from me."

Would she? I swallow a sob. What if it's all true? I flip through pages aimlessly to distract myself. I need sleep. Maybe Durvla will somehow dreamwalk to me again. Maybe if I fall asleep focusing on her. "I need more wine."

The bed shifts as Lowri walks away. I'm confused for a moment until she reaches for the bottle of wine left on my vanity. I didn't even realize I'd spoken aloud.

"You do *not* need more wine," Ellynne says.

Lowri returns with a goblet, but before I can take it, Ellynne snatches it and downs the whole thing.

I stare at her, exasperated, before snatching the goblet back from her. "My own advisor and the Queen's Guards have turned against me. I need more wine." I don't turn away from Ellynne as I hand the goblet back to Lowri.

Ellynne sighs heavily in resignation. "Fine."

I lose track of time as I pore over the books, trying to cram as much of the information into my mind as I can, trying to commit it all to memory in case I need to wield it like a weapon somehow. My eyes grow heavier and heavier, my stomach churning, my head woozy. I've yawned so much by now that my jaw aches. I close the books and set them in the drawer of my nightstand.

Beside me, Ellynne is dozing off as well. I glance to the window to find the sun still shining, but the fight to stay awake grows futile. "I'm … going to take a nap," I tell the ladies. I try to focus my dizzying thoughts but it's difficult.

I throw out Durvla's name to the universe: *Durvla, dreamwalk to me. Please. Please, Durvla.*

I don't even get the chance to get into a comfortable position before Sunlagh whisks me away.

Chapter 57
CARYS

"OH, CAAAAAAARYS ..." THE SINGSONG voice sounds distant, eerie, dreamlike. "Wake up, Princess."

There's a strange odor, coppery and unpleasant. I can't quite put my finger on it, nor on the voice that speaks to me. I'm groggy, disoriented. My limbs are too heavy, my thoughts lethargic. Who's speaking to me?

"Open your eyes, Princess."

I swat at whoever is trying to wake me. I peel my eyelids open with much effort and it takes a moment for my vision to clear. "Lowri?"

The smile that the woman returns is nothing like Lowri's. It's vulpine, sinister. "Lowri ... Eefa ... Whichever you prefer," she says.

"I don't understand."

The woman's appearance changes. Her blue eyes turn green; her dark brown hair, honey blond. Her petite frame stretches until she's taller and more filled out, and suddenly I'm staring at Eefa. I swear under my breath and bolt upright. Beside me, there's a whimper. As I propel myself back, my hand hits something warm and wet. I lift my hand to find it coated in crimson … The coppery stench overwhelms my senses … Blood. My heart drops into my roiling stomach.

My head whips toward where Ellynne had been sleeping beside me. She's slumped back against the pillow, her breathing too shallow, her face paler than ever, and her eyes bulging. Her hands clutch at a wound in her stomach, blood pooling beneath her and soaking into my sheets.

A sob catches in my throat. "Ellynne!" I turn to Lowri, no, Eefa. "Did you do this to her?!" A bloody kitchen knife lays beside Ellynne. I need to do something. I need to call for help.

I jump out of bed and run to my bell, yanking on the rope. A weighty metal band of some sort is clamped around my left wrist. But I have other things to worry about.

"No one's coming," Eefa says.

I spin to face her, noting the amusement on her face. This *must* be a nightmare.

My legs move on their own accord, running toward my door. I yank it open and bellow Callum's name, but he's nowhere in sight. I run back toward the bed, that coppery odor filling my nostrils again as coagulated blood coats my hands, my dress. The scent consumes my senses, and bile rises in my throat. I'm a sobbing mess as I press my hands to Ellynne's wound.

She doesn't even cry out. I have to save her. Even though this is a nightmare, I can't let her die. "It's going to be alright," I manage to choke out through my sobs.

"Sweet Carys." Her voice is gravelly and effortful. "It's no use. I'm sorry … I didn't know. Lowri … She's …"

"Shh, you're going to be alright."

"I'm not." Her lips tug up momentarily. "Listen," she says as firmly as she can. She stares into my very soul. She wets her lips and takes another shallow breath, but no words make it past her lips.

The light goes out from olive green eyes that will never see again. "No … Ellynne, please no." She's all I have left. I press my hands to her face, willing her back to life. Her face is ghostly, and there's just so much blood. My entire body is trembling.

My stomach heaves, threatening to evacuate all the wine I drank in the past … however long it's been.

"Well …"

My head whips back to Eefa sitting casually on the edge of the bed. I'd forgotten she was still here.

"That was quite a heroic effort, if you ask me. Impressive for an entitled princess who acts like she's better than everyone."

Chest heaving, I gape at her, unsure of how to process anything. It's all too much.

She shifts, turning her body so that her back is against my headboard, her arms behind her head as she lounges. "You know what'll make this moment even more theatrical right now?" She pauses as though for dramatic effect. "A fire show!"

I can't stop staring at her. Please let this nightmare end.

"Not impressed? Maybe *fireworks* would've been a better pun, but …" She shifts again and leans toward me, her face too close to mine. "Let's see what you've got."

With one hard yank, she breaks my necklace and rips it right off my neck.

Chapter 58
DURVLA

ONE MINUTE, WE'RE WALKING, and the next I drop like a stone. I hardly register the pain that flares through my hands, then my cheek, as I try and fail to catch myself before my vision goes white.

I find myself in a dark tunnel with weepy, stone walls. My heart pounds, and I break out in a cold sweat as I seek the end of the burrow. Fear grips my heart, and a voice echoes eerily. "Durvla, dreamwalk to me. Please. Please, Durvla."

The voice wavers in and out, my surroundings spotting and disintegrating in front of me, only to restructure again. It feels like I'm continually falling. Replaying the same moment over and over again.

I turn left into another part of the tunnel and look around wildly. I've been here before ... haven't I?

The voice returns, fragmented. "Durvla, please." There's so much pain in that voice.

Carys's voice.

Sadistic laughter echoes from someone else.

My surroundings collapse again and reform, and I want to scream from this never-ending dreamscape.

"Oh Caaaaaarys."

Goddess, am I walking in circles? The voices persist, but I don't know which direction they're coming from. There's no light, no end in sight. I veer toward the right side this time, where the tunnel forks, my boots pounding against the damp ground for what feels like forever.

Dead end after dead end taunts me, and I bite back a scream of frustration.

"Wake up, Princess—"

I wake with a gasp, the scent of blood in my nostrils. Gagging, I roll to the side, dry heaving while my stomach spasms. My heart flutters in my chest, fear pulsing through me.

Someone takes hold of my arm, and I wildly swat them away. *"Garrick, it's me,"* Kilkenny mind-speaks. I startle, though I force myself to pay attention to my surroundings. I'm on a riverbank, dirt and patchy grass beneath me. Kilkenny looms over me, and as I lurch upright, he straightens, sitting back against his heels.

My heart is still racing, and I can't catch my breath. My legs burn as though I've truly been running, but cold trepidation skitters across my skin. Each breath is shallower than the last, and I fear I'll soon stop breathing all together. I fear my world will cease to exist completely.

I'm going to die. Right here.

My heart is going to give out. I draw in another ragged breath, clutching at my aching chest.

Alys appears beside me. "Describe what you see right now, sweetling," she signs.

"Grass," I choke out. "River. Mountains." I try to make a full sentence, but it's like I've forgotten how to speak properly.

"Good. Keep going." She places a hand gently on my forehead and a warm sensation flows through my body, soothing and calming me. "What else?"

"Kilkenny."

He smiles tightly at me. I hate the worry on his face.

In turn, I focus on each of them. "Chiyo … Osheen." They're both sitting nearby, concern radiating from them. My cheeks heat up even as I fight the tears filling my eyes. Slowly, my breathing regulates, my heart beginning to steady.

"Welcome back," Kilkenny motions. "You gave us a scare."

I can only blink back tears and focus on steeling myself. Chiyo rises from her haunches and brings over my waterskin. She hands it to me, and I thank her before guzzling down the whole thing. The voices from that bizarre tunnel echo in my mind again. I inhale shakily.

"Are you alright?" Chiyo asks. "You just … fell. Out of the blue. Thud." She shrugs, perplexed. Apparently, we all are.

I face Osheen, who nods in confirmation and signs, "I thought you were having an episode, but then you wouldn't wake up." He swallows hard. He wants to say more. I know him, but now he's guarded, choosing his words carefully.

I frown up at the sky. The sun is setting, fiery orange and dark purples streaking across the navy blue. "I was in a tunnel," I say. "There were voices. Carys and … another voice. It was disturbing. Like my life was in danger, but I didn't know why. The dream just kept sort of fragmenting or repeating or something."

A deep gulch appears between Alys's brows when I turn to her again. "Has that ever happened before?" she asks.

I shake my head. "I've had episodes before—dizzy attacks that make me suddenly fall over or leave me literally unable to move without fainting or vomiting."

The blood drains from Osheen's face, giving away just how much those moments affected him as well. Yet, he'd never left my side when they happened.

"It's been about two months since I've had an episode, but this certainly isn't the same. It wasn't even the same as the other dreams from Carys I've walked into. I didn't see her, but I heard her."

Alys makes a thoughtful face. "You were awake when this happened so maybe …" She twists her lips to the side for a moment. "Perhaps, you were pulled into her dreamscape."

"That can happen?"

"Yes. It could be daywalking—same as dreamwalking, but while you're awake."

Great.

"It's complicated. In your case, it could also be in part because you're still wearing your dampener, so your powers are sort of fragmented. It means you're getting stronger, overpowering the runes."

I glance down at my bracelet, then back up at everyone again.

Chiyo laughs. "Lugda's hells, Durvla, you're going to be *terrifying* once you get some training."

I wince. Being terrifying is the last thing I want.

Kilkenny and Alys exchange glances, and I want to shake them both because it's not the first time they've done that. Their expressions speak of a multitude of things. About *me*. But I barely have the energy to be annoyed with the very obvious fact that they're keeping something from me; I certainly don't have the energy to speak out about it.

"Chiyo is right, you know," Kilkenny signs. "You're getting stronger." Pride crosses his face for a split second before it's replaced with concern again. Or maybe I've even imagined it.

Then the meaning behind their words really hits me. My dampener didn't work, or only half worked? "I don't want this to happen again."

"I understand." He nods compassionately. "We need to start training more when you're awake."

I heave a sigh. Lovely.

Just moments after we begin riding, the onset of a raging headache renders me almost incapacitated. So, training doesn't happen. I barely manage to keep myself atop Ghendor, though by the next stop we make further down the river, I can at least make sense of my surroundings. We're closer to the larger body of water, as well as the mountains looming ahead beneath the night sky. Everyone takes their turn relieving themselves and even washing up as quickly as possible in the river.

Afterward, Osheen starts a fire and sits beside it, warming his hands as Chiyo and Kilkenny do a terrible job trying to catch fish. Alys has retired to her bedroll to "rest her eyes."

I join Osheen in front of the fire and sigh blissfully from the warmth that radiates from it. I've not been able to get the dampness out of my body since that miserable maze of a dreamscape, and my head is steadily pounding, my body exhausted. I hate that training has again been delayed, this time because of my ailment.

Osheen does a double take when he catches sight of me. He waves, a small, tentative smile on his lips. His blue eyes are dark in the weak light of the flames. "How are you feeling?" he signs.

"Confused." I fiddle with my dampener and shrug my shoulders. "I just can't wait to get to the Verge and see Taig again."

"Same." He smiles and I believe him. Then his smile drops. "I'm sorry you have to put up with those dreams. They sound awful."

Awful is an understatement.

"I'm not sorry about you having powers, for the record. I just mean—"

I rest my hand on his arm gently. "Please stop being overly cautious about everything you say. Let's move past that."

The tension melts off his body and his shoulders droop. "Thank you." He smiles warmly as he signs.

For a moment, I stare into the flames. Carys had truly sounded so pained in the dreamscape. The paralyzing fear starts to seep back into my body, and I quickly wrangle my thoughts and redirect them. I turn back to Osheen. "So ... you and Chiyo ..." I quirk a brow at him.

He makes a face as color rushes into his cheeks. It's adorable, honestly, but a moment later, he heaves a sigh and says, "No romantic prospect."

"Why not?"

"Because she's not interested in men."

"... Oh. Well, that's unfortunate for you."

"Indeed." He shrugs. "It's fine. Probably not the time for rom—" He stops talking as I glance over his shoulder. Chiyo and Kilkenny approach again, each of them with a few fish in hand. They drop the fish beside the fire and Chiyo proudly announces, "Salmon and trout are on the menu tonight, boys!" She beams and pulls a dagger from her belt, tossing it so it lands in front of Osheen's boot. "Make yourself useful, mate."

Kilkenny turns to me with a small smile. I can't resist smiling back at him, but then another dagger lands point first in the dirt in front of me. My heart jumps. "How many daggers do you have?" I ask Chiyo.

She grins. "You don't want to know."

I scoff, but a spurt of laughter slips through. "Fine, but maybe stop throwing them at us."

Chiyo bursts out laughing. "Maybe if you people stop loafing about, I wouldn't have to throw daggers at you." A fish comes flying at me, and I barely deflect it from my face. Kilkenny scowls at his sister, but she only grins at him. Honestly, I appreciate that she doesn't treat me like an invalid.

For the next hour or so, we gut the fish and roast them over the fire, making sure to leave a serving for Alys, who is fast asleep on her bedroll.

"So, what are your thoughts on this prophecy business?" Chiyo asks us.

Kilkenny shrugs and Osheen purses his lips.

"I'm not sure if I believe it," I say.

"It reminds me of that rhyme … *The Land Beyond the Veil*?"

I'm swept up in a stream of nostalgia, staring at Chiyo's lips as she hums out a tune and begins to sing the lyrics of a song that my mam used to sing to me as a child. The melody is still fresh in my mind as though I've heard it just yesterday.

Beneath the pale moon's eyes, she rode
On embers black as night,
With ire, greed, and wrath she cried
O, save me from the light

Beneath the rays of sun, she stood
In dusk as bright as day,
With misery and fear she cried
O, save me from dismay

The sun has gone, the shadows dance,
Let moonlight chase the dusk away,
Dwell not in umbra's brutal grasp
That keeps you in a trance.

O, rest your head, relent your dread
Let nightly dreams take you away,
To a land that's far beyond this realm
Where the Other-worlders play

May Sunlagh take you by the hand,
To where Other-worlders play

Let Sunlagh take you by the hand
To the land beyond the veil

We all stare at Chiyo, mesmerized by the words, the men clearly captivated by her voice. Chiyo gives a seated flourish and announces, "Thank you! Feel free to toss a coin for your humble bard."

We laugh and chat about songs we grew up with, exchanging stories. Kilkenny tells us the legend of the war goddess Damarlach, who wed a mortal man and made an undefeatable warrior of him. Osheen shares the story of Ostanha, the god of spring and love. Clearly, Ostanha is struggling this year, based on the blight that's slowly spreading.

We discuss a few things regarding our journey, Kilkenny showing us the map that Alys has entrusted him with. We still have quite a way to go, including another mountainous trek.

As summer approaches, the weather should be a little more bearable, but the closer we get to the Verge, the colder it becomes. I fidget with my fingers and my dampener once we finish eating. The tedium that was my life is so distant—I yearn for the simpler things. I wish I'd packed some knitting needles and wool. I could use a channel for my nervous energy.

Each day that brings us closer to Taig also brings a greater possibility of danger. At least, it feels that way. We've managed to somehow stay ahead of the Forayers. Maybe they've even lost our trail by now, but there's a constant sinking in my stomach.

I'm so lost in thought that when I glance up, Chiyo and Osheen are on their feet, Chiyo tugging him by the sleeve toward the water. Kilkenny's questioning look lands on me. "A shilling for your thoughts?" he asks, turning so that he's fully facing me, his legs crisscrossed.

I'm not sure what to say without sounding like I'm indulging in self-pity. Kilkenny wouldn't appreciate it. I turn so that I'm facing him as well, our knees touching. "It's nothing."

"I don't even need to be a Whisperer to know you're lying." He fixes me with a stern expression. "What's *really* on your mind?" he signs.

I face the riverbank where the silhouettes of Osheen and Chiyo are practicing fighting skills—or rather where Chiyo is trying to teach Osheen how to fight. I'm not sure which of us is the worse student. Kilkenny waves his hand in front of my face very gently and I turn to him again.

"I know I haven't been the friendliest."

"That's an understatement." The words fly past my lips so quickly, I'm not even able to filter them. Gods, I should stick to solely signing—at least that may give me a chance to stop myself. Maybe. But I've been so used to speaking aloud for so long.

Kilkenny grins at me. "How did that feel?" he asks.

"How did what feel?"

"Saying what's actually on your mind rather than bottling it up?"

I wrinkle my nose at him. "Who says I do that?"

"You may keep your thoughts to yourself, but your face is an open book, Durvla."

My jaw slackens for a moment before I catch my lower lip between my teeth. *Durvla.* My name on his hands is like a warm hug.

It's so pleasant, so affable, so unlike Kilkenny that I don't know what to do with myself for a moment. Then, I'm grinning like a fool while fighting the urge to hide.

"What are you grinning at?"

"You called me Durvla."

He stares at me as though I've jumped up and started doing a jig or something. "It is your name, isn't it?"

"Gods …" I sigh. "You're impossible, Kilkenny." There's no way he didn't realize it's the first time he's not called me *Garrick*. The glint in his eyes is clear, even by firelight.

"I have to keep you on your toes, Garrick. Good for practice."

I huff out an exasperated sigh and he laughs. *Laughs*. My annoyance quickly disappears, and I smile again. "I would love to hear your laughter …" As soon as the words are out there, I regret it. Heat floods my face, and the laughter dies on Kilkenny's lips. But it isn't an unpleasant expression that remains—it's curiosity.

No words are exchanged between us for a while. I stare at him, wishing that I had mind whispering rather than dreamwalking. Wishing that I could just catch a glimpse of his innermost thoughts. More facial hair has grown along his cheeks and jaw, hardening his features, but his eyes hold such warmth. His lips move as if to say something, but even if he did, I'm too busy wondering what they'd feel like against mine.

Ostanha, spare me. I need to keep my resolve.

"Why?" he asks.

My brows furrow.

"Why do you want to hear me laugh?"

"Oh …" The question catches me off guard. "It's just … the joy on your face. It seems … infrequent. Sort of priceless, in a way." I lower my hands for a moment, gathering my thoughts. "I'm glad that I can *see* it though. You look like a different person when you laugh. Like someone I could've—" Could've what? Where was I going with that? I let my hands fall but the unfinished sentence hangs in the air.

"… You could've?"

I peer over my shoulder at Chiyo and Osheen. Chiyo is doubled over at the waist. Has Osheen landed a blow? My brows begin to rise, but no, Chiyo is laughing so hard that her petite frame shakes. Osheen stands off to the side, arms crossed. Their friendship was forged so quickly, so naturally. The way my friendship with Osheen had been formed.

This … *thing* with Kilkenny has been quite the contrary. Rocky from the start. I didn't trust him at first—now I would gladly fall backward off a cliff knowing he'd be there to catch me. My breath snags. It's illogical. I've known him for nearly two months, and yet I trust him as much as I trust my best friend. Perhaps more … My stomach knots at the internal admittance.

When I turn back to Kilkenny, curiosity is still etched into his features. Did I just almost confess that I can imagine him as someone I could've made a life with? If we were in different circumstances. If I was … typical.

Gods, I just need to get to the Verge and thank the rebels that saved Taig before moving on with our lives. Whatever that may look like. But I know Kilkenny has another calling.

He's a hero and I'm a weakling.

"Durvla …"

The name startles me again and I laugh sardonically. "What?"

"Stop thinking so hard. I have my shields up, and yet you're making it very difficult for my mind to stay out of yours."

I press my hands against my head, and he starts laughing again.

"Your hands aren't going to do a thing to keep your thoughts hidden," he signs. His laughter is so contagious that I can't resist joining in. He grins so widely that his eyes disappear and, gods damn me, it's so endearing.

"I'm glad I can hear your laughter," he says.

My smile falters and I want to tell him that I know for a fact that my laughter is atrocious. I snort, without fail, whenever I giggle even remotely hard.

"It's beautiful." The smile slowly fades from his lips, replaced by an intensity that causes flutters deep in my belly. My heart kicks and my breath hitches as his face draws closer to mine and his gaze drifts down to my mouth. His face is so close. I want his lips on mine. Eagerness rolls off him in thick waves, mirroring my own sudden impatience. The implications no longer matter to me. I want this. Whatever *this* is.

A shadow appears in my peripheral vision. Sword drawn, Kilkenny jumps to his feet so quickly, it's a wonder he doesn't knock me over.

But it's Alys. Just Alys, her eyes wide with surprise, her salt-and-pepper hair peeking out from beneath her headscarf. "I am so very sorry to interrupt. I just came to claim my supper."

I glance between the two of them—Kilkenny with his sword still drawn, Alys with amusement written all over her face. It's such a sight that I burst out laughing. I feel the snort as it happens and I groan, making a face. Kilkenny smirks at me as he sheaths his sword again. He doesn't speak into my mind, but I swear I can read his. *I'm glad I can hear your laughter.*

It doesn't take the fire to warm me all over again.

Chapter 59
CARYS

THERE'S AN INCESSANT DRIP, *drip, drip* sound that grates on my nerves. Cold creeps into my bones, and shivers rack my body. Peeling my eyelids open takes effort, my arms too heavy, my mind sluggish. I stare into the darkness, my heart pounding as I fear that I've lost my sight. But slowly I register a faint flicker of a firelight, a candle in the distance. My joints protest as I push myself up, my hands against a cold, hard surface that has me aching all over.

I lift my hand to rub my achy head, but the cumbersome metal wristband makes the movement awkward. My palms are stiff and gritty from the blood caked on my skin. A sob catches in my throat, a choked sound echoing in the small space as my memory returns in a dizzying rush.

Ellynne is dead. I've known her my whole life. She's always been more friend than servant, exuding as much confidence as the queen herself. I already miss her cheeky wit and exuberant dedication. The tug of her hands through my hair and the godsawful fortunes she told. I'll never see the glee on her face at the prospect of fresh gossip or hear the wildly inappropriate retellings of her sexual conquests again.

My gut lurches, and I scrub my palms against my lap, desperately hoping to remove the blood of the woman who had so lovingly served me.

After Lowri—Eefa—snatched the necklace from my neck, she slammed something hard against my temple. She could've killed me.

She should've killed me.

I'd trade my life any day to save Ellynne, my mother. Aneirin.

The death toll continues to grow. Their blood is on my hands.

There's a clang and the terrible, grating sound of metal against stone. A small flame shines in the darkness and heavy boots thud against the stone floor, growing louder as a figure approaches. My heart speeds up, and I scoot on my rump until my back connects with the wall. Moisture seeps into my dress.

My eyes adjust to the dark, and I make out the silhouette of prison bars as the slide open. But this is not the brig.

"Hello, Princess." The voice is familiar, yet foreign at the same time. "Sorry it had to be this way, but you didn't exactly make this easy."

I glare at Iywan, his face slightly illuminated by the lantern he holds as he steps into my cell. Lowri stands at his side. "What do you want from me?" I spit as bitter betrayal fills my mouth.

"Your cooperation." He says it like we're having a cup of tea on a regular morning.

Uncertainty furrows my brows; I'm not sure what to make of his statement.

"Tell me everything you know about magic."

My laughter echoes in the cell, and Iywan blinks and leans back. "I hate to dash your hopes, Iywan, but I'm almost certain that you know more about magic than I do."

A small muscle in his cheek twitches and he clicks his tongue. "I wouldn't lie in your situation, Princess." Every time my title is spoken, it's even more of a mockery. "What is in that godsdamned book of fairytales?"

I sneer at him. "*Fairytales*, you pretentious fool." I pray my voice sounds steady enough.

"And *The Book of Agryna*?"

My heart jumps. "Another book of fairytales."

Drip, drip, drip.

It takes an eternity for Iywan to speak again. "Fetch Briony."

Lowri nods and hurries back toward the exit, leaving me with a simmering Iywan. "Can you summon your powers?"

There's no point in hiding it. He knows. They've removed my necklace, imprisoned me. "No, but if I could, I would set fire to your hideous face."

Iywan tsks. "No need for violence, Princess. I only want to unlock your full potential. You've been complaining about not having the power you so rightfully deserve. Am I right, Carys Meredyth fa Rhodri, Princess of Erleya, sole heir to the throne? What would you say if I told you that you weren't the sole heir to the throne?"

"I'd say that you're lying out of your despicable mouth."

He grins and his white teeth practically glint in the dim light. It's a grin that promises unpleasantries. I immediately regret my words. "Be that as it may," he drawls. "We need each other, so you'd better stop hurling useless insults at me and cooperate."

Boots sound against the ground again as Lowri and Briony approach. "You called, Lord Iywan?"

Gods, how I hate her sugary little voice.

"I wanted to properly introduce you to the princess." Iywan doesn't look away from me. "Princess, meet Briony, High Priestess of Lugda. She's going to help us reclaim power and restore Erleya to its former glory."

I roll my eyes. "Hells, what are you talking about?"

"Briony is going to help you unlock your powers so we can dismantle the wards of Fiada Purlieu and reclaim the power that once belonged to the realm. Our worlds were never meant to be separated. Those wards, which were erected to banish Enidwen and keep the Otherworld out, have drained Erleya. You will know this all in time, but first, you need to learn how to use your powers, and you're going to tell us what we need to know about magic. Do we have an accord?"

"I don't know what you're talking about."

"I see we're going to have to do this the hard way." He sighs and nods to Briony.

It's all she needs to step forward and crouch in front of me. Her smile is no less sweet than it's always been. "I really don't want to do this, Your Highness."

"Do we have an accord?" Iywan repeats, firmer this time.

"Not on your sorry arse."

Briony presses a hand to my shoulder, and blinding pain shoots down my arm. I bite the inside of my cheek and refuse to scream as my vision goes bright white.

"Enough," says Iywan, and Briony removes her hand. The pain ceases as though it was never there.

I draw in a shaky breath and press my cuffed hand to my shoulder.

"That's just a sample." Iywan is too pleased with himself.

My blood runs cold. Briony stands and steps back, regarding me.

"I'll have someone bring you fresh clothing in the morning. You'll start training then. And you *will* tell us what we need to know."

I press my lips together.

"Welcome to the Zenith, Princess."

Chapter 60
CARYS

SLEEP NEVER FINDS ME. I lay awake in the small bed in the corner of the cell. The mattress is so hard that I might as well sleep on the floor, but at least it's dry.

Drip, drip, drip.

I roll onto my side, my back facing the wall, and try not to focus on the infuriating sound. Being left here with my own thoughts is torture within itself. This morning—at least I think it was this morning—a servant lit a few more oil lanterns in the brackets on the walls. It leaves the cell a little brighter, enabling me to gauge my surroundings. There is just this one cell with a bed and chamber pot. *A. Chamber. Pot.*

I shudder.

Welcome to the Zenith, Iywan's words echo in my head. The Zenith. I've never heard about whatever that is. All I know is that I want nothing to do with it.

Outside the cell, a long walkway leads to a metal door.

For the longest while, I stare at the door. What more could possibly happen? How is my mother faring up there? How are Durvla, Alys, and Tiernan managing? Are they safe? Maybe Durvla has reunited with her brother.

I hope for their safety, all while hating myself for being wildly jealous of them.

"Oh, Princess. Wake up."

I jump up so quickly that my head spins.

Lowri is smiling down at me, fresh clothing in her arms. "Time to change out of those clothes."

There are a couple of guards outside of my cell. One is a younger lad who I vaguely recognize, with a pale, bald head. I don't recognize the other, but she's tall and lanky, with a dark complexion and boredom on her face.

I turn back to Lowri. "What if I say no?"

"Then Lieutenant Bronn and Cadet Aela will step in." Only then do I notice the shackles in Lieutenant Bronn's hands.

I start to remove my dress, ungracefully unlacing the bodice and letting it fall to the ground. The hem crunches in my hands from the dried blood. I shove down the nausea and hold my breath to escape the stench. I could use a bath, but there's no water in sight despite the incessant dripping, so I snatch the fresh clothing from Lowri and glower at her.

"I trusted you." My voice is a mere whisper as I stare at the Skinchanger. I climb into the too-big trousers and pull the strings as tight as I can.

Lowri shrugs. "I know."

I fumble with the ties, making a knot as my stiff fingers won't allow for a bow. After dragging the tunic over my head, I pull my braid out of the clothing and push it back over my shoulder. Like my hands and the dress I've just removed, my hair has taken on its share of blood. I try my hardest not to cringe. Ellynne did such a good job styling it, and now her blood is all over her handiwork. I close my eyes and breathe through the memory of Ellynne dead in my bed.

"It's easy to trust someone who you think is beneath you, isn't it?" Lowri asks, and my eyes fly open.

"I never treated you as subservient."

"You claim to be so accepting, to treat your servants like equals, yet you send for us at any given time of the night. For your pleasure." Something sparks in her eyes and my stomach turns. Oh gods, I've almost forgotten that she's also Eefa. It suddenly makes sense now—Lowri's constant tardiness, her reluctance to join us for meals in the dining hall. *Lowri*, however, always looked away from me during dressings—this monster is quite the actress.

"Did Ellynne know?"

Lowri scrunches her nose. "Of course not. That bitch was more loyal to you than she's ever been to me. She let our father send me away to that cruel duke in Darragh. Even when I sent her letters telling her how miserable I was, she didn't seem to care. She told me to tough it out."

My hands pause on the laces of the tunic. That doesn't sound like Ellynne at all.

"When my powers manifested, I kept it a secret. To protect *her*. Yet she left me there with that cruel man. She deserved what she got."

Her voice is so harsh, so cold. Nothing like the Lowri I thought I knew. "But she got you your position here."

"I got *myself* my position here. I created my alter, Eefa. From a portrait hanging in my husband's house, if you'll believe that. I asked Ellynne to vouch for me, Lowri, after I murdered my husband and stashed his gold."

No wonder it had been so easy for her to kill Ellynne. It wasn't the first time she'd done such a thing.

"I'd already joined the Zenith, so worming my way into Paramount with Master Iywan practically in power was simple. Ellynne didn't question my sudden appearance here. She accepted it because she felt guilty about failing me as an older sister."

Gods … I shudder as I imagine Ellynne's reaction when her own sister attacked her.

And there's the mention of the Zenith again. I draw in a breath to ask about it, but Lowri speaks again.

"Briony will be here soon, but keep this in mind: if you try anything, it's not just the guards who won't hesitate to hurt you." Her focus darts down to the metal band on my wrist and then back to my face, a sneer of satisfaction on her lips.

A chill runs through me.

"You're no pampered princess down here."

With that, she marches off, leaving me to my own thoughts again. I examine the bracelet closer—there are symbols etched into the metal. There is no definitive clasp or place to unlock it. Then it dawns on me: these are runes. But what for? It's unlikely to be a dampener—why would Lowri go through the trouble of removing the one I already wore?

My heart constricts at the possibility that it could be an amplifier like in the tale of the Lightweaver, Osha, who went in search of something to strengthen her powers. I'm reminded of the blaze that took out my brother. At the monstrosity I was as a little girl with no control of my powers. No different than I am now. I clutch my manacled wrist against my churning stomach and begin pacing the cell, my bare feet sticking to the damp floor with each step.

The sound of boots stops me from pacing. I turn as Briony approaches with Lieutenant Bronn and Cadet Aela again. Unlike the Lowri I thought I knew, Briony is no different than when I'd always been so quick to dismiss her. The guards carry high-backed chairs that appear to be from a dining set.

Briony draws closer, the ruby of my amulet around her neck winking at me. The rage that fills me is so swift, I'm rendered breathless. "Give me back my necklace," I hiss.

"I can't do that, Your Highness. You put this on, and the result will be catastrophic."

"What the fuck are you getting at?" I demand.

The guards place the chairs facing each other and retreat silently.

"All in due time," Briony says sweetly.

I stare down my nose at her. "I've never trusted you."

"You're very clever then. Now, sit."

"I don't answer to the likes of you." I fold my arms across my chest and remain rooted to my spot.

Briony points toward the ceiling "Up there, you are the heir to the throne." She points at the floor. "Down here, I am the High Priestess of Lugda, and you *do* answer to the likes of me. For your own good. Please. Sit."

High Priestess … The title still baffles me. We stare at each other for what feels like eons, the tension thick in the air.

Drip, drip, drip.

At last, I huff out a breath and plop into one of the chairs. Briony takes a seat in front of me, her knees touching mine. "Alright," she says airily. "Show me what you've got."

"I'm sorry, what?"

"Summon your flamewielding."

I stare down at my hands, still discolored from the dried blood I've scrubbed off. "I don't know how to … do it on purpose." But if I did, perhaps I can get out of here.

"Reach deep inside yourself and feel for your powers. Then envision yourself physically drawing it out." She holds her hand up and a small ball of pale blue light forms in the palm of her hand. I try not to appear alarmed or even impressed, but the smile on her face tells me that I've failed at that. "Your turn," she says.

"You aren't afraid I'll scorch your pathetic arse?"

"You couldn't even if you tried." She's so sure of herself that it gives me pause. "We don't have all day, Your Highness."

I hold my palm up just as she showed me, and I close my eyes. Focusing deep within my being, I find something warm and foreign, yet familiar. As I reach for it, uncontrolled infernos and screams fill my mind, and repulsion drives the warmth away. I clench my fist as cold creeps into my bones again.

"Hmm …" Briony stares down at my fist and then back up at my face, lightly tapping her thin lips. "Try again."

"No."

She sighs. "If you're not successful with this method, we'll have to move on to less gentle approaches."

"Try me."

She raises a fine brow and makes a small sound in the back of her throat. "I'll give you one more chance. What do you say?"

I glare at her. "Kiss. My. Arse."

Another tight smile. "Suit yourself." She pushes her chair back and calls for the guards. "Take her."

My chest knots as the guards barge into my cell, one grabbing me, the other shackling my hands behind my back. The shackle on my right hand presses over the wristband underneath, and the metal bites into my skin. I draw in a sharp breath.

"Walk," Briony says, nudging my back before stepping around me to walk ahead. The guards trail us as Briony takes the lead, the small magical light in her palm illuminating our way through the twists and turns of the tunnel. I try to make sense of the directions, to commit them to memory, but by the time we enter another chamber, I've forgotten every turn.

Briony flicks her hand toward the walls, and a ball of magelight illuminates a couple of small glass lamps. The space is barely large enough to fit the four of us. It's even colder than my cell, and the stink of urine and fear makes my throat spasm. An armchair sits in the center, its metal legs nailed to the stone floor. The walls are drab grey, and one side has a metal rack filled with weapons. I quickly turn away from them as I'm shoved into the chair. My manacles are removed long enough only for my forearms to be strapped into a metal contraption on the arms of the chair, my palms facing up. My ankles are next, immobilized by chains around the base of the chair.

On instinct, I tug against the bonds, my heart pounding in my ears, my stomach twisting into knots. The guards step away, standing on either side of the door, while Briony crouches and stares into my eyes. "What did you discover in *The Book of Agryna*?"

I don't so much as blink.

She sighs like I'm a minor annoyance and straightens so she's towering over me. "You won't cooperate for training. You won't answer questions. What will you answer to?"

Ironically, I don't have an answer to that, so I keep staring at her. I don't know what they're going to do to me if I continue to show defiance, but I fear telling them about *The Book of Agryna* will put more people than just me in danger.

"Send for Iywan," Briony says.

My muscles tense and her sandy brown hair sways as she walks toward the door. She takes the place of Cadet Aela, who steps out of the small space. Time ticks by for an eternity before footsteps approach. Briony moves aside for Cadet Aela to reclaim her place, and Iywan enters with his hands behind his back. The royal advisor broach is still pinned against the breast pocket of his robe. What an insult.

"You're not worthy of your title, *royal advisor*. What would my mother say to you if she knew what you were up to?"

"I'm doing what she didn't have the courage to do," he says plainly. "To actually teach you how to access your power. All you have to do is give us some answers."

"I don't know anything."

He pulls a book out from behind his back and the gold symbol in the worn leather cover glints in the magelight. *The Book of Agryna*. My pulse scurries as Iywan opens the book to a page I've earmarked and holds it up in front of my face.

The passage reads: *The daughter of Agryna and Ehlach shall stand resolute and restore balance to the realm*. It's quite vague really. But a handwritten note in the margins of a different page implies that the prophecy is incomplete, and the mythos of Enidwen redacted—it redirects the reader to the full text found in *The Song of Moonlight*. A book I've never seen or even heard of.

"Read." There's no room for argument in Iywan's voice.

"I can't."

"Don't lie to me. You've been reading in the Ancient Tongue without even knowing it all this time."

I bite the inside of my cheek. Of course he had to have been there for that discovery. I lift my chin a little higher. I will not be reduced to meekness.

"Read it!"

I scowl at him, then focus on the symbols that should logically be foreign to me. The words naturally infiltrate my mind and pour from my lips—a series of rolled consonants and guttural vowels that are so satisfying to utter. *How's that for reading the passage, Iywan?*

I barely register his raised hand before pain flares in my cheek. He shakes his hand out, clearly pained, and I catch a glimpse of the large ring on his finger. I start to lift my hand to my throbbing face, but I'm still bound to this godsdamned chair. I stare back with all the defiance I can muster.

"One more chance," Iywan says.

"Fuck you."

The next slap, I should've seen coming.

This time bright spots pulse in my vision and incoherent speech reaches my ears as multiple footsteps grow more distant. There's a slam, and the room plunges into near darkness, save for the oddly flickering magelight left behind.

Chapter 61
DURVLA

I'VE BEEN DEEP BREATHING for ages, trying to get my mind to somehow find Carys's subconscious—or anyone's, really. I'm bored out of my mind. Cracking one eyelid open, I stare at Kilkenny where he sits in front of me with his eyes closed. His legs are crisscrossed, as mine are, and the grass beneath us is slightly damp—it's starting to seep into my trousers. Above us, pink and lilac blend into the grey-blue sky as the sun slowly wakes.

"I think it'll rain today," I say.

Kilkenny's eyes open and his chest heaves with an impatient sigh. "Your focus is terrible," he motions.

Around us, the others are beginning to prepare for our day of travel. Alys was the first to wake and ensured that I took my tincture before she began her morning routine.

I pull a face at Kilkenny. "Sorry, but nothing is happening. I don't know how this daywalking works."

"You aren't trying hard enough." I don't have to be able to hear to know his tone is sharp. He sighs again and holds up his hands in apology before raking his fingers through his hair. "Neither of us knows what we're doing. It isn't your fault."

I gasp theatrically, feigning shock. "The great Tiernan Kilkenny admits he doesn't know how to do something? Alert the town crier!" He scowls at me, and I smile with mocking sweetness for a second before my shoulders droop. "Maybe I'll never be able to control it."

The wheels in his mind begin to turn. "Let's try a different approach. Close your eyes and let your mind wander. That shouldn't be hard with your focus."

Now *I* scowl before closing my eyes. Deep breath in, and out, in, and … I've never been this far from home before. Will I ever see Cluain Baile again? How tall is Taig by now? Will he be happy to be reunited with me? What will life be like for us after this? I envision wrapping my arms around Taig's little body and hugging him tightly. He'll probably growl at me. I chuckle, imagining Kilkenny's face right now.

He's probably rolling his eyes at me. I'm tempted to peek at what emotions play over his face. I'd love to see that dazzling smile of his again.

Instead, it's my own face I see.

My eyes are closed, a smirk on my lips. My hair is wild and messy, dark coils tumbling over my forehead and onto my shoulders. Impatience and admiration fill my body. No, not *my* body; it's as though I'm looking at myself through …

"Whoa!" I force my eyes open and scoot back on my bum. Soil makes its way underneath my fingernails as I clutch at the grass, needing to hold onto something, anything.

Kilkenny leaps up to his feet, his face frantic. Our gazes clash and we share one very loud thought: *What in Ludga's hells was that?*

"Stop that." Kilkenny points a finger at me.

"Stop *what?!*" I don't even bother to lift my hands to sign, but clearly I was loud enough to draw everyone's attention.

"Everything alright?" Osheen signs.

I shrug and Kilkenny shakes out his limbs before steepling his fingers atop his head. He walks back and forth a couple of times before spinning back to me so quickly that I recoil. "Did you ... You ... Were you ..." He can't form words.

Honestly, neither can I. All I can do is shrug uselessly again. "You said let my mind wander, so I did."

He peers over my shoulder. "Alys! A word, please."

I glance at Alys, who approaches as she ties a scarf over the front of her hair, securing any frizzy strands. "What's going on?"

"Durvla ..." He points to me, but his words run away again. He exhales slowly and tries again. "She was in my head a moment ago." His rushed signs follow soon after.

"As in mind whispering?" Her eyes bulge.

"No, this was different. I asked her to let her mind wander, but then I felt her presence in my head. As though she'd taken over my mind for a moment."

Gods, I didn't know it was that involved. "I ... didn't mean to."

Alys presses her lips into a line. "This seems to be a newly developed part of your daywalking."

I try not to sigh heavily, but my control fails me.

"For someone in the early days of developing her powers, it's likely that you're only able to make such connections with those you feel ... bonded to. Like Carys ... and Tiernan."

Kilkenny smirks at me and a flush creeps into my cheeks.

"It means you're on the right path to figuring out these powers." She faces Kilkenny and signs for my understanding. "How about you take a break, and I'll work with Durvla for a while?"

"I'm fine," he snaps. He turns away again and my heart sinks. Is he afraid of me? *Kilkenny* afraid of *me?*

"I know you're fine, but you both need to learn to delegate sometimes. Just because you have the ability to do something, doesn't mean you have to do it. We're a team. Asking for help is not an admittance of weakness."

Kilkenny and I exchange glances. I hate asking for help. I nod, but I know I'm the weakest link here, and if I ask for help, it's essentially proving that. Alys raises her perfectly arched brows at Kilkenny, and he also nods before sulking away.

With a cheery smile, she turns to me, "So, where were you?"

"I don't even know at this point."

Alys chuckles. "I'll tell you what," she signs. "I'll teach you to shield your mind. It comes in handy when in the company of a Whisperer." She winks and I giggle.

"It sounds handy. Thank you, Alys."

Chapter 62
CARYS

MY ARSE HAS LONG fallen asleep, the sensation of pins and needles shooting down my legs and into my feet, turning into unbearable discomfort. I can't sit still. I've shifted countless times, trying to relieve the prickling sensation, but it's no use. The dull aching in my back has gotten sharper, and my arms are starting to tingle now. I fear the others have left me here to rot.

As I shift again, the door slams, disrupting the silence as Briony and *Eefa* waltz into the tiny space. At least Iywan isn't among them this time, but the wicked glint on Eefa's face is unsettling.

"Missed me?" she asks, twirling on the spot. "I think I'll stick to this body. It's way more alluring than Lowri's, don't you think?" Her wink makes my gut curdle.

I don't bother to respond as she leans back against the wall beside the door, propping her foot against it.

SOLACE OF DUSK

"Lessons first, translation later?" Briony asks. As if I have a choice. I scoff at her. "First, I need some answers myself."

"Alright." Briony's face is stern. "You get one answer to *one* question. Then you give me one minute of your full cooperation to start."

I frown at her, considering the options. Perhaps it would be wise for me to learn to draw on my power, just not for the reasons they want. "Deal." I gnaw on my inner cheek for a few beats, then ask, "What is this wristband for?"

"It's a conduit."

"What is a—"

"One. Question." She says it firmly, but there's no edge to her voice.

I bite back a brazen response and stare at her. She straightens, smoothing out the skirt of her dress. "Right, so let's get started. Try to imagine your fire appearing in the palm of your hand. Reach inside yourself and find that energy."

I frown in focus. "There's nothing inside of me."

Eefa scoffs from her spot near the wall. "You're right about that."

I glare at her.

Briony waves her hand with a heavy sigh. "Ignore her. Try to focus."

My arms are fastened to the chair still, but my palms are face up. I try my hardest to focus on the center of my palm. Reaching inside myself, I search for any semblance of power, for that heat. It's there, glowing brightly inside of me, but when I try to grab a hold of it, it dances mockingly out of my reach. Sweat beads on my forehead and slowly trickles down my face. My hand remains cool, free of flames, ordinary. I release a breath, and the tension dissipates along with that energy.

If disappointment had an embodiment, it would be Briony. Her narrow shoulders slump, her focus still on my hand. "Again."

"I gave you one minute. You owe me another question."

Briony sighs and, behind her, Eefa cackles. "You are *terrible* at this, Priestess," Eefa says. "Tag me in."

"Not yet." Briony gnaws on her lower lip.

"I can go get Iywan …"

Annoyance, and something that looks surprisingly like sympathy, plays over Briony's long face. She heaves another sigh and turns from me, walking toward the wall.

A brilliant smile stretches across Eefa's lips. "At long last!" She steps toward me, aggressive excitement radiating off her. "You have three seconds to summon your powers. And I won't ask nicely again."

"That was nicely?"

She slaps me across my face, and it *stings*. I'm certain she's slapped right over where Iywan last struck. "Summon them willingly or I'll force it out of you."

I huff out a sigh and I reach inside myself for that ball of energy. I call it forth to my fingers, but nothing happens.

Another blow from Eefa. "Again!"

Once more I try, and once more I fail. Eefa's fist flies at me and, with a sickening *crunch*, pain flares in my nose. I growl in frustration, tugging against my bonds, desperate to quell the pain. "Stop it," I grind out, my voice nasal. "I can't do it. I'm *trying*." Hot blood flows unstaunched, dripping off my chin. My whole face is on fire.

Eefa lifts her hand again and Briony calmly says, "Enough."

Eefa steps back with an annoyed grunt. But then she bends so that her face is level with mine and says, "Your face isn't so beautiful anymore."

I'm lost for words, but I hope my expression comes across as unbothered.

"I think it's time to take things up a notch," Eefa says to Briony.

Briony sighs and approaches me. "I don't want to do this, but you're not giving me much of a choice."

I wince as she reaches for me, but when her hand connects with my cheek, the pain is quick and sharp before cool relief flows into my face. Warm drowsiness counteracts the cooling sensation, and everything fades away.

$$\cdots \circ \,) \, \ast \, (\circ \cdots$$

Drip, drip, drip.

My mind is slightly groggy as I come to. As much as I want to open my eyes, they're reluctant to do so.

"Maybe the Zenith is wrong about her. Maybe she's not the one." Eefa's voice.

My pulse quickens, my palms going clammy. My arse and back ache, and my arms are starting to chafe from the bindings anchored to the chair.

"She is the one," Briony says.

"She can't even summon a little bit of fire."

"She's never had to before, and her powers have been dampened for years. She just needs time."

Eefa sighs heavily. "We don't have time. The summer solstice will be here before we know it. If we fail, we'll have to wait until the autumn equinox. Master Iywan would never forgive us."

There's silence for a moment.

Drip. Drip. Drip.

That incessant dripping has me alarmingly aware of how full my bladder is. I breathe through it, though when a few footsteps come my way, I hold my breath.

"She's awake," says Eefa.

As much as I want to continue pretending to sleep, I quit the charade. I'm back in my cell, except the chair from the torture chamber is now rooted to this floor.

"Welcome back, Your Highness. Let's give the fire summoning another try, shall we?" Briony says with a too-cheerful smile.

"I can't do it. I think we've already established that. I reach for the damn energy you keep talking about, and it rejects me."

"But it *is* there?" Hope blooms in her icy blue eyes.

"I suppose so."

Briony casts an I-told-you-so glare at Eefa, who crosses her arms and huffs a breath. Briony turns to me again. "Find that power and try again."

I cannot find another way out of this, so I reach deep inside again, searching for that source of energy. The heat grows stronger and stronger, the power surging beneath my skin, and I try to draw the energy to my palms. Suddenly there's a blast of fire in my mind alongside Aneirin's screams. My heart races, my body cools, and I clench my fist. I lift my head to Briony again and her shoulders slump.

Eefa cackles and steps away from the bars to strut toward us. "You've had your turn, now step aside." She pulls a dagger from her boot and crouches, holding the blade a mere whisper from my face. I press my head back against the chair as hard as I can, my heart threatening to give out. "Let's see how high your pain tolerance is, darling princess." She touches the tip of the dagger to my cheek, and there's a cool sensation at first, until the blade bites into my flesh.

"Eefa, don't," I hear myself say with a gasp.

"Oh, a command. How predictable. Maybe if you beg, I won't do it." Her vulpine grin makes my pulse skitter again, but I steel my nerves.

She will not get a plea out of me.

The blade bites deeper into my cheek as Eefa drags it slowly across my skin. I clench my jaw and fight the urge to whimper.

"Stubborn bitch," Eefa coos. Her tone is confusing, almost affectionate. It makes me shudder. "Imagine what you can do with that power."

I squeeze my eyes shut, pushing away the memories. Aneirin.

"Just summon the damn power. Prove what you've always wanted to prove. Be that warrior princess that Ellynne claimed you were."

The sound of Ellynne's name on her lips pulls fervent rage from my core. "Don't you dare say her name."

"*El-lynne.*"

She steps back, and though the cut from her dagger still stings, the memory of Ellynne bleeding to death in my bed hurts even more. "You're a disgrace," I say. "You deserved every bit of mistreatment in your marriage."

A glint of amusement appears on her face. "Ah, the claws have come out," she says with a grin. She taps the flat of the blade against her cheek, leaving a smear of my blood on her olive skin.

"Once I figure out how to summon my powers, you'll be the first person that I burn."

She laughs. "I'm looking forward to it, darling." She sighs happily, a smile still on her lips. "She begged for your life, you know. *Ellynne.* Before I shoved my knife into her belly."

Heat floods my hands, but it doesn't go beyond that. I want to stick my fingers into her eyes and burn her from the inside out. I want her brain to melt and her flesh to blister and burst.

Briony suddenly stands at full attention, focused on something beneath me. Eefa's attention shifts as well, not to me but to the shackles binding my wrists.

They glow bright orange with my own summoned heat.

I stare at the bonds in shock before I find the nerve to face Briony and Eefa again. Briony's shoulders sag with relief, but Eefa's chest puffs out.

She smirks at me. "Good girl."

And again, my flame dies.

Chapter 63
CARYS

IYWAN HOLDS THE BOOK so close to my face that the words are barely visible. "Read it. In the common tongue this time."

"I can't *see* it!" I protest. I'm back to sitting in this damn chair after they let me loose for a moment to relieve my bladder. I am so bone-tired that I could probably fall asleep in this.

Iywan pulls the book back a small distance. Two guards, plus Briony and Eefa, stand nearby. "What does it say?"

"It says that you are a pretentious bastard."

I expect him to strike me, but he does something even worse. He summons Eefa.

She practically skips to his side like an overeager child. Her dagger is in her hand before Iywan can say anything else.

"Read," Iywan repeats.

I glimpse something animalistic in Eefa's eyes, sending my heart leaping into my throat. "Alright, fine." I fix my focus on Iywan for a moment before taking in the text. "It says that the mighty shall fall with the coming of the new age. The Heirs of Dusk and Embers shall rise again and dismantle the very foundation of the realm." I shrug a shoulder.

Iywan stares at me for the longest while, and I cannot figure out what's going through his mind. He doesn't turn away from me. He simply says Eefa's name.

Without hesitation, she slices through the sleeve of my tunic. The blade grazes my skin, and I hiss from the sting. The upper portion of my sleeve is fully ripped open, blood bright against my pale skin.

I glare at Iywan. "I read you the passage!"

"You're lying."

"How can you be so sure?"

He only glances at Eefa, and she slices swiftly just below the last cut. I grit my teeth as more bright red blooms.

"Read it properly," says Iywan.

I grunt. "That passage isn't even important, you idiot! I earmarked it because that's where I left off."

He crouches so that his face is close to mine and says, "Then tell me what is important."

"How am I supposed to know what's important when you haven't explained a thing to me?"

He straightens and, as Eefa lunges to mar me again, Iywan catches her wrist. She pouts but lowers the dagger, and I release a breath.

"It was said that the daughter of Agryna will restore power to Erleya—and the only way to do that is by piercing the Veil of Fiada Purlieu," Iywan says.

Shit, I still can't believe this is true. My stomach squirms.

"As far as everyone knows, the magical bloodline ended with the royals a millennium ago, yet here you are. A Flamewielder, in the flesh." Iywan gestures vaguely to me.

"What clued you in that I'm a Flamewielder? Not even *I* knew."

"After I discovered that you could read the Ancient Tongue, it narrowed things down. It's in your bloodline. Not to mention that your mother gave you the necklace after Aneirin mysteriously died in *an accident*, and you haven't taken it off since."

My stomach sours and I force myself to swallow. I grit my teeth against my brother's screams in my head.

"The stench of smoke lingered for days around the time of Aneirin's death. Yet, no one could remember there being a fire. I suppose that's Morwenna's particular skillset." He lets out a dry chuckle and scratches his chin. "It was you reading the Ancient Tongue that triggered my memory again."

I fight to keep my breathing steady.

"The texts declare that a Mage of royal blood has the ability to tear down those wards and summon the Enchantress Queen, just as she'd summoned the Underling Prince a thousand years ago."

"So ... you think *I* can tear down the wards and summon *Enidwen*?"

"Yes, and as a reward for her release, you will obtain ultimate power. Enidwen's spirit fused with the Underling Prince's, so you'd have twice the power that either of them ever had. And this time, there are no *Heirs of Dusk and Embers* to stop your reign. You will be not only the queen, but the empress of the realm. Erleya will be invincible."

I can't help but laugh. "You've forgotten one very important detail about that story. When Enidwen released the Underling Prince, he overpowered her. She no longer had control. What makes you think that the combined spirits of Enidwen and the Underling Prince won't overpower *me*? More importantly, what makes you think I even *want* this?"

His oily smile makes my skin crawl. "Because, Princess, this time her spirit will be tethered to a mortal body with a conduit."

My brows draw close before the metal band on my wrist grows heavier. My pulse triples. "Conduit … is that what's on my wrist?" My voice hitches and I wince at the sound.

"First, tell me what the prophecy says."

"Didn't *you* just tell me the prophecy?"

"I told you the redacted version that's known by anyone who still believes the words of the ancient oracles."

Part of me wants to tell him. To end this all. To find out what this device on my wrist does. But his desperation indicates that the information is clearly important for his twisted mission to open the Veil. I can't let that happen, I can't let him unleash Enidwen or let her infiltrate me. The Book of Agryna spoke of the moon and sun falling if the Veil were opened. It could be symbolic, but there is no room for risks. I've caused enough messes in my twenty-one years—I refuse to destroy the world.

Iywan glances at the sadist beside him. "Eefa—"

She eagerly slices into my arm, right through the last two cuts. I grit my teeth and keep my focus away from the pain.

"What does the prophecy say?" Iywan asks.

"That the daughter of Agryna shall restore power to—"

More pain. I clench my teeth and breathe through the searing sensation. Blood darkens my light grey tunic and my vision blurs.

"Cutting me over and over again isn't going to change what the book says," I grind out.

Another slice, this time through my trousers. The blade nicks my thigh but it's nothing compared to the slashes on my arm.

"Keep going until she tells the truth," Iywan instructs.

Bile rises into my throat. They're never going to stop.

Eefa grins as she presses the point of the blade into my upper thigh. I steel my resolve and imagine myself far away, on a ship in the middle of the ocean, gazing out at the beautiful blue waters. Still, pain tears through my leg as Eefa languidly pushes the knife deeper and deeper and deeper. I bite my lip and a coppery tang springs onto my tongue. My heart threatens to burst from my chest, and a strangled cry of pain fills the space.

It takes a while before I realize that the screams are coming from me. Tears pour down my cheeks, and the dagger slowly sinking into my thigh encompasses all my thoughts. I clench my jaw, cutting off the scream and emitting a prolonged, almost animalistic grunt instead.

"She can't bloody think if you're shoving a blade into her leg!" Briony yells.

Eefa yanks the blade from my flesh and blood spurts, drawing another scream from me.

Briony swears colorfully as she rushes to my side, pushing Eefa away. "You've severed an artery, you doltish girl," she says, casting a heated glance at Eefa while she presses her hand against my leg.

I bite back another cry.

Eefa shrugs. "Good thing we have a Healer around."

Briony glances sidelong at her as a pale blue light glows around her hands. The pain slowly dissolves, leaving behind a faint throbbing. Then Briony rocks back onto her ankles and stares silently at my newly healed leg, trying to regain her own composure as I try to regain mine.

I'm dizzy and heavy-limbed, barely able to register what's happening as Briony reaches for my injured arm.

"Leave those." Iywan's voice is cold.

Briony balks. "With all due respect, Master Iywan, we're not going to get much out of her if she's in pain."

Master Iywan?

"Quite the contrary, Briony," he says. "This one *only* responds to pain."

·· ◦ ☽ ☀ ☾ ◦ ··

This time, my solitude is short. I try to focus on anything other than the sense of foreboding and the pain, but the situation is hopeless. Finally, everyone files back into the room. First, Iywan, Eefa, and Briony. Then Cadet Aela and Lieutenant Bronn enter, dragging a tall man between them, his hands behind his back and chained, judging from the sound of the metallic jangle. I take in the brawny figure beneath the maroon livery of the Queen's Guards, but there's no black sash, meaning he's …

My guard.

No no no. Not Callum. My heart skips a beat, panic rushing through my blood as I meet his uneven, tormented, bloodshot gaze.

He winces as he attempts to stand fully, but his knees buckle, wrenching his shoulders as the guards hold him up. Blood mats his ashy blond hair and smears his grimy face. His right eye is swollen shut, but his good eye holds such intensity.

"Princess," he chokes out, and the soldiers yank on his shackles, overarching his back. Callum grits his teeth, breathing harshly, but he doesn't cry out. "Don't tell them anything," he says. His voice is gravelly, nearly unrecognizable.

I sit up straighter, my chest too tight, my stomach sour. Callum is hardly able to stand on his own. There must be so much damage hidden beneath his uniform. What have they done to him? What *will* they do to him? The heavy rasp of his breathing fills the space, and with each intake of breath, pain crosses his face.

I tug hard against my bonds.

"Are you ready to cooperate now, Princess?" Iywan asks.

If I don't cooperate, they're going to hurt Callum. Or worse.

Iywan glances at Eefa and she steps toward Callum, her dagger at the ready. I yank against my bonds again silently, as if I can jump from this chair and whisk Callum away.

"Don't touch him." My voice is a mere whisper, my eyes stinging. I tear my gaze away from Eefa and Callum, forcing myself to focus on Iywan again.

He isn't even recognizable to me anymore. The coldness, the hatred—how could this be the same man who'd once been like a father to me?

"What does the prophecy say?" he asks. "The *full* prophecy, in the common tongue."

My chest tightens more, but I know I have to say *something* to give Callum a chance. Maybe a half truth. "It says that the daughter of Agryna and Ehlach will restore balance to the realm." I leave out the part where the entire prophecy is in *The Song of Moonlight*.

"Agryna *and* Ehlach?" Iywan asks.

I nod. "Yes, now let him go."

"Is that the whole prophecy?"

I nod again. "Yes. And everything you've already said. The Heirs. The Daughters. Let Callum go. He doesn't know anything."

Iywan glances over his shoulder, and I *know* what will happen before it even does. Eefa sets the knife against Callum's throat, and he strains to get as far away from her as possible.

"Don't!" I blurt. My breaths come in quick bursts, my pulse hammering behind my eyes, my vision turning wavery. "The prophecy in *The Book of Agryna* is incomplete." My mouth waters as I speak, and I swallow, afraid I'll be sick. "The rest of the prophecy is in another book."

Iywan straightens, his brows arched. Briony and Eefa appear equally intrigued. "Which book?" Iywan asks.

I can't tell them. I can't ... "I don't know."

Iywan lifts his hand, and as I draw in a breath to protest, Eefa presses the blade against Callum's throat, the soldiers holding him tighter. I yank so hard against my bonds that my arse leaves the seat. "Eefa, *please*!"

She sneers. "Oh, *now* you beg?"

Callum's full attention is on me, his broad chest rising and falling rapidly with each shallow intake of breath. A single tear rolls down his cheek, carving a path through the blood and grime.

"I'm sorry," I say, my voice breaking as I fight the urge to spill the truth. To spare Callum's life.

"I have no regrets," he says calmly.

"Callum—"

"I will love you even in death."

A deep-rooted ache tears through my tightening chest, and I grapple for that power Briony has been coaching me to use. If I can just get a hold of it. If I can figure out how to wield the flames, I can maybe, *maybe* get us out of here.

Please, gods. Please Agryna. Please.

At first, nothing happens. Callum's muscles are taut as he's held firmly by the soldiers, as Eefa's knife remains against his skin. But then Iywan raises a hand. Everything slows as Eefa carves a deliberate line across his throat. I scream for her to stop, as if it would do anything to staunch the blood that rushes down his neck and drenches his livery.

The coward that I am, I shut my eyes. I don't want this to be my last image of him. I don't want to witness the life drained from his body. A nauseating gurgle emits from where he stood before a heavy *thud* sounds.

Each forceful beat of my heart pumps remorse and sorrow into my blood, until my body is so heavy that I'm certain I'll sink right through the chair. There is no sound except for the screaming in my head and the roaring of my pulse in my ears.

When I dare to open my eyes again, Callum is slumped on the floor. A puddle of scarlet spreads around him.

First Ellynne …

Now … Callum …

Guilt, regret, and sorrow wrench tears from me, the silent sobs trapped in my heaving chest, threatening to strangle me. A surge of nausea rushes up from my stomach. I hunch over in the chair as bile scorches its way out of my throat.

Briony steps toward me, and I don't even feel her touch before merciful darkness takes me.

Chapter 64
DURVLA

WE SIT ON THE side of the road and munch on underripe strawberries as Alys briefs us on entering the Verge. She draws an image in the dirt with a stick, showing mountains and a forest, then she makes a line at the base of the mountain. "This is the entrance. It's *heavily* warded. In fact, anyone entering without the proper knowledge of how will be torn apart by the wards."

I make a face. "As in *literally* torn apart?"

Alys glances up at me, sternness on her face. "Yes." She draws three Xs beneath the line, each a small distance apart. "The runes have to be drawn here, here, and here, with the enchantments spoken at each. Very old magic. It's all written down on a scroll in my pack—in case for some reason I'm unable to do it. Once beyond the wards, there are guards trained to kill on sight. Immediately take a knee and lower your gaze. It's a sign of reverence. It sounds complicated, but for good reason, of course."

"Of course," Chiyo agrees.

A strange, metallic taste suddenly fills my mouth and colors dance before me. My limbs grow heavy, and I must make a sound or something because everyone turns to me.

"Durvla? Are you alright?" Osheen signs. My focus darts between his concerned face and then Kilkenny's.

Still crouching, Kilkenny moves closer, his focus on me as he urgently calls to Alys. "She's going to—"

Then the world around me whirls and morphs.

By the time the world stops warping, I find myself standing in dark tunnels again. I gag from the wringing in my gut and swallow hard. This time, I don't try to run. I drop to my knees and press my hands against my ears to block out the screams.

Why is this happening? Why can't I control it? I want to join in the scream-ing—out of frustration, out of helplessness. When I want to dreamwalk, I can't? When I least expect it—

Pain lances through my leg, my arms, my face. Everything hurts, and soon I'm sobbing right along with a disembodied voice.

This is a dream, I remind myself. Not my dream but a dream, nonetheless. I pull my hands from my ears and try to gauge my surroundings. A candle flickers in the distance. That must be my exit. I struggle to my feet, ignoring the aches, and hobble toward the candle. "Carys!" I call, assuming this is her dreamscape. "If you can hear me, please answer."

Nothing.

More howls of pain come from her, wherever she is. Moments like these make me grateful that I usually exist in silence. Carys's screams hurt even worse than the phantom pain attacking my body. "Carys! Think of yourself somewhere else! Anywhere else. Far away from the pain. Carys?"

The screams stop, but I barely have a moment of relief before pressure builds in my head. I squeeze my eyes shut, pressing the heels of my hands against my temples. A breeze brushes my cheeks, and when I open my eyes, I'm on a boat. Carys stands at the bow, gazing out at the ocean.

"Carys!" I call.

She spins toward me, her hair billowing out behind her, distress on her face. "Durvla," she says with breathless relief. "Thank the gods." I step toward her, and she grasps my hand.

I give her a quick once-over. "What is going on?"

"Ellynne and Callum are dead. Lowri is a Skinchanger; she's also Eefa. I've been captured. I'm somewhere under the castle, I believe. They're torturing me, Durvla. Iywan, Eefa, and bloody Briony." She chokes back sobs, irrational laughter cutting through with a harsh sound that makes me wince.

I'm lost for words, unsure what comfort I can offer. "Did anyone tell you why?"

"The book of Folklore and Fairytales that I own, it's in the Ancient Tongue. The passage that mentioned Lightweavers mentions the Heirs of Dusk and Embers and something about the solace of dusk. Iywan and the others ... they want me to summon Enidwen and ... absorb her powers? Like she tried to do with the Underling Prince."

"What?" My eyes nearly pop out of my head.

She wipes tears off her cheeks. "Yes, exactly."

"But Enidwen failed and then the Heirs of—"

The entire dreamscape shudders and I shut my eyes to ward off the dizziness. "I think we're running out of time," Carys shouts.

I open my eyes as the world settles again, but things are a little blurry.

"Durvla, this is important. The Book of Agryna *seems to have a companion tome called* The Song of Moonlight. *I don't know where it can be found. It's not in our library at the palace, but there's an important passage regarding Enidwen there, and an addendum to the prophecy."*

Her words start to sound distant. It's reminiscent of when my hearing first started to wane. I focus on Carys's lips, but the entire image blurs. "Is there more?" I ask.

"Yes, when Iywan captured me, he told me ..." She pauses to find her words. "Welcome to the Zenith."

I barely make out the word. "Zenith?"

"Yes!" She's shouting now as wind whips around us, drowning out most of her words, contorting my surroundings. "Durvla, I'm scared."

"I know."

"I feel so alone."

The statement resonates so deeply with me that it aches. "Don't give up. We'll figure something out. You're not alone."

More wind whips around us, and the ship floor begins to shift. I try to remain upright, to grasp for Carys, but as I reach out, I meet nothing but air. I collapse, and before I land, I awake with a gasp again—

The bright sun hurts. I squint and vaguely make out Alys's full-figured silhouette. "Hello again, sweetling," she says.

I sit up and look around wildly. I don't have time to ground myself right now. I need to tell them everything that Carys told me. "Carys is being tortured," I blurt out.

The color drains from everyone's face. Alys's hand clutches her chest, and she turns away for a while, blinking back tears. Tiernan clenches his jaw and runs a shaky hand through his hair. I spew out what I can remember, including Callum and Ellynne's deaths, the Zenith, Lowri the Skinchanger, the missing prophecy about Enidwen and *The Song of Moonlight*, Iywan wanting Carys to summon Enidwen, the solace of dusk ...

All the while, my chest grows tighter and tighter with each word. I don't even know if anything I say is coherent at this point, but there are so many names and titles and terminology that signing and fingerspelling would take forever or be incomprehensible.

"I need to take a walk," I say. I don't wait for anyone to reply, even as I catch the tears glistening on Alys's face. I clamber to my feet and rush down the grassy path we'd just come from. My eyes sting and my chest aches, but I hold back the tears. I try to focus on the road ahead, despite walking in the wrong direction. I just need to put space between myself and everyone else. I need to get rid of this uneasiness.

How can we help Carys? By now, we're nearly at the northern tip of Erleya. We're so close to the Verge that I can taste freedom. Yet Carys is being tortured.

Guilt wraps around my heart and squeezes until I'm breathless. I stop walking and place my hands on my head.

Grass. Trees. Sky. Breeze against my skin … fear, hopelessness, anxiety. My body trembles and I turn my face to the sky and close my eyes.

Just as I'm about to lose it completely, cold water drips onto my face and I gasp. I open my eyes as rain pours down.

It's like the sky has opened. I rush back to the group. Kilkenny is readying Ghendor, and by the time I get to him, he helps me mount the stallion without even trying to get me to talk.

Before long, we're racing through the rain, the horses kicking up grass and mud. For once, I couldn't be more grateful for the cold that drenches my clothes and shocks my body out of a spiral.

Chapter 65
CARYS

WHY DID HIS HEART yearn for mine? Why was mine so reluctant to stretch beyond the pangs of lust? His last words haunt me, branding guilt onto my heart. *I will love you even in death.*

I didn't deserve his love.

He didn't deserve such a death.

I'll never feel his arms around me again, nor the whisper of his breath against my skin. Yet, I can still see his blood pooling around him. There will never truly be an *us*.

Staring down numbly at Briony as she finishes patching my arms, I note the tremor in her hands and the pallor of her usually tan complexion. I want to ask her why she's bothering, but I'm unable to. For days, maybe even weeks, it's been the same thing; My power continues to flee from me no matter how hard I try to summon it.

There have been threats to whip me, put me in a torture rack to stretch my limbs apart, and even kill off my servants in front of me, one by one. Thankfully, none of those extremes occur. Instead, I've had bones broken, joints dislocated, splinters shoved beneath my fingernails. My body hurts *constantly*, despite the repeated healing sessions from Briony.

Still, I refuse to tell them that I know the rest of the prophecy is in *The Song of Moonlight.*

This is my life now. Daily, as I'm marred and mended again and again, I pray for death more than I ever have. At least then my knowledge would die with me. Then they would be out of options, out of magical royal blood.

I keep my focus on Briony. "You're a priestess of Lugda, right?" My voice is coarse, strained—like I've swallowed grit.

"Yes?"

"Then kill me."

She peers up at me with surprising softness in her icy blue eyes, dark half-moons underneath. "Just because I'm a priestess to the god of death, that doesn't mean I cause it," she says.

Of course, it bloody doesn't.

"And you're too important to kill." She sits back on her heels. "They're going to tear you apart until you're a shell of your former self and willing to give them any information they seek. Just tell them what you know. It's for the greater good."

I mull over her words. For the greater good. Iywan wants to open the Veil and unleash the enchantress who sought to destroy our realm. "How could opening the Veil possibly be for the greater good?" I snap.

"I never said *opening the Veil* was for the greater good."

I blink at her, but she says nothing more.

· · ◦ ☽ ☀ ☾ ◦ · ·

Eefa's voice crawls across my skin as I slowly wake from a restless sleep.

"Do you think she could be Basduun?"

"No." Briony's voice.

I remain as still as possible, feigning sleep.

"How are you so sure?" Eefa asks.

"I'm not sure, but I don't think she is."

My mind is so sluggish from the lack of proper food and water that it takes a while for me to remember the tales about the Basduunai. It was never actually outright written, but most people believed that Enidwen was a Basduun—a Dark Mage with an impressive set of powers. Probably the most powerful Dark Mages to have ever existed. It's laughable that Eefa thinks that I could be a Basduun when I can hardly even summon flamewielding.

"Look," she says. "I think Her Highness is awake." Even though I can't see her, I know she's mocking me. "Let's begin."

"It's on my terms this time," says Briony. "You don't interfere."

I don't know whether to be relieved or even more afraid.

Chapter 66
DURVLA

BENEATH THE CLOUDY SKY, a gentle breeze rustles the shrubbery around me. Sweat breaks out across my brow as I focus on the tree several paces ahead of me. I've lost track of how many times my dagger has landed in the grass. A moment ago, it landed directly in front of me as if I hadn't even thrown it. I could've lost a toe.

Kilkenny gives me the space I need, but his focus on me is tangible.

"Stop looking at me," I say.

"How am I supposed to teach you if I don't look at you?"

He has a point, but I don't admit it. These dagger-throwing lessons are overdue—I know it's important that I'm able to defend myself in the case of another ambush or something, but I hate this. I cannot fathom ever throwing a dagger at someone.

I adjust my stance again, one foot forward, my knees slightly bent. I have the blade of the dagger lightly in my hand just as Kilkenny showed me. The tree is far away, and I need to lift my arm higher, or is it lower? Perhaps I need to bend my elbow more so that my hand reaches my ear or is it supposed to be above my head? My mind buzzes with all the information that I thought I knew.

I'm not cut out for this. Better I just quit rather than continue to embarrass myself.

"You're not embarrassing yourself."

Kilkenny's voice in my head still startles me, and I flinch, the blade of the dagger biting into my skin. I suck in a sharp breath and drop the dagger to the ground as blood wells and trickles between my fingers. I clutch the wound with my other hand and turn to face Kilkenny. He's already right beside me and I nearly jump out of my skin. "Gods, Kilkenny …" I mumble.

He frowns at me. "You're extra skittish today."

"Well, it's hard not to be when I can get pulled into a terrifying dreamscape at any moment." It's been a couple of days since that happened, but it still has me on edge.

Kilkenny's expression softens.

"I hate that I can't control it. I keep thinking I'm going to drop again. What if I fall off Ghendor?"

"I won't let that happen," he signs. He extends his hand to me. "Let me see."

Blood is still dripping, and the sight makes me slightly woozy as I extend my injured hand to Kilkenny. I turn my head away, but he waves my attention back to him. "Permission to heal you?" he asks.

My brows knit together before I remember he can mimic any power in the vicinity.

I shrug, but he says, "I need you to say it."

"By the gods, Kilkenny. Please heal me before I collapse."

The corners of his eyes crinkle. "Are you afraid of blood?"

"Not afraid. I just don't like it."

He smirks as he places his hand over my wound. A slight wince plays over his face as my pain melts away, and my palm itches as the skin is mended. When he releases my hand, the ache is gone but it's still covered in blood.

"Does it hurt?" I ask. "Healing, I mean."

"I'm not entirely sure about Healers in general—you'll have to ask Alys. But as a Whisperer, I can feel what others feel."

"I didn't realize that," I say, frowning. "So, it's more than mind reading."

"Right. It's also empathy. Reading or speaking into someone's mind takes a lot of energy. Except with you … Sometimes, your thoughts just *jump* into my mind."

I'm not sure I like that …

"*Sometimes!*" He holds up a hand as though making an oath. "When your thoughts are particularly loud. But please know that the last thing I want to do is invade your privacy."

That's sweet of him.

"We should work on your shielding more."

I roll my eyes, though I cannot help but smile. "Clearly."

He takes my hand in his again. "How does your hand feel?"

My lips tug up in a small smile. "I'm beginning to think you're just using this as an excuse to hold my hand."

Kilkenny chuckles. "Maybe I am."

My smile widens.

"Let's just see if I did an Alys-worthy job or not." He reaches for the waterskin on his belt and opens it without releasing me.

I gawk at him in disbelief. "How did you open that with one hand so easily?"

"What can I say? I'm very skilled with my hands." His eyes meet mine with an air of mischief, and my heart dithers.

I don't shy away from his onyx gaze, even as it intensifies. A heart-beat later, he pours cool water over my palm and pulls a clean rag from his trouser pocket. As he rubs the cloth over my bloodied skin, the tip of his tongue pokes out from the corner of his lips. His focused face is so endearing that I can't tear myself away. His silver streaks slip free from the rest of his dark hair and partially cover his eye. I want so much to brush the strands back, but I restrain myself, clenching my free hand.

When he lifts the rag, there's just smooth, clean skin. No blood, no scar. It's incredible. Kilkenny gently slides his thumb over my palm and my stomach flutters.

Gods, what other kind of magic does this man have that he affects me so? I've never felt this way before. I'm not even sure I want to.

"There," he says as I'm still trying to pull myself together. "Good as new." He tilts his head slightly, regarding me. "All good?"

I nod and gently pull my hand from his grasp.

Kilkenny runs his fingers through his dark hair, mussing it up, and I can't figure out for the life of me how he makes that so captivating. He bends to pick up my dagger and cleans it off with the damp cloth he used on my hand. He dries the blade with two smooth swipes across his trousers, then holds it out to me. I thank him and slide it back into the sheath on my belt before wrapping my arms around my torso as if I'm cold.

He stares off to the left, somewhere through the trees before turning back to me again. I start to ask him what he heard, but he gestures before I can say anything. "Were you and Osheen ever … More than friends?"

"No!" I speak perhaps a little too hastily. "He's been my best friend for as long as I can remember. Or, well …" I worry at my lower lip and motion, "I don't know what we are anymore." Osheen is out hunting with Chiyo. I'm not jealous, but their new friendship draws attention to the fact that the last relationship from my old life is dwindling.

Kilkenny rubs his stubble idly as he observes me for a while. "Did you have a lover back home? Or someone you were interested in?" His curiosity is genuine, but his body is taut.

"Maybe I do," I say, flicking my braid off my shoulder. I have every intention of walking away with an air of mystery. To leave him guessing. But as I start to strut past him, my boot catches on a tree root. I throw my arms out for balance, the back of my hand connecting with Kilkenny's face. Then the ground is rushing up toward me for the umpteenth time. Kilkenny's arms wrap around my middle, tugging me upright.

He saves me from a nasty fall. *Again.*

My face can't be any warmer right now. I can't trust myself to move, so I remain standing there, held upright by Kilkenny's arms, overly aware that my back is flush against his front. He turns me to face him, his arm still encircling my waist. "How many times do I have to catch you?" he asks, biting his lip over a restrained smirk.

Feigning nonchalance, I shrug. "You *could* just let me fall."

"No, I can't." His smile is slow, purposeful. "I'll gladly catch you a million more times if I have to."

My traitorous heart flutters. He doesn't release me, and I don't object. I melt into his hold, my gaze drawn to his.

And there's that subtle pull again. I wish I were truly brave enough to explore whatever this is.

"To answer your question …" I start, stepping back from him.

Kilkenny blinks and lets his arms fall, as though he's only just remembered that we'd been speaking before my clumsy moment.

"… there's no lover back home. I'm an Undesirable—"

"Durvla—"

Kilkenny crosses his arms. "You're not a liability, nor is Taig."

"Kilkenny, if Forayers discover either of us, anyone involved in keeping our secrets would either be hanged or sent to the Wastelands to die. I'd call that a liability."

He presses his lips into a line. His cheek twitches in either uncertainty or an attempt at restraint.

After a moment, I say, "Taig lost both his parents. I'm all he has left. He's my responsibility, and his happiness is essential to me."

"You also lost both your parents. What about *your* happiness?"

I huff out a dry laugh. "I was surviving just fine."

"I didn't ask about your survival. I asked about your happiness."

The silence is thick between us for quite some time. I rub my hand over my arm. "If I could go back in time and somehow avoid being brought to Paramount, I would be truly happy. It would be incredible if I could erase the past couple of months."

A strange expression flickers across his face, but it dies before I can decipher it. His stoic mask slips back into place, and gone is the Kilkenny I've gotten to know since leaving Paramount.

Oh …

Erasing the past months would mean I would've never met Carys, or Ellynne, Alys, Kilkenny …

"We should get going," he signs sharply, his lips still a firm line.

"Kilkenny, I didn't mean—"

But his back is already to me as he moves with quick steps.

I'm glad that I met you, I want to say, but maybe it's best that he thinks otherwise.

Chapter 67
DURVLA

THE OCEAN STRETCHES OUT below us as we navigate the green cliffs of Moicriach. Never in my wildest dreams did I think I would be this far from home. My heart is constantly in my throat—not just from the fear of our uncertain future, but because we are so unnaturally high up. Even the air is thinner up here, and I try my hardest not to look down at the deep waters reflecting the early morning rays.

Alys has predicted that the Verge is another two days' ride away at the rate we've been going. Every now and then, we make a stop to relieve ourselves, get some nourishment into our bodies, and give the horses a break. To think that Ghendor and Ffion have carried two riders each this far is impressive. Mirren must be more than pleased to have Alys as her rider.

Since the discussion that Kilkenny and I had a couple of days ago, he's been guarded. At least Osheen has become a little less tense, but unease is already high given our knowledge of Carys's situation.

It's hard to swallow the details of the last time I spoke with her—Carys's torture, in particular. As much as we all wish there was something we could do, right now we're powerless.

Much like my magical abilities …

There is something else looming inside me. Something cold and worrying. I'm certain that Alys is keeping her knowledge from me, because she has *that* expression on her face quite often whenever I train with her and Kilkenny.

I'm too afraid to ask and give up my blissful ignorance.

I've been riding in front of Kilkenny since my first daywalking incident, just in case it happens again. His hand appears in my view, calling for a stop. I pull on Ghendor's reins and can't get off his back fast enough. We're all exhausted.

There's no direct source of water for our horses, but as we remove our packs from them, they happily graze on the moist grass.

I'm bone-tired, but I sense there's something menacing coming. Something that I'm not going to be prepared for because I don't know the full extent of whatever power I have. I'm a cynic by nature, and as much as I try to shake it, that worry remains like a nagging voice in the back of my mind.

A light sea breeze blows through my braids as I stretch my arms up to the sky, taking the time to breathe. Chiyo approaches me as I'm stretching my legs, pulling my ankle back toward my bum and, naturally, nearly falling over. A smile brightens Chiyo's face. Alys has had to heal her sunburn so many times, but now a gentle tan graces her skin. The blue is fading from the roots of her hair and silver shines through beautifully in the sunlight.

"How are you doing?" she signs to me. Her signing has gotten more fluent—everyone's has.

"Fine," I reply.

"Right." She lifts a thin brow, dubious. She begins stretching along with me, bending over with her back straight, one hand reaching across her body to the opposite foot. She straightens and switches sides before turning her face to me again. "How are you *really* doing?"

I fidget with my sleeve since I no longer wear my dampener. "I'm … anxious. I think your brother and Alys are hiding something from me."

She glances over her shoulder at them as they converse a small distance away. "You should ask them."

I gnaw on my lower lip and shake my head.

"How do you feel about the rebellion now? You know, as we draw closer to the Verge?"

I shrug, wanting to look away as my neck and face grow warm.

"I know you're not able to fully control your powers yet, but think about how rewarding it would be. To be able to be a part of the group who rescued your brother? It can't be that bad, right?" Her smile is too wide, almost comical.

To keep from smiling, I press my lips together. "I don't think it's for me. I just want to get back to a mundane life. I'm no warrior. I'm just … Durvla. If there's anything I'm good at, it's taking care of my brother."

Chiyo giggles. "And making the princess's *Feast dress*. You didn't know you had that in you before you did it. You're not just an older sister. You have your own things."

Still reluctant to give in to the romanticization of joining the rebellion, I remain silent. Chiyo crosses her arms over her small frame, her face etched in deep thought before she glances over her shoulder again at the others and then back to me. "Would you like me to talk to them?"

I appreciate the change in topic, but I heave a sigh. "I'll ask … soon. I just need to find the courage."

Osheen strolls toward us. His auburn hair has grown, curling around his ears, and he has a thick beard that makes him appear older than twenty-four. The dark circles beneath his eyes do nothing to help. He smiles at me, but it lacks the warmth I'm used to. I mentally swat away the small pang in my chest and smile back at him, hoping that mine makes up for the warmth that his is missing. I doubt it.

"Are you alright?" he asks.

I sigh heavily. "I am fine. Please, stop asking me."

He blinks, slightly taken aback.

"I'm sorry." For so long, only Osheen and Orla knew about my struggles, and now more struggles have been added to my plate. The constant barrage of questions about my wellbeing is a reminder of how much weaker I am than everyone else. It's a hint that my life will never go back to the comfort I was familiar with, even if I could return to Cluain Baile. I don't know my next steps. My guilt lingers for wanting to run away from it all when Carys is being tortured. How long can she endure?

"Durvla?" I refocus on Osheen and Chiyo's concerned faces. "Are you—" Chiyo stops abruptly, the question intentionally left unfinished.

"I need to walk," I tell them. I turn away as a tear escapes and start walking in a random direction, keeping far away from the edge of the cliff. A couple more days. I just need to keep it together for a couple more days, then I can regroup and figure out my next steps.

I walk with my hands on my head, breathing slowly like I've been taught, bringing my mind back to the present things rather than the past or the future.

Our surroundings are beautiful. The frightening height allows a wide view of the land. Across the sea, far in the distance, exists another land. I'm not entirely sure which.

In my periphery, someone approaches. My heart lifts as I expect it to be Kilkenny, but it's Alys. A mild disappointment settles over me, but I smile softly at her.

"Hello, sweetling," she says, holding out a bright red apple. Her grey eyes are weary, lacking the usual brilliance. Her salt-and-pepper hair is piled atop her head, a pink and orange patterned scarf wrapped around it with the tail ends peeking over her shoulder. It's such a cheerful accessory for such a dreary day and the overall somber mood of everyone in our little party.

"Thank you," I say, taking the apple. "I just need a moment to myself ... if you don't mind?"

She smiles and nods, then pats me on the shoulder and retreats.

I sit in the grass, intending to eat the apple, but my appetite runs away. I cross my legs and close my eyes, recalling everything I've learned about shielding. Pull up a mental wall, block everything out. It shouldn't be hard when I've spent most of my life blocking everything out. Slowly, steadily, I breathe, focusing on each inhalation and exhalation, letting the world fall away.

Then suddenly, it's as if I'm falling, my mind propelled into another setting. I open my eyes, and rather than cliffs and beautiful waters shining in the sunlight, there are two tree trunks in a dark forest. Kilkenny and Alys stand between them ... where I'd worked on dagger throwing not long ago.

"I don't want to tell her unless we're certain," Alys says to Kilkenny.

He runs his fingers through his hair, a tremor in his hand. "I can feel it. I'm certain."

Then I'm back where I started, sunlight, cliffs ... My head throbbing, and ... I'm in the grass with Alys crouching in front of me, panic written all over her face. Mistrust propels me to pull away as she reaches out to me, and she blinks, confused.

"Are you alright?" she signs.

I draw in a tremulous breath and shake my head. "Where is Kilkenny?" I ask.

Uncertainty appears on her face. "He's doing some meditation right over there." She points, but I don't follow her finger.

"Tell me the full extent of my powers," I say. "No lies, please. I need to know everything."

Alys's eyes widen, but rather than avoid the statement or deny anything, she nods. "Alright, sweetling. Let me get Tiernan and we'll talk."

Chapter 68
CARYS

I PROMISE THAT I won't scream. Over and over, I try and fail to swallow the agony, to fight the pain and avoid giving them the satisfaction of breaking me.

Over and over again, Eefa mars me and Briony mends me. Iywan stands by, ordering each cruel action. Sleep hardly comes, and I swear I'm beginning to hallucinate.

A day ago, I awoke in my cell with my wrists and ankles bound to each segment of a wooden X-shaped contraption that keeps me upright. My wrists chafe, and the muscles in my legs have turned to gelatin, the weight of my exhausted body putting pressure on my shoulders. My very soul aches, and every time Eefa carves into my flesh, I hope with all my heart that I'll bleed out.

Today, I've not been let out of the contraption, and I wait impatiently to relieve the overwhelming, painful pressure in my bladder that's starting to outdo the pain in my shoulders. The *drip, drip, drip* does nothing to help, and for the life of me, I cannot figure out where the bloody sound is coming from or how the cell isn't flooded by now.

I wait. And wait. And wait, but no one comes.

Time ticks by, lasting eons. I rehearse my resistance. I rehearse all the ways I can defy them. All the ways to say no to the same requests I've gotten over and over again. Forcing me to translate the ancient texts hasn't been as easy as they thought it would be. Neither has getting me to summon my powers. Every time I try, Aneirin's screams echo in my head, and the guilt consumes that fire inside of me.

Drowsiness is starting to settle over me when the heavy metal door slams. My head jerks up and I clench my muscles as my bladder threatens to release. Soon … soon I can relieve myself and get back to torture as usual. To think that I find comfort in being able to use the chamber pot, only to be cut into again … It's so ridiculous, it nearly makes me laugh.

This is my life. Unbelievable.

"Good morning," Eefa sings as she waltzes toward me with Briony in tow. No Iywan. I didn't see him yesterday either. What the fuck is going on above ground? What has become of the kingdom, of the castle? Of my mother?

I catch the glint of the dagger as Eefa pulls it from her belt. My heart pounds hard against my ribs. Eefa steps up to me with purpose in her stride. I'm taller than her, yet she intimidates me more than anyone over six feet ever could.

"We need that translation," she says smoothly. "No more faffing around. What does the passage about the prophecy say? And don't leave anything out."

I stare down at her. No point in wasting my breath on lies; I know what's coming.

Eefa lifts the blade, and my pulse jumps in fearful anticipation. Instead, she pulls a fistful of my hair that has come unraveled from its braid and saws through it, delight in her wild gaze. My breath stalls as ebony and gold strands fall to the ground. She grabs another fistful from the other side and does the same, then again for good measure. I stare at the hair on the floor, my heart aching in Ellynne's stead—she would've loathed this awful moment.

The next slice of Eefa's knife goes straight down the front of my tunic. The sound of the fabric tearing only heightens my unease, and all my muscles tense as I stand before Eefa and Briony with my torso bare. Gooseflesh breaks out along my skin from the kiss of the air in the dank cell.

"*Ee-fa*," Briony punctuates, but Eefa doesn't even turn.

Eefa drags her gaze slowly over my frame before she lifts the dagger and presses it against the base of my throat. I draw in a sharp breath and hold it, terrified to move. Eefa grins up at me. Her grin is so inhuman that I shudder, and the blade pierces my skin. I groan through my teeth.

"Oh, the many times I've coaxed that very sound from you, darling," she says with an airy laugh. A sensual smirk plays across her lips. "Only under … different circumstances."

Repulsion crawls in my blood, turning my stomach, but I force myself not to look away from the predatory beast before me.

"Funny how you long to be worshipped—always taking on another lover, calling to your servants at all hours of the night, and drinking yourself into a stupor at any given moment. You claim to have rescued an innocent woman from the brig, only to keep her away from her friends and family, from her home, just so she could make you a bloody dress. You don't give a damn about how your actions affect others … Yet you're offered ultimate power, and you choose *now* to show weakness? Heart of a warrior, my arse."

Heart of a warrior. Ellynne's words on her lips causes a different kind of flush to rise within me.

A trickle of warm blood runs from the small cut on my neck before cold steel replaces it, this time whispering across my abdomen. "You really think everyone is so obsessed with you, don't you? Me? Wynn? *Callum?*"

My heart clenches and I squeeze my eyes shut as if that can eradicate the image of Callum's throat being slit from my mind.

"How many others have you cajoled into your bed for *fun?*" Then her voice suddenly changes, becoming raspier—a familiar, soothing voice. Instead of Eefa before me, it's Ellynne's wavy red hair and curvaceous figure I'm staring at.

My heart stammers as I force air into my lungs.

"*Eefa,* enough." I've never heard Briony speak with such firmness.

"Master Iywan gave me the lead on this one, Priestess." She keeps her focus on me as she speaks in Ellynne's voice.

I fight to keep my tears at bay. I can't do this. I cannot look at Ellynne's face, but as I turn away, Eefa forces my face back to hers.

"If only Erleya knew what a whore their future queen is."

Future queen ... My chest constricts painfully. "My mother," I say breathlessly. "What's become of my mother?"

"Alive." Eefa shrugs, unbothered. "Sort of. Kept alive by magic." She wiggles her fingers, delight on her face. I turn an accusatory look Briony's way, but she shows no sign of guilt. Figures.

Ellynne's olive green eyes morph back to bright green, her red hair replaced by honey blond, her curves lessening until the face and body of Eefa stands before me again.

"What do you want with me if you have her blood or whatever?"

"Well ..." Eefa's grin spreads slowly across her face. "Her blood provides the medium we need, just in case. But it can only tear down the wards that protect the Veil; it does nothing to the Veil itself. Your living, breathing body provides the tether and the command we need to permeate the Veil and summon the enchantress."

"What makes you lot think that I will cooperate with this world domination nonsense once I have Enidwen's power. Aren't you afraid I'd just smite you?"

"No." She flips the dagger in her hand and catches it casually without even looking. "Not when you're leashed like the rabid dog that you are." She homes in on my wrist and my blood chills as I put together everything they've told me about this piece of metal.

"Leash?" I whisper.

"Yes …" She slowly drags the dagger over my skin, drawing imaginary patterns. The blade grazes me every now and then, and even though I tense every muscle in my body to avoid shuddering, my body acts on its own accord, and blood wells beneath the knife.

"Tell me this, Carys. Which of your lovers were you most attached to? Did you call out my name when Callum fucked you?"

I cringe so hard that my shoulders scream at me.

"What did you think of his last words? That he *loved* you? What a pathetic little puppy dog."

Poor Callum. Poor Ellynne. I should've done more to show them how much I cared about them. But I don't want Eefa to know how deeply guilt has its claws in me. I muster a smile down at her and say, "And you call *me* obsessed."

Ire flares on her face. She draws back her hand and slams the pommel of her dagger into my ribs. I scream as pain bursts across my abdomen and stars dance before me.

"Eefa!" Briony shouts. "Stand down!"

Oh, *now* she intercedes.

I blink, trying to clear my vision, but Eefa rams the dagger pommel into my ribs again. The air rushes out of me and I'm unable to even catch my breath before she strikes me for a third time. My lungs struggle to inflate, my chest burning from the effort.

Over the roar of my pulse in my ears, I'm able to make out Eefa's sneering words. "You can fight all you want to, Carys, but with that conduit on your wrist, not only are we immune to your flamewielding, but you're anchored to Master Iywan."

So, that's why they've been unbothered by the possibility of me summoning these powers. But … *anchored?*

The corner of Eefa's lips twitch upward. "I can see you thinking … Let me spell it out for you, darling. As long as you wear that, you're his puppet. He can *will* you to do whatever he pleases. He just hasn't done it yet because he hoped you would come around on your own. But by all means, keep fighting. Keep being the stubborn bitch you are. Soon you will be a vessel for ultimate power, and you won't be able to do a damn thing of your own volition. Ironic, hmm?"

My body goes numb.

"You might be a Flamewielder, darling, but Master Iywan will wield your very soul."

Briony swears and storms out of the cell, her footsteps echoing. Each jagged breath sends a shooting pain through my abdomen and my head grows woozy, nausea gnawing on the pit of my stomach.

All the defiance and rage rush out of my body, only to be replaced with icy cold trepidation. *Iywan will wield your very soul.*

The strong scent of urine fills the cell as warmth spreads down the front of my trousers.

I dare to face Eefa again, and the most satisfied grin stretches across her wicked face while the very last of my dignity is lost along with my bladder control.

Hot tears sear my cheeks as the door slams shut.

I beg Lugda for death to come.

Chapter 69
DURVLA

SEATED IN THE GRASS in front of me, Kilkenny's hands clench and unclench. Alys sits to my right, and Chiyo and Osheen are a small distance away, sparring. He's actually starting to get the hang of it now, deflecting her blows more often and even landing a few punches himself. I turn away from them and face Kilkenny, who has been avoiding any one-on-one time with me since I accidentally implied that I'd rather not have met him or anyone else from Mainland.

He slowly releases a breath, grimacing slightly. "We didn't tell you everything because we were afraid of how you would react," he motions.

"Well, that makes me feel so much better …" I pause, surprised at myself for even voicing such a disdainful comment. But I'm so tired of people hiding things from me.

"Do you remember back in Paramount when I provoked you during your first training? When I told you all those lies and irritated you enough that you'd be willing to hit me? You aimed to punch me, but what you really did was shove your powers at me."

In that moment, I'd been so confused about how he'd fallen over when I couldn't remember my fist making contact. *Did you feel that?* he'd asked. I hadn't, but I'd thought I was just so angry that it masked any pain.

"Think about all the times that your vision went a little dark, or when you saw shadows that no one else saw. When you got angry with Carys the day she called you a waste of time. She was too preoccupied to notice, but I saw everything …"

That day, Kilkenny had been guarding the door. My vision had indeed gone dark around the edges, but seeing dark isn't abnormal for me; it often precedes fainting. Kilkenny had glanced back at me and slowly shaken his head. After that, he'd insisted on training me under the cover of night.

I'm frowning deeply at him now. What is he trying to tell me?

"Each time, you'd felt something physical, inexplicable, right? A tingle in your hands? A buzz beneath your skin? A chill?"

I nod.

He breathes out again and glances over at Alys, who has been focused on me the whole time. Kilkenny turns back to me. "You're not just a Dreamwalker. You're also a Shadow Wielder."

My chest constricts. "*What?*" I ask aloud.

"The daywalking is also not typical of a Dreamwalker. Not necessarily. Nor is puppet mastery—when you somehow managed to slip into my mind. There's so much more about you that we don't yet know. That I've been trying to figure out. But we're finally certain that …"

He hesitates. I shift uncomfortably, impatiently, unable to stay still. "That what?"

"We believe you're a Basduun."

I jump to my feet, panic lancing through me. My head protests and I stumble back, my arms flailing. Kilkenny is up in less than a second, reaching out to me, but I maintain my balance and shove my hands toward him, keeping him at bay. "Don't," I sign firmly. I don't want him to touch me. I hardly want him to look at me.

My heart hammers, and I try to recall everything that had been explained to me about the Basduunai.

Dark magic. Corruption. *Basduunai were feared and usually executed.*

My stomach churns. Even when magic was accepted, Basduunai were not. I swallow hard as uncontrollable shivers rack my body, cold dread dancing up and down my spine.

Alys stands, but I glare at her as well. "You both kept this from me!" My signs are tense, my lips firmly sealed. I fear opening my mouth because I'm certain I'll vomit on both of them if I do.

"I didn't want to tell you because I feared this was how you'd react," Kilkenny says.

A humorless laugh bursts from me, and I stare at him with all the appreciation of a cantankerous house cat. "You just told me I'm a Dark Mage that may one day be hells-bent on destroying the realm."

"I didn't say that."

"You might as well have!"

"That's not how it works, sweetling," Alys interjects.

"Haruka said it herself." My throat constricts, my hands shaking as I sign. "That the good Basduunai refused to use their powers because they feared corruption. That they pushed down their powers so much, they often went mad."

Kilkenny swears and aggressively swipes his hair from his fore-head. "Gods, you have an annoyingly good memory, but you're looking at this too black and white. It's much more complex. Remember how Carys mentioned something about the solace of dusk? Think of that. There's something that can be comforting about your powers."

Comforting? I scoff.

"Being a Basduun does not automatically mean that you crave power. You're not like that. Your personality isn't going to change just because you're aware that you possess these gifts."

"Gifts …" Laughter swells in my throat even as tears threaten to spill. I turn my face away, but Kilkenny tilts his head back into my view, and it takes all my control not to shove him and walk away.

"I've waited to see if your shadow wielding would unintentionally manifest again like it did in Paramount, or when those headhunters attacked us a while back."

It's happened *more than once* and I didn't even notice? My heart pounds, cold sweat beading on my back.

"I was waiting for the right time to tell you. I was hoping that you would come to terms with the dreamwalking, but I never expected the daywalking. You were already so unnerved by the powers you knew existed. I didn't want to add to your plate."

"What's new?" I say. No one ever wants to *add to my plate*. "I don't want this. Any of this!" I sign so hard that when I jab my finger at my chest, it hurts.

I've spent my entire life keeping my emotions obscured. The last thing I ever wanted to do was draw attention to myself, so I shoved everything down into the deepest recesses of my being until it became second nature to hold back. Drawing attention to this ridiculous Undesirable label forced upon me was too dangerous. So, I played the hardworking botanist, the one who sacrificed the little free time she had to make deliveries to Ballybaeg. I played the dutiful dressmaker in Paramount, the passive young woman who allows secrets about *herself* to be kept from her. The *asset* to the rebellion.

But I've had enough.

Anger and frustration ambush me, thrashing against barriers of self-control that I've taken years to build. I want to scream until I can't anymore, to hit something, to cry. I need to get away, but Kilkenny starts toward me again as soon as I turn.

No! I swing my hand toward him, and the fury inside of me breaks through.

A black shadow arcs from my hand. Kilkenny flies backward, landing a short distance away. His hands take the brunt of the fall, and pain sparks on his face.

I clutch my left hand to my chest as it heaves with panicked breaths. "I'm sorry!"

It takes me a moment before I run toward him. I plop down in the grass beside him at the same moment as Alys does. Osheen and Chiyo come running. My heart matches their pace. As frustrated as I am, I didn't mean to hurt Kilkenny. What if it happens again? What if I hurt more people? If I lose control ... Dark clouds swirl around my knees.

Dark clouds ... of death. Of destruction. Shadow wielding is malevolent. What good could come from it? *Solace* is the antithesis of this power.

Haruka's words loop in my mind. *The name is literally translated from the old language as "death bringer."*

I'm a *death bringer*.

I jump up and step back quickly, my chest heaving more. Every muscle in my body is pulled too tightly.

"I'm fine," Kilkenny signs, getting to his feet again. He dusts off his hands and the back of his trousers. "I need you to calm down." He walks toward me, and I keep my hand clutched to my chest as I take a few more steps back. More shadows swirl around me even as I keep my hands clasped. I will my powers to stop, will that wall to go back up, but nothing happens. Osheen's fear is almost tangible.

Chiyo regards me as though I'm a wonder of the world. "Lugda's hells, Durvla."

Kilkenny glowers at her. "Not helping. Give her space."

I *am* a Dark Mage.

A Shadow Wielder.

I try to steady my breathing. Closing my eyes, I step backward. The tingling in my fingers intensifies, but I clench my fists even harder. I don't want this power. I don't want any of it. Wind whips around me, tugging free coils from my braids onto my face. I stand my ground, eyes squeezed shut.

Please, Sunlagh, let this be a nightmare!

Swallowing my emotions, I shove them down deep inside, along with the shadows and whatever other sources of darkness lay dormant. I plop down in the grass and slam the door on those feelings. A moment later, there's a gentle hand on my knee. "*It's me,*" Kilkenny says into my mind. "*I have your dampener.*"

I open my eyes, and indeed, the bracelet dangles from its strings which are pinched between his fingers. My shoulders drop with relief. I take it, but the moment the leather circles my wrist, pressure forces its way into my head. I grit my teeth and yank it from my wrist, dropping it into the grass. "I can't," I whisper.

He nods. "Funny how that works, hmm? Once your body accepts your powers, it becomes harder and harder to smother them." He smiles hesitantly before holding his hand out. I don't take it, and he drops it to his side. "You have every right to be cross with me."

"You're damn right I do."

"I should've told you sooner."

I want to hold on to the anger and resentment. It would make everything so much easier. This overeager heart of mine would be calm. I lift my hands to say something, my lips firmly pressed together, but I don't know what I even want to say.

"Can you forgive me?" Kilkenny asks, extending his hand to me again.

I don't respond right away, but after a while, I finally take his hand and let him pull me to my feet. "No more secrets."

"No more secrets," he agrees. He gives my hand a little squeeze and I revel in the warmth of the gesture.

I glance around at each of the others in our group. Alys, Osheen, Chiyo. "No more secrets," I echo.

They all agree, but I watch as Osheen's hand presses over the pocket of his trousers where he keeps Carys's wristlet. As that hand trembles and guilt replaces the concern on his face.

"Give me the wristlet," I say, holding out my hand.

Osheen's eyes widen. "What?"

I turn sharply to Kilkenny. "What is he feeling?"

Osheen's focus shifts back and forth between us. Kilkenny seems ready to protest, but he must see something on my face because he exhales and turns to Osheen. A moment later, he faces me and says, "Fear. Anxiety. Guilt."

My chest heaves with shallow breaths. "Osheen, give me Carys's wristlet."

Chiyo says something to me, but I don't bother to figure it out.

Osheen takes a step back, his hands shaking as he signs, "Durvla, let me explain. Please."

I swallow around the lump in my throat as I move toward him, Kilkenny by my side. "Give me the wristlet!"

Chiyo suddenly shoves her hand into his pocket and yanks out the golden band, tossing it to me. I miss the catch by an embarrassingly large margin, but Kilkenny catches it instead and drops it into my hand as though it's scalding.

At first, there's an uncomfortable buzzing sensation that makes me want to drop it as well. But then I'm forced to my knees, images flooding my mind as I hold on to the wristlet.

Lord Iywan is standing behind a woman with sepia skin and wavy grey hair. A charcoal-colored cloak is draped over narrow shoulders as she stares intently into a mirror radiating a gentle purple glow. Within the mirror, a scene of five figures standing among green hills and steep cliffs plays out like a vivid memory.

The woman and the strange mirror disappear from my mind, replaced with a vision of Osheen in the brig. Iywan hands him the gold wristlet. "Will you do it?" Iywan asks.

There are tears on Osheen's cheeks as he nods. "Just tell me that her brother will be safe."

"He's already dead. I sent Forayers to intercept those rebels immediately. Things turned ugly; there were no survivors."

Osheen's face goes white, and he hesitates, wiping tears shakily from his face before asking, "Then why should I do this?"

"Because if you don't, I will dispatch Forayers to your home to execute your mother and grandmother. You just need to find the others and get to the rebel base. Then your family's lives will be spared. That piece of jewelry will track your whereabouts; no need for you to report anything to us. This is for the greater good, boy. The rebellion must fall."

The image crumbles, and I draw in a breath that rattles my chest. I'm on my hands and knees, trembling as I try to make sense of everything. I stare up at Osheen, tears brimming, my heart aching.

He lied to me. He's been lying to all of us all this time.

Tears trickle down my cheeks as I push myself up onto one knee, leaving the wristlet in the grass. I swat at Kilkenny as he reaches out to me, unable to fathom being touched right now. I'm too exhausted to speak or even to sign. I cast my thoughts out to Kilkenny, hoping he'll hear. *"Can you see what I saw?"*

"No," his voice in my head responds. *"But tell me."*

"There was a woman with Iywan, looking at us through a mirror. Us ... here ... now ..."

Kilkenny winces. "Fuck ..." He scrubs his hand over his face. "It's a scrying tether. He's been spying on us for Iywan."

Something breaks like a dam within me, and the next thing I know, I'm on my feet, screaming at Osheen. "You've been working for Iywan all this time!"

"Yes, well no ... I ..."

All logic abandons me, and I charge at Osheen, shoving him as hard as I can. Once, twice. On the third time, I pound my fists against his broad chest. Again and again, until I'm swinging like a mad woman, shouting at him. "You betrayed us, you coward!"

I shut my eyes as I pummel him with my fists. He doesn't fight me or step away. He just stands there and takes it. When I dare to look at him again, thick bands of shadows are coiled around his body, from his ankles up to his mouth. His eyes bulge frantically, his arms bound beneath the dark bands. I step away from him, dropping my hands as pain creeps into the back of my skull and moves to the front of my head.

A high-pitched sound erupts in my ear, bringing along agonizing pressure that makes my gut roil as though I'm being tossed about on a boat. I press the heels of my hands against my ears as the world around me spins and I completely lose track of where I am in space.

This isn't magic.

It's an episode, and it hits me like a satchel of bricks—with more force than ever before.

I stagger back, but strong hands grasp my arms from behind. My stomach lurches again as everything tilts on its axis. My mouth waters unpleasantly, and as the world spins around me, vomit rushes up my throat. I double over, spewing the contents of my stomach.

I don't have a clue about what goes on around me, but a firm arm envelopes me, holding me upright even as my legs give in. *"I've got you,"* Kilkenny says into my aching head.

Then darkness yanks me into its cold embrace.

Chapter 70
DURVLA

OSHEEN BETRAYED US.

Taig isn't safe. He may not even be alive.

Osheen came along on this journey with us, knowing that the Forayers had already been sent in pursuit of my little brother. He'd agreed to spy on us in exchange for the safety of his family.

I hate him so much that it hurts.

The scent of marjoram and a hint of musk floods my nose, and a warm presence surrounds me even as the world jostles and shifts. My head feels like it's been split open with an axe, and nausea ripples through me in waves that leave me clutching my stomach. I groan and the presence around me tightens.

When I try to open my eyes, blinding agony erupts through my forehead. I clench my jaw and swallow the bile that rises into my throat. More tears leak.

The thought that I may never see Taig again rips at my heart, shattering my purpose.

I am weightless, and at the same time, more laden than ever before. What's the point of continuing this journey? I might as well just lie down in the road and wait for Forayers to pick my body apart like the buzzards they are.

My head falls back against a solid, warm something, and I let unconsciousness tug me under again.

The next time pain lances through my head and my ears, there's a soft surface beneath me. I slide my hand out, reaching to feel anything. Fabric bunches beneath my exploring fingers, and the fresh scent of linen fills my nose. Something warm settles over my hand, and I almost pull back before Kilkenny's voice fills my head. "*It's alright. You're safe.*"

Safe. Unlike Taig.

I turn my face into the pillow to stifle the sob that escapes. A moment later, the soft surface that I'm on sinks in and Kilkenny wraps his arm around me. The scent of fresh marjoram and peppermint envelopes me. I focus on the scent, on the weight of his arm around my waist, and his solid form pressed against mine. Soon I drift off again, leaving behind the hammering in my skull.

The next time I wake, bright, blinding light pours in and everything spins. I lean over the edge of the bed and retch, the bitterness triggering even more nausea. My stomach tries to wring itself dry, competing with the searing, repeated stabbing in my head and chest.

Alys is here, tending to me. I know the gentle touch of her hand and the warmth of her magic. It trickles into my head as she presses her hand to my clammy skin, and the overwhelming pounding dies down to a subtle throb. She leads me to the bathing chamber, taking on the brunt of my weight, since my sight is unreliable.

Then, I'm back in bed, my senses still on edge. I partially meet Alys's steady, grey gaze. "I wish I could take it all away, sweetling," she says.

My throat swells, and I turn my face away again. I can't handle her sympathy right now. It only reminds me of how futile this all is. I might as well have stayed in the brig under Paramount.

I don't realize that I've fallen asleep until I awaken to a warm hand on my face. Kilkenny's lips move, but I don't make out what he says as I seek sleep again.

It's that way for a while. I wake, see someone, maybe sip a bit of lukewarm water, then give in to oblivion again. Over and over until it no longer feels like sticking a hot poker through my ear and into my brain every time I open my eyes. I draw in a breath. Physically I'm feeling better, but my very spirit still aches.

I slowly roll onto my back, and it's like the world has been flipped upside down.

Taking a deep breath, I push up onto my elbows, then slowly turn to find Chiyo sprawled out on an armchair. Her head hangs back, her mouth agape, and her legs are splayed with her arms hanging down at her sides. Her bum is dangerously close to the edge of the seat. I fear she'll slide right off. The sight is so comical, I nearly smile.

The door opens and Kilkenny steps in. A smile slowly spreads across his face as he one-handedly signs, "It's good to see those brown eyes of yours again." He holds a metal pitcher in his other hand, which he sets down on a bureau before walking over to his sister. He taps her on the shoulder, and she jumps up, her hand moving toward a dagger sheathed in her leather vest.

"Whoa," Kilkenny says, immediately getting into a defensive stance.

The siblings are just alike—always ready to fight.

Where are Alys and … Osheen? I lay flat again, pressing my hands over my eyes. Saliva fills my mouth, and my throat feels like it's been scorched. The bed compresses. When I look, Kilkenny is sitting at the edge beside me. Chiyo is gone.

"Alys suggested that you have a nice, hot bath and get some broth into your stomach. I can call for the tub to be filled, if you like?"

A bath sounds wonderful. I push myself upright slowly and lean back against the headboard. Not wanting to move my head too much, I survey my surroundings with my eyes, but even that makes everything wavery. The bed takes up most of the small room. There's a massive bureau against the wall next to the door, and the curtains behind the bed are drawn, keeping the room dark save for the few candles on the side table and bureau. To my right, there's another door—the bathing chamber, I believe—and the walls are covered with gaudy framed paintings of landscapes.

"Where are we?"

"Dead Man's Inn," Kilkenny says.

I make a face. "That's an awful name."

He chuckles and motions, "It is. But the services are more than decent."

"How long has it been?"

"Two days," he says. "No word of any Forayers, raids, or anything like that, though."

Panic returns as I remember what happened on the cliffs. "Carys's wristlet."

"Chiyoko destroyed it and flung it off the cliff."

I relax and rub my hands down my face. Then I remember the shadows that shot from my hands and I pull them away abruptly. My hands are weapons … of darkness. A tremor runs through me as I stare down at my palms. The shaking intensifies until Kilkenny takes both of my hands into his. "Don't," I say quickly, my fear spiking. "I don't want to hurt you."

"You won't."

He turns my hands over, palms up, and gently runs his thumbs over the map of lines. If he were a palm reader, what would he see? Destruction? Violence? Corruption? Death?

"Kindness," he says to me. "Selflessness, bravery, far too much self-loathing …"

I stare at his lips, at the words he carefully speaks. "Did you just—?"

"Yes, sorry." He smiles wryly. "It's hard not to when you're thinking so loudly."

I breathe out the smallest of laughs.

"Now …" says Kilkenny. "I regret to say that you are in desperate need of a bath."

My jaw drops. "Are you saying that I stink?"

"You're … a tad ripe." A small smile touches his lips.

He's not wrong, sadly. "Alright, then I guess we should get that bath going."

Kilkenny lowers my hands, but as he stands, he leans over and kisses my forehead. The gesture is so achingly tender that I don't know what to say or do. He pours me a cup of water, and I sip it slowly as he leaves the room. Once the cup is empty, I very slowly sit up from the headboard, turning so that my legs hang off the bed. My head is light, so I remain still, getting used to the sensation of sitting up again.

It isn't long before Kilkenny returns with a wooden bucket of water in hand. "This is Seren," he says, stepping aside to reveal a woman behind him. He discretely fingerspells her name before bending to lift the second bucket of water at his feet. The fair-skinned woman has short strawberry blond hair and an endearingly crooked smile. She follows Kilkenny into the room.

"Hello, miss," she says.

"Hello. And thank you."

"No problem, miss." They head to the adjoining bathing chamber. Slowly, I cross one foot over my knee and painstakingly remove my socks. It takes so much effort, but if I keep my movements unhurried and smooth, it shouldn't exacerbate my headache or dizziness. Kilkenny returns just moments later. He raises a brow at me as if to ask how things are going.

"I'm fine," I tell him.

"Alright."

Seren smiles at me, and I thank her once more before she leaves the room.

Kilkenny starts to head toward the door as well, but he pauses, turning to face me. "Do you … want to wait for Alys to help you? She's out gathering herbs at the moment but—"

"No, I'll be alright."

But as soon as I stand, everything seems to slowly rotate upside down. I reach back and grip the headboard, steadying myself.

Kilkenny is at my side in no time, his arm around me. "Are you certain?" he asks.

I'm not. I slowly inhale and then exhale. "I'm certain."

"Alright, at least let me walk you there."

There's no point in declining his offer, so I agree, and we head toward the bathing chamber together. Each step is cumbersome, my limbs feeling oddly separate from my body. But with Kilkenny's arm around me and my focus directly ahead, we make it to the room. It's a simple bathing chamber with a levered commode and a rather large clawfoot tub.

For a moment, we both just stand there, staring at the water in the tub.

At last, Kilkenny turns to face me. "I can get Chiyoko if you're comfortable with that. Or we can still wait for Alys, and I can get more hot water once she returns."

"No, I don't want to bother Chiyo. Or waste any water," I object.

Kilkenny visibly battles his thoughts for a moment before saying, "I can help you in and leave you alone. I'll be a respectful gentleman. Knight's honor." He salutes.

A small bubble of laughter slips past my lips, but I immediately rein it in; it's wrong of me to even smile.

I untie the laces of my tunic with shaky hands. Removing it proves to be more exhausting than I expected, and by the time it's off, my arms are like gelatin. I hug the tunic to my chest, covering up. Kilkenny keeps his focus on my face, not daring to let his gaze wander.

"My balance is even worse than usual," I warn him. "I'm not sure how well ..." I can't even finish the sentence because it already sounds so pitiful and so foolish in my own head. I cannot even remove my own trousers or undergarments. Embarrassment burns in my chest.

"Are your episodes usually like this?" Kilkenny signs.

"This one is a little worse than usual."

"I'm sorry." His brows draw close. "Alright ... Hold on to my shoulders. I'll slide these off you and you'll just have to step out of them." He smiles gently before taking a knee.

My heart thuds. I don't hold on to his shoulders; I keep the tunic hugged against my chest and shut my eyes against the dizziness that threatens to knock me over.

I've got you," Kilkenny says into my achy head, and I sway, caught off guard.

"Don't do that mind-speak thing while I'm trying to balance."

He smiles up at me. "Stop trying to balance and hang on to me, then," he says calmly. He's considerate enough to turn away from me as he settles his hands on my hips.

I sigh and drop my tunic to hold on to his strong shoulders. As he slides my trousers and undergarments down in one go, his fingers brush against my skin and I shiver. The pleasant sensation that settles in my stomach takes me by surprise, and I stare at him wide-eyed.

Kilkenny glances up at me, a brow arched. "Everything alright?"

I clear my throat, tensing as I fling my arm across my breasts. "Yes."

He straightens and offers me his hand. "Right, let's get you into that water before it gets cold."

Stepping into the tub is another challenge. But once the warmth of the water surrounds me, I release a blissful sigh and slowly lay my head back against the lip of the tub. My fingers grip the edges on either side, as I'm not completely comfortable with my balance even while I'm sitting.

Kilkenny sinks down onto the floor beside the tub and regards me with such warmth that my chest quickly becomes crowded. A hot tear slips down my cheek. As soothing as this bath is, I hate how vulnerable I am right now.

Kilkenny's back straightens—he's immediately ready to jump into action. "What hurts?"

"What doesn't?"

His posture deflates. He reaches out to place a hand atop mine. "Give yourself some grace."

"I hate being helpless."

He smiles softly. "And yet you think *I'm* stubborn."

I start to laugh, but my breath catches and a sob breaks free instead. I pull my knees close to my chest and bury my face. For a while, there's just stillness. Then warm water flows over my back, and something smooth and cool slides across my skin. It takes me a moment to realize that Kilkenny is lathering my back with a ball of soap. Then my shoulders. He pours water over my hair and coaxes me out of my position so he can unbraid and wash it.

The whole time, I sit there, holding back tears as best as I can. It takes all my energy, sapping any lingering shyness over my nudity. I remain still as Kilkenny lathers the front of my body with the soapy rag. By the time the lavender soap conquers the sweat and my hair is tons lighter, my chest aches from continuously swallowing sobs.

Kilkenny helps me out of the tub and wraps a towel around me. I expect it to be thin and hardly absorbent like the ones back in Cluain Baile, but this one is plush and so soft it makes me want to curl up in bed with it and never get up again.

I hardly register anything as Kilkenny helps me get dressed. He applies soothing balms to bruises I didn't realize I had. As he wrestles my hair into a thick braid, Iywan's voice from my vision echoes in my mind: *Things turned ugly; there were no survivors.*

It feels as if someone has reached into my chest cavity and clenched an iron fist around my heart. I focus on breathing slowly through the heaviness, but the tension doesn't loosen—it only moves up my throat, to my head.

Kilkenny sits in front of me on the bed with his legs crossed, and I stare at him with heavy, bone-tired resignation. I want to thank him, but my voice doesn't obey me.

I can't do this anymore, I want to say. *Just leave me here.*

As I open my mouth to say it aloud, what comes out instead is, "I don't know how to go on anymore. Who do I fight for now if not for Taig?"

Kilkenny brushes a tear from my cheek and says, "*Yourself.* You fight for yourself."

I'm trembling as I try to contain the ugly cry that is threatening to shatter me. I wrap my arms around my legs, attempting to physically hold myself together.

"I know I told you not to break," he starts. "But this is the part where you give yourself permission to do so. For now. I'll be right here to help you pick up the pieces afterward. I promise. We'll do this together."

My breath falters. Each word dismantles my carefully constructed dam of emotional repression, brick by brick. A tidal wave of hurt, anger, and betrayal rises up inside of me—burning, aching, thrashing against my crumbling blockade. Instinctively, I start to shove it all back, but then, recalling Kilkenny's words, I give myself permission to break. I release a shaky breath, tears following, and the emotions rush through. The first sob loosens, and before I know it, I'm in Kilkenny's strong embrace, crushed against his chest. I weep for my father, my mother, my brother. For Ellynne, Callum. For Carys. Osheen.

I weep for the Durvla I thought I was.

And for the Durvla I need to find.

The sobs endure until I have no tears left, until my throat is raw, and my eyes are swollen. My chest feels as though it's been over-stretched from the inside out.

At the end of it all, Kilkenny is still there, his arms offering me comfort in my moment of weakness.

I take one steadying breath after another and wrap my arms around him, not just because I need his comfort.

But because I *want* it.

Chapter 71
CARYS

DRIP, DRIP, DRIP.

With each droplet of water hitting the stone floor that never floods, I grow a little more on edge. I'm no longer bound to the torture contraption nor to the metal chair. Instead, I'm sitting on the very corner of the bed, rocking back and forth to distract myself from the millions of scenarios running through my mind.

I've considered charging head-first into the metal bars of my cell, repeatedly if needed.

I've thought of standing on this very bed and diving into the stone floor as one would into deep waters.

Of taking Eefa's dagger when she returns and shoving it into her heart before dealing myself the same blow.

Or of summoning my flamewielding and incinerating myself—if only I can figure out how.

The images play through my mind again and again despite the many times I've willed them away.

Durvla doesn't dreamwalk to me anymore.

It's rare that anyone comes in here anymore, and the same routine repeats endlessly. Wake. Use the chamber pot. Sip very little water or broth that's somehow been placed in my cell whenever I doze for a moment. Pace my cell. Plot my death. Try to sleep.

Again, and again, and again—as incessant as that bloody dripping that reverberates inside my head.

For years, surrounded by servants and so-called friends, advisors and royal staff, I felt so very alone. Now, for the first time, I know what it truly is like to be alone. For the first time, I've been forced to come to terms with the dark thoughts that have always plagued me. The scream in my mind, vying for my attention, with no warm body in my bed nor strong drink to distract me. I even miss that strange internal voice I've gotten so used to hearing; it's abandoned me, as everyone else has.

A scraping sound fills the silence, and I jump so hard that all my muscles protest. Heavy footsteps approach, and I squint at the ball of light that grows closer.

Bloody Briony.

Her steps are hurried, her face frantic in the glow of the mage-light. "Your Highness, Iywan and Eefa are on their way."

My blood runs cold, and I gulp.

"Listen, I need you to trust me for a moment."

Laughter fills the cell before I realize the sound is coming from me. "Trust you? Why on earth would I trust any of you? I don't know your motives, healer-priestess woman, but you've played a part in my torture. There's no way in hells that I'll ever trust you."

She plants her fists on her hips and stares at me, her face flustered. "That is fair enough, but—"

The door scrapes open again and footsteps thunder down the walkway toward me. With each step, my heart beats a little faster. I hate the effect they have on me.

"Good morning, Miss Carys," says Iywan.

I frown at this new title as I try to still my restless hands in my lap.

"I am done playing games. If you do not give us the answers we seek, Queen Morwenna Meredyth, the Good, is going to make a miraculous recovery. In three days' time, the queen will make a public appearance and announce her engagement and forthcoming marriage to me."

The words swirl around in my messy head for a moment before settling in with sharp realization. "What?" My voice is coarse. I'm so parched.

Iywan turns to Eefa, and my heart jumps into my throat, my pulse leaping. I expect pain, harassment, and insults to be hurled at me. Instead, Eefa grows taller, her hair lightening to a golden sheen, her eyes darkening from green to brown. Suddenly, Eefa is gone, and my mother stands before me. It's so uncanny that my jaw drops and my heart flutters in my chest like a fish out of water. I blink and remind myself that this is not my mother. This is a monster.

She poses. "Just imagine me with a crown, darling."

"Stop," I whisper.

"Tell us what we need to know, Carys." Iywan steps toward me and I recoil.

Eefa laughs again. "Oh, poor kitten." Her sweet tone makes me want to carve out her sadistic heart.

I run my tongue along my chapped lips. "What do you gain with this ruse? What happened to the ultimate power plan that you have?" My voice sounds so unsteady that it makes me wince. Gods, I want to carve out my own heart.

"I gain time, Miss Carys. You will sit down here for as long as it takes to get the prophecy out of you, and up there, Eefa will pose as the queen until you're ready to take your place. There's always the autumnal equinox to open the Veil. We'll wait if we have to. If not the autumnal equinox, then winter solstice. How long would you like to postpone the inevitable?"

Shit … he *has* found a workaround.

"So, what will it be? Do you want to stay down here as Miss Carys until you give in, or will you join the Zenith as our empress?"

"I'd sooner end my own life than do anything for you or the Zenith," I say, my voice breaking.

The slap is hard enough to make my teeth rattle. I turn back to him, my lip stinging as I press my fingers to it. They come away bloody.

"Get her back onto the saltire," Iywan says.

I swallow hard, my stomach threatening to revolt, but I don't fight.

"Briony." Iywan sweeps out of the room while Briony approaches me. I swear regret surfaces on her face before she places her hand on my shoulder and sends me into darkness.

Chapter 72
DURVLA

I WAKE TO THE weight of Kilkenny's arm around my waist, my back pressed against his front. I don't even remember falling asleep, let alone still having him in my bed. As I shift, he presses his hand against the outside of my thigh, halting my movement. "*You don't want to do that,*" he says into my head. Even his mental voice is laden with sleep.

"*What?*"

"*You shifting against me is making it very difficult for things to remain ... chaste.*"

It takes me a moment to figure out what he's talking about, but then it hits me. "Oh!" I shift once more, but this time it's to put some distance between our bodies. The ache in my head has died down to a dull throb. My stomach is a little more settled, and while my vision is still a little blurry, the room isn't spinning. My face is still puffy, and exhaustion has a hold on me, but I am far better than before.

I sit up slowly, Kilkenny following suit. "What time do you think it is?" I ask.

"Well, no one has come in to get us, so I'd say it can't be that late." He smiles and runs his fingers through his hair, mussing it up.

I smile at him. "How do you manage to make messy hair look so good?"

His fingers pause in his hair, and he raises his brows at me.

Heat immediately floods my face. I clear my throat. "Thank you for … earlier," I say. I can imagine it couldn't have been easy, given that he can literally feel what others feel.

"Any time," he says. His arm reaches around my back as he pulls me closer against his side. It completely takes me by surprise, but I rest my head against his shoulder and breathe him in. The scent of his marjoram soap still clings to his skin and mingles with my lavender soap. I commit the combined scents to my memory, knowing that soon we'll all be sweaty again as we commence our journey.

My heart drops. I sit upright so I can glimpse his face again, and his hand falls away. "Kilkenny?"

"Yes?" He loosens the tie from his hair, only to smooth the strands back and retie it.

"Do you really think that I won't become corrupt like other Basduunai?"

"I have no doubt," he signs with sincerity.

"What makes you so certain?"

"I've been in your head, remember?" A smile slowly spreads across his face. It's sunshine and flowers and meadows. His eyes twinkle like moonlight reflecting off the dark ocean, and my pulse leaps eagerly. He's so humble, so gallant, so selfless. He's everything a knight should be, but he's so much more.

I'm almost afraid to breathe too deeply as that hypnotic pull reemerges between us. His lips draw closer to mine, and I find myself unsure what to do with my hands. Or my head, for that matter.

"*You think too loudly*," his voice says into my mind, and I can't help but laugh.

His lips claim mine, swallowing my laughter as my stomach lurches pleasantly and my breath hitches. His arm wraps around my back, one hand cradling my head, and I melt into his embrace as delight dances along my spine. My arms snake around him, pulling him even closer, until my back is against the soft sheets beneath us and Kilkenny's weight presses into me.

I'm not even sure when or how exactly we got here, but our tongues meet, and my thoughts try to intercede. I shove logic aside, dampening the noise of my mind and making room for instinct to take over. Desire ignites, consuming me, quelling any residual angst. I wrap my legs around his waist, and with our hips flush against each other, everything south of my naval clenches. The world falls away.

A multitude of sensations war within me, lust rising above reason and surfacing as victor. Kilkenny pulls away, leaving me bereft and flustered. His chest heaves as he gently disentangles my legs from around his waist. "Gods, Durvla," he says. Two simple words, but there's so much longing in his eyes that I ache for more.

But then he moves to sit beside me, trying to gather his composure, and I find myself staring at him, marveling that his lips and body were just on mine.

So *that's* what it's like.

Attraction. Yearning. Something greater that I don't want to confront right now.

"Are you alright?" he asks, and I can't help but grin.

"Yes, of course. Are *you*?" He's the one that stopped.

He smiles unevenly and takes my hand in his. His lips brush against my fingers and my heart flutters. He swears and shakes his head, the smile still on his face. "What are you doing to me, woman?"

He scrubs his free hand down his face, then draws in a breath to say something, but suddenly his focus shifts toward the door.

He reaches for his waist, but he's not armed with any weapons. "Who is it?" he calls out. Then he sighs and signs Chiyo's name for me. He gets out of bed, and I settle back against the headboard, my mind still reeling from the taste of his lips.

Kilkenny opens the door to Chiyo tapping her foot, her arms crossed, her face pinched. Her attention drifts over his shoulder, pausing when she spots me. Her focus shifts from him to me, then to him again. She grins and pumps her fist in the air. "Finally!"

Kilkenny steers her back out the door and closes it before turning to face me.

The realization hits. "Does she think that we … ?" I can't even finish the sentence without my face heating.

Kilkenny laughs and shrugs his broad shoulders.

I ease myself off the bed, and he saunters toward me with a smile that has me almost melting into a puddle. "I'm not sure if she thinks *that*. But if that happens, I'd prefer that it's not in some place called Dead Man's Inn."

My mouth goes dry, the flush in my cheeks unrelated to shyness or embarrassment. My breathless laughter is delayed and Kilkenny grins as he closes the gap between us again.

He pulls me close once more and kisses me until I'm weak in the knees. He releases a breath, then steps back and clasps his hands together, the picture of self-control. "Let's get dressed and get out of here before we prove Chiyo right."

I grin despite the heat flooding my cheeks. With the space between Kilkenny and I, reality hits me in the face. I lock my knees to keep from staggering back. We'll be getting on the road again soon, and I don't even know what's become of Osheen. I clench my fists. As much as part of me wants to walk away and never look back, I ask, "Where's Osheen?"

The desire completely disappears, and Kilkenny's face hardens with anger. "He's here, somewhere."

"Here?" I point to the floor.

"Yes. Alys and Chiyo didn't want to just leave him exposed out there—I was more than happy to do so. He's gotten a job helping the innkeeper. It'll give him a roof over his head and food. A new start for him—far more than he deserves. In the end, though, it's up to you whether he continues traveling with us or not."

I freeze. "It's up to *me*?"

He nods.

I clasp my hands together and exhale slowly, expelling the tension that worms its way back into my muscles. Osheen has been my best friend, the most trusted person in my life after my parents died. He looked after Taig, and then he knowingly came along on this journey with us after Iywan informed him that Taig was …

Pain sears my heart again, and I step back, plopping onto the bed as I try to catch my breath. Kilkenny sits beside me, turning to face me slightly. He seems conflicted, like he's unsure of what to say.

Osheen willingly carried a magical relic that enabled Iywan and whoever that woman was to track us. He's the reason the Forayers found us in Dubh Carrig, the reason we could still be very much in danger even though the wristlet was destroyed.

Turning my tearful face to Kilkenny, I take a deep breath. "I can't trust him anymore," I motion.

Kilkenny nods, his shoulders relaxing slightly. "Alright," he says. "Then we go on without him."

Chapter 73
DURVLA

MY GAZE MEETS OSHEEN'S red-rimmed eyes as I mount Ghendor in front of the Dead Man's Inn. Osheen stands in the doorway of the building, his splotchy face drawn, his knuckles turning white on the doorjamb. My body goes cold, and my throat tightens painfully as he takes a step forward. Quickly, I turn away from him—away from the last surviving person from my old life.

"Let's go," I whisper to Tiernan, who gently nudges the black stallion's sides and sends the horse into a canter. I wipe my sweaty palms against my trousers, ignoring the tremor in my hands. The more distance we put between the inn and us, the easier it becomes to breathe, but the more my chest aches. It's as though I've sawed off one of my own appendages.

Chiyo now rides Ffion on her own, her posture stiff and her face puffy. Despite Osheen's betrayal, we've both lost a friend. Dawn is still hours away, and I'm grateful for the darkness. My head is still adjusting after the massive episode I had.

It set us back by nearly three days. I've cost us precious time—

Kilkenny gives my thigh a little squeeze as if to tell me to stop thinking so loud.

A couple of days go by with minimum stops and a few quick moments of rest beneath the stars. No dreams fill my nights, as though my body is too tired to dreamwalk, and while a part of me is grateful for the break, I long to know how Carys is doing.

We've not heard any word of Paramount. The kingdom doesn't seem to be in any more unrest than usual, so we continue as we have been. The terrain rises and falls as we ride across the land. We're riding across an extensive bridge as the sun begins to rise. I squint, briefly catching a quick glimpse of the mysteriously dark loch that reminds me of Kilkenny's eyes. The thought alone makes me blush, and I swear laughter reverberates from him through my back.

We make it to the other side of the bridge. Somewhere around noon, we find a stopping point. Similar to Dubh Carrig, rolling hills and mountains surround us, but there aren't any houses or stables. Or people, for that matter. Not as far as we can see.

Kilkenny helps me off Ghendor and holds on to me for a little longer than necessary. I don't complain, of course.

He peers down at me thoughtfully. "You should try to eat something."

I smile half-heartedly. "Now don't start being all overprotective, Kilkenny."

He smiles back and presses a kiss to my forehead. I want to wrap my arms around him and soak up his warmth. It would be so much easier to just pretend that Osheen didn't betray us all and that Taig is safe and sound. I suck in a shaky breath and Kilkenny gently pulls away, his face searching mine for signs of pain or injury.

I don't bother to put on a brave face, but I assure him that I'm alright.

While we munch on apples and stale bread, no one speaks. None of us has the energy to talk about much. It isn't until we're getting ready to leave again that Alys signs, "How are you feeling?"

I shrug one shoulder. Numb at times, I want to say. Distraught at other times, and overall exhausted. Instead, I say, "My head still throbs a little, but I don't want you to use any more of your healing. You've been spending a lot of energy on me, and you need it for the rest of this journey."

She doesn't argue, knowing that it's true. Each time she's tended to me, she's drained a bit of her own energy. Still, just as Kilkenny did, she wordlessly assesses me for any signs of pain.

"Alys, I'm alright."

She nods and slides her colorful headscarf back from her forehead. "When we get to the Verge, you need a nice, long rest."

"We all do."

She smiles. "Absolutely. We should be there before night falls tomorrow."

To my surprise, it's not relief that fills me, but dread. I fight to forget Lord Iywan's words— *there were no survivors*—and focus on making it to the Verge. With other Mages there, it should be safe for me to exist as a Basduun. But will I need protection, or will others need to be protected from me? A slight shudder hits me as I tuck the terrifying thought away.

Still, I smile back at Alys before she saunters off to prepare Mirren. Chiyo stands in front of Ffion, gently caressing the horse's snout. She looks my way as I'm about to walk past. There's so much I want to say to her. I want to apologize for the friendship that she also lost. I want to ask her how she's holding up, but my mind fixates on the silver at the roots of her hair, even more pronounced now with the blue dye almost completely faded.

"I like your hair," I sign to her. "The silver looks good."

She makes a face. "I hate it. Mam was completely grey by the time she was twenty-two. So, I guess that gives me two more years until I look like an old woman myself. Or like old man Tiernan." She smirks.

I chuckle. "You don't look old. Neither does your brother, or even your mam."

Kilkenny walks by, waving his arm my way before hurriedly motioning, "Are you two finished gossiping? Let's go."

I exhale heavily. "Killjoy." The light that appears on his face is unmistakable before a smile crawls across his lips. The time I first accidentally called him *Killjoy* could be a lifetime ago. It's unbelievable that it has been almost two months since I was taken from my home.

A multitude of emotions plays over his face. Before I can mull over it for too long, Kilkenny takes my hand and gives it a squeeze.

I'm grateful for the gesture as it draws my mind away from our problems. "To the Verge?" I say.

He nods. "To the Verge."

Navy blue clouds glide past the nearly full moon and I'm mesmerized by the gentle yellow-orange glow that lightens the otherwise dark sky. I lean back against the tree, staring up at the scattering of stars while anxiety swirls through my mind. Alys and Chiyo are asleep, but I'm unable to find much rest, so I volunteer to keep Kilkenny company while he takes the first watch.

He sighs as he plops down beside me with a magically lit lantern and holds out an apple. I shake my head. Not only am I sick and tired of apples, but I doubt my stomach can handle food. He sets the lantern down in front of us and signs single-handedly, "You have to eat something."

I take the apple from him and turn it over in my hands.

"What's on your mind?"

I offer him a half smile. "That's an ironic question coming from a Whisperer."

He grins, his high cheekbones accentuated in the moonlight, even beneath his stubble. He bites into his apple, glances up at the moon for a moment, and then faces me again. The question is written clearly on his face—he still wants to know what I'm thinking.

I heave a sigh. "I can't help but feel like something ominous is coming."

He pauses mid-bite and lowers the apple. "Anything specific?"

Staring down at my apple, I shake my head slowly. "Just ... ominous."

When I look back at him, his lips are pressed together before he takes another bite out of his apple. "Is there anything that you *see* when you have these ominous feelings?"

"No." I sign more firmly than I mean to.

A silent apology ghosts over Kilkenny's face. "I don't mean to pressure you," he motions. "Alys says that Dreamwalkers sometimes also have the gift of sight. Like an oracle."

I wrinkle my nose and shake my head. "No gift of sight here. It's just ... it feels wrong to make my way to safety when ..." Taig didn't have a chance. I cannot finish the sentence aloud, and grief grips me again.

Kilkenny nods. "I know."

I've already let myself break once, and it was much needed. Now I need to hold it together until we get to the Verge.

Kilkenny tosses his apple core a small distance away, and I idly follow its trail as it lands in the grass.

My jaw drops. "How on earth did you finish that apple already?"

A small burst of laughter escapes him. "I was hungry." He smiles and shrugs.

"You *just* started eating it."

He presses a fist over his mouth to stifle his laughter, glancing at the other two who are still fast asleep. Then he scoots closer to me, the side of his hip against mine. He puts an arm around me, and I let my head rest on his shoulder as he holds me close. His warmth erases the chill in my body.

"I'm worried about Carys," I say aloud.

His reluctance is evident as he slowly releases me and gives us just a bit of space for communication. "So am I," he signs.

"I wish we could rescue her the way she rescued me and Alys. I hate that there's nothing we can do about the horrors she's enduring."

"I know." His shoulders slump, his jaw tightening.

My teeth sink into my lower lip. "Do you believe in prophecies? And don't say 'I know.'"

A small smile curves his lips. "I do." He tucks a bit of stray hair behind his ear.

"Do you believe that Carys is an actual descendant of Agryna?" I sign. "Is that even possible after the Purge?"

He wrinkles his nose. "Perhaps."

I squint at him as the teeniest of smiles plays on his lips. "How can you possibly be amused at a time like this? There is so much to figure out. So much I don't understand. Carys is being tortured, and the whole kingdom may be in peril."

There's such a softness in his gaze that I want to weep again just as I had back at the Dead Man's Inn. "You cannot bear the weight of the entire kingdom on your shoulders. You place everyone's needs and woes above your own until there's no room for your own thoughts in there." He gently taps my forehead, and I sigh.

"It's easier to focus on other people's woes rather than my own." The words slip past my lips without permission, and I cringe.

He tilts his head at me and puts his hand on my knee. "Then maybe you ought to share some of your own woes with someone. Perhaps a certain killjoy who happens to be rather fond of you?"

My chest flutters pleasantly. "You're rather fond of me, hmm?"

"Did I say that?" He looks so bewildered.

Have I misunderstood? I frown at him, but then a slow, teasing smile melts onto his face.

I smile back. "Well … you're *alright*, I guess."

He grins, nudging my shoulder gently with his, but it's futile to have any sort of attachment to this man. Never in my life have I been physically attracted to anyone, let alone contemplated what it would be like to have a relationship that goes beyond friendship. Now is not the time for such thoughts.

Kilkenny fixes me with a troubled expression. "Durvla?"

"I … it's trivial."

"Your woes aren't trivial."

Gnawing on my lower lip, I stare up at the moon again as more clouds float by, eclipsing the celestial body repeatedly. It's oddly reflective of my life—my joy continuously obscured by tragedy, misfortune, or ill-health. I have smiled in the face of adversity daily, tending to the plants back home in Cluain Baile, cataloguing, volunteering to make solo deliveries to Ballybaeg even though it sapped the little time I had left to wind down.

Ma had been my greatest role model. When she was alive, she took great care of us. She taught me to read, shared her love of knitting and embroidery. My father was brave and loving, and even though I was a rubbish hunter, he still took me on excursions to bond with me. Often, Osheen came along—his own father deceased and mine stepping in.

My throat swells as a gentle breeze chills my damp face. There's so much compassion in Kilkenny's eyes that I have to turn away to gather my composure. I brush my hand lightly over wind-dried tears crusting on my cheek and find the nerve to face him again.

"I had two loving parents and a wonderful childhood. There should be no reason for me to have anything to complain about. You've been in the Royal Brigade, lost your lover and—" I choose not to finish the sentence, to mention his lost unborn child, but pain already shadows his features.

"You lost your parents," he signs. "And you were left with the responsibility of looking after a child this kingdom has made it entirely too difficult to care for."

I wave a dismissive hand. "Many people are in that position."

"Don't do that," he says.

"What?"

"Don't diminish your own pain based on the pain of others."

It's hard not to. My lips tug down.

"You've been the sole caregiver to your brother. And yes, other people have been through that. You've done so while also handling your own ailment and while navigating losing your hearing." He pauses and hesitates for a moment. After a little while, he asks, "Does your ailment or your deafness scare you?"

"Yes and no to both." I worry at my lower lip for a moment. "We live in a world not built for people like me or like Taig. That's what scares me more."

"Then let's change it."

"Change what?" I gesture.

"The world."

I laugh light-heartedly, but he doesn't crack a smile. "Us? Maybe *you*, but I'm nobody. Besides, no two people can just change the world."

"You're somebody to me. And change starts with one small drop of water with the potential to become a storm."

I scoff at him. "What grandiose ideals."

"What can I say? I'm a dreamer."

"Hmm … Actually, *I'm* the dreamer, remember?" I crack a small smile, and he laughs.

He leans in as if to kiss me, but he stops and pulls back a bit, his full face in view again. I can't help but release a small, disappointed breath having had his lips so close to mine for a second.

"You are worth far more than you believe."

My chest clenches. "I want to believe it."

"Then believe *me*." He smiles and it's devastatingly charming.

"Alright," I say.

"Alright?" He leans in close again.

"Alright."

When our lips meet, it's soft, tender, and filled with unspoken promises. His arms wrap around my waist, and I shift, straddling him as my arms loop over his shoulders. When our lips part, he presses his forehead against mine.

"For what it's worth, I'm glad to have met you, Durvla Garrick."

Chapter 74
DURVLA

A FLOCK OF SHEEP roams through the winding green valley as we walk in the shadow of the towering mountains. A monstrous slope of steep, black stone looms ahead of us like a fortified wall, the peak beyond what I can see. It would take scaling the face of the mountain to make it through without magical means. A lush forest is somewhere to our right and the ocean is to our left.

"Here we are," Alys signs.

I stop walking and grip Ghendor's reins perhaps a bit too tightly. The horse paws the ground restlessly and Kilkenny takes the reins from me. Doom hangs above my head like a guillotine set to fall, and my skin crawls. "Durvla, what is it?" Kilkenny signs.

"I don't know."

Chiyo releases Ffion's reins and turns to fully face me. "If you sense something ..." she begins.

Everyone's attention shifts to me, and I resist the urge to cower. "I'm just anxious," I admit.

We continue onward, following Alys since she knows the exact point of the entrance to the Verge. I cannot fathom what lies beyond the wards, because as far as I can see, there are just mountains, pastures, and woodland. Alys gave us a refresher on the runes and the incantations earlier, before we got in the vicinity of the wards. There's a winding path up the mountain that makes my stomach dip with anxiety.

Kilkenny slips his free hand into mine and gives it a small squeeze.

The closer we get to the base of the mountain, the more nervous I become. Each step makes my pulse quicken and my stomach churns with dread. We let go of our horses' reins as we make it to the rocky face of the steep mountain. We're so close we can touch it, and I can already *feel* the energy sizzling before us. I recoil, daunted.

Kilkenny shifts his focus to me. "I feel it, too."

"Let's get started," Alys says.

We all stare up at the rocky mountain as Alys takes a stance, her legs shoulder-width apart. She flexes her fingers a few times as if warming them up, then takes a deep breath. An immense sense of foreboding burrows into my head, and Alys collapses to her knees.

I barely have time to register anything before Kilkenny unsheathes his swords and whirls around. Chiyo grabs a few daggers, getting into a fighting stance as six figures in black cloaks materialize before us. Alys is on her hands and knees. An arrow has gone straight through her back, the tip protruding from the right side of her chest. She places a shaky hand against the mountain's side.

"Alys!" I start to move toward her, but Kilkenny shoves me behind him as his voice fills my mind. "*She can heal herself. You can't.*" He charges toward a figure with spiky white hair and an oddly curved blade in hand. I force shallow breaths into my lungs as the fight unfolds. The man doesn't remain in one place. He disappears and reappears every time Kilkenny's sword gets close to striking him. Gods, that's … shocking. Terrifying.

I stand frozen, watching the clash of swords, the whiz of arrows and daggers. I count six attackers, nearly doubling our small party, and with Alys and myself unskilled in weaponry, that impending sense of doom surges in my chest again. As if things aren't dire enough, three others in bright white cloaks appear. I stare for a moment at the startling contrast.

The horses are uneasy, pawing at the ground and tossing their heads. Ffion rears back on her hind legs before running away, but somehow Ghendor and Mirren stand their ground.

"They're Dispellers," Kilkenny says into my mind, his mental voice breathless. *"If they get close, use your dagger. Don't let them touch you—they can vanish you to wherever they desire."*

One of Chiyo's daggers finds its place in the forehead of one of the white-clad figures and they drop. Another white-cloaked figure faces the same end just as they turn on Chiyo. Seven attackers remain.

The remaining assailant in white takes out one in black. Six.

Then five as Kilkenny's sword goes straight through another in black.

My back to the mountain, I sidestep toward Alys. She snaps off the arrowhead protruding from beneath her clavicle. "I need you to pull the shaft out," she says.

What? "Alys, I can't," I say, shaking my head firmly.

"Yes, you can. Make it quick, sweetling."

I scrub my sweaty palms on my trousers and grasp the shaft, closing my eyes before wrenching it free from Alys's back. I toss the arrow aside, swallowing the bitterness in my mouth. It takes a moment for Alys to gather her composure, but then she struggles to her feet.

"Are you alright?" I ask.

Her smile is almost convincing. "It'll take more than an arrow to stop me."

A black-cloaked assailant comes at us, a spear in hand. Alys shoves a ball of light at him, sending him staggering backward right into the path of Chiyo's dagger. But the blade never hits as he disappears and reappears in front of Chiyo. My heart skips a beat, but she's quick and dodges each jab of his spear. She pulls another dagger free from her belt and slams it into the man's forearm. His spear rolls a short distance away down a small swell of land behind Chiyo as she ducks and dances out of the man's reach.

He yanks the blade from his arm, blood spraying, and slashes at her. She dodges and sinks her fist into his stomach. When he doubles over, she grabs his hair and shoves his head down, driving her knee into his face. Blood spurts from his nose, and he grabs at it, falling to the ground. Chiyo retrieves the spear, twirling it in her hands. Her foot lands on his chest as she lifts the weapon. I turn away to avoid what happens next.

Four remain. Kilkenny takes it down to three—two in black and one in white.

Wrestling to find some semblance of focus, I turn to Alys. "We can't breach the wards with them here, right?" I sign quickly. We wouldn't want them to follow us in somehow.

Sweat beads on her forehead, making her mahogany skin shine. "Even if they follow us, they wouldn't make it past the stronghold. But we need an uninterrupted moment. Can you summon your powers?"

My stomach dips. "I can't." I've only done so in times of anger—and it wasn't even intentional.

I chance a peek over my shoulder to where Kilkenny is locked in combat with the white-haired figure. The man disappears from in front of Kilkenny, only to appear behind him. As Kilkenny spins, ready to deal a blow, the lone survivor in white turns her attention his way. She's lithe, with dark hair spilling out from her white hood. Even though she's still some distance from him, her focus on him is singular—determined. Oh gods …

My lungs seize, but I shake the fear long enough to scream. *"Tiernan!* Look out!"

He whirls, panning to me before he turns toward the woman who lets two daggers loose. Tiernan deflects one of the daggers with his sword, but the other sinks deep into his stomach. He cries out, his face contorting with shock and agony as he grasps the hilt and drops to his knees.

Icy panic ripples through me.

The man behind Tiernan falls to the ground with an arrow lodged in his throat. I don't register that my legs are moving until I'm beside Tiernan. I fall onto my knees and place a hand on his shoulder. His chest heaves with effortful breaths, his hand shaking violently as he grapples for a dagger from his vest.

The woman appears before us, drawing a sword from beneath her robes. I throw out my hand to block her.

A wall of translucent black shadows shoots up and arches over Tiernan and me like a dome, plunging us into semi-darkness. The woman's sword bounces off the shield as though clashing against solid stone.

Tiernan's jaw drops as he stares up at the dome. His voice touches my mind: *"Solace of dusk* …" He's still clutching the hilt of the dagger protruding from his stomach. My heart somersaults as my mind grapples for the relevance of his words. He's bleeding profusely from a gash across his upper thigh, and I'm not sure what's worse—the amount of blood leaking from his leg or the dagger currently keeping more blood at bay. "Can you hold that shield?" he says, nodding toward the shadow dome.

"Not for long." My arms are already trembling, and I don't even know how I summoned it.

Beyond the force field, the white-clad woman drops listlessly to the ground, two daggers in her back. Chiyo has one more figure in a headlock, and I stare through the wavering wall of shadows as she twists the man's head with one swift motion. His body crumples to the ground as my arms turn to gelatin, falling to my side. The wall of shadows dissipates.

Tiernan peers up at me, his knuckles white on the hilt of the dagger that he still grips, his face even whiter. But he offers me a pained smile. "You amaze me."

A despairing laugh escapes me, tears slipping down my cheeks. My joints are too loose, my muscles worn—but Tiernan is worse. "Just don't die on me, alright?"

He salutes, his smile more brilliant than it should be at a time like this. I turn away from him and discover Alys beginning to draw invisible symbols on the face of the mountain with renewed focus.

When I turn back to Tiernan, he has the crimson coated dagger from his abdomen in his hand. He chucks it aside into the grass, and my heart stops as blood pools through his fingers pressed against the opened wound.

"Have you lost your mind? You're going to bleed out!"

He shakily shrugs a shoulder. "I'm a Mimic, remember? Thank Ehlach for Alys's healing powers." His hand glows with a gentle blue healing light as he presses it to his abdomen then his thigh.

Mimic, Mind Whisperer, Empath … And yet, I still fear for his life. There are bodies around us now. The dark-haired woman whose dagger bested Tiernan is uncomfortably close, her unseeing eyes staring at us.

Tiernan's breathing is still ragged as he struggles to his feet. "We need to get to the mountain."

I nod, shifting to stand as well, though it proves to be harder than I imagined. My legs nearly give out, my body so worn I could lie in the grass and fall right asleep. With one arm around Tiernan's back, and his draped over my shoulders, we hurry as best we can toward the mountain ... as it begins to fade.

I blink forcefully as my vision wavers and pray that another episode isn't on the horizon. There's no time for my body to rebel right now, for the gods' sake. Tiernan slips his hand into mine, his fingers slick with blood. I push back the nausea that threatens to evacuate my stomach. "*Alys says hold hands,*" he tells me. "*Sorry about the blood.*"

I nod, trying not to think about it.

"*Step forward,*" Tiernan mind-speaks. My brows knit in confusion. There's still a mountain before us, though it ripples as if it's made of water. The hair stands on the back of my neck and the world seems to tilt. I am weightless for a moment. My skin prickles almost painfully, my vision wavering.

When my sight clears, a defensive wall of wooden planks stretches in front of us, and archers aim their weapons scaffolds just beyond the barrier. We all drop to a knee simultaneously. My head is bent while my heart thunders, and my whole body begins to shake—the aftereffects of the attack. I dare to glance at Tiernan beside me. Pain ghosts across his too-pale face with every strained breath.

I'm afraid he'll soon pass out or worse, but to my right Alys collapses in the dirt.

Chapter 75
DURVLA

ALYS IS WHISKED AWAY to the infirmary—a small building just beyond the barrier—and we're told that our horses will be brought through the wards for us. Chiyo, Tiernan, and I are ushered to a mysteriously well-lit room with bare wooden wall panels. We sit on one of the pristine, wine-colored couches facing a lean woman with warm brown skin, leather armor, and a sword on her hip.

She regards us with intimidating eyes, a greenish shade of hazel. Her shiny black hair is in thick braids that fall to her waist. She hurls questions at us about our relationship with Alys—Elviera—our reasons for seeking sanctuary, and even our powers. We leave out the Basduun detail, of course. When she's pleased with our responses, she stands and meanders from the room.

I glance at Tiernan who immediately hides a grimace of pain with an artificial smile. As I start to say something about him needing to see a healer, the couch sinks in a little. Chiyo has shifted and is staring in the direction where the young woman just left. When she turns her bruised face back to me, her thin brows are drawn close together. She doesn't say anything, but the woman reenters the room before I can ask anything.

This time she's with a tall man who is practically just an older version of her; they have the same warm brown skin and hazel green eyes. He turns to me and halts, taken aback by something. As the woman tilts her head at him, he blinks as though a spell has been broken and speaks up at last. I focus on his signed words, some of it a tad odd for my mind to translate, but I get the gist of it. "My sincerest apologies for the interrogation. We just want to keep the Verge safe for all our inhabitants. My name is Dayfyd O'Hara."

Dayfyd ... the name rings a bell. I recall the conversation I had with Alys back at that marketplace we'd walked through. *His eyes are a gorgeous hazel green,* she'd said. I blink at him. "You're Alys's husband."

Now he's truly taken aback. "Yes."

"It's nice to meet you," I say, smiling. "Your wife has told me about you."

Chiyo scoots to the edge of the couch. "Is she alright?"

"Stable," Dayfyd says. "It seems the arrowheads were poisoned, but her Healer's blood is fighting it off as best as it can."

The arrowheads were poisoned? But not the dagger ... I glance at Tiernan, who at least isn't declining, then back to Dayfyd. He's still regarding me with a strange expression that I can't figure out. "Ava will lead you three to your housing. Try to get some rest, and you can visit the infirmary tomorrow during visitation hours."

Ava ... My head snaps to the lean woman who watches us stoically. So, this must be Alys's daughter. I get to my feet and extend my hand to Tiernan to help him up. "Tiernan needs to see a healer as well," I say, ignoring his scowl. "He's just too stubborn to admit it."

With a smirk in his direction, I remember him saying very similar words to Alys about me back in Paramount.

"I'll have a Healer come by," Dayfyd says.

"Thank you." Tiernan offers a pained smile.

We start to follow Ava out of the building, but I stop, my heart tugging on me. I have to know. I turn back to Dayfyd. "My little brother was taken from Cluain Baile by Forayers a few weeks ago, but the rebels managed to rescue him on the way to Paramount. I was told that they'd been intercepted again, but … Is it possible that he still made it here? Somehow?"

Tiernan places his hand gently on my shoulder, and I place my hand over his.

Dayfyd looks thoughtful. "How old is he? What does he look like?"

"He's five years old and has chestnut curls and big, brown eyes. He walks, though not well, and he doesn't speak."

Dayfyd glances at Ava who shrugs her shoulders. But then she says, "We have a home for children here—the Hatchling's Nest. We can visit in the morning and see if your brother is there."

I nod, hope blooming in my chest even though I know it's unlikely, given the circumstances. "I'd like that, thank you."

It's completely dark outside now, but the sky is flecked with countless stars surrounding the full moon. I can't make out much of the landscape, but silhouettes of trees surround a mixture of buildings, meadows, and a body of water beneath thick mist. My attention is drawn to the fog as we follow Ava's long strides. Tiernan hobbles beside me, too stubborn to ask Ava to slow down—and admittedly my legs are now truly as wobbly as a newborn foal's. Luckily, we don't have to walk too far before we arrive at a two-story house of whitewashed stone. Ava stops and pulls a key from her pocket to open the door.

"There are a few rooms," she says, slipping the key into my hand. "Make yourselves at home. I can bring you all some fresh clothing until you can get your own."

We all thank her and step into the house. A domed light of some sort is nestled in the ceiling, illuminating the sitting room. I stare up at the light until spots fleck my vision. When I face Ava again, she's fighting a smile.

"Magelight," she says. "It automatically turns on and off according to your needs." She shrugs, then turns to Tiernan. "I'll make sure a Healer has already been dispatched."

Tiernan doesn't even get the chance to thank her again before she turns on her heels and strides off with purpose. Chiyo watches her go, then lumbers further into the sitting room and collapses on the couch. She puts her feet up, crossing her ankles and pressing her hands over her face. She mumbles something that I don't quite make out, but I don't bother to ask as I take in the rest of our surroundings.

Like the other building, the floors and walls are wood, and there's a fireplace in front of the couch. There isn't much decor, but a few paintings of flora and fauna hang on the walls. Tiernan turns to me, one hand still over his abdomen. He pulls me close with his free arm, but his grip tenses before his arm falls away, a grimace on his face.

I huff out a sigh. "Alright, you need to get off your feet and wait for the Healer. Chiyo—"

I don't even have to say anything more before she swings her legs off the couch and stands up. "In that case, I get to choose a bedroom first," she signs with a grin before sauntering away.

I put an arm around Tiernan's lower back, and we walk over to the couch together. He's favoring his right leg where his pants are slashed open. Thank the gods that he didn't get hit with any arrows. "Do you think Alys will be alright?" I ask as he sinks into the couch cushions.

"I hope so," he says. I get down onto my knees and begin to unlace his boots. He reaches out to grasp my arms and shakes his head. "You don't have to do that."

I smile at him. "I want to. You've helped me *bathe*—the least I can do is help you remove your shoes."

He returns my smile, and I take a moment to admire the light in his eyes before I turn my attention back to the task at hand. I unlace his boots and pull them off his feet before peeling his socks off and setting them aside.

"Take your armor off," I sign gently.

He doesn't argue, sitting up with a wince. He's slow and clumsy, fumbling with the buckles and laces of his leather vest. I lean over to help him. It's a slow process, but eventually we get both his armor and his tunic off. His fair skin is marred with black and blue bruises, the warm undertone faded. His lower abdomen is bloody, the stab wound still raw. My stomach roils, and he takes my hand, bringing it to his own cheek before gently kissing my fingertips. "Don't worry about the wound," he says. "Sit with me." He pats the spot on the couch beside him.

I sit and he turns slightly so that he's fully facing me. "That shadow shield was brilliant."

I smile sheepishly. "Too bad I have no clue how I summoned it."

"You'll learn. But I hope you can see now that shadow wielding doesn't just bring death .... You saved my ass out there."

By sheer luck. Could I truly become good enough at wielding to be useful ... purposely? For a few moments, I entertain the notion. Though I have to keep drawing my focus away from his chest, his muscles rippling with each intake of breath.

"My eyes are up here, beautiful," he teases. "I'm trying to give a wise, motivational speech about your incredible powers."

My cheeks burn as a little laugh escapes me. "Oh, hush," I say. A trail of dried blood is tangled in the silver strands of his hair, his lip is split, and I'm almost certain he'll have a black eye tomorrow. "You're such a bloody mess."

He smirks and winces. "It's not that bad."

"No, I mean you are *literally* a bloody mess. Let me at least help you clean up before the Healer gets here."

I scoot to the edge of the couch to stand, but he grabs my hand. "Durvla, for Lierwen's sake, relax for a moment. I'm alright, and I'm certain the Healer has seen plenty of bloody messes."

My chest tightens and my throat swells, and as much as I try to convince myself to move past the emotions, the tears begin to flow. Tiernan sits up with urgency, a grimace on his face. "Durvla, what is it?"

"I thought I was going to lose you for a moment back there."

He smirks. "You can't get rid of me that easily."

"Thank the gods." I chuckle and wipe tears from my cheeks.

He tilts his head side to side, as if stretching his neck. The scars there grab my attention. "When I walked into your dream back in Paramount ... Was it ... just a nightmare or ..."

His body stiffens, a fleeting look of deep pain crossing his face before that familiar mask covers it all. My stomach sinks a little. "A memory," he says. He's even paler, if possible. His fingers brush against the scars on his neck. "A story for another time."

I nod and snuggle up beside him, resting my head on his shoulder. We remain like that until the Healer comes to tend to Tiernan's wounds. She brings clothing, mentioning which outfits are intended for each of us. I gratefully take the pair of light grey trousers and olive green tunic intended for me and set off to find the bathing room. It's just outside the sitting room, and it's small but has everything we'll need.

I fill the tub with a strange lever system, and to my surprise, the water is warm. Magic, I suppose, as I strip my filthy clothing off and eagerly get into the water. When I no longer reek like a barn, I hang my towel and washcloth to dry, clean my teeth, and rinse my mouth before gathering my dirty clothing and heading off to find the bedrooms.

Passing one bedroom, I spot Chiyo lying in the middle of the bed, sprawled out, fast asleep. I hold in my laughter and proceed to the other bedrooms…

Bedroom.

For a moment, I stand in the middle of the corridor, glancing between the doors.

Two bedrooms only.

Somehow, I'd expected there to be three from the casual way Ava mentioned that there were *a few rooms*. As I step into the unoccupied room, a magelight turns on, gently illuminating a large bed, a dresser, and a sizeable window covered by dark blue drapes. I drop my filthy clothing into a wicker basket near the door and saunter over to the window. Drawing back the curtains doesn't reveal much—it's too dark outside to make out any details, but it's peaceful here.

I pull the curtains closed again and make my way over to the bed. It's inviting, and I climb right in.

My intention is to relax for a moment, but the next thing I know, it's pitch dark. Moonlight peeks through the very corner of the window where the drapes aren't fully drawn.

Beside me, Tiernan is flat on his back and shirtless. Citrus with a familiar hint of marjoram drifts from him. Even with all the options of soap, he stuck with what he's known. His beard has been trimmed, with only stubble remaining. I smile and consider rousing him, but he's sleeping so soundly, his chest steadily rising and falling. The magelight flickers to life, shining faintly. The blood is gone from Tiernan's abdomen, and there's barely a sign of the stab wound.

My heart stutters when I drag my eyes up to a small circular scar on his chest—from the arrow he took for Carys, I assume—and the jagged scar that starts at his clavicle and climbs up the side of his neck. I swallow thickly and I roll onto my side so that I'm staring at the window.

The bed shifts, and Tiernan's arm snakes around my waist. I want to say something to him, but my mind is too exhausted. He pulls me closer, and his chin settles over my shoulder. "*Sleep*," he says gently into my mind.

It doesn't take any convincing at all. Soon, I drift off into a deep slumber.

I expected to sleep better than I have in a long time, but instead, I'm jarred awake by images flashing rapidly through my mind. Decaying flowers and dying greenery, fissures in the earth, ice spider-webbing across the land, and dripping icicles … in the middle of the summer. Fear holds on to me as I wake to a lingering presence that's both strange and familiar.

My limbs are heavy and sore as I roll onto my side to find that I'm alone. Sitting up stiffly, I wait for my head to settle before slowly getting out of bed. I stop by the bathing chamber and wash my face and mouth before heading into the main room. My stomach is a bundle of nerves about seeing the children's home Dayfyd mentioned—I'm afraid that I won't be able to handle it.

Tiernan in the kitchen is a welcome sight. He's pouring hot water into one of two mugs on the counter when I enter. A stream of sunlight filters in through the window over the counters. Tiernan turns to me with an equally radiant smile. "Good morning. I've made you some tea. Ava already came by with freshly baked bread and some more clean clothing."

I lift my brows. "Wow. She really is efficient."

"Yes, and slightly intimidating." Tiernan leaves the cups on the counter and walks toward me. "How did you sleep?"

I shrug. "Not very well, but the bed was comfortable. You?"

"Same. We're probably still on edge from our travels." He smiles and gently places his fingers beneath my chin, tilting my face up to his. "But I think I've lost the ability to function like a normal human being in your presence during waking hours."

I wrinkle my nose at him. "What do you mean?"

He lowers his hand, but I keep my face angled toward his. "Every time I look at you, I have a strong desire to taste your lips."

My cheeks flush. "So, what's stopping you, Tiernan Kilkenny?" I can feel the hitch in my voice, and the amused spark on Tiernan's face verifies it. I lace my fingers behind his neck and his arms wrap around my waist. Our lips meet, and the kiss is slow and leisurely, as if we could stop time. He pulls my hips to his, and I melt into him, desire igniting deep in my belly. My lips part, and just as his tongue touches mine, he withdraws.

My head is still reeling as I glance up at him, confused. "Why did you—?"

His head turns toward the kitchen entrance, and I follow his stare to Chiyo. She stands with her hands on her hips, smirking. Finally, she signs, "Well, good morning."

Tiernan lowers his forehead to mine, and laughter vibrates through him. He pulls back and straightens up, reluctantly releasing me from his grip. "We ought to put a bell on this one," he says to me.

I smirk and glance from him to Chiyo, who says, "Or keep your affections in the privacy of the bedroom? Just putting that out there."

A laugh is on my lips as I turn away without a clue about what the siblings say next. I grab a knife to start carving into the golden crust of the sourdough loaf on the counter. The knife breaks through the crust with a satisfying crunch that I feel through the handle, and my mouth waters expectantly.

While my mind whirls, I cut several slices. I don't know what this thing is between Tiernan and me. We haven't had the chance to discuss anything, and I have no clue how to let him know that I am completely new to this world of attraction. He knows I've never been in a relationship, but I'm not sure if he knows just how inexperienced I truly am. Doubt and nervous energy fill me.

The weight of Tiernan's hand settles on my shoulder. I glance back at him and there's a question on his face. "Chiyo's gone," he signs. "You're giving off some very intense feelings. Everything alright?"

I slide the knife aside and turn so my back is against the counter. "I'm just … A lot has happened, and I don't quite know what to make of … us."

He smiles slowly. "Me neither. But, for now, we don't have to rush into anything or figure it all out. I have self-control. Knight's oath." He places one hand over his chest and raises the other.

I roll my eyes fondly at him. "We better eat and get ready for the day. Did Ava give any updates on Alys?"

"No, but I assume no news is good news. You're right though. Let's get going."

We all eat and dress in our fresh daytime clothing. Not long after, Dayfyd meets us outside. He smiles a bit shakily. My lips curve up in response. "Welcome to the Verge in the daytime," he signs.

The Verge is unlike any place I've been before. A bog runs through the land with dense fog rolling over the shallow, murky surface and the surrounding banks. There are small houses and other buildings scattered, and there are lush forests and majestic grassy mountains all around. A damp scent clings to the humid air, like the earth after a downpour.

The sun shines brightly, and there are people *everywhere*. Children run around freely, their faces gleeful. People of all ages, backgrounds, appearances, and abilities interact with each other. For a while, I stand there, absorbing our surroundings. A group of people converse in signed language a small distance away and my heart leaps.

A young man walks with a carved stick in each hand. His footsteps are unsteady, but the smile on his face is so genuine. He approaches a young woman with startlingly white hair and alabaster skin who wears a hat over her head and long sleeves despite the warm weather. She tiptoes to peck him on the lips, and they continue their journey. A couple pushes a child just a little younger than Taig in a pram and my heart flips.

Taig. Oh, how he would thrive here. I force air into my chest and turn my attention back to Dayfyd. "How's Alys?"

"Still stable. Her Healer blood is staving off the worst of the poison. She's already sitting up and asked how you all are faring. We can visit after, if you'd like."

I sigh with relief, then nod and glance at Tiernan.

He smiles encouragingly and hooks his elbow through mine. "Ready?"

My throat is too knotted up for speech, so I nod again.

As we pass other inhabitants of the Verge, they either smile or gawk at us with curiosity. Farther across the land, we come upon a pasture with a large, two-story building in the background with the words Hatchling's Nest above the double-door entrance. Children are playing happily, working on little crafts in small groups with an adult chaperone, or being pushed in wooden swings and hammocks hanging between trees and handmade structures.

I spot a small child with a hat over her head, much like the one I once made for Taig. Sound-muffling, I presume. She flaps her hands happily as she spins in circles and my heart just about bursts to witness her so openly able to express her joy in her own unique way.

There is no such thing as an *Undesirable* here.

I reach out for Tiernan's hand, needing the extra boost of courage as I prepare for disappointment and heartbreak. I'm just about to say that maybe we should go back to the house when a flash of big hair catches my attention. I take in the scrawny body and teetering gait. The chestnut curls and the small grabby hands that reach out in front of him. The little boy turns full circle, nearly falling over, and I catch a glimpse of his perfect little face. His light brown skin has a healthy glow to it, his cheeks even filling out a little.

I stumble back on wobbly legs, my thoughts jumbled, limbs weightless. Giddy warmth floods my chest, tears welling behind my eyelids.

Let this be real. Please, let this be real.

It's only Tiernan's arm around my waist that keeps me upright as my knees buckle. I blink, tears streaming down my face as a sob breaks free.

"Taig," I manage to say, my throat too tight, my body seemingly unsure of exactly how to process what is right in front of me. "Taig!"

He turns to face me very slowly. His expression remains unchanged at first, but then a radiant smile spreads across his face, dimples blossoming in his cheeks.

My heart bursts.

I break free from Tiernan's grasp and run toward my little brother. My knees hit the grass, and I throw my arms around him. His skinny arms wrap around my neck. I bury my face in his shoulder, my body shaking with sobs of joy and relief.

"My sweet boy, my sweet Taig." I can't stop the repetitive words.

My Taig. He's alive. Thank the gods, thank the rebels, thank goodness he's alive.

I push him an arm's distance away to study him, but he shoves me away and walks off. I stare at him, slack-jawed as he hobbles away from me. Then I collapse onto my bottom.

I can't stop laughing and I can't stop crying.

Tiernan joins me on one side and Chiyo on the other. We watch together as Taig walks in circles and Dayfyd speaks to the very concerned caregiver who had witnessed the whole thing. I hold up a hand in apology to her as Dayfyd seems to be explaining the situation. She nods to me in acknowledgement.

My face aches from smiling so much, and I reach out to take Chiyo's hand, squeezing it once while I lean against Tiernan's shoulder. Eventually, Taig totters back over to us and plops down into my lap, knocking the air out of me. He sits still for about five seconds before he tries to get loose again. "Sweet boy," I say. "Can I just introduce you to my friends?" I point to each of them. "This is Tiernan and Chiyo. They helped me find my way to you again."

Even Osheen. My throat constricts, but I swallow down the heartache.

Taig stares at Tiernan and then reaches out as though he means to caress his cheek. But rather than caress his cheek, he grabs hold of Tiernan's hair and tugs *hard*.

"Ow!" Tiernan exclaims, and Chiyo bursts out laughing. Taig laughs as well, then struggles to his feet and walks off once more.

I apologize to Tiernan as he tucks his hair behind his ear, but he shakes his head and smiles brightly. "He'd make a good fighter, that one."

I laugh. "He already is."

It's amazing that he is outside. Free, happy, thriving.

I can live my life here with him, protected by the wards. It seems so simple.

But what about all the other children out there? All the others who are *Undesirable* and struggling to keep their lives a secret? Or the baby in Ballybaeg who died in my arms. The rebels seek to help those who do not have the means to help themselves. To rise up against the laws that make it impossible for people like us to live with a sense of safety.

I dry the tears on my face, take a deep breath, and slowly get to my feet. Brushing grass off my trousers and hands, I gather my composure and turn to Chiyo and Tiernan.

"I've made a decision," I tell them. "I'm ready to join the rebellion."

Chapter 76
DURVLA

NIGHT FALLS AND I continue to stare down at Taig as he slumbers peacefully in the middle of the large bed. Tiernan stands beside me, an arm around my shoulders. He tilts his head into my view and signs to me, "He's adorable. But where are *we* sleeping?"

I snort a laugh, swiping at a stray tear that slips down my cheek.

Concern immediately wipes the amusement from Tiernan's face. He gently turns me to face him. "Taig is safe. You are safe. We made it to the Verge, and you saw those wards and the fortifications … They've fortified it even *more* now since our arrival. We're protected here."

"Yes, but we have no idea how strong those people who attacked us are. For how long will we be safe?"

He shakes his head, his lips curving up into a soft smile. "Optimistic as ever."

I shrug and smile wryly at him. Just as I turn back to Taig, my mouth waters unpleasantly from a sudden tang of metal. Colors swirl in my vision and I grab Tiernan's shoulder. "Ti—" It's all I can say before invisible hands tug me into an abyss.

The world warps, and I find myself, once again, standing in the middle of dark tunnels. I'm on the cold ground, pulling in harsh breaths. Think, *I tell myself.* Haruka said something about Dreamwalkers and dreamscapes. I just need to remember.

I draw in breath after breath and rein in my thoughts.

A practiced Dreamwalker can also interact with the person dreaming, and sometimes, influence their dreams.

I search for any sign of light—any indication of the right direction. A candle flickers in the distance. No, not a candle. A strange flame of orange and black, seemingly floating in midair. It flickers until I blink, then it's gone. I draw in a shuddery breath.

Haruka's words come back to mind: there are also certain Mages able to distort another person's dreamscape or even what they see while they're awake.

Like Basduunai.

Closing my eyes, I pour all my focus into blocking out the panic of this familiar darkness. An ethereal voice emanates from everywhere and nowhere all at once—the haunting sound fills the void, singing the same lullaby I'm so familiar with.

"Let Sunlagh take you by the hand

To the land beyond the veil."

The voice continues, speaking rather than singing, but its tone is musical, soothing. "There is a fine line between the realm of dreams and the realm of the dead ...

Let Sunlagh take you by the hand

To the land beyond the veil."

The strange, yet familiar presence disappears, and Carys's pours in, her distress, despair, anger, and melancholy so pungent that I can almost taste them. A taunting voice mocks Ellynne's death. Grief kicks me in the gut, and I press my hand against the cool, moist wall, one arm around my middle as though the blow were physical.

Pain lances through my body.

But this is not my pain. I repeat the reminder. It's not my *pain.*

A new disembodied voice fills my head. A memory that isn't mine. A man's voice that I don't recognize: "It's not your fault." Then Ellynne's voice: "You have the hair of a princess, but the heart of a warrior."

I latch on to the voices, tapping into those particular memories—Carys's memories. Of her brother. Of Ellynne. More words that aren't mine pour into my mind, equal parts meaningless and perfectly comprehensible. They're not just words of the past, not just memories—they're too relevant, omniscient.

Like they're coming from beyond.

The land beyond ... the Veil? Chills whisper against the back of my neck.

"Sunlagh ... ? Was that really your voice?" I say into the void, but there's no response. She's already given me the answer—I just need to figure out how to do what I need to do. Goddess, give me strength.

With great hesitation, I walk toward the strange black and orange flame in the distance. Carys has been utterly abandoned by everyone she's ever cared about and everyone who's cared about her.

She needs to know that she's not alone, and it seems I have a message for her. I must lose myself to become who she needs me to be.

The lonesomeness floods my consciousness as I press on toward that flame. Toward Carys.

When I come to, I'm on the floor, Tiernan cradling my head in his lap. I bolt upright and my head swims. Scrambling to my feet, I barely make it to the rubbish bin as my stomach upends itself. The words from beyond that I projected into Carys's mind replay in my own memory. Tiernan is at my side seconds later, one hand holding my hair away from my face, the other rubbing between my shoulder blades as my stomach continues to revolt. As the energy continues to drain from me, my body trembles uncontrollably. I wipe the back of my hand across my mouth and turn my wavering gaze to Tiernan.

"Carys?" he asks.

I nod, making the room spin.

"Paramount," I sign. I sit there on the floor, fighting the darkness that tries to pull me under so I can tell Tiernan everything I fear will come to pass tonight.

Chapter 77
CARYS

THE FAMILIAR STRAINING ACHE of my shoulders is what yanks me out of oblivion. Again, my arms and legs are splayed and bound to the merciless X-shaped apparatus. My pulse races, trepidation rushing through my veins. As much as I try to steady my breathing, my chest grows tighter.

"You might as well open your eyes," a singsong voice says. "I know you're awake."

My stomach dips, my throat closing up. Before I face this torture, I need to think. I don't budge; I search the crevices of my mind for a way to get out of this. Eefa craves attention. Her face was ecstatic when she imagined masquerading as the queen at Iywan's side. Perhaps her loyalties don't lie with the Zenith, but with herself. That wouldn't surprise me.

Eefa accused me of being obsessed with the devotion of others, but perhaps she was only projecting her own desires.

Eefa is face to face with me. I jump so hard that the shackles dig into my wrists and ankles. I bite back a cry of pain and stare her down.

"You know the drill, darling," she croons, flipping her dagger. I track the blade as it spins and lands in her grasp again and again. "Master Iywan is upstairs arranging a council meeting as we speak, so you don't have much time. What will it be?"

"What has Iywan offered to make you so enthusiastic about torturing me?"

She cocks a brow, and the blade spins once more.

"You do know that once Iywan's plan comes to fruition, he'll just marry you off to some stuffy lord, right?" I pour my focus into speaking steadily even as sweat gathers in the small of my back.

"Nonsense, I'm his most useful weapon." She isn't quite convinced of her own words. The dagger spins in the air again before she catches it. I track the motion while I try to figure out my next move.

"I'm glad you got rid of Callum," I say, my throat tensing as I speak. "He was always so sulky whenever you showed up."

"Hmm, yes he was quite the sulker, that one."

"How did you overpower an ordained knight? Did you change into the form of a man?"

She laughs. "Oh Carys, who would've thought you were a misogynist. I'll have you know that I overpowered him with this magnificent body you love so much, but yes, I can transform into a man. You'd like that, wouldn't you, darling? Someone to replace your sweet, chivalrous Callum?"

Don't let her get to you, says a voice.

A breath rushes out of me at the return of that voice.

Patience.

"Can you change into Iywan?" I force myself to ask Eefa.

Eefa's brows raise.

"We can execute his plan together. You can be my right hand. We can rule this realm as the emperor and empress. We don't need Iywan."

Desperation has its talons in me as Eefa mulls over my words, her lips pursed as she idly twirls the dagger between her fingers. Then at last, she peers up at me and grins predatorily. "I am aware that you knew me as Lowri, the mousy little servant girl who didn't have a mind of her own. Yet … I'm still offended that you think I'm daft enough to trust your little half-arsed ploy."

My gulp is audible. I barely manage to blink before Eefa's blade is at my throat. I hold my breath and try not to swallow.

"Nice try, darling," she says. "But I can slit your throat right here, go upstairs and announce to Master Iywan that he can go ahead and execute his plan. *I* can be queen without you. Hells, I can be *you*."

She's delusional! My heart is racing so fast that my head grows light. All I've wanted to do for so long now is die, yet as I'm confronted with my mortality, I'm scared stiff. I haven't had anything to drink in quite a while, yet my bladder aches, a reminder of the moment when my pride had been completely stripped from me.

Drip, drip, drip.

"What are you waiting for?" I whisper.

"What? You're not afraid?" There's a hint of disappointment in her voice.

"Yes."

She draws the blade back slightly, and I suck in a breath. Uncertainty shows in Eefa's expression, as if my admittance has thrown her off her game. Her perfectly arched brows draw close together and she steps back. She starts pacing the length of the cell, tapping the blade against her face and muttering something under her breath.

Then she whirls on me. "You're a disgrace to the crown. You don't even care to fight for what's yours. You're a coward. *I* should be the one to hold the power. *I* know how to get what I deserve!"

The tip of her blade presses into my cheek. I wince at the first sting. She draws an excruciatingly slow line down my cheek. I barely breathe, afraid that if I move, she'll take out my eye. As she lowers the blade, I ask breathlessly, "Does Iywan even know you're down here?"

Eefa lifts the blade again and, this time, she carelessly slashes across my face. My scream echoes through the cell, and the satisfaction on Eefa's face is apparent. My breath comes in ragged pants, my face throbbing and stinging as warmth spreads from the blood oozing down my cheek. Heat rises in my chest, that pulsating power beckoning to me, but I try to keep my focus away from it. I stifle the screams of my brother in my head and breathe through the suffocating fear.

"First, my own bloody sister puts her life on the line to save you when she's never so much as lifted a finger to help me. Now Master Iywan chooses you, a pitiful Wielder who cannot even summon her own powers. Why choose a Flamewielder when he can have a Skinchanger? I can be anybody he desires. Literally!"

Gods, she really is delusional.

"Say something!" The wild intensity in her glare makes me wither.

I open my mouth to say something, but my lips close again as nothing comes to mind. I barely register her movement before she madly slashes her dagger across my face again. Had I closed my eyes just a heartbeat later, the blade would've blinded me. Instead, pain sears across my eyelid, my nose, and down to my jaw.

A sob tears free as I dare to look at her again. "Eefa, please!"

Everything slows down, a chill running through me. One moment, I'm staring at the vulpine grin on Eefa's face and the next, a figure in my peripheral vision catches my attention. As I blink, my eyes stinging from the blood, I'm standing, unbound somehow, in a dark tunnel.

The figure materializes before me. I take in his tall, lean stature, his black hair, and brown eyes like our mother's. He's wearing the same loose tunic and trousers as the last time I saw him, a small crown around his head, and a sword belted to his narrow waist. Just the way he looked before … Oh, gods.

I draw in a shuddery breath, gulping back the emotions. "Aneirin?"

"Hello, sister," he says.

Chapter 78
CARYS

I SINK TO MY *knees, sobbing before my brother.* "*But you're dead …*"

"*I am,*" *he says.* "*I know you feel guilty about what happened, but it was not your fault. You were a child then, and not in control. But you are now.*"

I can only blubber in response.

"*Carys, don't let your guilt destroy you. I have to leave again, but I love you with all my soul and I forgive you.*"

The words begin mending the torn pieces of my heart back together as he disappears. I jump to my feet, as a different figure materializes where Aneirin just stood. I take in the mane of red hair, the playful glimmer in olive eyes, and the dazzling smile playing on painted red lips.

Ellynne.

"*Hello, sweet girl,*" *she says.*

I want to laugh, to cry. I step toward her and throw my arms around her body, only to be met with air. I step back, befuddled.

"Am I hallucinating?" I ask.

"No, sweet girl. But listen, there's something you need to know."

Shoving my thoughts away, I focus on her words.

"That conduit on your wrist can only work as long as you continue to fear your powers."

"But—"

"I know it's scary, but you can do scary things. I've seen your struggles, and I know your pain. Dig deep down and grab ahold of the power that Iywan wants to take from you. He cannot reign over what you already dominate. You are Carys Meredyth fa Rhodri, daughter of Queen Morwenna, the Good, heir to the throne of the kingdom of Erleya. The power that Iywan seeks is already within you. Use it."

I blink, tears flushing the blood from my eyes, flowing freely down my face and stinging every gash inflicted by Eefa's blade. The tunnels disintegrate around me, and I find myself bound to the saltire in my cell again. With sickening realization, I find neither Aneirin nor Ellynne present.

Instead, I'm left with Eefa.

Her head is tilted, and she regards me as if I'm some rare creature to behold. "Oooh, goodie, there you are," she purrs. "I thought I'd lost you for a moment. Now where were we? Maybe this time I'll destroy those pretty, golden eyes of yours." She lifts the dagger, this time with the intention to stab.

I draw in a breath, finding that heat in the center of my chest. I grab ahold of it, but my memories taunt me.

Aneirin's screams.

My mother placing the amulet around my neck.

Years of discordance within myself, shame, guilt, hopelessness, worthlessness, and instability, all filling me to the brim until I fear I may implode.

Don't run from your memories; reign over them.

My pulse roars in my ears. Energy vibrates through me. I clench and unclench my shackled hands, torridity overwhelming my body as anger and frustration sear a path up my throat. A conflagration flares at my wrists, and I scream in rage. I yank my wrists free as the manacles melt away.

Terror flashes across Eefa's face. She turns to run, but I grab her as I step out of the molten shackles binding my ankles. I knock her dagger aside with my wrist as she lifts her hand again. Grabbing her face, I stare into her soul, my body trembling with ire. "Ellynne says hello," I drawl.

She starts to scream as my hands glow bright orange. The sound of skin sizzling reaches my ears. Her fear morphs into pain and her pain back into horror. She claws at my hands, the whites of her eyes showing, but her palms come away blistered and seared. When her screaming subsides and her body goes limp, I release her. She drops to the ground, her head hitting the stones with a sharp *thud*.

Her formerly pretty face is unrecognizably charred. I stare down at my palms, expecting flames. Instead, a thick web of black veins runs from the palms of my hands up my arms, disappearing where my tunic is rolled at my inner elbow. Icy hot rage unlike anything I've felt before sinks its teeth into me, and I let out a scream for all the torment I've endured in this godsforsaken dungeon.

A cold presence strokes the boundaries of my mind, promising me strength, fueling my fury. Even as blood, tears, and sweat stream down my face, I find myself numbly striding through the gates that Eefa hadn't bothered to close. I advance down the corridor to the door and burn a hole straight through it, ripping metal shards away, before stepping over to the other side. Steely determination lances up my spine and I turn, snarling at Lieutenant Bronn and Cadet Aela as they come at me.

One swipe of my hand, and they scream as black flames lick up their ankles, slowly creeping up their bodies. Their garbled cries are music to my ears. A smile tugs at my lips. But they're on the ground, gasping for air, begging for death, and the black flames have not even singed their clothing.

How unsatisfying.

My head tilts, and that familiar caress in my mind nudges me. *Burn them.*

I throw my palms out toward them. Orange flames engulf their bodies. Not looking back, I stride onward, their cries following me down the tunnels.

Get Iywan.

I run through the tunnels, the darkness welcoming me like an old friend, eagerness dancing along my skin as I think of what Iywan's face will look like when I burn him alive.

My bare feet pound against the ground as I hurry through the tunnels beneath Paramount. When I find the stairs, I take them two bounding steps at a time. My heart cannot beat any faster, but no fatigue touches my body, no tension—no fear—remains.

"The princess has escaped!" a voice calls out from somewhere to my left.

Squinting, I make out a silhouette approaching me. I stretch my hand out, and his screams fill the small atrium. I rub my face and turn to the other guard who approaches from my right. It's the brawny woman with the one unseeing eye. She holds up her hands in surrender, slightly bending a knee in a curtsy far worse than Durvla's. "Your Highness, I'm on your side," she says quickly.

Take her dagger.

I hold my hand out. "Give me your dagger." My voice is low and surprisingly calm.

The soldier woman doesn't hesitate but quickly removes the dagger from her belt and presses it into my palm.

I smile slowly at her. "Thank you."

Then I'm running again, taking the secret entrance into the castle. I skid into the hallway of the palace, and anyone who dares to get in my way is met with a wall of fire that fills me with more satisfaction than I've had in eons. I strut down the halls of the castle, past my bedchamber where I last saw Ellynne's dead body and ... I pause for a moment, my heart filling with sorrow before I'm reminded of the corrupt bastard that tried to control me. I glance down at my wrist—the conduit is gone, destroyed along with the shackles that once held me.

With the gleeful realization of how limitless I am, I sprint across the castle, scorching anyone who stands in my path. Shrieks follow me as I climb the winding stairs of the tower. I shove the double doors of the council chamber, and they fly open, hitting the stone walls with a loud *bang*.

Iywan lurches out of his seat at the head of the table. He has the audacity to still be wearing his advisor pin.

"Your Highness," he says, and there's not just surprise in his voice but fear.

Good.

I snarl as I advance on him, my footsteps heavy, my power pulsating and tugging on me as my ire rises again.

Briony jumps to her feet and backs away from the table as others rise from where they sit. Everyone stares, time stretching out for several beats.

"Briony, the princess needs healing," Iywan says.

My head snaps toward Briony, and she drops down to her knees, placing her hands against the tiled floor and lowering her forehead between. She glances up at me from her groveling posture, meeting my gaze steadily.

"I am your humble servant, Enchantress," she says.

A grin stretches across my face. *Enchantress*, I like the sound of that.

"Carys, stand down." Iywan speaks in a commanding tone that carries across the chamber. He's clutching a metal wristband around his own wrist—an exact match to the one I once wore.

I raise my brows at him, then the corner of my lips tugs up again. I *tsk* softly and raise my bare wrist for him to see. "Bad news, Iywan … no conduit." I wink, and delicious terror sinks into him. I can almost *taste* it.

I hold my palms up, black and orange flames dancing across my skin. Gasps fill the room, and Councilor Belhan dares to make a run for it. I blast fire into his round face, and he goes down screaming and clawing at his head. More energy surges inside me. Red hot.

Burn them all.

I turn to Briony. "Run."

Without hesitation, she scampers off.

I draw in a breath, and, like the breaking of a dam, I unleash my flames on all the councilors. Iywan backs away while his accomplices burn around him. Their screams echo through the chamber, fueling my energy. I walk through the fire, extinguishing a path to get to Iywan. The flames reanimate behind me.

Iywan stands with his back flush against the wall as though he could phase right through it.

While the chamber burns, I press my forearm against Iywan's chest, shadowfire binding his arms to his torso. He roars in agony, and I lift the dagger to my lips. "Shh …"

Mouthwatering fear radiates off his loathsome body.

"You wanted to release the Enchantress Queen, didn't you?" I hear myself ask. I tilt my head at him as he cowers. "Well, here I am."

The pungent scent of urine fills my nose and, oh how delectable retribution is. I dig the dagger into the fabric beneath his advisor's pin and rip it right off. The pin clatters to the ground and his face drops down to it for a moment.

"Now, you are *nothing*," I say with vehemence. "Any last words?"

His throat bobs and tears brim. "Please—" he says. "I can be of use to you."

I scoff.

"I'm not the man you're looking for. I'm only second-in-command of the Zenith."

The flames are closing in around us and the screams of the councilors have subsided. Iywan's heart is beating so loudly that I can *hear* it.

"Who's the leader of the Zenith?"

Sweat streams down his face. "Lord Commander Rheon."

I furrow my brows at him. "Thank you, Iywan." I step back and inhale deeply, reveling in the heat of the flames all around us. Iywan's head darts left and right, taking in the growing blaze so close to engulfing him. I want to watch him burn. I want to watch the skin melt off his bones and his bones turn to ashes.

"Your mother would be so horrified," Iywan says.

His words douse me like icy water. I draw in a shuddery breath as the overpowering heat inside me flickers. "My mother would be horrified?" I ask. "By *me*?" I point the dagger at my chest and he follows the movement. "*You* kept her alive with magic, prolonged her suffering, turned the entire Council, the entire royal staff against her daughter. She trusted you. *I* trusted you; you were once like the father I'd lost. You were supposed to be on *my* side. You were supposed to help me."

The fires around me begin to dwindle and Iywan slumps against the wall, hope washing over his face. "I did what neither of you could," he says. "For our kingdom. For your own good. I did what I had to!"

FINISH THIS, the cold voice in my head roars, and that heat rises within me like the high tide.

"Well, then ... I suppose you'll understand that I'm doing what *I* have to."

Iywan's eyes widen, a question parting his lips. I step back and clench my fists, sending up a wall of flames that aren't nearly as powerful as moments ago, but Iywan's shrieks follow.

I back away, the flames behind me parting like water around a boulder as I make my way toward the door.

Iywan's screams die by the time I'm past the charred bodies and ash of the councilors and out of the chamber. The doors slam behind me, and I press my back against it, trying to catch my breath as the cold presence within me fades away.

A tremor runs through me, jarring my bones, pain radiating everywhere. My face smarts, my vision spots, and my stomach churns. I double over and dry heave uncontrollably. I have nothing to give, but the heaving doesn't stop for a while. I take a few steps forward and drop to the floor as sobs render me immobile.

I never want to sense that cold, alluring presence in my mind again.

Enchantress ... it's what Briony had called me and what I'd heard my own voice speak.

As if I've summoned her, Briony's soft voice travels down the corridor. "Princess?"

I lift my head as she approaches. "What's happening to me?" My head pounds in time with my erratic heart.

"The fulfillment of a prophecy," she says.

My vision begins to wane, and I blink repeatedly.

"We need to get you healed. May I touch your face? You're bleeding rather profusely."

My stomach dips and roils as my body recalls Eefa slicing me across my face. I nod and everything wavers, my body becoming both heavy and light at the same time. Then I succumb to unconsciousness.

When I come to again, Briony's face hovers over mine. I'm flat on my back, and the pain in my face is gone.

"Here, let's sit you up. You need to drink something," she says. She slides a hand beneath my shoulder blades and helps me sit up. Then she hands me a goblet that was sitting on the floor beside her. "Recovery elixir," she says. "It'll help a little as … everything wears off."

Without question I lift it to my lips.

"Drink slowly," she warns.

I take a sip and fight the urge to guzzle down the sweet, lukewarm elixir. After a few sips, I try to focus on the priestess through my dizziness. Slowly, my head starts to clear.

"Briony? Were you ever on Iywan's side?"

She winces at the question. "Yes. I believed in the mission of the Zenith until I realized that they had it all wrong."

"You called me Enchantress," I say. I called *myself* Enchantress. I shiver.

"Years ago, it was believed that the Heirs of Dusk and Embers banished Enidwen from the realm. The jury's still out. The truth is that she wasn't banished right away. A lot is still left to discover, but what has been speculated for years among priests and scholars of the old religion, what has become startlingly clear, is that her spirit—in fact, hers and the Underling Prince's—lived on. Passing through the generations, through the descendants of the Heirs.

"Her spirit has lain semi-dormant, but it was prophesied that one day it would awaken within one of Agryna's Chosen—that is, one touched by fire. You bear the curse of Enidwen through your mother's bloodline and firewielding from the sun goddess through your father's. The Zenith has been looking for the one who is going to continue Enidwen's mission to open the Veil. They thought they'd found her through your mother, but soon they realized there's more than one person who shares her blood."

My body is weighty and my mind too sluggish perhaps to fully process this new information. Agryna's Chosen? Curse of Enidwen? A true descendant of the sun goddess?

I should be in denial of all these ridiculous claims.

Instead, I feel nothing. I take another, larger sip from the goblet and close my eyes as the elixir slides down my aching throat. "Did my mother know?"

"Yes. Iywan ensured that I kept her asleep, but she appeared to me in a dream when there was a lapse in the effects of the potion that I was giving her. It's how I came to realize the dire mistake the Zenith was making. If they used you to open the Veil, who's to know what would come forth. It would be catastrophic."

I watch her uneasily as I finish the elixir. "Why should I trust a word of what you say?"

"Because, Princess, I have seen your power, and I can assure you that I do not want to awaken the enchantress again."

My heart plummets into my stomach. Gods, neither do I.

Suddenly remembering the thick black veins that had lined my arms back in the dungeons, I flip my arms over. My skin is speckled with cuts and bruises but nothing else. I search within myself for power, for that cold presence, but there's only nervous energy coursing through my veins.

Briony takes the cup from me. "Princess, I'd like to answer more of your questions, but as we speak, Lord Commander Rheon and a few of his men are riding to Paramount. He expects a bride tethered to a conduit for his wielding, and if he doesn't get that ... well, he has the entire Royal Brigade and the Zenith at his fingertips. I'm afraid Paramount is not safe for you anymore. In fact, the whole kingdom will be in danger if the Zenith gets their hands on you."

I'm a weapon to be wielded. Gods ... I expect to be more moved by this news, but fatigue has thrown a blanket over my emotions. "Are you suggesting that I run, *Priestess*?" I still have so many questions about her loyalty, her title, her dedication to the god of death.

She nods. "Respectfully … Not suggesting—*telling*. Angharad is already prepared to get you to safety." She stands and helps me to my feet. My legs are reluctant to support my weight, and I'm overcome with nauseating exhaustion. Briony slings my arm around her, and we start down the hallway.

Then her words circle back to me. *More than one that shares her blood.* More than one? As in more than me? My thoughts all meld together into a mess.

"Is my mother still alive?" I ask, already struggling to keep my breathing steady.

Briony catches her lower lip between her teeth, then slowly shakes her head. "I'm sorry …"

My chest constricts, sensation trickling back into me for a moment before ebbing away. "What did you mean when you said more than one shares my mother's blood. Are you referring to my brother? Because he's—" A brawny soldier clad in charcoal livery rounds on us, and I nearly swallow my tongue from the startled yelp I bite back. Her uninjured brown eye regards me with a respectful intensity.

"Sorry to scare you, Your Highness," she says. For her intimidating appearance, her voice is warm and melodic. "But we must hurry."

This must be Angharad.

I nod and Briony releases me to the soldier. I glance over my shoulder to thank Briony, but Angharad yanks me down the hallway so aggressively that my feet leave the ground for a moment. Everything aches. Even my soul aches. I want to lie down on the floor and never get up.

Don't you dare, says that cool voice in my head.

My back jolts straight, my muscles straining, and I bite back a grunt as I'm half dragged down the hallway. Feet pounding on the floor, we launch ourselves into the cool night air. Pains shoot through my shins as I struggle to keep up with Angharad's racing steps across the small, covered bridge from the castle.

I open my mouth to ask where we're going, but I can hardly breathe, let alone speak. I try to make sense of Angharad's direction. Rather than taking a more secluded path, she moves right to the front of the castle, through the hedge-lined pathways and past oddly wilting flowers, straight toward the rocky trail that runs alongside the loch below.

Hugging myself against the wind that whips around me, I drag uneven breaths into my lungs. My chest burns, my throat is raw.

"There she is!" a voice calls. Briony?

Angharad and I turn toward Briony whose arm is outstretched, her finger pointing at me.

A stocky man in brown Royal Brigade livery stands beside her, a few other soldiers at his back. The dozens of stripes and patches on his uniform clearly denotes his high rank. The *highest* rank.

Lord Commander Rheon.

Shit …

All hopes of catching my breath vanish, and my pulse skitters.

Angharad's unaffected eye is intent, almost … regretful? "Stay alive," she says, gently placing her hands on my shoulders.

As I pull in a ragged breath to question her, she shoves me.

I stagger backward, throwing my arms out to catch myself, but the back of my heel slams into the low wall behind me. I get one last look at the castle looming ahead, at the bright, full moon in the inky sky. The breeze chills my body as I tumble off the edge of the cliff. My stomach lurches, my hands grasping at anything, at everything.

This is it.

All of that for nothing.

All of that for everything, says the enchantress's voice. *Hold your breath.*

So, I do.

My body plunges into the dark loch below, and the icy water forces me to draw in a breath. My mouth fills, my lungs object. I fight to propel myself back to the surface.

But there's no fight left in me.

Find the daughter of Dusk again. Find your sister.

The world begins to fade.

Rest now, the voice croons. *For when you wake, the world will burn.*

To be Continued

Pronunciation Guide

<u>Characters</u>

Alys: AH-lis

Aneirin: ah-NYE-rin

Angharad: ang-HA-rad

Briony: BRY-uh-nee

Caedmon: KAYD-mon

Callum: CAL-uhm

Carys: CAR-is

Chiyoko: chee-OH-co

Dayfyd: day-FID

Durvla: DERV-la

Eefa: EE-fa

Eemer: EE-mer

Ellynne: EL-in

Elviera: el-vee-YEA-rah

Enidwen: EE-nid-wen

Ffion: FEE-on

Gethin: GEH-thin

Ghendor: GEHN-dor

Grawnye: GRO-nyuh

Haruka: ha-ROO-kah

Iywan: EYE-wahn

Lowri: l-OW-ree

Mirren: MEER-en

Morwenna: mor-WEN-ah

Odgar: OHD-gar
Orla: OR-la
Osheen: Oh-SHEEN
Rheon: REE-on
Sessaley: SES-ah-lee
Taig: TIE-g
Taliesin: tah-lee-EH-sin
Tiernan: TEER-nan

Pantheon

Agryna (Ah-GRIN-ah): goddess of the summer and sun

Bhugearan (byoo-GEAR-ahn): god of Autumn and harvest

Damarlach (da-MAR-loch): goddess of war, blacksmithing, fire, revenge, terror

Ehlach (EH-loch): god of the moon, healing, mysticism

Lierwen (LEER-win): The Father; King of the Overworld; the protector; god of justice and honor

Lugda (loog-DA): god of death and the Underworld

Magdin (MAG-din): goddess of winter; the veiled one

Ostanha (us-TA-na): god of spring, rebirth, flowers, youth, love

Rhianu (ree-AH-nu): Queen of the Overworld; The Mother; goddess of fertility and children, life, birth

Sunlagh (soon-LA): goddess of dreams

Places

Ardall: ARD-all

Ballybaeg: BA-lee-bayg

Ballygort: BA-lee-gort

Barr na Cahar: Bar nah ca-HAR

Bayenbar: BAY-en-bar

Caldeon: cal-dee-ON

Cluain Baile: CLOO-in bail

Daehan: DAY-han

Darragh: DA-rah

Dubh Carrig: dove CAR-ig

Erleya: ear-LAY-ah

Fiada Purlieu: fee-AH-da per-LOO

Glinrew: GLIN-roo

Moicriach: moy-CREE-ak

Uldarvik: OOL-dar-vik

Other

Basduun: bas-DOON

Basdunnai: bas-DOO-nye

Acknowledgements

AAAAAND BOOK 1 IS complete. Thank God!

What a wild ride this has been! Writing a book has been adream in the making since I was eight years old. My mother has been asking me for years, "When are you going to publish a book?" So, thanks, Mum, for believing in me. But also sorry for the swear words and the *coughs*other things …

To my sweet husband, my love, you have read every single version—from the hot garbage first draft to the final draft. I am bewildered in the best way, my wonderful weirdo. You even put up with all my super late-night rambles about plot holes and world building. (Sorry).

Thank you to my writer friends Hayley, H.E., Jay, Kaila, and Lindsey for encouraging me through this entire process. You too, Sam! Thanks for the peptalks haha. To my alpha readers and beta readers, you're all the best!

Thank you to my incredible editors for helping me hone this manuscript into what it is now. Editors are the real MVPs! And, to Kirsten, one word… ellipses LOL (and TYSM for so much more!)

Lastly, but certainly not least, thank you to you, my wonderful readers!! I hope you've enjoyed Solace of Dusk and that you'll be back for the next book in the Dusk and Embers series.

About the Author

K. V. MEADOWS IS the proud wife and the mother of two young children. With both children on the Autism Spectrum, and one with multiple disabilities, she longed to see more disability inclusion in fantasy.

When she's not pouring over words, plotting, or spending hours upon hours making playlists and Pinterest boards for multiple interests, K.V. enjoy spending time with her family, knitting, crocheting, sewing, and playing video games.

You can follow K.V. on Instagram or Threads @authorkvmeadows. For bonus content like soundtracks and character art, or to sign up for her newsletter, check out www.authorkvmeadows.com

instagram.com/authorkvmeadows
pinterest.com/authorkvmeadows
goodreads.com/author/show/54616771.K_V_Meadows

www.ingramcontent.com/pod-product-compliance
Lightning Source LLC
Chambersburg PA
CBHW020537120726
47903CB00001B/11